THE END OF THE STORY

Joyce Muriel

ATHENA PRESS
LONDON

THE END OF THE STORY
Copyright © Joyce Muriel 2004

All Rights Reserved

No part of this book may be reproduced in any form
by photocopying or by any electronic or mechanical means,
including information storage or retrieval systems,
without permission in writing from both the copyright
owner and the publisher of this book.

ISBN 1 84401 310 3

First Published 2004
ATHENA PRESS
Queen's House, 2 Holly Road
Twickenham TW1 4EG
United Kingdom

Printed for Athena Press

THE END OF THE STORY

Also by the author:

Who Is My Enemy?
Ellie's Story
Ripeness is All

Introduction

'I am the resurrection. Anyone who believes in me, though that person dies, he will live.' As I sat between Patrick, my husband, and Dominic, my son, at Eloise's funeral these words spoken by the priest at the beginning of his sermon reverberated in my mind. I had always simply believed, but now I was wondering. Even the last few certainties I had clung to now seemed to be slipping away.

On this morning in early September, although the sun was shining outside, it was gloomy and chilly in the crematorium chapel. There were only a few people present. No close friends, apart from us; only casual acquaintances and some colleagues had bothered to come, all obviously longing to get away as soon as they decently could. I couldn't blame them for I knew that Eloise would have expected no more and would only have been amused.

How inappropriate seemed the lesson I had so carefully read: 'Let not your hearts be troubled.' There were surely no troubled hearts here!

The priest was continuing with his perfunctory address, equally suitable for everyone and appropriate for no one.

Staring at the coffin I tried to convince myself that Eloise was truly dead. What had all this to do with the golden-haired, brilliant, ruthlessly successful person I had known for nearly forty years? How could it all be over so soon? How could she be dead of breast cancer when she was only forty-six and at the height of her success as a journalist? What was the point of it all, I asked myself?

To the accompaniment of canned music that Eloise would have detested the coffin began to slide slowly out of view. This is the moment for many when death becomes real and grief overwhelming. Patrick took my hand, obviously intending to show his sympathy. Dominic gave me a comforting smile. Why had he insisted on coming with us, I wondered? It was almost as if

5

he knew the truth. But that was impossible. That was one of the secrets I must keep.

Patrick and Dominic thought I was grieving, as I had expected I would be. They could not know that I wasn't thinking about Eloise, I was thinking about myself. I was only a few months younger than Eloise and the thought of our mortality pierced me to the heart. How vulnerable we all are! I had never realised so clearly before how short our little lives are.

Suddenly as the coffin finally disappeared I asked myself, why do we waste so much of life when it is so precious? Why do we so often squander our golden youth? Why do we so often accept what we recognise to be inferior? I had once been so different. How had I come to this arid place in which I now lived and had lived for nearly eight years? Why had I allowed myself to stay there?

Tears filled my eyes. It was then that I remembered the only other funeral which had been important to me – my grandfather's funeral when I was seven. On that occasion, however, I had felt so differently. That had been for me a joyful occasion. Now, my chief sensations were sorrow for myself and a shameful feeling that at last I was free from Eloise, from the burden of her love which had forced me in the end to share her sufferings.

Picking up my handbag I took Patrick's arm as we walked out of the chapel and assumed a suitably hypocritical manner with which to greet our fellow 'mourners' at the buffet lunch which we had arranged for them in a nearby hotel.

It was only on the journey home that I was free to think and to remember not only my grandfather's funeral but also that more important day two years earlier when I was only five. It was then that certain truths hit me. I don't mean the usual realities of life and death, but something even more overwhelming – the power of love and faith. The point where words fail.

Chapter One

It was one of those unexpectedly spring-like days, which sometimes come at the end of February. I still remembered it vividly The last grimy remains of the previous week's snow were still visible but on this Saturday morning the sky was an almost cloudless blue and the sunlight was golden with a deceptive promise of warmth. It was possible to believe that spring was coming.

As my mother and I walked down the garden path on our return from shopping, I was skipping happily. Suddenly, I stopped as I realised that the delicate, tiny snowdrop buds had all opened that morning. I was impressed. Winter must be over at last. There were even one or two brave touches of yellow on the daffodils. My mother, impatient to start cooking the Saturday dinner ready for my father's return from work, called me imperatively and I reluctantly followed her. I would far rather have talked to the flowers as I often did. But I was usually an obedient child.

It must have been about half an hour later when there was an impatient knock at the kitchen door. On opening it, I was surprised to see my Uncle Bill, my father's eldest brother. 'Is your mother around?' he asked. Without waiting for my answer he came straight into the kitchen where my mother was busy making the lid for a steak and kidney pie.

'Is something wrong?' She was as surprised to see him as I was for he rarely called on us.

'It's the old man. The doctor's been again and Eliza says she's sure he's dying and that our John had better come as soon as he can.' He looked round as if he expected to see my father.

'He isn't back yet but he should be here any minute now.' She carefully put the pie in the oven. Dad would be sure to want his dinner. 'Can you wait?'

Uncle Bill hesitated for a minute. 'Better not,' he answered finally. 'Eliza'll be mad with me if I'm away too long but tell John, won't you, that he must come straight away. Eliza says the end can't be far away and she's usually right.' He moved towards the door, then stopped by me. 'You'd better bring your Stella too. The old man will want to see her. She's his favourite.'

I thought Mother was doubtful but she only said, 'I'll tell John as soon as he comes home and we'll get there as fast as we can.' Uncle Bill vanished through the door and she turned back to the dinner preparations without a word to me. She was like that but I wasn't put off. 'Does Uncle Bill mean that Grandad is dying?' The thought seemed exciting somehow. 'Shall we go there? Does he really want to see me?'

Mother sighed. 'I don't know. We'll have to see what your Dad says.' She always said that so I asked no more but busied myself putting the dinner mats on the table together with the knives and forks which meant tackling my usual problems about left and right.

Dad, as always, wasted no time in making up his mind. Apart from a quick sandwich, dinner was postponed and we set off on the long bus journey to the other side of the manufacturing town where Grandad lived. It was only when dinner was postponed that I realised that Uncle Bill's message was being taken very seriously, even by my normally imperturbable father.

Grandad lived on the older and grimmer side of the town close to the moors. In spite of the still blue sky, the wind seemed fiercer and colder here. He lived with my Auntie Polly and her brother, my Uncle Bill, in an old terraced house, very different from the newly built semi-detached we lived in. Auntie Maggy and Auntie Eliza were there too. Their husbands were probably somewhere around but not noticeable, as usual. Auntie Eliza, the eldest daughter was the real boss; even my father, I noticed, treated her with a certain respect, as did his two other brothers, Tom and Jim, both working overseas and therefore unavailable. Auntie Maggy was a younger, plumper, rosier version of Auntie Eliza. She too could be very sharp tongued but she was sometimes kind, which Auntie Eliza never seemed to be. As for Auntie Polly, the youngest in the family next to my father, she was my friend. She never seemed to be one of the grown ups to me.

As we walked through the dark parlour into the kitchen we were faced by Auntie Eliza, dark and stiffly straight in her long black skirt and spotless, starched white blouse. 'I was beginning to wonder if you'd decided not to come, after all,' was her greeting. Mother shrank away as she always did, but my father was not intimidated. 'Don't be daft, Eliza! We came as fast as we could. You know what the buses are like this time of day. It's not easy to get here.'

'Well it was you who decided to move to the other side of town, away from your family as if this wasn't good enough for you.' She put her arms on her hips. 'So you'll have to put up with it. At least you're here now.' She moved aside so that we could at last go into the kitchen out of the cold passage between it and the parlour.

My father only laughed, then moved over to the brightly burning fire in the kitchen range to warm his hands. 'How is the old man?' he asked. 'I imagine he's still alive?'

'Yes, but only just.' It was Auntie Maggy who replied, coming forward from behind her elder sister.

'I've sent for the priest,' Auntie Eliza announced grimly. 'He should be here very soon.'

'The priest?' My father raised his eyebrows. 'I can't imagine the old man will be very pleased about that. It must be twenty years or more since he went near a church.'

'I told her it was a daft idea,' Uncle Bill muttered. 'But you know what she's like.'

Sensing a family storm, my mother sidled away and sat down in a distant corner. I walked over to Auntie Polly who was standing in the doorway to the scullery. She said nothing but took my hand comfortingly. Auntie Maggy too said nothing.

'Whatever he is now, he was a Catholic once, a good one too. Remember he was an altar server.' Auntie Eliza was sure and definite as always.

'You're talking of seventy years ago or more.' My father rubbed his hands. 'I doubt if he remembers a word now.'

'He does,' I said suddenly. Everyone stared at me but I still thought I should speak the truth. 'He recited some prayers to me once – all in Latin! You must remember, Dad, I told you.' A sharp

9

glance from my father's vivid blue eyes was enough to make me realise that it would have been better if I hadn't spoken. He only answered Auntie Eliza, however.

'Well, you've sent for him already, so there's not much use in arguing, is there? Even if it seems pretty useless.' He looked round at everyone with a challenging look. Auntie Eliza contented herself with merely returning his look but Auntie Maggy spoke in her deceptively soft soothing tones.

'I don't see why you're so upset, our John. I can't see any harm in giving Father a last chance to repent of his sins before he dies. What's wrong with that?'

My father shrugged. 'Nothing I suppose, except that it's a lot of useless mumbo jumbo, which we all stopped believing in years ago.'

'We're all Christians, I think,' Auntie Eliza snapped, 'even if we no longer worship in the way our father does.'

'Doesn't you mean,' Uncle Bill muttered in the background.

'And as Christians we have a duty to be merciful,' Auntie Eliza continued, undeterred.

'Well, that's settled then,' my father said suddenly moving into the centre of the kitchen. Obviously, he was bored with the discussion. 'Since you've invited this priest around, how about taking us all upstairs to see the old devil before he arrives? We won't be wanted then.'

'Of course.' Auntie Eliza was very majestic. 'I'd have done it straightaway, if you hadn't thought fit to argue.' She sailed towards the door. 'You might as well come too Maggy.'

'What about me?' Auntie Polly spoke for the first time as I moved and took my father's hand.'

'You'd better make a pot of tea and perhaps Mary will help you.' Mary was my mother. I was not surprised that she was excluded as she and my grandad never got on, chiefly because my mother, timid though she was, had always made her disapproval of him quite clear. With the arrangements now settled, Auntie Eliza led the way up the steep, narrow stairs, followed by my father and me, with Auntie Maggy in the rear.

Grandad's bedroom was dark and stuffy. No cheering sunlight penetrated here for the curtains were almost entirely drawn.

There was just enough light for me to see his gaunt figure in the bed covered with many blankets and an eiderdown and propped up with pillows. There was an old shawl round his shoulders. On a small cupboard next to his bed there were several bottles of medicine. He wheezed as he breathed but when he spoke his voice was as loud and harsh as always. 'So you've come to see me, John, have you? Things must be bad.' He tried to laugh but was stopped by a fit of coughing.

'That's our Eliza's idea.' My father approached the bed. 'She always was one for a bit of drama. You know that. But you don't look too bad to me. I reckon you'll have a few more years yet.' He picked up one of the bottles with a spoon and gave Grandad something out of it to ease his cough, I supposed.

'Ay, you needn't worry,' Grandad said as soon as he could speak again, 'I intend to be around a bit longer to torment you all.' I was just deciding that he didn't really seem to be very ill at all when he suddenly slumped back on his pillows and closed his eyes, dropping the spoon out of his hand. I was sure he was dead but no one moved or said anything.

It was Grandad who spoke first to my father. 'Have you got little Stella with you? I want to see her.'

'Here she is.' My father pushed me in front of him. Grandad opened his eyes slowly and gazed at me. His eyes under their bushy brows were blue like my father's but paler and bloodshot. His glance was penetrating too but without Dad's friendly twinkle. Apart from his rather large nose the rest of his face seemed to be covered with hair. It was hard, in fact, to see his mouth between the bristling moustache and the luxuriant whiskers. He held out his hand. 'Come a bit nearer, Stella so I can see you properly.'

I suppose he meant to sound kind but his voice was harsh and grating. Nevertheless, I approached him timidly and put my hand in his hard one. 'That's better. Now I can see you. Are you sorry your grandad's ill?'

'Of course.' That was easily answered. 'I hope you'll soon be better. I'll pray to Jesus for you tonight.' Feeling that I had done all that could be expected of me, especially since I had rarely seen him, I tried to draw my hand away gently.

11

Grandad, however, was not so easily satisfied. 'Aren't you going to give your old grandad a kiss?' he asked, pulling me closer and leaning a little towards me still fixing his pale blue eyes on me. Suddenly I was terrified. He was ugly, old and threatening. Even his own children talked of him as wicked. I could not kiss him! I stared back at him for a moment, then violently pulled my hand away from his. 'No!' I shouted. 'I'm not going to kiss you! I don't want to kiss you!'

I rushed out of the room, ignoring Auntie Eliza's furious look, then down the narrow stairs into the kitchen followed closely by Auntie Maggy shouting after me. 'You're a wicked girl! Do you want your grandad to die thinking you don't love him?' Auntie Polly who was just about to warm the teapot with some water from the kettle on the hob put out a hand to stop me but I ignored even her.

It was the loud knocking on the front door, which saved me temporarily. 'That will be Father Regan,' Auntie Maggy said hastily assuming a holy expression as she hurried to answer the door. Without pausing, I seized my chance and fled out of the kitchen through the scullery and into the yard. I didn't stop until I had reached the small garden Auntie Polly had managed to create at the end of the yard. Safe at last I sat down on a large flat stone.

The biting wind, which came straight off the moors, was bitterly cold, although the sun was still shining. I shivered a little in spite of my warm coat and gaiters but here at least it was quiet and there were flowers to comfort me. I counted at least ten snowdrops and several golden crocuses then suddenly I realised what a terrible thing I had done. I had refused to kiss my grandad and he might die thinking that I didn't love him. Even now he was receiving the last rites from the priest. I wasn't quite sure what the last rites were but I knew that you didn't get them unless the priest thought you were dying.

Auntie Maggy was right. I was a wicked girl and, because of me, Grandad might die unhappy. Everyone had always told me that I was his favourite grandchild. But, if it was true and I supposed it must be, then I really was wicked. What could I do about it? Slowly I stood up then knelt down on the hard stone. Putting my hands together I recited the 'Our Father' which my mother had recently taught me and explained to me. For a moment, I felt happier. At least I had asked God to forgive me. But was that enough for it wouldn't really help Grandad?

The words of the only other prayer I knew came into my head. 'Gentle Jesus, meek and mild, look upon a little child.' That was it! Jesus who was always so kind would help me and show me the right way. I knew no more prayers so it was obvious that I had to use my own words. I explained the situation to Jesus and asked Him to show me what to do. I waited, shivering. Then suddenly it was as if someone was holding me gently and wrapping me in a warm blanket. I knew what to say. 'Please Jesus, don't let Grandad die until I've told him I'm sorry and he knows I love him. And please let him have time to be good before he dies!' But that wasn't the end. More was expected. Words were not enough. I understood that I must kiss Grandad lovingly.

I was still kneeling when Auntie Polly called out to me as she hurried down the yard. 'Stella. Love, you must come in or you'll catch your death of cold! What are you doing?' she asked as she saw me getting up from my knees.

'I was asking Jesus to forgive me for being such a naughty girl. Auntie Maggy said I was wicked!'

Auntie Polly came and put her arm round me. 'She didn't really mean it, love. We're all a bit upset, you see. But do come in now. You must be freezing. Look I've brought you a sweetie.' She produced a pear drop from her large apron. She always seemed to have a supply of sweets to comfort me. I took it gratefully and we walked together towards the house.

When we came into the kitchen Father Regan was just going. He spoke mostly to Auntie Eliza. 'It was a good idea to send for me. Your father seems to be more peaceful since I spoke to him. I don't think the end can be far away.'

'Should I go and speak to him?' Auntie Eliza asked.

'In a little while, yes. But I think you should leave him in peace for a while. He told me he would like a little quiet time alone.' Nodding to us all, he gave us his blessing and he and Auntie Eliza walked through the parlour to the front door.

'How about that pot of tea, Polly?' my father asked. 'I reckon we could all do with it now after all this emotion.' He sounded so cheerful that my mother looked a little shocked but she didn't say anything.

'It won't be a minute, John. Mary and I have got everything ready on the table. I just need to pour the water in the pot.' She jumped up ready as always to do something. With my mother's help everyone was soon served with a cup of tea and a slice of Auntie Maggy's home made cake. After Mother had taken off my coat, I sat on a stool by the fire enjoying the cake. Auntie Polly sat on a small chair near me. The others, even Auntie Eliza were all sitting round the table laughing and joking, as if they had forgotten Grandad. I hadn't and I was determined to see him soon, if I could.

I suppose it was because we were sitting quietly by ourselves that Auntie Polly and I were the only ones to hear the noise. We looked at each other the Auntie Polly said, 'That sounds just like the front door being opened.'

'Don't be silly, Polly,' Auntie Maggy said in her slow drawl. 'There's no one there it must be the wind.' No one else took the slightest notice. Accepting this rebuke, Auntie Polly took the kettle into the kitchen to refill it then put it back on the hob. 'Are you alright now, Stella?' she asked me. I nodded.

It must have been about ten minutes later that we heard a similar noise again. Putting down her cup and saucer, Auntie Polly stood up. 'There's that noise again. I'm going to look.' She went towards the parlour and I followed her. The streetlight shone through the window; we could see that the room was empty and the front door firmly shut. As we looked at one another we heard a noise upstairs. 'Father must be out of bed,' Auntie Polly exclaimed. 'I'm going to see what's going on!' Going back to the kitchen, she called out to the others then began to run up the steep stairs closely followed by me. Auntie Eliza and my father came close behind.

An amazing sight met our eyes. My dying grandad, now wearing a coat over his pyjamas was sitting up in bed with a bottle of whisky in one hand and a half-full glass in the other. As we came towards the bed he quickly emptied the glass. Auntie Polly stared at him. 'I was right then. I did hear the front door.'

'Don't tell me, Father,' Auntie Eliza said majestically, 'that you've been out in the street dressed like that?'

'Ay, I've been in the street and to the off-licence as well. What's wrong with that?'

'You disgust me, as you always have done.' Auntie Eliza began to turn away. 'I did think that now...'

'You mean you hoped I'd be dying quietly at last. Well, I'm not. It's all your fault, Eliza, for getting that priest. These last rites are bloody good.' He took another gulp of whisky.

It was then I stepped forward. I knew I had to speak. 'May I talk to you, Grandad?'

'Of course, lass, but you'd better come closer.'

Without hesitating, I walked straight up to his bed and, after closing my eyes so as not to see the ferocious whiskers, I bent down and kissed him firmly. 'I'm glad you're better, Grandad. Though I knew you would be.'

'You're a good lass!' Grandad put his arm round me. 'Can we have a little talk?' I looked round at the assembled family, wondering what to say. Grandad understood. He was in control, as always. He looked round too with a grim smile. 'You might as well go down and enjoy your tea again, while Stella and I have a chat. Don't worry, I won't corrupt her!'

'You'd better make a start by putting down that whisky, then,' Auntie Eliza retorted as she swept out followed by the others. As he went my father smiled as if he was enjoying one of his secret jokes.

After putting down his glass, Grandad suggested that I sat on the bed. For a few moments we were both silent. Grandad spoke first. 'Come on, lass. Spit it out. You don't need to be afraid.'

'I'm not afraid. I don't know how to start, that's all.'

'Then just let it come straight out. It won't do any harm, if it's true.'

'It is true, Grandad.' Then I told him all that had happened to me in the garden. When I had finished, Grandad said nothing. After a while, I looked at him timidly. 'You're not cross, are you, Grandad?'

'Cross? Of course not, lass.' I'd never heard him speak so gently. 'You've shown more love for me than anyone's done for years. Not that I blame them, mind you. I've never been an easy man to live with. A bit of an old devil, if the truth be told.'

I was shocked. 'Don't talk like that now.' I wanted to make things clear. 'It wasn't Father Regan who healed you or the last rites. It was Jesus himself. He did it because I was so sorry and because I asked him. He did it, like he did in the stories Mum has told me because he loves us both and wants us to be happy. You do understand, don't you?' As I looked at him, I almost thought there might be tears in his eyes. But that wasn't very likely.

'I understand.' He still spoke gently. 'But it was your love first that did it, lass. I'll remember that until the day I die.'

I was still not quite satisfied. 'But it means that you've got to try to be good, don't you see, Grandad. And so have I. We have to do that to thank Jesus.'

'And I have to thank you.' he added. He was silent for a time, then he spoke, almost as if he was talking to himself. 'And it's about time, too. I haven't much time left. I always worked very hard to make sure we all had a roof over our heads and enough food. But it was difficult and as the years passed, I couldn't seem to keep it up without the whisky. That made me nasty but I still wanted it.' He paused. 'Do you think there's any hope for your old grandad?'

'Of course there is!' I was completely sure. 'I'll pray to Jesus for you every day and he'll help us.'

'If you say so. Then I'll have a go at it.' He took my hand. Let's shake hands on it. But it's to be our secret. Do you agree?' I nodded and we shook hands.

'Good. Then you'd better take this whisky to your Auntie Eliza and tell her that Grandad doesn't need this any more. He's had his last drink.' He chuckled wickedly. 'I'd love to see her face when you tell her, the old hypocrite! Will you do that for me?' I nodded again. He kissed me and leaned back on his pillows. 'I think I'll have a sleep now. Off you go!'

Picking up the bottle, I tiptoed out of the room and down the stairs. As I came into the kitchen, I heard my father saying cheerfully, 'Well you have to admit it, Eliza, the old man's put one over us again.'

At that moment Auntie Maggy seeing me exclaimed, 'Whatever have you got there?'

Without answering her I went straight over to Auntie Eliza

and gave her the bottle with Grandad's message. Grandad was right, he would have enjoyed seeing her expression. I thought for one moment that she was going to throw it at me but she just managed to say, 'The old devil! He doesn't expect us to believe that, does he?'

'You never know, it might just be true,' Auntie Polly said softly, smiling at me. I said nothing because of my promise. I wasn't sure they would have believed me anyway!

Chapter Two

Of course, I told Patrick about it but not until three months later, when Grandad had just died and I felt freed from my promise. Patrick and I had always confided in each other since the time we had first met nearly two years before.

We were sitting at the bottom of his garden in the wild part where we had a secret hideout among the trees. I had just given him one of my pieces of toffee so that he couldn't say much but he listened carefully, as he always did, with his large brown eyes fixed earnestly on me. 'What do you think?' I asked as I came to the end of my story.

When he didn't answer straightaway I became a little cross. 'You do believe me, don't you?'

'Of course I believe you.' Patrick spoke slowly as if trying to make up his mind. 'You've told me and I know you don't tell fibs.'

'That would be wrong. You know I wouldn't do that. So, what do you think about what I've told you?' I looked at my sticky bag of toffee lumps and shook them so that Patrick would notice. Although I knew he wanted another one, I wasn't going to give it to him until he answered me.

At last he gave his opinion. 'It must have been wonderful.' He wasn't even looking at the toffees now. 'I wish something like that would happen to me. But I don't suppose it will, because I don't know about Jesus and the Bible like you do. My parents never seem to talk about things like that. And we hardly ever go to Church. I've never felt anything like that. You must be very special, Stella. I think you are, anyway.' For a moment he held my hand and we were silent.

At last I moved my hand away. 'Don't worry,' I said, wanting to comfort him, because I knew what really made him sad. 'I'll tell you all I know. And I expect they'll soon teach you lots at school.' As he still looked sad, I offered him another piece of toffee and didn't make a fuss, as I usually did, when he absentmindedly took the largest lump.

Before he put the toffee in his mouth, he asked me another question. 'Did it really happen? I mean did your grandad really try to be good?'

For a moment, I considered this carefully. 'Well, I only saw him about three times but he was always nice to me and asked me if I still prayed for him and he seemed pleased when I said I did. Auntie Polly said he never did drink any more whisky and, although he was sometimes cross, he was never as bad as he had been and he didn't use wicked words any more. So I think it did. And, what do you think?' I opened my eyes very wide. 'He left me his old prayer book. It's very fine and it's got his name in it and the date when the priest gave it to him for being the best altar server when he was eight. Mum's put it away but I'll ask her to show it to you when you come to our house.'

'He must have really liked you a lot. Patrick sighed deeply. 'I wish someone felt like that about me.' I knew why he said this and I knew that my parents thought it was true. His mother and father didn't seem to love him very much. Certainly not, like mine loved me, and I always had Auntie Polly as well.

I put my arm round him. 'Never mind, I love you. You're my best friend.'

'And you're mine.' He hesitated for a moment, then he asked, 'Will you marry me one day, so we can always be together?'

I wasn't sure exactly what this meant but it seemed a nice idea, so I agreed, and then we happily finished the toffee together. I didn't realise it but I had made my first serious commitment to Patrick.

Patrick and I should never really have become friends because the children who lived in my very new street of little semi-detached houses never mixed with the few children who lived in the large Victorian villas which together with the Norman church and the cemetery were the remainders of the original village, which had gradually become a genteel suburb of the town. Patrick and I, however, were both rebels in our very different ways.

It had been a sunny Sunday afternoon nearly two years before when we had first accidentally met. I had been with my father to visit my Auntie Maggy and her husband, as we sometimes did when Mother had a rest. We were walking home from the bus stop when we overtook Patrick, who was standing in the middle of the pavement. My father stopped at once. 'Hello, young man! Where are going then?' My father was always easy and friendly and most people seemed to trust him, as Patrick did now.

Patrick stared solemnly at my father and then seemed to decide that he could safely speak to him. 'I've been for a walk.'

'By yourself?' My father was surprised. 'How old are you?'

'I'll be four in August.' Patrick announced proudly. 'How old is your little girl?'

I was annoyed. I might not be quite as old as he was and I was a bit smaller but I could speak for myself. 'I'm three and a half!' My eyes flashed. 'And my name is Stella. What's yours?

'Patrick.' He looked upset that I was cross and I felt sorry.

Smiling, my father interrupted our exchange. 'Well, Patrick, you seemed to have stopped walking. Don't you think you ought to go home now?'

'I suppose so.' He looked up at my father. 'I think I'm lost.'

'Perhaps Stella and I can help you. Where do you live?'

'In a big house not far from the church.' Patrick replied vaguely.

There are several houses near the church. Can't you tell me which one?'

'We haven't lived there very long. It's painted black and white.'

That wasn't much help. 'Well, we'll walk that way,' my father said. 'Do you think you'll know it when you see it?'

'I think so. It's got my father's name on the gate.'

'And what's that? What's your name?'

'Gestenge.'

'Good.' At last my father had the information he needed. 'You must be Dr Gestenge's little boy then?' Patrick nodded agreement. 'Then we'd better take you home. Your mum and dad will be getting worried.'

'I don't think they will be.' Patrick said as he trustingly took the hand my father offered him. 'My father's out on a call and my mother's having a rest, so I went for a walk. I don't suppose they've noticed.'

'They will be glad to have you back anyway, don't you think?'

'I expect so.' Patrick didn't sound very convinced.

'Well, I think we'd better take you there,' my father decided. It was not a long journey to Patrick's house and my father managed to keep talking cheerfully. 'You haven't lived here very long, have you?' he asked Patrick.

'No, we only moved here just after Christmas.'

'We've only been in our house a few months,' I volunteered, anxious to have my say.

'Where did you live before?' Patrick seemed interested.

Before I could answer, my father said, 'We only came from the other side of town but you've come much further haven't you?'

'Yes, we used to live in London. Have you ever been to London?'

'I have,' my father said, 'but Stella here hasn't.'

I felt that Patrick pitied me which didn't please me. 'It's a big place. Where we lived it was very nice much nicer than here.'

'Don't you like it here?' my father asked.

'No. I hate it. It's lonely. I don't know anyone.'

'Well, you know me and Stella now. That's a start, isn't it?'

'Yes.' We had reached Patrick's gate now with a brass plate on it as he had said. It was a large house with a long drive to the front door. Patrick didn't seem eager to go in. 'Do you think I can see you again?' he asked.

'Shall we ask your mum if you and Stella can play together?' my father asked.

Patrick smiled. 'Do you think she would? I'd like that.' He turned to me. 'Would you like it?'

I considered the idea carefully. 'Yes, I think so, if you're good.'

'That's settled then,' my father said quickly. 'We'll take you back and see what your mum thinks, shall we?'

The front door was surrounded with a big porch and there was a large, brass bell which my father rang vigorously. A very small maid in cap and apron opened the door and stared at us. Suddenly she recognised my father and smiled at him.

'Why are you standing at the door, Susan?' a cold voice asked, as Mrs Gestenge came into the hall. 'Do we have a visitor or not? I've told you many times what to do.' She sounded very impatient.

'It's Mr Fitzgerald, Ma'am and his little girl. They've got Master Patrick too,' she added as Patrick came from behind my father.

Mrs Gestenge came quickly down the hall and confronted us, as Susan seemed to disappear. As soon as I saw her and heard her, I knew why Patrick hadn't wanted to come home. She was very well dressed and good looking, I suppose, but she simply didn't look or sound like a mother should or so I thought.

My father was unruffled by her very discouraging look. He smiled pleasantly. 'We've brought your young man back. He seems to have been wandering a little.'

'That's very kind of you.' Immediately she turned to Patrick. Her tone was cold and angry. 'You're a very naughty boy. I'm always telling you not to go out of the garden. I shall have to tell your father, since you don't seem to care how much you worry me. You'd better go to the kitchen now and ask Susan to get you some tea.' I would have been very upset if my mother had spoken to me in that way but Patrick seemed unmoved. In fact, he didn't move but still clutched my father's hand.

My father still smiled pleasantly. 'Well, you know how it is, Mrs Gestenge. You mustn't be too hard on the young lad. Boys will be boys! I expect he was just looking for a bit of an adventure. It was lucky he found us.'

Mrs Gestenge suddenly seemed to make an effort to be more amiable. 'Indeed, it was and I'm very grateful to you.' She looked more closely at my father. 'Did I hear Susan say your name was Fitzgerald? I seem to know the name but I don't think we've met, have we?'

My father laughed a little. 'I'm sure we haven't met,' he said, 'but I expect you've seen my name on the posters.' As she still looked puzzled, he explained. 'John Fitzgerald, Labour Party Candidate in the local elections.'

Mrs Gestenge, studying my well-dressed, well-spoken father seemed to be more puzzled than ever. 'You don't look like a Labour Party man,' she announced.

'We come in all shapes and sizes.' Dad seemed to be even more amused as he smiled back at her.

'Well, you're a brave man,' she conceded finally, 'standing in this Ward. You haven't a hope surely? It's always been Conservative, I'm told.'

'It has. But I think the time is coming for a change. If not this time, perhaps next—'

'Mummy,' Patrick interrupted boldly. 'Can Stella have some tea too? I was amazed at his asking and wondered if this might make his mother even angrier.

She looked as if she might refuse but suddenly to my surprise she agreed. As Patrick led me to the kitchen, I heard her say to my father. 'Susan has just brought some tea into the lounge. May I invite you to join me? I should like to hear more about your political ideas.'

I don't know how my father managed it but he must have spent about twenty minutes talking to Mrs Gestenge, while Patrick and I ate homemade buns and drank lemonade, and he showed me some of his toys. He hadn't any dolls of course but I liked his train set, especially as no one ever gave me presents like that. We were building a bridge together when my father came into the kitchen with Patrick's mother. She was actually smiling when she told Patrick and me that my father had agreed that Patrick should come round to play at our house the next morning. Susan would take him and bring him back, as she was very busy.

And that's how it started. In a short time Patrick and I were spending most mornings together. Sometimes Susan brought him to our house and on the other days my mother took me to his house, which was very grand. He actually had a small room where his toys were kept and where we could play. Mother sometimes stopped to chat with Susan but we very rarely saw Mrs Gestenge.

One day when she had a free afternoon, Susan came to have a cup of tea with my mother. She began to talk to my mother about the Gestenges. I was playing with my dolls behind the armchair and I think they forgot I was there or perhaps they thought I wouldn't understand.

I noticed first when Susan said crossly that she didn't like Mrs Gestenge and that she was 'a nasty old cow'. My mother was shocked and told her not to say things like that. 'Well, she is, anyway,' Susan retorted. 'I do my best but she's always finding fault and never says she pleased. I don't wonder her husband doesn't stay home much.'

'Doctors often have to go out. People expect them to call when they're ill at all sorts of times.' My mother didn't seem very pleased with the way Susan was talking but Susan was determined to let off steam. 'Well, everyone knows he likes a drink and a pretty face, my mum says. Still, I don't mind him; he's always pleasant. He's not a snob like her. But what I hate most is the way she treats Patrick.'

'Is she cruel to him?' Mother sounded worried.

'No, not as you might say "cruel", though she's pretty unkind sometimes but most of the day she hardly seems to know he exists. Poor little mite. It's been lovely for him to have your Stella to play with. It has really. He often tells me.'

'Yes. I'm surprised how well they get on together. I was rather nervous about it at first, especially as we don't usually mix with people like them. I thought Stella might feel out of place.'

'Not she!' Susan exclaimed. 'She's like her dad. Look how he got on with Mrs Gestenge! And him a Labour Party man and all! I couldn't believe my eyes!'

'Yes, my husband does seem to get on with most people. He says it doesn't matter who they are; it's what they are, that counts.'

'And little Stella's just like him. Patrick always seemed such a lonely kid but he liked her straightaway. She's a bit bossy sometimes but he doesn't mind. I fair killed myself with laughing the other day when I heard her say to him, "If you don't play properly, Patrick Gestenge, I shall go home." And I think she would have done too, if Patrick hadn't stopped her.'

'Oh dear!' Mother seemed a little upset. 'That wasn't very nice of her. Perhaps I should talk to her.'

'I shouldn't if I were you. Girls need a bit of confidence or so my mum says. Patrick doesn't mind anyway. He knows she's his friend. And that's what matters to him. He thinks a lot of you and Mr Fitzgerald too.'

'Poor, little boy he doesn't seem to have a very happy life at home. Isn't his father kind to him either?'

'When he's there, but he's mostly out. Prefers it that way, I reckon. Of course she was a nurse and she does help in the

Surgery in the mornings but in the afternoons, she either goes out or rests. I keep my eye on Patrick. I can't think why she needs to rest. Some do say she likes a drink then, but…'

I was interested in what they were saying but at that moment, I dropped my favourite doll and the noise reminded them that I was there. There was no more talk of the Gestenges and Susan left soon afterwards.

Now, two years later sitting at the bottom of the garden with Patrick sharing toffee and secrets, I knew that all Susan had said that day was true, not only because Patrick had told me, but because I had discovered for myself that his mother could be very unpleasant indeed when she was in a bad mood, as she often seemed to be. Sometimes I was impatient with him but I was always sorry because he cared so much. I knew that I could never have a more loyal friend. What I didn't realise of course when I was five was how much of a responsibility that can be.

Suddenly my reverie was interrupted as I noticed that Patrick was slowing down. Opening my eyes I saw that we were entering a motorway service station. 'We're about half way home,' he said. 'I thought it might be a good idea to have a break.' After sliding skilfully into a conveniently empty parking space, he switched off the engine and undid his seat belt.

'Thank God for that,' Dominic emerged from his doze on the back seat. 'If you don't mind, I'll have a walk round and buy myself a coke.'

'Don't be longer than ten minutes,' Patrick warned him.

Since I hated all motorway service stations I had provided us with a thermos of coffee and some biscuits. I carefully poured out two cups. Fortunately, we both liked black coffee which made it easier. Still feeling lost in the past, I didn't speak. After sipping his coffee for a few moments, Patrick turned to me 'You're not feeling too bad, are you? I know the funeral must have upset you, since you've been friends so long, especially when you think what might have been. I suppose it's hard not to think about her as she was years ago?' He kissed me gently on the cheek.

'I was thinking about the past but not about Eloise, more about you and me years ago, when we used to play together and I didn't know Eloise. Do you remember asking me to marry you when you were six?'

25

'Of course I do. It still amazes me that I had such good sense even at that age.' He smiled at me. 'It was the best thing I ever did to put my claim in early, though perhaps you're not so sure?'

I evaded him slightly. 'Why not? It made me different and I always liked being different. No other girl that I knew was engaged at such an early age.'

He laughed. 'Don't tell me you boasted about it? That's something I never knew!'

'Of course not! How can you even hint at such awful behaviour on my part, Patrick Gestenge? It was just that it was lovely to have such a secret!'

He was suddenly serious. 'You still like having a few secrets, don't you, Stella?'

I drew back from that dangerous place. There are some questions that shouldn't be asked, and others that can't be answered except at the right time if it ever comes. 'Who doesn't? Even you do, at times. You can't deny it!'

'I suppose not.' We were both silent for a few moments while we finished off our coffee. As he handed his cup back to me, Patrick continued thoughtfully, 'I don't even know the truth about myself, except for one thing, I love you.'

'I love you too,' I replied quickly. I was afraid that my words sounded perfunctory and I wished I could have made a more convincing response. I knew that he meant what he said and wanted to console me, knowing that I wanted to be consoled. Oh, how I wished it could be different! If I made one encouraging move perhaps he would hug me tightly as he had done when we were young and all might be well. But it was impossible! I couldn't make that move because, in spite of all we said, there was still a barrier between us. I was glad to be saved from answering further by the sight of Dominic returning with his drink and a packet of crisps. One more chance for reconciliation had passed but it wasn't all my fault.

As Patrick restarted the car, I leaned back shutting my eyes. My thoughts returned to Eloise. How much had she affected my life? Would I have been a better person if I hadn't known her?

Chapter Three

'Why do you always ask that stupid Margery to play with us?' Eloise was cross and her deep blue eyes were flashing. We had just met in the playground at the beginning of our morning playtime, as we usually did. Margery had not yet come out.

I was surprised. It had not occurred to me that Eloise would object to Margery. 'We have always played together since I first started school two years ago. She looked after me because she was older and we became friends. I've only known you since the beginning of this term.'

'I know that but you don't have to go on playing with her now you've got me.'

'But she won't have anyone to play with.'

'I'm not surprised. No one likes her, except you. I don't think you really do either.'

Seeing Margery hurrying towards us fortunately I didn't have to answer this. It was a difficult playtime. Eloise refused to agree to anything and Margery feeling herself pushed out got sulkier and sulkier. I think we were all glad when the bell went. I know I was.

Margery and I always walked home together, while our mothers walked behind chatting. On this particular evening, Margery was silent at first, then she suddenly said grimly, 'If you don't want to play with me, you don't have to. I don't care.'

Although I was only seven I knew she did care, because I was her only friend. She was unattractive, ugly or so Eloise said, and withdrawn, and other children didn't like her. She was a year older than me and in her gruff way had mothered me since my first day at school. I knew this and I didn't want to be disloyal nor did I want to lose my new friend, Eloise, who had only just come to my school. 'Of course, I want to play with you,' I replied.

'It didn't look like it this playtime. You were much more interested in that Eloise. And what she wanted to do.'

'That's not true.' I felt cross. 'You just wouldn't speak. You disagreed with everything.'

'So did she.'

I couldn't deny that. 'I don't see why we can't all three play together.' I really hoped that this could be possible. Although I liked Eloise, I could not desert Margery, who had never had a friend until I had made her mine.

'You know we can't.' Margery's face was set in familiar stubborn lines. She was never pretty but at times like this she could look almost ugly.

'Why not?'

'Because she doesn't like me. She thinks I'm dull.'

'Why don't you try to be pleasant and show her you aren't?' We had reached the place where we had to cross the main road and then part but our mothers were a little way behind so we still had time.

'If people don't like me as I am, they can lump it!' Margery folded her arms defiantly. 'But, anyway, it wouldn't make any difference. Don't you see, Stella? She wants you to herself. She wants to get rid of me.' I stared at her. I simply couldn't believe this. 'It's true,' Margery said. 'And I expect you'll choose her. Most people would.'

'Don't be silly. I'm not going to do any such thing. You're both my friends.'

As our mothers now joined us, Margery had only time to say, 'It won't be any good. You'll have to decide.' She sounded so certain that I felt worried. I didn't want to choose. I saw no reason why all three of us shouldn't be friends.

After tea I shared my worries with Patrick. We still shared things, as we had always done. Most evenings we met for a short time either at his house or mine. We could not meet during the daytime because Patrick had been sent to a small private school, while I went to the local council school, as my father could not afford to pay fees and would have thought it a silly thing to do in any case. Even this had not separated us, since Patrick thought that the people who went to his school were stupid and he would much rather have come to my school.

That evening he came to my house and we talked in the living room while my father was having a rest upstairs and my mother was washing up. I told him about my miserable playtime and also what Margery had said. 'Don't you think she's silly?' I was sure of his approval.

'I don't know,' he replied slowly. 'What's this Eloise like? I've met Margery a few times but I've never met her. Where's she come from?'

I didn't see what difference that made but I told him. 'She's just come here from some place in the North and she came to our school a few weeks ago. She was lonely so I talked to her.'

'But what's she like?'

I thought. 'Well, she's very pretty. She's got curly golden hair and blue eyes. She smiles and laughs a lot. She's clever and was only a few marks behind me last week.'

'And you like her?'

'I suppose so.' The truth was, although I didn't like to admit it, that I was flattered that she who seemed so exciting had chosen me. 'We like reading the same books and she invents stories like me. I don't see why that should upset Margery; she's always liked my stories and my games.'

'But don't you see,' Patrick explained with all the wisdom of his eight years, 'when Eloise is there she isn't special any more. She feels the odd one out. I expect you'll have to choose. People do.'

I was disappointed. 'I think it's silly! I don't see why people don't try to like each other. It would be much nicer! Don't you think so?'

'That's because you always try to like people and they don't understand. I'll never have that difficulty. I don't like people much, except you and you're my best friend, just like you've always been.'

'And you're mine!' I was relieved. The problem was solved. Neither Margery nor Eloise was my best friend, so I didn't have to worry. I would try to keep them both as friends; Margery because I couldn't bear to let her down and Eloise because she was fun. It was difficult to do this but fortunately a few months later Eloise left again for the North where her father had been offered a more secure job.

Times were hard then in 1930–1931. Seeing the queues of men in the centre of the town I asked my dad why they were standing there. 'Because the poor blighters have nothing else to do. They've lost their jobs and they're queuing for the dole so they won't starve.' He answered bitterly. He was angry that men who like himself had fought in the war should be begging in the streets. Margery's father was unemployed for a time and that was another reason for not letting her down. My father, because he was skilled and very capable didn't lose his job. He even made good his boast to Mrs Gestenge and, on his third attempt, was elected to the council. She actually congratulated him. Although she didn't approve of his politics, she apparently admired his forceful character. I think that was why she never actually objected to Patrick and me being friends.

Now, years later, leaning back in the car I wondered why I had remembered this episode so vividly and why it seemed important. Was it perhaps because it illustrated two things that had always been important to me; my friendship with Patrick which had always given me as well as him a feeling of security and secondly my dislike of rejecting people? Was it, as Patrick had suggested because I always wanted to like people or was it because even then, I didn't want to separate myself entirely from Eloise? Even at that early age I had often been upset by her when she teased people and especially when she imitated Margery behind her back and made me laugh in spite of my guilty feelings.

I didn't have to decide that when I was eight because Eloise went away and Margery and I resumed our earlier friendship. It was not until I was fifteen that Eloise came back into my life. During those years Margery had left school at fourteen and become a shop assistant, while I at the age of eleven had been fortunate enough to win a scholarship to a prestigious independent girls' school, so we were no longer close friends. Patrick, at the age of nine, had moved to the Prep. Department of a famous boys' school where he had later been awarded a Foundation scholarship. We had miraculously remained friends, although we only saw each other mainly at the weekends and in the holidays. We tried to keep our friendship secret, fearing the stupid talk there might be.

Eloise's father had returned to work in our town. He was obviously doing well for they now had, as Eloise told me, a large house in one of the better suburbs, plus a car and a telephone, luxuries which I had never imagined ordinary families would possess. She also came to my school as a fee-paying pupil, two or three weeks after the beginning of our Lower Fifth year. I recognised her immediately. She seemed to have become even prettier. I wondered if she would remember me.

As soon as break arrived I walked over to her desk, where she was still sitting looking rather lost. As soon as she saw me, her face lit up. 'Stella!' She exclaimed jumping to her feet. 'I never expected to see you here! How lovely! Now I don't feel like a lonely new girl anymore!'

Flattered by her obvious pleasure in meeting me again, I introduced her to my friend, Elizabeth. I doubted if they would get on very well, as Elizabeth was the quiet studious daughter of a teacher. Eloise, however, was delighted to be shown round by us and to share the chocolate we bought. After a few minutes, Elizabeth left us, as she wanted to go back to the form room to revise her French verbs for a test. Eloise and I were now able to renew our old friendship, remembering our past times together and also exchanging some of our news. We were still chatting happily when we came back to the classroom at the end of break. As I sat down in the desk next to her, Elizabeth gave me a slightly reproachful look and I remembered I had promised to test her before the end of break.

The next day Eloise managed to get herself moved so that she was sitting at the desk on the other side of me. As I was sitting between her and Elizabeth, I was suddenly reminded of Margery. I need not have worried. This new, sophisticated Eloise had no desire to exclude anyone. Her intention seemed to be, in fact, to attract as many people as possible. In this she was very successful. For not only was she pretty and elegant but she was lively and entertaining. She liked to charm and she was good at it, always being able to adapt herself to the person she was talking to. With Elizabeth she was serious, with less intelligent girls frivolous.

With me she was different – I was her best friend – and she always made this clear. She talked as if before we had had a much closer relationship than we had ever had. Although I was puzzled, I accepted this position. There seemed to be no way of avoiding it. By the time we reached the Fifth Form, we were accepted as a pair with Elizabeth as a third who was apparently content to trail behind. We vied for the top position in most subjects and always took the lead in discussions, although Eloise sometimes annoyed me by the extreme views she put forward, often I suspected for effect. She even expressed Communist views to my Labour father on the first occasion I invited her to my home for tea. Dad was amused and enjoyed himself by asking her awkward questions but afterwards he warned me not to take her too seriously. 'She's a bright girl', he said, 'but she hasn't much depth. I don't want you to get like that. I want you to do something worthwhile with your life.'

I did not tell her about Patrick and carefully avoided meeting her on Sundays when Patrick and I often took a bus on to the moors where we walked and talked about serious matters such as why we were on this earth and what we should do, especially in this time when war seemed to be coming very close.

At this time Patrick was extremely unhappy. His home life had never been relaxed and loving like mine but for several months now it had been getting worse. His parents had always quarrelled but in the last months the quarrels had been more frequent and sometimes quite violent. He confessed to me his fears that his mother had taken to drinking secretly and that his father spent more and more time out of the home, possibly with other women. He knew as I did that there was much gossip about them, although when they appeared in public they always behaved most correctly.

But, although they were opposed on most matters they were united on one. And that was that Patrick must become a doctor like his father and grandfather before him. To my surprise, Patrick was completely opposed to the idea. 'Why?' I asked him. 'You can help a lot of people, especially poor people. I think it's a wonderful job.'

'It is, for those who can do it but I can't.'

'Why not?' I questioned him again. 'You're clever enough and you do care about people, don't you?'

'I don't, at least not like you do, Stella. I don't even like people much. Sometimes I hate them for their selfishness and cruelty. And then I feel so depressed that I don't want to do anything. Nothing seems worth doing any way. I certainly don't want to study for years and take endless exams just to become a useless doctor. Even you don't seem to understand that I'm not capable of doing it, any way.'

'I don't see why not', I began, not really knowing how to help him as I longed to do.

'In that case why don't you just go away and leave me?' Sounding bitter and angry, he turned his back on me.

'Because I'm your friend. Perhaps I'm not clever enough to understand but I do care.' Taking hold of him, I forced him to turn and look at me. I was afraid he was going to pull himself away but after a moment he seemed to relax a little and said quite quietly, 'You'd be better without me, Stella.'

'I don't think so.' My stubborn refusal to quarrel or to go away always seemed to put him into a better mood, for a time at least. I was very worried about him, however, so much so that I even consulted Auntie Polly. She was the only adult I still found possible to approach because she had remained young at heart and treated me as an equal, as she had done when I was a small child. I knew also that she would never repeat anything I told her.

'What can I do?' I asked her finally. 'Surely there must be something?'

Auntie Polly was silent for a few moments. 'There isn't a simple answer, Stella love. Sometimes, however much we want to, we can't put things right. You're doing the best you can, if you continue being his friend, even when it seems hard. He needs you.'

I stared at her disappointed. 'But there must be something more than that?' I was young enough to believe that there was an answer to every problem.

'There is. You must pray to Jesus for him. Pray specially, I mean with all your heart and believe that you'll get an answer.' When I didn't reply, she asked me a direct question: 'You still do say your prayers, don't you?'

'Sometimes.' As I thought about it, however, I had to admit that I had not thought much about such things particularly in the last two years since Eloise had been my close friend. Unlike Elizabeth she never went to church, and she scoffed at such old fashioned ideas. I was ashamed to realise that I had not stood up to her and didn't therefore seem a suitable person to pray for Patrick.

Suddenly I remembered Grandad and the prayers I had made for him. I had been at fault then but, when I had admitted it, Jesus had forgiven me and my prayers had been answered. As if reading my thought, Auntie Polly said, 'You'll have to pray with all your heart, really believing. Your prayers will then be answered but don't expect it to be straightaway. Patrick's is a difficult problem You'll have to keep on trying.'

I promised that I would and that night, alone in my bedroom, I began. At first it was very hard, especially when I had to admit how wrong I had been and to ask forgiveness. But when I began to talk of Patrick it became easier and gradually I became convinced that someone was listening and caring. I felt enclosed in love as I had done as a small child. I became convinced that my prayers would be answered but the way was going to be long and hard. I knew I had to persevere. That night I had the first of those vivid dreams, which were to come to me through many years. They were always the same, always comforting, yet challenging.

★

At this moment, I became aware that Patrick was speaking to me. 'Wake up, Stella. We're nearly home. You, too, Dominic,' he added, turning to our recumbent son on the back seat. I sat up and looked quickly out of window. We were just entering the Kentish village where we had lived now for several years. I felt rather guilty for having been such a poor companion. 'I'm sorry for being so silent. I haven't really been asleep, I've been thinking about everything.'

'That's a good one,' Dominic exclaimed as he sat up yawning. 'You don't believe her, do you, Dad?'

Patrick only smiled. 'It doesn't matter. I prefer people to be quiet when I'm driving, particularly at night.' Turning to me, he added, 'You'll feel better at home, Stella.'

As we entered our carport, the kitchen lights were switched on and the kitchen door was flung open. Our three younger children, Cordelia, Julia and Ben had obviously been awaiting our return and worried that we were later than they had expected. Cordelia, the eldest, proudly told us that there was a hot meal waiting for us and very quickly she was serving out Spaghetti Bolognese in the kitchen dining area while Julia was busy making coffee. Ben produced warmed rolls and in a very short time we were all sitting cosily around the pine kitchen table. Even Dominic, often more taciturn than the others, seemed relaxed. Patrick and I smiled at each other. It was good to be home.

Cordelia led the others in asking tactful questions about the funeral. They all knew that Eloise was one of my oldest friends and they did not want to upset me. As soon as possible Patrick changed the conversation by asking them what they had been doing. 'It's been pretty boring,' eleven-year-old Ben said. 'School all day and Cordelia wouldn't let me watch the television until I'd done my homework. I nearly missed part of my favourite programme. She was really bossy. Worse than you, Mum!'

'She was quite right too,' Patrick comforted Cordelia who looked a little upset.

'It was your own fault,' Julia said quickly. She always supported the more sensitive Cordelia. 'You shouldn't have wasted time arguing. But you always do.'

Dominic suddenly stood. 'Forget it Ben. You can't win with two women against you!' He moved away from the table towards the door. 'Since I've got to travel back to college in the morning, I think I'll go to bed. See you at breakfast, maybe!'

It wasn't long before the others followed him, leaving Patrick and me to clear away the supper. I suggested that he leave it to me, since he must be very tired with all the driving, but he refused, as I rather suspected he would. He was concerned about me, I knew, and about my unusual silence. I tried to convince him that there was nothing wrong, that I was simply feeling a bit sad about the way Eloise's life had ended. He accepted this but reluctantly, although he asked no further questions. 'I expect you'll tell me when you're ready', was all he said.

As I was watching him making his last preparations before

coming to bed, I said suddenly. 'You never really liked Eloise anyway, did you? Not even when you met her for the first time?'

He frowned a little. 'Probably not. But when was the first time? I'm afraid I don't remember it.'

'You can never remember anything!' I exclaimed crossly. I was tempted to wonder if he was speaking the truth, even though I knew his recollections were often hazier than mine.

He sat on the bed near me. 'There's no need to be cross.' He took my hand comfortingly. 'Just remind me.'

'I don't know how you can have forgotten.' It all seemed so clear to me and important.

'I don't suppose it seemed very significant to me. Not if you were there anyway.'

'Of course I was there. It was the end of year dance for the Fifth and Sixth Forms at my school. I persuaded you to come and do the lighting. I thought we might even have a dance together since we'd both recently had dancing lessons.'

'I remember now we did dance a waltz together. I was pretty terrified, I can tell you. I thought I might let you down. But it all went well, didn't it? We've always been good together, haven't we?'

I smiled back at him. 'Yes, it was good. But you don't remember Eloise?'

'Dimly. I seem to remember her coming into that little room when you were helping me to repair a switch or something. Yes, it comes back to me now. She annoyed me with a lot of clever talk and silly questions. I would have been rude to her, if she hadn't been your friend.'

'You were pretty rude anyway.'

Patrick laughed. 'Well at least I got rid of her which was what I wanted. I couldn't think why you wanted me to meet her. Why did you?'

I evaded that for the moment. 'But didn't you notice how lovely she looked?' As I asked him the question it was all still so clear to me. I could see her standing in the doorway wearing a new elegant deep blue dress which accentuated the blue of her eyes. Her bright golden hair was arranged in soft shining waves which framed her oval face. Her red lips were a perfect bow. She was brilliant and I felt very dull in comparison.

Patrick was making an effort to remember. 'I suppose she was pretty but it all seemed rather artificial to me, not like you. You're just naturally beautiful and you don't change. Although I wasn't quite seventeen, I appreciated the difference between the real and the false. I thought I made that clear to you then, didn't I? I think I asked you how you could possibly be friendly with such an artificial person and you seemed surprised. Why ever did you want me to meet her?'

For the first time in all these years I realised why this meeting had seemed so important to me but I hesitated to admit it even now. But Patrick was not going to let me off. 'I think I must have been afraid.'

'Afraid? Of what?'

'Afraid that you might prefer her to me, because I thought she was so attractive.'

Putting his arms around me, Patrick began to laugh. 'So why didn't you keep us apart then?' He kissed me.' You don't have to tell me, I know why. It's your fighting spirit. You never run away from anything, do you? That's one of the things I've always loved about you.'

I returned his kiss but without saying anything because I knew that it was no longer completely true. There were some things I didn't have the courage to face, at least not yet.

Chapter Four

By nine o'clock the next morning the house was empty. Dominic had returned to college before anyone, except me, was awake; the others had managed to catch the school bus and Patrick had with the usual difficulty been persuaded to catch the London train. Everything was normal except that I was restless and dissatisfied. I had work to do but could not force myself to do it. It all seemed suddenly pointless. The questions I had asked myself after the funeral had not been answered. Furthermore there were several others I didn't even dare to look at.

But wasn't this all rather ridiculous, I asked myself? I wasn't a girl just starting out in life. On the contrary, I was forty-five years old, and had been married to Patrick for twenty-three years. We had four children; lived in a large, comfortable house in a pleasant village in Mid Kent, where we were pillars of the Catholic Church. Patrick, in the last six years seemed to have settled finally as the assistant editor of a respectable scientific journal. The salary was not large but that didn't matter since I earned money teaching German part-time in a local independent school and in recent years had increased my earnings by writing and illustrating children's stories with the help of an artist friend of ours, Lucas Graham.

With determination, I settled down at my desk. I had a story to revise before I went off to teach in the afternoon. Fifteen minutes later with a still untouched paper in front of me, I gratefully accepted a cup of coffee from my daily help, Mrs Austin, and was tempted to gossip for a few minutes with her. It passed some more time but it didn't help. Finally, I was forced to admit that I was not going to be able to work that morning. For years I had resolutely refused to look honestly at certain questions. Now, after Eloise's death, I knew that I could no longer do this.

Looking back at my early years had shown me in some degree where the difficulties had started but now I had to face far bigger questions. Had I been right to carry on, as I had done? Should I have made a clean break? What was right to do now?

I walked across the room and looked through the patio windows into the garden. In the clear blue sky the mid-September sun cast a golden glow on the remaining flowers and the trees. The fuchsias and geraniums were still brilliant around the patio. This room had once been the children's playroom but, as they had grown older and my workload had increased, it had been turned into a study for me and a comfortable refuge for Patrick too when he was at home.

Opening the patio door, I walked outside and sat in one of the garden chairs. The air was fresh but warm. Nothing disturbed the dreaming stillness of the garden. It was a time to remember. Before I was seventeen, in my second term in the Sixth Form, my teachers and my father had settled my future. I, the daughter of an ordinary working man, was to take a degree in French and German and, most amazingly of all to me, it was suggested that I should try for Oxford or Cambridge. This meant hard work. Not only had I to prepare for College Entrance but I must study for scholarships to pay for the cost of this education. My mother and other women thought this was ridiculous. Eloise who had decided to leave school at sixteen scoffed at the idea.

'You'll turn into a ghastly blue stocking', she said, 'and into a boring old maid teacher too whose greatest excitement is the antics of the Lower Fourth. Why don't you give it up and have fun with me?' Eloise intended one day to become a journalist, preferably on a woman's paper. In the meantime she was learning shorthand and typing, reading whatever she fancied and drifting through life as easily as she could in the first year of the war. Sometimes I was tempted by her but fortunately I was sensible enough to realise that my only chance was to go to University, since I didn't have a father who was sufficiently wealthy or easygoing to keep me comfortably at home as long as I wanted to be there.

When I was tempted in this way, I confided in Patrick. His confidence in me helped me to carry on even in my most depressed moments. One day when I was considering whether to apply for a job, he was almost angry with me. 'Don't be an idiot,

Stella! You'd hate it. You're far too intelligent to waste your time in some office. This is your great chance. For God's sake don't throw it away!'

'But supposing I fail?'

'Fail! Of course you won't. Who put that idea in your head? Don't tell me. It was Eloise, wasn't it? Why do you waste your time with her? She doesn't know what she's talking about. She hasn't even got the guts to try, has she?'

'Patrick! You've only met her once a year ago at the dance. How can you possibly know what she's really like?'

'It was obvious, especially when she told me when you'd gone off for more food, that her ambition in life was to be rich and enjoy herself. When I asked her how she proposed to achieve it, she said she might earn it herself but she thought a rich husband would be the best solution.' He spoke with considerable scorn.

'She does say things like that, I know but she doesn't expect to be taken too seriously. She thinks it's amusing. She's actually very ambitious in her own way and can work very hard.'

'As far as I'm concerned, she can do what she likes but I won't let her have a bad influence on you. I'm your real friend, Stella, you know that and I don't want you to waste the gifts you have been given. Promise me you'll forget about jobs and all that nonsense. You know how much I care about you. Don't turn away. Look at me!'

As I stared into his earnest, brown eyes I was filled with compunction. It was obvious from his expression that he really cared and remembering his much greater difficulties I was ashamed of the stupid fuss I had been making. He was right; of course, it was Eloise who had encouraged my rebellious feelings. 'I promise I won't try to run away again. I'll do my best to succeed.'

He continued to look steadily at me for a moment and then he smiled. I remembered then how Eloise had once said how handsome he was but before I could say anything he completely surprised me by bending down and kissing me. When we were small children we had often kissed quite naturally but never since our primary school days until now. I didn't move but I couldn't think of anything to say. As I looked up at him, I began to realise that Patrick had surprised himself too.

'I didn't plan that,' he said finally. 'It just happened. I hope you don't mind. If you do, I'm sorry but I don't regret it. Do you mind?'

Suddenly, I felt very happy. 'Of course I don't mind. I rather liked it, in fact.' Although shocked at my own boldness, I was determined to be truthful. This was not any boy; this was Patrick, my oldest and dearest friend.

For a moment we stood there smiling at one another then, without another word, he kissed me again. Only this time, his arms went round me and the kiss lasted longer. Slowly he released me, then took my hand and we continued our walk uphill together. It was a Sunday afternoon and, as we often did, we had a taken a bus out of the smoky town to the nearest small town on the moors. Once there we had set out on one of our favourite walks, uphill all the way to a bare outcrop of rocks, from which there was a splendid view.

We had been almost there when he had stopped to expostulate with me. Now we continued hand in hand without a word until we reached the top. Once there, we sat down on the short rough grass and leaned back on a convenient rock. Obviously something needed to be said. But what? I decided to leave it to Patrick. After all, he was the one who had changed our situation.

Patrick, however, seemed to have difficulty in knowing what to say. This also was unusual because, except when deeply depressed, he was a fluent and ready talker. I stole a look at him. He definitely didn't look depressed. 'Don't you think you ought to explain yourself?' I asked finally.

'I've wanted to kiss you for sometime but now it just happened.' He stopped.

Surely, he didn't think that was a sufficient explanation? As I looked at him, he took my hand in his. 'It was bound to happen sometime, I suppose. We're growing older and people do fall in love. You can't pretend you don't know that, Stella.'

'Of course I know that but I hadn't...'

'You hadn't expected it to happen to us. Is that what you mean? Why ever not?' He sounded almost indignant. 'Isn't it romantic enough for you?'

'People fall out of love too, sometimes. I wouldn't like that to

41

happen to us. We might not be friends any more.' I found it difficult to explain my feelings.

'It won't happen to me.' He was very confident. 'You're not only my best friend but I think you're the loveliest and most attractive girl I'm ever likely to know. How could I find anyone better? And why should I even want to try? You do like me, don't you Stella?' Looking at me almost pleadingly he ended far less confidently than he had begun.

I saw no reason not to tell the truth. 'You know I do. You took me by surprise, that's all. I don't see how I could find anyone better.'

'You should ask Eloise. I'm sure she'll tell you that there are plenty of people you could find who would be better.'

'Do you mean someone rich or very likely to become rich?'

'Obviously, if one is to judge from her own ambitions, as she expressed them to me once and probably many times to you.'

'I have heard her say that. Her mother always says that it's just as easy to fall in love with a rich man as with poor man and much more sensible. So you see, Eloise hasn't been brought up with the right ideas.'

'Neither have I.' Patrick paused for a moment. 'But then I've been lucky to learn them from you and from your family.'

'Eloise thinks I'm so naïve and romantic that I don't sufficiently appreciate the importance of security. I really think she worries that I'm not worldly wise and will do something silly.'

'Well no one could accuse you of being worldly wise if you chose me. I'm sure that Eloise will clearly point that out if you discuss your intentions with her.'

'But I shan't.' I was surprised that he should say this. 'I never discuss you with Eloise.'

'But you talk about her to me, don't you?'

'Yes, but you're my best friend. She's only a friend.' Looking back now I wondered how truthful I'd been when I made that declaration. I always wanted to make Patrick happy.

Patrick smiled at me. 'I'm sure these distinctions are quite clear to you. But seriously, Stella, she would be right if she told you that you couldn't probably choose anyone less likely to promise you a settled future. You know how chaotic my ideas about the future are.'

This was something that had worried me for several months and I had hoped that his ideas would change. 'But you do believe in doing something worthwhile, don't you?'

'Yes, if I can.'

I hesitated, then I decided to be bold. 'But you can be a doctor, Patrick, if you want to be. You have a helpful background and you are intelligent.'

He gripped my hand tightly but didn't at first say anything. Then, turning to me, he spoke vehemently. 'I don't really care what anyone thinks but I do want you to understand me. I'm not just being awkward or trying to annoy my parents. I can do that any time simply by existing. It isn't that I don't want to be a doctor. I know I'm not capable of being one.'

'What do you mean?' I realised he was trying to be honest but I was puzzled.

'I know I couldn't stand the discipline of it – the long years of training and all those examinations. I hope I'm intelligent as you say. It's true I like reading and discussing ideas and all that but I'm not academic. I'm not like you. I wish I were. Perhaps, I'm simply lazy. That's what my parents think and some of my teachers. They may be right.'

'I don't think it's just that. You work very hard sometimes.'

'Sometimes, yes, but not regularly. That's one of my difficulties. There are times when I'm so depressed that I can hardly persuade myself that it's worth doing anything or even bothering with anybody. You know that's been true for years. You're the only person I've ever known who can put up with me. I'm very grateful for that. But you can surely see what a rotten doctor I would make, even if I managed by some miracle to force myself through the course. My father's not a model doctor but he's hard working and easygoing and that gets him through. You know that what I'm saying is right, don't you, Stella?'

I was reluctant to admit it but I could hardly deny it. 'I suppose so but don't you think you might change, Patrick?'

'No! Don't think of it, Stella! If you can't like me as I am – neurotic, depressed and unreliable – then you'd better forget about being my friend or anything else.' He stood up and seemed about to move off down the slope.

43

Shocked, I caught hold of his hand again. 'Please, Patrick, don't talk like that! You know I don't mean that. I can't bear you to say such things. You are probably all the things you say but I also know you are honest and kind and I've always been able to trust you.' I was very upset. 'You're my dearest friend and I thought I was yours!'

'Of course you are and whatever you decide about the future you'll always be mine.'

Reassured I began to clamber down the slope with him. It was time for us to leave if we were to catch the bus home. Just before we emerged on the road, he put his arm round me and kissed me once more. 'You seem to be making a habit of this,' I remarked a little primly. I wasn't sure how much I approved of this.

'No need to worry, Stella. I do know how to be sensible and I shall be.' He was cheerful again.

'I don't want to say anything to my parents. It would upset them, I think.'

'You're probably right. We should wait until we're sure. And it would be a disaster to say anything to mine, as you know. I tell them as little as possible, especially my mother.'

It was only when we were on the bus that I again brought up the subject of his future. 'But what are you thinking of doing? You've got to do something.'

'I realise that. Fortunately, there's a war on, so like most of men of my age I intend to take part in it. I suppose that seems like a convenient excuse but I'm not simply opting out of making a decision. I honestly feel that is something I should do. You know that's true. I think that as this war had to be fought, so it has to be won. If we believe in democracy and freedom, then we must be prepared to defend them. I think that I should play my part. I've already spent two years in the OTC so I'm pretty well prepared. Furthermore, it's something I'm ready to do.'

'Well, if you don't go in for medicine, you will be called up when you've taken your Higher Schools, won't you?'

'I'm not waiting for that. I'm volunteering this coming week. I've been told that if I volunteer, I can opt for the Army unit I want. I'd prefer that. You don't think that's a bad idea, do you?'

I was very surprised and a little annoyed. 'Why haven't you

said anything to me? I tell you everything but you always like to have your secrets.'

'I'm telling you now.' He smiled at me. 'You're the first person to know and the only one until I have to tell my parents, sometime next year. I've only just decided that it's obviously the best thing for me to do. Don't be angry with me, Stella.'

'I'm not really. If you're sure you can't be a doctor, it's probably the right thing to do. What are you going to volunteer for?'

'The Royal Corps of Signals. A cousin of mine has done well in that. And my Maths and Physics should be useful.'

A familiar guilty feeling came back to me. I felt that by going to University, I was removing myself from the problems of most people of my age. Patrick as always was vehemently against such an idea. 'You're going to be a teacher,' he said, 'and that's a very necessary job, particularly as more and more men have to go into the army. You'd be wasted doing some clerical job, which is probably all they'd offer you in the forces. Don't waste your time thinking about it, get on with what you should be doing.'

'Which is?' I smiled up at him.

'Cheering me up, especially when I'm a gallant soldier. I shall need regular letters and lots of love and encouragement.'

'I suspected it would be something like that.' I tucked my arm through his, feeling very happy.

★

'Good morning, Stella,' a familiar voice brought me back suddenly to the present. I looked up and saw my artistic partner, Lucas Graham, standing a few feet away. 'I'm sorry, Lucas,' I explained, 'I haven't finished the story and I'm not likely to do so today.'

'Don't worry. I didn't expect you would have done. I only came to see how you are feeling after the funeral. I expect you found it upsetting?'

'Yes, in a way. It has started me thinking about the past, remembering things I'd almost forgotten.' I sighed. 'And wondering too.'

'How things might have been different, I suppose?' His

sombre dark eyes under their heavy black brows regarded me steadily. His black hair, now streaked with silver, was untidy as always. It was generally difficult to know what he was thinking. His face was habitually set in austere, almost stern lines, except for his mouth which was fuller and gentler than one would have expected. He was wearing his usual denim shirt and paint stained overalls. Suddenly he smiled. 'Don't,' he advised. 'It's a waste of time. You are here now and that's all that matters.' He sat down opposite me.

I offered him a cup of coffee but he refused it. 'Eloise and I go back a long way. I can't help remembering. We talked a lot before she died, more than we'd been free to do for years.' I paused. It was difficult to tell him the decision I had only recently been considering. 'I ought to tell you,' I said finally, 'that I don't think I shall write any more stories. It's not really what I want to do.'

His answer surprised me. 'It never was. I knew that. It was Eloise's idea not yours.'

'Yes. Cordelia showed her the stories I had jotted down for the children.'

'And Eloise saw the commercial possibilities at once, especially with my being conveniently near and ready to help. She managed us both beautifully.'

'Did you mind?'

He shrugged. 'Why should I have done? It brought us both money which we needed and enabled me to get to know you much better which I enjoyed.'

'What do you mean? Are you saying that Eloise planned that?

'Of course! Don't tell me that it never occurred to you that this was the other part of her experiment?'

'I just thought that she wanted to help me.'

'She did, I'm sure. But she was also amused to see what would happen. She thought that you ought to have some fun and that I would be the right person to help.'

'How do you know?'

'She told me when I asked her. She recognised a fellow sinner, you see.'

I stared at him, as if I had never seen him properly before. 'Why didn't you tell me?'

'You wouldn't have believed me and it would have spoilt our relationship.'

Suddenly I decided that I didn't want to ask any more questions, for I was afraid of the answers. I would keep to the clearly defined path and avoid the dangerous bog. At the same time I acknowledged to myself I had been doing this for years. Was that perhaps why I now inhabited this arid, grey world? Why had I come to believe that the desert was safer than the marsh? Quickly I avoided the invitation to turn off the path. 'Eloise always liked playing with people. I should have guessed there was more to it. We go back a long way, as I said.'

'Am I right in thinking,' Lucas asked, 'that she enjoyed stirring up trouble even when she was near to death?'

'Yes and I had known her a long time, so she was important,'

'But not as long as Patrick?'

'No.'

'So there were some things she couldn't affect?'

'Yes. Patrick has always been part of my life, as you know, or so it seems. She couldn't change that.'

'But she would have liked to have done so? After all, she had her claims, didn't she?'

'Perhaps,' I refused to be drawn. I was clinging to my firm ground.

'And I've only been in your life for eight years, so I don't feel I have a right to probe or do you think differently?'

I looked at him silently for I wasn't ready to answer. It was eight years since Lucas had come into our lives, introduced by our priest as a man without home or family who was just recovering from a serious illness, a breakdown, I imagined, but the priest didn't actually say. Knowing that we had a large house, Father Donovan had suggested that we might be willing to take him in for a time and give him an opportunity to experience family life. Patrick had agreed immediately for he was always generous and I had seen no objections to it.

He had arrived with his old car packed with all his worldly possessions, chiefly a potter's wheel and painting gear. In his previous life, he had somehow been a potter and a painter. We asked no questions, however, but accepted him as he was. For his part, he asked no questions either but quickly became a helpful and agreeable member of the family with an unexpected fund of funny stories, which delighted the children.

It was when that Eloise discovered that I could write children's stories but needed an illustrator, that he offered his services. Our partnership had been successful. He now lived in our garage which had been converted into a studio flat. In many ways we had become close but I wasn't ready now to confide further in him. Finally, therefore, I said, 'No, I don't think differently at the moment. I don't believe that you can help me.'

As he stood up, Lucas appeared to have accepted his dismissal but unexpectedly he paused. 'I think I might be allowed to ask one more question. Since you have decided to give up writing stories, what is it that you now want to do?'

'I'm considering accepting a full-time teaching post if it's offered to me as I think it might be.'

'Are you sure that's what you really want to do? Without waiting for an answer, he left.

I was glad that he didn't insist on my answering him, because I couldn't have done so. Once I had had a dream of myself happily married with a large family. We would not be rich in worldly goods but we would be a family united by love, helping one another and ready to love others. For several years I seemed to have achieved this dream with Patrick. Eight years ago it had been cruelly shattered and since then there had been no dream. It's difficult to live without a dream and never to be able to speak of it.

Chapter Five

After Lucas had gone, I walked slowly back to my study. Memories were tantalising and eluding me. Perhaps a look at some old snapshots might help my powers of recall? Delving into the capacious bottom drawer of my desk, I finally found an old album of photographs. These might help.

As I turned the pages I came unexpectedly on a close up of myself, aged eighteen. Smooth, dark hair framed my oval-shaped face. Large hazel eyes under level brows gazed seriously at me. My mouth was curved only into the slightest of smiles. I had a remote air as if my mind was on a search for eternal truths. It was an unusual face for one so young for it looked not only thoughtful but also strangely serene and happy.

This then was the young Stella Fitzgerald; the girl Patrick loved and whose good looks even Eloise had admired. It was the memory of this girl that had haunted me during the last few weeks of Eloise's life and again at her funeral. What had happened to this girl of dreams and visions? Who or what had changed her? Had it been inevitable? These were the questions that refused to go away.

Turning the pages I came upon a photograph of Patrick and me standing at my garden gate. This was in the summer of 1941 some weeks before I was due to go to Oxford. We looked very happy. Patrick had his arm around my shoulders and I was clearly holding my left hand so that the little ring sparkling on the third finger could easily be seen. I remembered now this photograph was taken on the day of our engagement.

It was I who had persuaded Patrick to buy the ring and to tell our parents of our intentions. He had several fits of depression as the time drew nearer for my departure to Oxford and one Saturday he seemed worse than usual. 'I have nothing to offer you, Stella,' he exclaimed. 'It's no use pretending any more. My father will tell me again that I'm a fool and your father will have every reason to despise me. You have an exciting future in front of you and it would be wrong for me to get in your way. You shouldn't feel yourself tied to someone like me.' I understood that he felt particularly unhappy that day because our examination results had just been announced. I had done sufficiently well to make certain that I would have enough scholarship money to go to Oxford. Patrick, however, although he had done brilliantly in Mathematics and Physics, had failed his Biology and only scraped a pass in Chemistry so he was not qualified to study medicine. His father had been angry but his mother had been cruel in her comments. He had not told me much but I could guess the kind of things she must have said.

He had that familiar obstinate inward look but I refused to be deterred, knowing from experience that this was the best way of dealing with him. We were sitting on a bench in a nearby park and, since Patrick had put a physical distance between us, I moved towards him taking his hand forcing him to look at me. 'I know your parents have been horrid but you mustn't let it affect us, really you mustn't.' I put my arm through his now and snuggled up to him. 'As for my parents, I know my mother will be sympathetic, although she will never oppose my father but, if you're honest with him, I don't think my dad will be angry. And, if he is, we'll survive.'

'But, if they say that I have no decent prospects and have no possibility for years of supporting a wife, they'll be right, won't they?'

'We're not thinking of marrying until I've obtained my degree,' I reminded him. We only want to make it clear that we care for each other. As for you supporting me, that's simply old-fashioned. I'm going to be an independent woman. You won't have to support me, until we're both ready. If you had to consider supporting a wife and a child soon afterwards, then it wouldn't be possible for years. But we know better than that now, don't we?'

Suddenly to my relief he smiled at me. 'So what do you think we should do? Should we buy the ring and then tell them or should we tell them first?'

'Let's buy the ring, since you've saved the money and then tell them. We needn't produce the ring straightaway.'

He stood up. 'Let's go now. We can take a bus into the town centre and go to the best jeweller. I can't afford a splendid ring but I'd like it to be something you can be proud of wearing.'

We spoke to my parents first since Patrick had been invited to tea that Saturday. When Patrick had told them simply what we wished to do and I had said that was what I also wanted, my father looked at us silently for a few moments. It was difficult to tell what he was thinking. He looked at my mother who smiled but said nothing, obviously waiting for him to make his views clear, as she usually did. At last he spoke. 'You say you would like to get engaged now but you haven't said when you think of getting married.'

'We can't be exactly sure,' Patrick looked straight at my father. 'But it certainly won't be before Stella has taken her degree in three years' time.'

'And what will you be doing during those three years, since you aren't qualified to study for medicine. Will you stay in this factory job? You might do quite well there, I imagine.'

'No, I don't intend to do that.' Patrick sounded quite sure of himself. 'I volunteered for the Royal Corps of Signals a year ago. I shall join them as soon as they send for me. The factory job is just to keep me going while I'm waiting.'

'I expect you could stay in the factory if you wanted to. They're doing war work now, I hear and your qualifications should be useful.'

'I don't want to.' Patrick looked straight at my father. 'I believe in the cause we're fighting for and I think that I should take an active part and be ready to defend my country.'

My father looked approvingly at him. 'I couldn't say more myself. In 1914 I volunteered and I gave four years of my life for this country and I don't regret it. You won't either, I'm sure.' He looked keenly at us both. 'But I must be sure that you won't interfere with Stella's studies. I want her to go as far as she can.'

'So do I.' Patrick answered with determination.

For the first time my mother intervened. 'You have to admit, John, that Patrick certainly hasn't held Stella back so far. In fact I think he's often encouraged her.' I admired her for being so unusually bold.

My father seemed to approve too. 'I think you're right, Mary.' He smiled at her then turned to us. Well, I'll trust you both but, if you let me down, I'll be very angry. Now let's have a bit of a celebration.' Suddenly, he seemed very pleased; so much so that he produced a treasured bottle of port, gave us all small helpings and proposed a toast to Patrick and me. 'It's a good thing,' he said to Patrick, 'for a young man to have a faithful sweetheart at home when he's off to the wars.'

After that, the photograph was taken. It was Mother's idea that I should wear my ring since she admired it so much.

At Patrick's request I didn't go with him when he told his parents. He knew his mother would be unpleasant and he didn't want me to hear her. If anything, she was worse than he expected but his father was kinder, seeming to decide finally that I might be a good influence, if anyone could be. I think this change of attitude might have been because he and my father had become friends in the Home Guard. Also not having the ridiculously snobbish attitude of his wife, Dr Gestenge understood that my father as the successful manager of the factory, where he had once been a workman and, as a town councillor for many years, was a respected member of the community, who felt no need to enhance his position by the marriage of his daughter to the local doctor's son. Whatever his reasons he invited Patrick and me to meet him in the local hotel for a drink and was extremely agreeable to me.

Surprisingly enough, I remembered, the only person who was openly difficult was Eloise. Her reaction, although it didn't surprise me, nevertheless disappointed me. For some time now, she had gradually become aware of a growing romance between Patrick and me. She had however refused to take it seriously, especially as she and I were still close friends and I made no girlish confidences to her.

A few days after my engagement I went on one of my usual tea time visits to see Eloise. As she had not yet returned from her typing class, I first showed my ring to her mother, Celia Marshall, an even more glamorous blonde than her daughter. She was delighted with it and with the news, for to her marriage was the only possible career for a girl. She was examining the ring closely as Eloise came in. 'It's very charming,' she exclaimed, 'and quite unusual. It was very clever of Patrick to choose it!'

'What was clever of Patrick?' Eloise asked, as she heard her mother's last words.

Celia laughed. 'Several things I would say! He's not only persuaded Stella to agree to marry him but he's also bought her a lovely engagement ring without spending too much money.' She handed the ring back to me and I put it on my finger. 'You must look at it Eloise and hear all the details while I get a little celebration for tea.'

As soon as her mother had left the room, Eloise turned quickly towards me. 'Why didn't you tell me that you were going to get engaged? I thought we were friends.' Although she kept her voice low, I was surprised to see that she was angry.

'You knew about Patrick,' I began but she interrupted me. 'Of course I knew about Patrick but I had no idea you were going to do something like *this*!' Her scorn was obvious. 'Why ever didn't you say something to me? I thought I was your best friend.'

'I couldn't really. I wasn't sure until Saturday. Then we both decided it would be a good thing and our parents agreed. I couldn't tell anyone before that.'

'I didn't think I was just anyone.' She spoke bitterly and I realised that she was hurt. 'Still,' she shrugged, 'that's not the main point. If you don't care about me, I care about you. And I simply can't believe you've done this.'

'Whatever do you mean?' I was bewildered and a little annoyed.

'How can you ask that? You surely can't be as naïve as you sound? I thought you were going to be an emancipated woman and now, when you're just starting out, you've fallen for the old male chauvinistic trick. He flatters the girl, puts a ring on her finger but leaves himself free. He doesn't wear a ring, does he?'

'Of course not. What are you talking about? All I've done is to get engaged to Patrick, whom I've know since I was three and who loves me and whom I love, whatever you may think.'

'OK. I don't mean to upset you. Let me ask you another question. You surely don't intend to go to Oxford wearing that ring?'

'Of course I do. There's nothing wrong with it, is there?' I looked proudly at it as it sparkled on my finger. 'I suppose it isn't expensive enough to suit your tastes?' I was hurt and angry.

'I think it's a very pretty ring,' Eloise said slowly. 'But you're mad if you go to Oxford wearing it. You're just starting out in life and most important; you're going to a place where you have a good chance of meeting some interesting and well-connected men. You're intelligent and attractive. It's the chance of a lifetime. You don't know who you might meet. What chances you'll have. You might even fall in love with someone completely different! Why not? After all, you've never met anyone except Patrick, so far. You and I might even have fun together for a time, as we sometimes thought we might.' She sat down, her brilliant blue eyes fixed seriously on me. 'I'm just trying to give you some good advice, that's all,'

'You simply don't understand, do you?' I burst out. 'I love Patrick and he loves me. Even if I didn't have the ring, I wouldn't be interested in anyone else.'

Eloise smiled mockingly. 'But do you think once he's in the Army that he'll be as faithful as you are? You have to admit that he'll be an unusual man if he is.'

'Patrick is unusual and I think he will be faithful just as I shall be.'

'I hope you're right. But I can't help remembering Shakespeare, "The lady doth protest too much methinks", so be careful. I don't want to hurt you. I only want to warn you, so don't quarrel with me, please.'

'Of course I don't want to quarrel with you. I think you're wrong that's all.'

A few days later, Eloise came back to the subject when we were alone together. 'I do wish you wouldn't do it, Stella.' She was looking unusually serious, almost sad.

'Do what? I don't know what you're talking about.'

'Tie yourself down publicly to Patrick just now. Why don't you wait at least until you've been away for a term or two?'

'I don't see why I should. We love one another. Even my parents have agreed, so why can't you?'

'They don't know you as well as I do. Or perhaps they don't want to. The truth is you're too innocent.'

'And you're so experienced, I suppose?' I mocked her.

She answered with unusual seriousness, refusing to be angry. 'I know more about love than you do.'

This shocked me. Ever since my early years when I had first discovered the power of God's love in my grandad's garden and had realised the need that people had for love, I had tried hard to be a loving person, whereas Eloise had always seemed indifferent to all of this. 'I don't think you know what you're talking about.' I was angry with her. 'I know I love Patrick.'

She replied more seriously than I'd expected. 'I believe you do but you're not "in love" with Patrick. And that's very important. Surely you realise that? Love between a man and a girl isn't just a spiritual thing, nor is it just romantic. Until you've understood that you shouldn't think of getting married.' I wasn't prepared to listen to her, however. It was a long time, in fact, before I understood what she was trying to tell me.

I turned another couple of pages in the album and found myself faced with our wedding photographs. The date was at the top of the page, 'August 14th 1945'. I was just twenty-two and Patrick a few months older. We made a good couple. Patrick was tall and handsome in his uniform. I looked very pretty in the simple dress and jacket, with the matching hat and its little veil. We both looked happy. It seemed as if everything had happened just as I had confidently predicted to Eloise. But it hadn't. The date on the photograph was a year later than had been intended. We had first planned to be married as soon as I had taken my degree in 1944.

What had happened? The simple explanation was the exigencies of war. D-Day had come and Patrick had suddenly been swept off to France. We had a brief meeting before he went, in my chilly, almost bare Oxford study. Everything seemed bleak. I tried to suggest that we could plan the wedding for October when he could reasonably expect another leave. There was a pause.

'If I'm still alive,' he replied chillingly.

'Don't be ridiculous,' I stormed, using anger to mask my fear. 'It's no use thinking like that in wartime. Anyway, we intend to be survivors.' We argued until suddenly it became clear to me that

Patrick was determined to put our plans on hold indefinitely or, at least, until everything was more settled. Finally, I demanded an explanation.

'You're too young to be tied down, especially to someone who has nothing and may not even return.'

'It's a bit late to think of that, isn't it?'

'But it's not too late. I don't want to deprive you of the opportunity to test yourself before you make a binding decision.'

It was then, unfortunately, that I remembered Eloise's cynical remarks about men. 'Don't you really mean that you don't want to tie yourself down? That you'd like a little freedom to experiment, after all?'

He looked sadly at me. 'No, I don't regret it and I know I never shall but I think you might and I would hate that.'

In the end, angry and hurt, I returned his ring, refusing to understand what he was trying to say.

Nevertheless, a year later we married and everything seemed just as it might have been. Only I knew it wasn't. A month after the wedding, Patrick, still in the army, was sent to Germany and we were apart for much of the next two years. During this time Eloise and I renewed our friendship, which had been interrupted by the war when she had joined the ATS.

Reluctantly, I put away the album. It was time for me to prepare to go to work. As I did, it occurred to me not for the first time that it was perhaps easier to face danger than the relentless monotony of ordinary life.

That evening, quite without warning, a storm broke over my head. If I had been wiser, I might perhaps have anticipated it but I hadn't. As was usual when I taught in the afternoon, the children had all returned from school shortly before I had. Lucas, as he often did, joined us for our cup of tea and biscuits. Afterwards, he willingly accompanied Cordelia on the piano while she tried out a new piece on her flute. She was studying music for one of her A levels and was a skilled pianist and flautist. Soon afterwards, he drifted away, refusing an invitation to join us for our evening meal.

Cordelia came to help me in the kitchen, as I cooked a meal, which would be ready, when Patrick returned from London. We didn't talk much, for I had a piece of good news, which I didn't want anyone to hear before Patrick did. Cordelia didn't seem to be in a communicative mood. If I hadn't been so absorbed with myself, I might have noticed this and questioned it but I didn't.

I planned to make my announcement at the end of the meal when everyone would be feeling relaxed or so I believed. Before I spoke I looked round at them all with some pleasure. All the children had changed into the now routine jeans and T-shirts but nevertheless they were different. Seventeen-year-old Cordelia, who had just started her second year in the Sixth form, was wearing a brilliant emerald shirt with golden scrolls on it. She liked to appear artistic and different. Her thick brown hair with its fascinating auburn tints hung loosely down to her shoulders. Her eyes were brown like Patrick's. In fact, she resembled Patrick in many ways.

In contrast, fifteen-year-old Julia, the intellectual one of the family wore a simple but tasteful cream shirt with a purple chiffon scarf effectively arranged. She looked more like me in spite of her fair hair and blue eyes. She was not a dreamer, however, but apparently logical and far more controlled than her more emotional elder sister.

Ben, at eleven had just started secondary school. In spite of his attempts to look grown up in his jeans and checked shirt, he still looked a cheerful boy. He was our peacemaker who tried to be loyal to everyone and a result sometimes found himself isolated. I suspected that he felt much lonelier since Dominic had gone to University a year ago.

Patrick, too, even though he had arrived home rather late, had changed into casual trousers and his favourite maroon hand-knitted jumper. I made a mental note that I must knit him another one or he would wear this one until it fell to pieces. 'That was very enjoyable,' he remarked as he put down his spoon and picked up his cup of coffee.

'Before you all go off,' I began, 'I have something to tell you.' As they all looked at me, I suddenly thought that I should have spoken to Patrick first but now it was too late. I had to continue.

'Fire away, Mum,' Ben grinned at me, 'unless you're going to give us all more jobs to do.'

'It's nothing like that. It's about me. This afternoon my headmistress, Miss Armstrong, offered me the post of Head of the Modern Languages Department. The present Head of the Department has decided to leave at Christmas because of ill-health and Miss Armstrong has decided that she would find it very difficult to find anyone better qualified or more experienced than me to take the job, especially as my work has always been so good.' I had been very pleased by all the compliments she had paid me and, although I didn't want to repeat me them all, I wanted my family to share some of the satisfaction I felt.

For a moment, there was silence, then Ben said, 'Jolly good, Mum!' And immediately after that Patrick said, 'It's about time she realised what a good teacher you are. I'm very pleased.'

'Does that mean you'll be working full time after Christmas?' Cordelia, to my surprise sounded almost angry.

'Yes, although I'll probably have one free afternoon a week.'

'So, we shall see even less of you than we do now? Or doesn't that matter to you?'

Before I could answer, Julia asked in her quiet cool, voice, 'Will you be paid a lot more?'

'Yes. A good deal more, so we'll be able to have a holiday overseas, perhaps and several other things.'

'Fine.' There was an obvious sarcasm in Cordelia's voice. 'That may satisfy the others but it doesn't satisfy me, especially as you have always urged us not to care too much for material things. You may have changed, Mum, but I haven't. I would rather have a mother who has time and love for me. Why should you work? None of my friends' mothers do.'

'Cordelia,' Patrick sounded angry. 'You are being very unpleasant and very rude to your mother. I suggest you apologise.'

Before she could answer, I spoke. 'Why are you saying these things, Cordelia? I have never wanted to hurt you. I have always loved you all very much.'

'Don't listen to her, Mum,' Ben began but before he could finish his sentence, Cordelia burst out again. 'Don't try to stop me, Ben!' She turned directly towards me. 'Don't fool yourself, Mum. They all agree with me but they haven't got the courage to say it. For months you've been preoccupied with your friend Eloise and her sufferings. You even spent nearly three weeks of the holidays looking after her.' Ignoring the protests from Ben and Julia, she continued. 'Well, at last, now she's dead and buried and we all thought that you might have some time for us again. I bet even Dad hoped that. But you're not going to, are you?' You've found something else to take up your time. You don't really care if we're unhappy and if we need you.'

'Of course I do.' I stared at her in amazement. 'If you are, why don't you tell me?'

She stood up, her eyes full of tears. 'When? Mum, when? For your information I am unhappy. I need some help. Although you didn't notice, Dominic went back to college early because he had no chance to speak to you about what was upsetting him. Ben needs more time. And even Julia does.'

'You don't need to speak for me,' Julia interrupted her. Julia hated scenes, unlike her more emotional sister. 'It's time you shut up.'

'I will in a minute.' Her eyes were full of tears. She turned suddenly towards Patrick. 'I'm sorry I've been rude, Dad but even you haven't anything to say. And I think I know why.' She turned to me. 'I bet you haven't told Dad about this before you told us. Have you?'

Before she could say more, Julia had seized her arm. 'Come with me. You've done enough damage already. Don't do any more.' Without saying any more Cordelia, sobbing, allowed Julia to lead her out of the room.

Patrick, Ben and I were left alone. Poor Ben. 'Don't take too much notice of her, Mum. You know how upset she can get.' But I noticed he didn't deny the truth of what she had been saying.

'That's alright, Ben,' Patrick said gently. 'I think you'd better go and do your homework, hadn't you?' In spite of his gallant smile, Ben was obviously upset when he left.

I longed for some consoling word from Patrick but it didn't come. Instead he stood up and began to collect the plates. 'You must be tired. I'll clear away and do the washing up. I'm sure you've got plenty to do.' It was kind but it was distant.

'So you agree with Cordelia then?' My tears were not far away.

'Not entirely. She has no idea of the whole truth.' He paused as he was going through the door. 'But I wish you had talked it over with me first. I felt like one of the children. Perhaps that's what I've rightfully become in your eyes. It's hard to accept. But I suppose the truth is that we haven't been close for a long time, have we?'

Without waiting for an answer, he went out. Tears rolled down my cheeks. I wanted to run after him but what could I say? What had happened to that happy young couple on the marriage photograph I had recently been looking at? For years we had been happy, my dream of a happy family seemed to have been realised, then it had all gone suddenly wrong. When had it started? Why? I realised that this was the question I'd been afraid to ask myself all the time. I had changed from that earnest young girl, even more perhaps than Patrick had changed. Was there any way back? Hoping to avoid everyone, even Patrick, I went to my study.

Chapter Six

Patrick worked slowly and methodically in the kitchen, sorting out the inevitable chaos after a family meal. No help was offered him and he wanted none. It seemed to him that he moved most of the time now in a world of grey shadows. The blackness hovered, never far away, but, if he were careful, he could keep it at bay and thus avoid being cruelly enveloped by it as he had been eight years previously.

A good protection was to involve himself in a practical job, which kept his mind so busy with superficial details that disturbing thoughts had little means of entry. That was all he had learned, it seemed to him, eight years ago during his weeks in a mental hospital. If that was not sufficient, there was always a pill.

It was with his own consent that he entered this world, to avoid the unendurable pain which had almost annihilated him before. Sometimes, he thought that if only he had the courage he might find the way out. Tonight he had become involved briefly because of Stella but he had quickly retreated, ignoring her appeal.

He needed help and who was there to help him? Stella? My star, he had sometimes called her when they were young. She still shone brightly but her warmth could no longer reach him because of the invisible curtain between them. Sometimes, he half hoped that she might tear it down in her old impetuous way and protect him with her love. But she never tried now and he thought he knew why. He had betrayed and wounded her too deeply. She was right. It was better this way.

As he scrupulously wiped the china and polished the glasses, he admitted to himself that at the end of supper he had temporarily cast aside his neutrality and had intervened quite forcibly. The injustice of the scene had roused him. Why had all the family turned on Stella? No, not all of them. The attack had been instigated and kept going by Cordelia, whose chief aim had seemed to be to wound her mother, who had seemed defenceless.

He had to intervene. It was a duty he could not ignore, for he alone, apart from Stella knew the whole truth. Stella moreover was defenceless because she would not attack him. She would never admit that it was she alone for several years who had kept the family together. When Lucas had introduced him to the editor of the well-known scientific journal, it was Stella who had given him the confidence to accept the amazing offer of a job. It was his first success. He had discovered that concentrating on mathematical and scientific theories was as therapeutic as washing up and far more interesting.

No one put any great pressure on him. His work had proved acceptable; he seemed to have found his true place at last. During the last few years his life had proceeded far more smoothly than it had ever done before. The price, however, had been great. Stella and he had remained together but apart. He could no longer believe that she truly needed him.

Her long-standing friendship with Eloise had definitely been one of the causes. It was Eloise who had helped when he was ill; it was Eloise who had helped to market Stella's children's books. Eloise always seemed to be available. It might have been possible if he had liked and trusted her but he never had. And his distrust had grown with the years. Now, however, Eloise was dead. It seemed a disgusting fact to admit even to himself but the truth was that Eloise's cruel illness and death had given him a flicker of hope that he and Stella might once again come closer. He knew that if Stella made a move towards him, he would be only too ready to respond but he could not call on her any more. If she would only stretch out a hand towards him, he could he thought manage that last steep slope to the firm ground where she walked.

But would it have that effect? Remembering Eloise as an attractive, golden haired girl with great ambitions for wealth and success, he had to admit that he had always been suspicious of her and of her influence on Stella, although in their early years Stella had never been that much influenced. In recent years, however, that had undoubtedly changed; especially if he was to judge by Stella's almost extravagant involvement in Eloise's final illness. Once Stella would have discussed her thoughts and feelings with him but in these years of withdrawal that was no longer possible.

All he had been able to do was to make it possible for her to visit her dying friend.

It was almost amazing how, after the war, Eloise had made her dreams come true. She had obtained an editorial job on a women's magazine, which brought her to London and within visiting distance of the first home that he and Stella had purchased. About a year later they had been forced to rent out a couple of rooms to help to pay the mortgage and Eloise had been their first tenant. He had reluctantly agreed because of the bitter knowledge that his failure to provide adequately had made this necessary. He had consoled himself with the thought that it would only be for a short time. Nevertheless, he had found it difficult not to resent her proximity and to fear it.

His fears, however, had come to seem foolish for she had clearly been more interested in her relationship with her editor, a married man, who had visited her regularly twice a week. After a few months she had departed, presumably to make a permanent life with him.

This, however, had not lasted long, for less than a year later she had departed for New York with the millionaire magazine proprietor, Conrad Lestrange, who after offering her an editor's job had soon made her his third wife. Eloise's dreams of wealth and success seemed at last to have been realised. The marriage had only lasted a couple of years but after a profitable divorce she had returned to London as the editor of a leading fashion magazine.

Since her return, she had rarely visited them, except when he was in hospital, although she and Stella had continued to meet several times a year. He knew that she had been helpful when he was ill but Stella had never told him exactly what she had done.

Fifteen years later still beautiful, rich and successful, she had retired to her Sussex home to die of breast cancer, without the comfort of relatives and friends, as her funeral had made painfully clear. Only Stella had remained faithful and, although he had wished that it might not have been so, he had understood that because of Stella's character it was inevitable. Now at least that was over; they were free of her influence.

'Dad!' It was Cordelia's voice that disturbed him. She was standing in the doorway, apparently now quite calm, although traces of her earlier tears could still be seen. 'Have you finished?'

'Practically.' He looked around. Everything was as it should be.

'Can I speak to you then?'

'Of course.' Feeling weary suddenly, he sat down on a convenient stool, as Cordelia came further into the room.

'I want to say I'm sorry.' She sounded nervous but determined.

'Isn't it more important for you to apologise to your mother? You annoyed me but you were very hurtful to her.'

'Yes, I suppose so.' She was impatient with him. 'I will do it later but I want to speak to you first.'

'Why?' He stared hard at her.

'It's hard to explain but I think you understand me. Years ago when it was just you and Mum, Dominic and me, we had lots of fun. I always thought we were special friends. Then everything changed.'

'That was a long time ago.' He sighed involuntarily. 'But I suppose you're scarcely old enough to know that everything changes, including people.'

'I do have enough sense to realise that. I just wish it wasn't so. Recently I've been thinking about those times a lot.' Her voice trembled and he was afraid she was going to start crying again but she controlled herself. 'I just wish we could go back. Everything seemed so simple then and we were happy. Now, I so often feel confused and depressed.' Her voice trailed away as she looked appealingly at him. 'You do understand, don't you, Dad?'

'We're all tempted to feel like that sometimes, especially when we look back but you have to realise that it's mostly an illusion. In a few years' time, you'll probably think how happy you were at eighteen.' He felt the triteness of what he said but he had so little comfort to give anyone.

'I doubt that.' She spoke vehemently. 'At times I feel so cut off from everybody, especially you. I've always loved Mum, of course but I used to think when I was little that we were especially close because we were similar. We still are similar, I think, but not close any more. Don't you like me now I've grown older?'

'Of course I do. You're a lovely girl.' He wished he could

throw off the heaviness in his head, then he might be able to speak more warmly. It seemed to be impossible, however.

'Is it because of Mum? Are you afraid she might be jealous? She always wants to be first, doesn't she?'

Patrick stood up quickly. This must be answered. 'You're being silly now, Cordelia. Do stop indulging in this amateur psychology or whatever it's supposed to be. You said some pretty cruel and untrue things to your Mother at supper. It's about time you realised that she is an intelligent, talented woman, who, I believe has every right to use her abilities. Furthermore by using them, she is enabling us all to have a better life than I could have provided for you alone. And don't give me any of that anti-materialist nonsense. You would not enjoy being poor, believe me.'

Cordelia was not to be put off. 'But don't you see, Dad,' she protested, 'she is forcing you into the background all the time. It isn't fair.'

Anger which he had thought he had succeeded in controlling almost overwhelmed him as it had so often in earlier years. Only his love for Stella helped him to control it, so that he could answer Cordelia with sufficient calmness. 'I'm afraid you don't know what you're talking about. It's a fault of yours. You get highly emotional and irrational and cease to consider the truth. Believe me, in this case, you're quite wrong. You'd better humble your pride and apologise to the right person. I don't want you to hurt your mother any more... Do you understand?'

'I'm sorry, Dad. I'll go now.' She was obviously upset by his unexpected vehemence.

'Good. And make sure the others go too.'

'They already have.' She moved quickly towards the door.

'And, if you have any real problems, why don't you try talking to your mother about them. You'll find that's she very good at helping, if only you ask her.' Why did he not apply that advice to himself, he wondered?

'I will. Goodnight, Dad.'

For some time after Cordelia had gone, Patrick stayed in the kitchen trying to understand what had happened. He had to admit to himself that the faults for which he had blamed Cordelia had too often been his own. She was right. She was like him and for that reason he could give her little help. They were almost bound to clash. It was better that she should despise him, if that would encourage her to turn to Stella for help. He felt that he could be of little use to anyone.

Coming out of the kitchen at last into the adjoining breakfast room, he found Julia still working at the table. He spoke gently to her because she always reminded him of the younger Stella who had worked so hard and so purposefully. She also resembled Stella closely. 'You ought to be in bed, you know. It's nearly half past ten.'

'I know I ought.' She looked up at him wearily. 'The trouble is that I was late starting because I had to try to sort Cordelia out a bit. She was so upset. But I've still got to get this Maths problem solved before tomorrow.'

Hesitantly, he approached her. 'Can I possibly help you?'

'Would you? It's probably quite simple really but my brain refuses to cope.'

'I expect it's because you're tired.' Looking over her shoulder, he quickly made some suggestions. In a few minutes it was done.

'Thanks, Dad. You're brilliant, you know.' She smiled at him and for almost the first time he felt close to her.

'Brilliant is hardly the word, I think but I'm willing to try any time you need help.'

As he was about to move off, she surprised him by appealing to him. 'Would you think I was mad if I told you that I was thinking of taking Sciences for my A levels, instead of languages?'

He was interested. 'Are you by any chance thinking of taking medicine for a career? Your grandad would be very pleased if you did.'

"Fraid not. Pure Science is what interests me – Maths, Physics and perhaps Chemistry. Was Grandad disappointed when you didn't take up medicine?'

'Very. And he didn't leave me in any doubt about it.'

'I bet that was horrid. Why didn't you, though?'

'I knew that I didn't have the right personality. But, apart from that, I couldn't face the stress of all those examinations.'

'Have you ever regretted your decision?'

'No. Better to be a mediocre scientific journalist than a failed doctor. I've hurt less people that way.'

'Why do you talk about yourself in that way, Dad? I think some of your articles are very interesting. You've obviously gone on learning without exams. I should think that's harder.'

'It took me several years of failure before I discovered my little talent. And even now I find it very hard.' He smiled at her. 'So don't flatter me too much. And don't try to distract me. It's still time for you to go to bed.'

'OK.' She grinned cheerfully at him, as she began to pack up her books. 'I'm glad we had this talk anyway. You'll support me about science, won't you?'

'Probably.' He laughed suddenly. 'You're a very persuasive, young woman, just like your mum was at your age.'

'Thanks. I know that is a compliment. By the way, Mum's still in the study, if you want to speak to her.'

'I was thinking it was about time for our late night drinks. When you say goodnight to her, ask her what she would like.' It must be obvious, he realised, that he was avoiding speaking to Stella. Julia however made no comment but went out, coming back with the answer: 'Mum would like hot milk with a dash of coffee. She's just going to bed, so you'd better take it up to the bedroom.'

'Thanks. As you go past, just tell her it'll be ready in about ten minutes.'

'Twenty, if I know you, Dad.' She gave him a last friendly grin.

'You know me only too well,' he responded as he walked towards the kitchen. Julia had begun to show an unusually mature ability for accepting people as they were. That was probably why he found it easier to deal with her. She reminded him of Stella but she had not as yet Stella's loving and hopeful confidence.

Julia had been right. It was nearly twenty minutes later before he climbed the stairs warily with his tray of hot drinks and biscuits. As he reached the landing, he noticed that the light was still on in the smallest bedroom – Ben's. Putting down his tray he quietly opened Ben's door. To his surprise, his son was not reading but simply lying there with his eyes wide open. 'You ought to be asleep,'

'I can't sleep. I thought if I put the light on, I might feel better. It's so miserable in the dark.'

Patrick sat on the bed, puzzled by this revelation of unexpected unhappiness. Ben was normally cheerful. 'What's wrong?'

Ben hesitated then the words burst out of him. 'I hate my new school. It's too big and I haven't any friends there. My best friends, Peter and Mike, have gone to St Ignatius College. They really like it there but...'

'It costs money.' Patrick finished the sentence for him. 'It might get better you know, Ben. You've only been there for less than four weeks.'

'It won't.' Ben was sure. 'I might get used to it but I'll never like it. I wish I was clever like the others. They all got scholarships and I wanted to go to St Ignatius especially because Dominic was there.'

'I understand. Have you said anything to your mum?'

'No. I don't want to worry her; she's had so many bad things lately to cope with. You mustn't say anything, Dad, promise me.'

'Has it occurred to you that it may be one of the reasons why she wants this new job, which you all seem so angry about?'

Ben stared at him. 'I never thought! I wouldn't want her to do it for me. It wouldn't be fair! Has she said anything to you?'

'No,' Patrick admitted sadly, 'but that doesn't mean she hasn't thought about it. I think we'd better wait and see, don't you?' He covered Ben up carefully. 'Goodnight and try to sleep. We'll talk about it another time.' As he went out, shutting the door quietly behind him, he realised that his talk with Ben had delayed him for at least another five minutes.

It was over half an hour since Julia had given Stella Patrick's message about the hot drink. After hugging her and kissing her goodnight, she had said cheerfully, 'He's bound to be at least twenty minutes! You know Dad!'

Her last words seemed especially ironic since it was precisely that which she had been wondering about since he had left her to go to the kitchen. 'Did she know Patrick at all any more?' Looking over the old photographs had reminded how much had changed. Then there was another question. Would that younger Stella have allowed them to drift on for years in this almost neutral relationship – asking few questions and answering none? Surely not!

Immediately after he had left her at the table, she had been bitterly hurt and angry. How could he leave her so coolly after what had happened? If he had any love left for her at all surely he would have understood how much she needed to be reassured and comforted? How could he think that doing a few household chores could replace that?

She had wanted to run after him and force him out of his unnatural calm. Once she would have shouted at him, shaken him and then kissed and hugged him until the cold, black mood was forced to depart and he returned her hugs, smiling in spite of himself as he did so. They had managed that way for the first fifteen years of their marriage then events had changed them and she had ignored this until the last few months and especially at Eloise's funeral.

She had continued to pray all those years but God had seemed distant. Now she had begun to feel that God was telling her that something big was required of her, if only she had sufficient love and humility to do it.

Her anger and resentment had evaporated as she got into bed but she had no ideas as to what she should do. As the door opened and Patrick came in, balancing the drinks carefully on the tray, she prayed.

Patrick was very conscious as he came in that he was at least fifteen minutes later than even Julia's estimate. Stella who was always so efficient had every right to be annoyed, particularly after the way he had failed to support her. She was sitting up in bed looking very beautiful, he thought in her delicate pale green nightdress. The years had changed her so little. The same large hazel eyes regarded him thoughtfully and he was comforted to notice that she was smiling slightly. 'I'm afraid I've been a long time even for me.' He walked across the room and placed her drink and biscuit on her bedside table.

'What happened?' She was still smiling.

'Julia wanted some help with her Maths and I was actually able to give it to her. Then I noticed that Ben's light was still on, so I went in and persuaded him to turn it off and settle down.'

To his surprise she put out her hand and touched him. 'I'll have to forgive you then, since you've been busy doing more important things, like being a good father.' Was there a reproach here he wondered for his inability to support her earlier?

As if divining his thought, however, she continued quickly. 'Bring your drink over here and sit on the bed, I could do with some comfort too.' As he hesitated, she begged him, 'Please Patrick.'

The first thing she said as he sat down, surprised him. 'I want to tell you how sorry I am for not telling you about the job. It wasn't planned. It was simply thoughtless. Your opinion matters very much. The trouble is that I've been thinking far too much about what concerns me. The children were quite right.'

'No,' he interrupted her. 'I don't agree with that. You've had a very difficult time lately, trying to help Eloise. The family has to learn that they can't always come first. And, if in the children you include Cordelia, you're very wrong. She was completely out of order. I made that clear to her when she came to talk to me in the kitchen.'

'Thank you. You're very good to me.'

'Why shouldn't I be?

'Because I hurt you. I didn't realise how much until you told me that you felt that I'd treated you like one of the children. It was cruel of me to do that to you. I can't find words to say how sorry I am. Can you forgive me?'

For a moment he was silent then hesitantly he put his arm round her. 'Surely, there's no need for you to ask me that? You have forgiven me so many worse things. All I want is for you to trust me again. You see, I don't believe that anyone could have a better wife than I have and I know that no one could have done less to deserve it. Nothing that has happened has changed my feelings. I love you as much as I ever did.'

'Why haven't you said that before?' She leaned her head against his shoulder.

Feeling that he was not rejected he was able to answer. 'Because I didn't think you would want to hear it or even be able to believe it after what had happened. I felt you had turned away from me and I couldn't blame you. I was only grateful that you let me stay with you and do what small things I could to help, even if you no longer really needed me.'

'I suppose it was like that for a while because we were both shattered. That was natural but we shouldn't have let it go on. I shouldn't at least. And I'm not going to let it go on any more. Just recently, I've been realising what an idiot I've been. And you're an even bigger idiot if you think I don't need you. I've always needed you and I still do. In my own way, Patrick, I love you as much as ever I did. Don't you ever forget that. It's been pretty hard in the last few years but it would have been much worse if you hadn't been here.' Quickly she put her arms round him and pulled him close to her. 'Now give me a real hug and kiss me properly,' she ordered.

He did not hesitate. After a few moments he released her slightly, so that he could look into her eyes. They smiled happily at each other. 'It's not so difficult is it?' she asked. 'Even if we are a bit out of practice.' To prove that it wasn't, he kissed her again. 'There are things we have to talk about,' he suggested after a few minutes. 'But we don't have to do it now, do we?' she asked. 'Can't we just be happy again tonight? I've been so afraid and lonely, lately. I suppose it's partly because of Eloise.'

'Well, that's all over now and we're together.' He was just about to kiss her again when the phone rang.

As Stella reached for it on her table he felt an irrational stab of fear. 'Leave it', he said but he was too late.

'It's very late for you to be ringing, Dominic.' She leaned comfortably against Patrick. 'We're just going to bed.' She smiled at Patrick while she listened. 'I see,' she said at last. 'Of course there's no reason why you shouldn't come. We'll expect you on Saturday morning. Good night, dear.'

'What was that all about?' Patrick asked, pulling her close to him again.

'I'm not sure. He wants to come home again on Saturday.' She sat up moving away from him a little. She seemed worried.

'Why on earth should he? He's only just dashed back, apparently because he had a lot of work to do.'

'And a girl friend to see,' Stella added.

'I'm damned if I can understand him.' Patrick was irritated.

'When I was his age, I only wanted to be with you whenever I could.'

Stella smiled. 'Perhaps he's not as lucky as you were!'

'How could he be? But what's his excuse?'

'He says something has happened which has upset him a lot and he must talk to us.'

'And he didn't give you a clue?'

'No, but he sounded very upset and that's not like him, is it?'

'I suppose not.' He wanted to be fair but he was still irritated. Dominic had not chosen a very good moment. A young man of twenty ought to be more independent, he thought. Before he could say more, Stella drove away his gloomier thoughts by kissing him. 'Don't let it worry you. Get undressed, then we can drink our milk before it's cold. After that, we can have a nice friendly hug, just like we used to have. It's too late now to talk but we can enjoy being together again.'

Chapter Seven

Dominic waited until the end of lunch before he dropped his bombshell, which only Patrick and I were expecting. As we were all still chatting happily, he stood up suddenly, pale and determined. 'If you don't mind, Dad,' his blue eyes were fixed on Patrick, 'I'd like to speak to you and Mum alone for a few minutes.' Ben broke off in the middle of a sentence to stare at him, while Julia and Cordelia exchanged surprised looks.

Patrick stood up immediately. 'Shall we go to the study then?' He turned to me and I nodded. We made our way in a rather solemn procession, Patrick leading and Dominic in the rear. The others still sat staring at us; obviously wondering whatever it could be that could not be said in front of them.

Once we were in the study Dominic shut the door firmly and remained standing in front of it. I sat down on the chair in front of my desk, while Patrick stood behind me with his hand resting lightly on my shoulder as if to reassure me. I was very pleased that we had seemed to come closer again in the last two days – closer than we had been for eight years. I felt more secure than I had done for a long time.

Dominic seemed unsure how to begin, so Patrick took control. 'Whatever you have to say, say it quickly. It's better that way, don't you think?'

Instead of answering, Dominic after searching in the pocket of his denim jacket produced a crumpled envelope and took out a letter. 'It would probably be best if you read this first.' After handing it to me, he stood and waited. Slowly I unfolded the letter with a horrible sick feeling. As soon as I saw Eloise's signature, I guessed what the contents must be. Patrick leaned down a little and read it over my shoulder. It was surprisingly short, considering the information that it gave. It was dated a few days before her death, just after I had last seen her, before she became unconscious.

'Dear Dominic,' Eloise had written, 'I'm afraid it will be something of a shock to you to receive a letter from the grave from me. I have asked my solicitor not to send it to you until after my funeral. I have thought about this a great deal and changed my mind several times but I feel that I do not want to die without sending you some word from me.

'You see, Dominic, I am your natural mother. I've never seen you since you were a baby but I've received regular news about you from your adopted mother. It was she, my dearest friend, who when I was in a desperate situation, helped me by taking you as her own son. I think that you should know that she only kept this secret because I insisted on her doing so. I could not possibly keep you but I couldn't endure the thought of your going to a Home or to some family who would not love you properly. I've never regretted it because I know you have had a good and happy home. Now, before I die, I don't want to interfere with that, I simply want you to know the truth and to tell you that I wish that you may have a long, successful and happy life. All my love, Eloise.'

Patrick took the letter from me and read it again slowly. Only I knew what a shock it must be to him. When he had finished, he folded it up carefully and handed it back to Dominic. His hands tightened on my shoulders but he said nothing.

'Why didn't you tell me?' Dominic almost shouted at us. 'Surely, you could have spared me the shock of this?'

'You always knew you were adopted. So it isn't such a terrible shock, is it?'

'You never told me Eloise was my mother.'

'Would it have made such a difference? I think you are tending to exaggerate the situation.'

'You don't understand, do you? I would have liked to have spoken to her before she died, instead of having this horrible letter when it's too late. You've both been wonderful to me but she was my natural mother. And she could have told me things, which might have helped me to understand myself, don't you see? I would have liked to have seen her once, and talked to her as my mother. It's horrible to know that you've both lied to me all these years. '

His words were mainly addressed to Patrick. It was time for me to intervene. 'You mustn't blame your father, Dominic. Until he read this letter, he didn't know that Eloise was your mother. He too has had a shock. Only Eloise and I knew the truth.'

Dominic stared at me as if he couldn't believe what I had said. 'Why are you saying such things, Mum? You can't expect me to believe that Dad knew nothing at all about it?' When I didn't answer, he burst out, 'So you lied to Dad as well as to me? I never imagined that you could do something like that.' He sat down suddenly. 'I don't feel that I really know you at all any more.'

'I didn't lie. It was just that I didn't tell the whole truth.'

'You know that doesn't make any real difference, Mum. You often told us that. So why did you do it?' He turned quickly to Patrick before I could reply. 'I'm very sorry, Dad, I wouldn't have done it this way, if I'd known.' Then he turned back to me. 'Why did you do it, Mum? It's so unlike you. At least I think it's unlike you.'

I tried to keep calm, clasping my hands to hide their trembling, blinking my eyelids to keep back my tears. 'My chief reason for doing it,' I told him, 'was because that was the way Eloise wanted it as she has told you. She made me promise to keep it a secret from everyone.'

'What even from Dad? Surely you didn't think that was right? And how could it possibly have been managed?' He looked to Patrick seeking information.

Patrick answered him quietly and apparently unemotionally but his hands tightened even more on my shoulders. 'I thought you came from the adoption agency. The papers were in order. Your name on the birth certificate was given as James Parker and your mother's name as Lucy Parker.' He turned to me.

'Lucy was Eloise's second name and "Parker" was her third name which was her mother's maiden name. Eloise arranged it all. I don't know how.'

'But you agreed to it. Why?' Dominic stared at me.

'I had known Eloise for years. She was my closest friend and she was desperate. She couldn't keep you but she wanted to know that you would have a good home. I was the only person who could help her.'

'What about her parents? They weren't poor, were they? Couldn't they have helped her?'

'You don't understand the situation,' Patrick intervened. 'Twenty years ago it was a great disgrace for a young woman to be in Eloise's situation. Her comfortable middle class parents wouldn't want their "respectability" compromised. I'm right, aren't I, Stella?'

'She didn't tell her parents. She knew what their reaction would be. I was her only close friend. She had left her job about four months before you were born. Her savings were very low but she had been offered this wonderful opportunity to go to New York to work for Conrad Lestrange but she obviously couldn't turn up with a tiny baby in tow, particularly as when he had met her some seven months before he had obviously been smitten by her.'

'She married him, didn't she?' Dominic asked.

'Yes. About eighteen months later.'

'And she couldn't do anything about me then, I suppose?'

'No. A small child wouldn't have fitted into her life and you had been legally our child for most of that time. Are you sorry that was so?' I looked anxiously at him.

'No I'm not.' He sounded very definite. 'I think she would have been a pretty selfish mother and I wouldn't have had you two and my sisters and brother. I think I had a good miss.'

'She always wanted to have news about you,' I said quickly. 'I sent her photographs and told her about you, whenever we met but we agreed that it would be wrong to tell anyone.'

'Did she never want to meet me?'

'No. When I last saw her she told me that she had decided not to write to you as she had been thinking of doing but apparently she changed her mind without telling me.'

'That was what I would have expected of Eloise.' Patrick sounded angry. 'She clearly thought doing it this way would cause the maximum trouble.'

'You didn't like her did you, Dad?' Dominic smiled unexpectedly at Patrick. 'I think I can understand why. She sounds a bit tricky.' Then he turned to me. 'But I still don't really understand you, Mum? Why did you agree to do it that way? I can see you wanted to help her but she had no right to insist that you kept it a secret, had she?'

'It seemed my best chance, perhaps my only chance of getting a baby.' I tried to continue but I couldn't. The tears rolled down my cheeks.

'I think you've asked enough questions for the moment, at least,' Patrick said quietly, stepping forward. 'But perhaps I should remind you that our first baby had died just before he was born and that your mother was told that she was unlikely ever to have a living child of her own. I'm sure it is difficult for a young man of your age to understand what pain and grief a woman can suffer at such a time but you should try to think about it before you make a judgment, don't you agree?'

Dominic was silent for a few moments, before he walked over and kissed me. 'I'm sorry, Mum', he whispered. Standing up again, he looked at Patrick. 'You're right, Dad. 'You've both been very straight with me and I think it's time for me to think how lucky I am instead of making a fuss about my "so-called mother". After all, I always knew I was adopted. It was just a bit of shock to learn like this who my birth mother was.' He walked towards the door and then stopped. 'What shall I tell the others? They're bound to be curious.'

'Perhaps as little as possible until we've all had time to think it out,' Patrick suggested. 'What do you think, Stella?'

Wiping my eyes, I lifted my head. 'I think it's better to tell the truth, though not necessarily all of it. Simply tell them that you had a letter from Eloise telling you she was your natural mother and you wanted to talk to us about it.'

'Right.' Dominic considered again. 'I'll tell them that but I shan't say anything about Dad not knowing. That's got nothing to do with them, has it?' He smiled at us both, then went out shutting the door behind him.

We were alone and I had no idea what to say. It seemed almost unbelievable that Eloise should finally have sent the letter and that it had arrived just at this moment, as if it was intended to destroy our new found trust. Patrick sat down opposite me. 'I'm very sorry,' was all I could think to say. 'I never intended that you should find out in this way.'

'That's obvious. But surely the real question is – did you intend me to find out at all? You don't seem to have been in any hurry to tell me the truth. I can just about understand how it happened in the beginning, as I tried to explain to Dominic, but I can't understand why you kept the secret from me long after the adoption had been finalised. There was a time once when you and I used to tell each other everything, or so I thought. I know that hasn't been so for the last eight years but apparently it had stopped long before that. When did Eloise take my place?' As he stopped speaking, he looked steadily at me, clearly not intending to say any more until I had answered him.

I wished he sounded angry instead of sad and depressed. 'She never took your place. How could she? I suppose, however that we became closer when you were sent to Germany just after our marriage. I was very lonely, in a strange town with no friends. She was stationed in London. I wasn't very far away, so we met as often as we could. I needed someone, especially as you scarcely communicated with me.'

'I know I failed you then but I thought you understood, as it had happened for a shorter time when I was in France. That was how separation from you affected me. I shut down all my feelings and lived a totally unreal life until I could be with you again. I was selfish. I expected too much even from you. When I got back, you were so welcoming that I didn't realise what had happened. I assumed that we were now back to normal and as close again as we always had been, as I had thought. It seems that I was wrong.'

He stood up slowly as if he were about to leave the room. I too stood up and caught hold of him. 'Don't go, Patrick, please, I must talk to you.'

'There is really nothing more to say, is there? While I was away our relationship had changed but you were too kind to tell me when I came back. Later you made a promise to your best friend when she was in a desperate situation and you naturally kept it. Now she is dead, I suppose you might have intended to tell me, only she has forestalled you in a somewhat cruel way. I'm afraid you've not been very lucky in your friends, Stella. Both of us have been selfish in different ways. I would like to put it behind us but I can't help wondering how many more secrets you have? And will they ever be revealed to me unless you're forced to reveal them? It makes nonsense of your pretending, as you did on Thursday that we can be close again. You must see that.' He tried to detach himself from me.

I still hung on to him, however. I knew that if he left now all the gains we had made in the last two days would be lost and we would be perhaps even further apart. I could not allow that to happen. 'You're wrong. There's a lot more to say.' I tried to sound strong and sure. This was no time for stupid tears. 'Please sit down and listen. As soon as you came back, neither Eloise nor anyone else mattered to me. You can't possibly believe she did. You know how happy we were. I couldn't possibly have pretended that, could I? Why on earth should I have done so?'

He turned and looked at me, as he had often done when we were young, wanting to know the truth. I tried to meet his gaze without flinching. Suddenly he relaxed. 'I can't think of any reason.' As I released him, he moved across the room and sat on the sofa. Immediately I went and sat next to him. For a moment we were both silent, then unexpectedly he took my hand in his. 'I've been much happier since Thursday night,' he said, 'when you told me you still wanted me. But how can I believe that it's really true.'

'It certainly is,' I assured him. 'I want us to go forward. We've wasted too much time. I suppose our baby's death affected me even more than I realised and I acted in a way I would not normally have done. I think I was afraid you might not agree and I couldn't bear the thought of that. Then, when it was all over and Eloise had gone away, perhaps for good, it didn't seem to matter any more. You now loved Dominic as I did, then Cordelia was born. It may seem a bit incredible but I didn't think about it. I was too busy and happy. When she did come back into my life, I had far more important things to think about and you weren't ready to be bothered with unnecessary worries.'

'And this letter was a great surprise to you?'

'A horrible shock. I can't understand why she did it, especially when she'd said she wouldn't. No good could come of it.'

'Poor Stella! You never understood her, did you? You always hoped she would do what was right, didn't you?'

'Yes. I always thought that if I cared for her and trusted her, she would respond. You know that's what I've always believed. Surely, you do?'

'Of course I do. And many people do respond to your love but Eloise was different.'

'How do you mean – different?'

'She never had any intention of responding to what I might call your missionary efforts.' His smile took out any sting there might have been in the words. 'You, on the other hand never understood what it was that she really wanted.'

'And that was?'

'To come between you and me. I suspected that the first time I met her. And she soon convinced me that I was right by many things that she said and did.'

'And that's why you never liked her? But are you sure you're right?'

'Of course. Don't you remember how she separated you from your friend at primary school and years later from you friend, Elizabeth, at secondary school. I was obviously a much bigger threat.'

'I don't understand you.' I frowned, still puzzled. Why should that be?'

'You were very important to her. She wanted you for herself.'

'You surely not suggesting that she was really a Lesbian, are you? I assure you there was never anything like that between us.'

'Not necessarily. She certainly used her sexual attractions to advance her career. I think it was probably power she wanted and she very much wanted to have you because you were so different. Having you would have been a real triumph. Think about it, Stella. You're intelligent enough to understand what I'm trying to say.'

I needed time to think about this and as Patrick was patient, I was able to look back over my past life and see many incidents in a different light. 'I think you may be right,' I said finally. 'But I really thought she was changing when she was so ill and that's why I gave her so much of my time. But she wasn't any different, was she? If she had been she wouldn't have sent this cruel letter.' Even as I said this, I knew I wasn't being entirely fair but I had to keep Patrick with me, especially now.

Patrick kissed me gently. 'I'm so very sorry. I know you really wanted to help her.'

'I did but I was a fool. I neglected you and the family for months because of her. It was a sort of pride. Saint Stella saving the sinner but forgetting her husband and family. I can understand their outburst now when I suggested that I might take a full-time job. It must have seemed that it was just another way of escaping from them and you. I'm so very sorry, Patrick. What can I do?'

'Just come back to loving us as you've always done. It won't matter any more. She's dead now. This was I imagine her last malicious gesture. You and I can come back together again. That is if you really do want to as you said you did on Thursday night.'

'You know I do. I would never want to be without you. Things have gone wrong in the last few years but I think that now we can begin to put them right with God's help.' We kissed each other and stayed together quietly for a few moments. 'I'm afraid,' I said at last, 'that I'll just have to leave more discussion for another time, I'm so tired and confused.'

'As long as we are together, we can wait,' he replied. 'In fact, I think it's time we had a happy family time without any questions.'

'What do you mean?' I leaned comfortably against him.

'I'm going to take you up to our room for a couple of hours quiet and rest. I'll deal with the family and then see if I can book some seats for the theatre tonight. They've just put on a revival of an old comedy but I read it wasn't heavily booked, so I should be lucky. How would you like that?'

'It would be heavenly.' It was the first time for years that Patrick had taken it upon himself to arrange an outing like this. It seemed a very good sign. I smiled at him. 'Have I ever told you I love you?'

'Occasionally but not often enough. I, of course, don't have to tell you because you know only too well that I've loved you since I was three and considered myself more or less married to you at five.'

'And you've never looked at anyone else?' I laughed.

'Never and it's too late to start now.' He pulled me to my feet. 'No more idle chatter now. I want you to have that rest.' Gratefully I went with him.

Chapter Eight

As soon as the door closed behind Patrick, Stella lay back intending to rest as he had advised her. Immediately she closed her eyes, however, there were questions clamouring to be answered. Why had she behaved as she had about Dominic? Why had she listened to Eloise and never confided in Patrick? Why even now did she avoid this? Was it really to protect Patrick as she had always told herself it was? Memories of that terrible day twenty years ago flooded over her.

She was still lying on a bed but the room was bare and sterile with a high ceiling. It was twilight, a time she had always disliked and she was in pain. The pain in her body was nothing, however compared with that other pain. The words that had been spoken to her by the doctor and the midwife echoed and re-echoed through her head. 'We are afraid that your baby is dead, Mrs Gestenge. We've been unable to find any trace of a heartbeat. We're very sorry.'

Somehow she must have asked a question but she couldn't remember it, only the answer. 'The best thing you can do is to try to have a normal birth. That will be better for you in the future. We'll help you all we can.' The doctor had departed. The midwife had lingered for a moment, obviously wanting to be consoling. She straightened the covers, shook the pillows, then with a final, 'I'm very sorry, dear,' she too left. Stella was completely alone.

'Your baby is dead. We're very sorry. We're very sorry.' She put her hands over her ears but the words could not be cut out. Even Patrick had gone away some time ago, promising to be back in the evening. Why was he not here? Frantically, she sat up. 'I can't stay here,' she almost shouted to drown the other words. 'I won't stay here. What is the point?' Without pausing to think, she scrambled awkwardly off the high bed and made for the door.

The corridor was long and deserted. The dusk was deepening. She looked through the window and far below saw normal happy people going about their lives. Scarcely pausing, she hurried on to the corner, without considering where she was going. All she knew was that she must get away. She must find Patrick. He would deal with this nightmare. Rounding the corner, she almost fell over him. He clutched her in his arms. 'Stella, what are you doing? Where are you going?'

Unable to answer him coherently at first, she clutched at him, trying to control her shuddering sobs. Realising that something must be very wrong, he did not attempt to get her to speak until he had gently helped her back to her room and on to her bed. Then holding her hand firmly in his and supporting her with his other arm around her shoulders, he spoke quietly. 'What is wrong, Stella, darling? Please try to tell me.'

Making a tremendous effort she answered him. 'The doctor and the midwife have just told me that our baby is dead. They can't hear its heart beating.' She stared at him, the tears rolling down her cheeks. Even as she spoke the words, she couldn't believe that they were true. And yet they must be.

'When did they tell you that?' He held her hand even more firmly.

'About five or ten minutes ago. The doctor said it would be best for me to try to have the baby naturally. And they said they were very sorry.'

'And then they left you – alone?'

'Yes, and I couldn't bear it, Patrick. I had to get away. I had to find you. I'm so glad you came just then.'

'So am I, darling.' He kissed her gently and wiped away her tears. 'Lie down and try to relax. There might be some mistake. You haven't seen Mr Brooke?' She shook her head. They sat quietly for a few minutes, holding hands, until suddenly Patrick stood up. 'The bastards!' He was very angry. 'How could they leave you alone after telling you that? Couldn't they at least have waited until I was here? They're not fit to look after anyone!' He walked towards the door.

'Don't leave me, Patrick!' She sat up.

'Of course I won't, at least not for more than a few minutes. I'm going to find Mr Brooke or his registrar and get the truth. I'll come straight back. I promise.' Without another word, he was gone and she was alone again but at least she knew that he was here and that he would defend her.

She waited a long fifteen minutes, trying to remember all she had learned about relaxing. As he came back, into the room, she sat up. There was no need to ask questions. She could tell from his face that he did not bring good news. 'I've seen Mr Brooke.' He paused.

'However did you manage that?'

'I was so angry and determined. They had to give way. I asked him to explain why you were told only two days ago by his registrar that everything was fine and now today you were given this news without any preparation or explanation. And then you were left alone and that when I met you, you were so distressed that you were running away. I told him that I was disgusted with the inhumane behaviour of his staff.' He sat down beside her again and took her hand gently.

'What did he say?'

'He seemed upset as well he might be. He then said he would first look into everything and come and see you himself in about ten minutes.'

At first she felt a glimmer of hope but as she looked into Patrick's set, white face, she doubted. 'You don't think he'll have anything different to say?'

'I hope so but I don't feel very confident, Stella, my darling.'

Patrick was right, as she had feared. Mr Brooke examined her carefully. He was kind and sympathetic but he could offer neither hope nor explanation. 'It seems to be,' he explained to Patrick, 'one of those inexplicable things that very occasionally happen.' He turned to Stella. 'You must try to be brave. We will do all we can to help you.' As he was leaving, he turned to Patrick. 'Are you able to stay for an hour or two?'

Without hesitation, Patrick answered him. 'I intend to stay to the end. I would never consider leaving my wife to face this alone.' He held her hand tightly and, even in her pain and misery, Stella felt the comfort of his love.

Mr Brooke appeared to consider the situation. 'I wouldn't encourage most husbands to do that. In fact, most of them prefer not to be around but, in your case, I'm prepared to leave the decision to you and your wife. I will be in to look at your wife later and I'll be present at the delivery.'

'You do want me to be here, don't you?' Patrick turned to her.

'I don't know how I could bear it, if you weren't. I feel so much stronger when you're holding my hand. I know you'll look after me.'

'I wish I could bear it all for you. But, since I can't, I'll do all I can and I won't leave you.'

The midwife seemed almost outraged at the thought of Patrick's presence but she could not gainsay Mr Brooke. As soon, as she realised however how calm and helpful he was and how much Stella wanted him she relented completely. And so the long, dark hours slowly passed. From years of practice, Stella knew how to withdraw into her inner being. It was a kind of prayerful meditation when she allowed suffering to happen without opposing it. Patrick's hand and his consoling words alone connected her to reality. She knew she could rely on him and she needed him.

She had begun to feel that the ordeal would never end but just before dawn they decided that it was time to move her to the Delivery Room. With a kiss Patrick reluctantly left her there. She scarcely noticed his leaving for by now the processes of birth had completely possessed her and everything else was forgotten. All seemed to be going well until suddenly they told her to stop pushing and she dimly heard a whispered consultation. After which, the midwife gently told her that there was a little unexpected difficulty but they would give her an anaesthetic and all would be well.

She emerged from the darkness to see a cradle standing in front of the window. Suddenly, she hoped foolishly. Surely there would not be a cradle without a baby? Then the midwife spoke, 'Your baby's dead. You know that, don't you?' From somewhere a quiet, little voice, it must be hers, said calmly, 'Yes, I know.' A few minutes later as they prepared her to go back to her ward, she asked timidly, as if the mother of a dead baby had no rights, 'Was my baby a boy or a girl?'

'It was a boy and he weighed nine pounds.'

What else was there for her to say? A strange kind of

numbness seemed to have fallen over her. The only thing she knew was that she must endure and to do that she would have to be quiet and controlled, in spite of her grief. Patrick was waiting for her but at that moment she had no more tears to shed. She could only cling to his hand, as he told her that at the end there had been a strange complication, a kind of contraction ring. If the baby had been alive they would have had to cut her but as he was not they had been able to cut his shoulders. She listened but it meant nothing.

It was then that she began to realise that Patrick was very angry. He wanted to find out what had happened and to pin the responsibility on to someone. While she sat writing neat, little notes explaining to anyone who needed to know that their nine-pound baby boy had been stillborn, he was constantly leaving her in order to gather information. He spoke at length to his father, who actually travelled to London to see them, borrowed relevant books from a scientific library, gleaning information from wherever he could so that he would be ready to confront Mr Brooke on a day already decided. His father tried to warn him to calm down, begging him not to get too obsessed with what had happened but to consider his wife more. It seemed, however that Patrick couldn't do this. He discussed everything with Stella, believing that she felt as he did. She listened but said very little, finding communication extremely difficult lost as she was in a dark tunnel of pain.

The day after the birth he told her that he had seen their baby. 'He's a lovely boy,' he told her. 'I couldn't see anything wrong with him. They intend to do a post-mortem, however, so we may learn something from that. He looks rather like you.' He seemed unaware of the greater pain she now felt. This was her baby she had known for so many months and so longed to see. She longed to ask if she could see him. Nobody suggested it, however, and she was held back by the feeling that a failed mother should keep quiet.

Just before she left the hated hospital, Patrick told her that the post-mortem had produced no definite results. 'What will they do with him now?' 'I don't know.' Patrick seemed surprised at her question. 'I believe they usually incinerate them.' There seemed to be no words she could find, so she accepted it mutely. There were to be no last rites for her baby; not even a moment in which to say farewell.

Patrick's interview with Mr Brooke produced nothing, except the opinion that if he had taken certain symptoms more seriously he would probably have arranged for a Caesarian to have been done. Mr Brooke also waived his fees, which seemed to give Patrick a momentary satisfaction.

He was still bitter and angry, however and now turned his rage against the God who had left his prayers unanswered. She would not agree with this. 'But you must be angry!' Patrick exclaimed. 'You don't deserve this.' He loved her, he wanted to comfort her but he didn't realise that his anger was separating him from her. She had thought that when they came home, things would be better but they weren't. She felt herself alone in a dark tunnel, struggling to find the light, while outwardly maintaining an apparent calm that amazed everyone. No one could reach her not even Patrick. Then one morning she awoke with the memory of a visitation. The One who had so often come to her in her dreams when she was younger had come again. He brought light and love. 'I am with you, Stella,' he said. I am always there in the darkest and loneliest places.' She felt his hand upon her. 'Good can always be brought out of evil, if you have the faith and the courage. You will know what I mean when the time comes.'

That morning she awoke for the first time with hope and did not begin the day by burying her head under her pillow. A few days later she met Mr Brooke for her final examination and he told her gently that he was afraid that she would never have a living baby. 'If you really want a child, why don't you adopt one?' He smiled at her. 'It's not so difficult, you know.'

As she travelled home, she realised that Mr Brooke had given her the answer. That was obviously the way to bring good out of evil. She who had a fully equipped nursery without a baby could offer it to a baby who had no place. It was hard at first to convince Patrick but when he understood how happy the idea made her, he quickly agreed, although their parents were opposed to it. All that was left was to find the baby.

The adoption society which they approached was willing to

help them but warned them that it might take some time. Unsatisfied though she was, Stella did not see what to do. She considered returning to teaching since the money would be helpful but decided that it would be more likely to take her away from her goal. Empty weeks passed slowly, then one morning she was surprised by a phone call from Eloise.

Since she had left the little flat in their house, early in Stella's pregnancy, Eloise had scarcely been in touch. She had not even responded to Stella's brief communication about the death of her baby. Now, however, she sounded both concerned and consoling. 'How soon can we meet? It might do you good to talk, I think, even to me. Beneath my glittering exterior a heart still beats, though you may find that difficult to believe some times. After all, I am a woman and still your best friend, I hope. Or have you found someone to replace me?'

'Of course not!' Suddenly Stella felt that it might be possible for her to talk to Eloise, even if it was mostly frivolous chatter. Even that would be better than the silent days when Patrick was away. 'I'd love to see you. When do you suggest?'

'Why not lunch today?' Eloise suggested immediately. 'We can eat at a little Italian place near where I'm living now and then we can go back to my place and have a real talk. What do you say?'

Stella was delighted. An empty day had suddenly become brighter. Eloise could always be relied on to be sparkling, however irritating she might be at times. After noting down time and directions carefully, she promised to be there. Putting down the phone she rushed upstairs to find the least dowdy outfit she could wear. There wasn't much choice but for the first time in weeks she made the effort.

Eloise was already there when she arrived. As Stella approached the table, she looked up with her customary bright smile from the menu she was studying. She was wearing a black coat in the 'new look'. Her golden hair gleamed in the latest style. Her beautifully manicured scarlet nails perfectly matched the scarlet bow of her lips. Her smile, however, was friendly and her welcome warm. In a few moments Stella had lost all feelings of inferiority.

During the simple meal they talked happily of the past,

remembering many amusing incidents of their schooldays. 'Do you remember the night before your wedding,' Eloise asked, 'when Elizabeth and I were staying with you?' she began to laugh.

'Could I ever forget it?' Stella too began to laugh.

'We'd just settled down to sleep, after exchanging our maidenly confidences when there was an almighty crash and your mother rushed on to the landing. We rushed out too and she was very embarrassed, saying something about their bed falling down. We asked no questions but it seemed a strange story to me. What could they have been up to?'

'If I remember aright, you had some naughty suggestions to make at the time.' The memory made Stella laugh even more.

'And if I remember,' Eloise retorted, 'you contributed to the merriment by disloyally telling me of her motherly advice to you as she said goodnight to the daughter about to be sacrificed on the altar of matrimony. What was it now?'

'She was very embarrassed but she finally managed to say that she didn't think she need tell me anything as I probably knew more than she did. I could only say demurely that could hardly be true, could it? But she didn't reply.'

'I imagine that you and Patrick already knew how to make love without bringing the bed down. Although you never quite confessed to me, I guessed.' They smiled at one another. 'Alas, for the carefree days of our youth,' Eloise sighed.

Suddenly they were silent. This could not be the conversation Eloise had meant, Stella thought. Looking unexpectedly sad, Eloise summoned the waiter, paid the bill and led Stella out into the street. 'We'll have coffee in my flat and then we can talk properly. That's what I really want us to do. I think we can help one another, perhaps.'

Eloise's flat was much smaller and plainer than Stella had expected, consisting as it did of one room and a tiny kitchenette. Noticing her surprised look, Eloise smiled slightly. 'It's not what you expected, is it?'

'Not really. It isn't the place you went to when you left us, is it? Have you been living here long?' Stella sat down on the divan as Eloise heated up the coffee on the gas ring.

'No, only a few weeks and I shan't be here for more than

another two or three weeks, I hope. I'm going to New York. Conrad Lestrange has renewed his offer on even more favourable terms and I don't think I can afford to turn him down again as I did six months ago. Refusal seemed to make him grow keener but one can't risk that too often.' Eloise turned her attention to the coffee. 'I think it's ready now.' She poured out two cups, handed one to Stella, then sat down at the table to drink hers. Stella waited for a few minutes then, when Eloise did not say any more, she decided to speak herself.

'You said you thought we could possibly help one another. What did you mean?'

Eloise hesitated. 'Can I ask you a question first? What do you intend to do now? You told me that the consultant didn't think you were likely to have a living baby. Is that really so?' Stella nodded, unwilling to speak. 'So, have you decided to give up and go back to teaching? Or have you some other idea?'

'I can't accept that. I want to have a baby.' Stella stopped as her eyes filled with tears.

'He had no right to say that to you when you are so unhappy.'

'Oh, but it was he who gave me the wonderful idea.'

'Whatever was that?'

'He suggested that I could adopt a baby. When I thought it over I realised that it was just the right thing to do.'

'Does Patrick agree?'

'He does after I've talked to him. He's now very keen. The trouble is the Adoption Society says there may be quite a long time to wait.'

'There needn't be.' Eloise moved over to the divan and sat next to Stella.

'How do you mean?'

Eloise replied softly without looking at her. 'I mean that I can offer you a baby.'

'I don't understand. Please don't torment me Eloise!'

'I wouldn't dream of doing that.' Eloise seized her hand. 'Especially when I know from my own experience something of what you are suffering.' Without waiting for Stella to respond she hurried on as if afraid to stop. 'I'm offering you my baby.'

'Your baby!' Stella stared at her. 'What do you mean, Eloise?'

'My baby son born nearly a month ago. He's with a foster mother but I need someone to adopt him before I go to New York.' She laughed bitterly as she saw Stella's horrified expression. 'Yes, your clever friend who said she knew all the answers actually made a fool of herself. I actually trusted someone and now I must pay the price.'

'Oh, Eloise, I'm so very sorry.' Stella put her arm round her friend. 'Won't the father help?'

'Don't mention him. I've put him right out of my life, not that he has any intention of being in it.' She tried to laugh but instead burst into tears. 'The silliest thing of all is that I didn't think I'd mind getting rid of the baby. I thought he had a right to life but that was all, but as soon as I saw him, I loved him. I must go to New York. I have scarcely any money and no job otherwise, but I can't bear to think of him going to just anyone. It's silly isn't it?'

'I can understand. I wasn't even allowed to see my baby but I still long for him.'

Suddenly, they were crying and hugging each other. For the first time since her baby's death Stella felt able to come out of her self imposed solitude and speak freely to someone who shared her feelings. Eloise too spoke simply without any of her usual pretence. They were closer than they had ever been. At last they sat up still tearful but able to smile at one another.

'You want me to adopt your baby?' Stella asked.

'I'm begging you to adopt him, then I'll be sure that he will be loved and properly cared for. I don't know how to leave him without knowing that. I love you far more than I ever loved his father, so it seems right to give him to you. You are my only hope, Stella. And perhaps you'll be happier with my baby because you'll know something about him. What do you think?'

'Of course I'll take him,' Stella replied immediately. 'And I promise you I'll love him as if he were my own son.'

Eloise kissed her. 'I knew you would, if only we could talk together and share our pain.'

'You were right. We have helped one another.'

'That's what friends are for, isn't it? But there's one thing I want you to promise me that you will keep my secret. Please, don't tell anyone I'm his mother. I couldn't bear that. And I promise that I'll never make any claim on him. I don't even want to see him after I've handed him over, although I'd like to hear sometimes how he's getting on. Do you understand? It would make the situation much more difficult if anyone knew he was your friend's son.'

'I suppose it would, if you're quite determined that you must give him up.'

'I am. It would be miserable for both of us if I didn't. I'm not the self-sacrificing type. You know that.'

'I suppose not. But what about Patrick? Surely, you don't mean that I can't tell him?'

'He's the last person I would want you to tell.' When Stella looked at her, very surprised, she continued, 'He doesn't like me. He never has. You know that. And, therefore, he might be angry at the idea of accepting my son.'

At first Stella was reluctant to accept this but, after some discussion, she agreed that Patrick might not be entirely willing to accept Eloise's son. Even if he did it for Stella's sake, it still might lead to difficulties in later years. At last they came to an agreement, Eloise promising to arrange everything with the adoption society.

It was now time for Stella to go so that she might arrive home before Patrick. As they kissed goodbye Eloise said, 'Thank you, Stella. I know my son will be safe with you for you have always been good and never a bad girl like me. Now I can return happily to my evil ways!'

'Don't be silly. You're exaggerating, as you always did. But I hope to hear that you're successful in New York.'

'You will. I promise you.' Seeing her bright smile Stella was almost tempted to believe that Eloise had never really been very upset but she dismissed that as very unkind. More likely Eloise was just resuming her normal mask. 'You'll hear from the adoption society in a few days,' Eloise assured her as she left. Everything had in fact, turned out just as she had predicted, but then Eloise was very good at arranging matters.

Chapter Nine

Patrick had accepted the unexpected information about Eloise and Dominic far more equably than I had any right to expect. As I drove home a few days later at lunchtime I felt happy as I thought over the events of the past weekend. It might have been disastrous. In fact, however, we had remained closer than we had been for a long time. Ben had been delighted to be told that my new job would provide enough money to send him to the College in January. Julia had been pleased that I had accepted her decision to study the Sciences. Cordelia was the only problem left to be tackled and I had Julia's support here. As I parked my car in the drive, I decided that I must have that talk with Cordelia as soon as possible, preferably that same evening.

Suddenly, as I walked into the house my mood changed. I had no idea why but, as I sat down, all the thoughts and feelings which I had had during the months of Eloise's illness and which had been so strong at her funeral now swept over me again. Where was the real Stella, I asked myself. Was this the life I had wanted? What was life all about anyway? What was love? It seemed so hard to be sure about anything. Patrick and I had certainly come closer in the last week than we had really been for years. But how far did that go now? Did I now want to go back to the way we had always been until our life had disastrously fallen apart eight years ago? Could I go back? I sat down in the study feeling depressed and hopeless. I was nearly forty-five and I didn't know any of the answers!

A knock on the garden door roused me, fortunately. I hurried to unlock it. Lucas was outside, carrying in one hand a saucepan and in the other a portfolio of illustrations. He was wearing his usual paint stained overalls and his black hair was unruly as always. He was smiling. Handing the saucepan over to me, he said cheerfully, 'I've brought my home made soup. We can have lunch together if you can produce some bread and cheese and apples.

And, after that, you can tell me what you think about these illustrations for your last work. It's about time we got together.'

Immediately cheered, I took the saucepan from him. 'Let's eat in the conservatory. It'll be sunny and warm in there.' Without further discussion, he followed me to the kitchen where we prepared a tray with our simple lunch and then he carried the tray to the conservatory which conveniently opened off the kitchen. It was pleasant in there and for a time we simply enjoyed the sunshine and the food with little conversation.

After we had finished eating I went into the kitchen to make the coffee. When I came back Lucas had stretched himself out comfortably in one of the cane armchairs. Handing him his cup I took an armchair opposite to him. For a moment we both looked down the long stretch of grass bordered by the apple trees which marked the boundary. There was a good crop of apples but they would not be ripe enough to pick for several weeks. The autumn sunshine gave a golden glow to everything. I felt relaxed.

Suddenly my peace was broken. 'Why were you looking so unhappy,' Lucas asked, 'when I arrived?'

'Was I?' I didn't look at him.

After putting his coffee cup down slowly and deliberately, he turned to face me, then put his hand firmly on mine. 'Don't play games with me, Stella. We know one another too well for that.' He smiled waiting for me to respond.

I didn't answer directly. 'Last night I was talking to Julia and she told me what I should have known that it was mainly you who kept things going when I was away looking after Eloise. It was too much for Patrick; Cordelia felt too much was being expected of her; so you stepped in, as I might have known you would. And I have never really thanked you, as I have been too absorbed in myself. I'm sorry and I do thank you very much.' I tried to smile at him.

'Don't be ridiculous.' He held my hand more firmly. 'Since you and Patrick so generously took me in nine years ago, I've been a member of the family – Uncle Lucas and all that. That has meant a lot to me so why shouldn't I act like an uncle when one is urgently needed?'

'No reason, I suppose. It's just that I have come to see that I have been taking everyone for granted, while Eloise was so ill and that it's not surprising that my family resented my suggestion that I should soon take a full time job. They were quite clear about that and actually defended Patrick against his bullying wife.'

'They simply didn't understand the choices you felt you had to make. You can't blame them; they're too young. In any case it seems to me that you and Patrick have become closer than you have been for years, as a result of that discussion. I'm right about that, aren't I?' I nodded. 'Then what is wrong? I come back to my original question. You seemed happier for some days but now you're not. Why is that?'

I didn't want to be evasive, especially not with Lucas, but it was difficult to answer this. 'I was probably just being childish or more accurately adolescent, pondering about life with a capital "L" of course. Asking myself those unanswerable questions. "What's it all about anyway? What really matters? What sort of a person am I?" etc., etc. You know the sort of thing, excusable at twenty but ridiculous at forty-four. Silly, isn't it?' I tried to laugh lightly.

Lucas didn't laugh. 'Not necessarily. Perhaps the truth is that you're just trying to face some problems for the first time.' Releasing my hand he turned to look down the garden again.

'It's not really sensible, is it, because I haven't any answers?'

'Perhaps you're not asking the right questions. Or, perhaps, more importantly, you're afraid to consider what might be the right questions. Sometimes it can be very frightening to think about that.' When I made no answer, he continued. 'I was only a little younger than you are now when I found the courage to ask myself the questions which I had been skilfully avoiding for years. The result was rather devastating, as I had feared, but it was the right thing to do.'

'You're talking about the time when you decided to leave the monastery?' Patrick and I had known that this was what he had done after about twenty years but, respecting his privacy, we had never really questioned him about it. The only information he had given us was that he had been very ill and that, while he was in hospital he had decided that he couldn't go back. 'It wasn't just because of your illness that you decided to leave?'

'Of course not. That simply made it easier. I'd been trying to ask myself the right questions for many months before that.'

'Have you ever regretted that decision?'

'Never.' He looked straight into my eyes. 'How could I when I was so fortunate as to meet you and Patrick and to be generously welcomed into your family? For the first time since I was a child I experienced the healing power of human love.' I dared not speak. 'I don't need to say any more, do I? I love Patrick and your children but, as you know, it is really you to whom my deepest love is given. You are the only woman I've ever truly loved. And because it is love and not just lust, I respected your wishes eight years ago and have remained your friend.'

'I thought we had agreed eight years ago not to speak of that any more?' I hadn't thought to be discussing this and I didn't want to now.

'We did. But perhaps the time has come when it might be better to look at it? It might help you to understand what are the questions you should be asking. And why you are still unsettled, even unhappy.'

'I can't. I don't want to do it, Lucas. It seems the wrong time when Patrick and I have a chance of coming closer together again and of being happy as we were before. Don't you see?'

'If you have that chance, Stella, and, if that is what you want, I would certainly not try to persuade you to do anything else. I've certainly no intention of suggesting some drastic action which could easily harm many people. Surely you know that?'

For the first time I looked directly into his eyes. 'I do know that and I rely on it. I also know that I love Patrick and I love you. And, of course I love my children. But,' I stopped because I still didn't know what the 'but' was; only that it existed.

'You loved Eloise too,' Lucas added.

'I don't know, I think I did, although I'm sure how much she loved me but perhaps I was always too ready to judge her.'

'Don't worry about that now. You acted as if you loved her and that's what really matters You did what you thought was right.'

Feeling very unsure of the true reasons for my actions, at first I made no answer then suddenly I turned to him. 'How can one be sure about things like that? I mean were you sure when you entered the religious life? Did you believe that you were doing God's will?'

'I was very sure. I didn't believe I was trying to escape from the world. On the contrary I was convinced that I was taking on something which although difficult, was indispensable to my happiness.'

'And yet twenty years later you left it. And you say you have no regrets?'

'I certainly have no regrets and I'm convinced that leaving then was right. We have to expect that we might change, especially if we gain a deeper understanding.'

'I don't want to think about that, Lucas. It frightens me.'

' And that is perhaps all the more reason why you should think about it. You're not the sort of person to let your life be dominated by fear.' He smiled lovingly at me. 'It might be more sensible for you to tackle the problem of Cordelia first. She needs a mother's advice.'

'How do you know?'

'From observation and from remembering how I was at her age.' He looked at his watch. 'We haven't much time left. I really must insist on your looking at these illustrations with me. I need your opinion and the publisher won't wait for ever.'

I seized the opportunity to return to 'normality' but I couldn't help realising how well Lucas seemed to understand me.

The discussion of the illustrations didn't take as long as we had expected and some half an hour later we had finished. After he had put them back into the portfolio, Lucas was about to clear away the dishes we had used for lunch but I stopped him. 'Sit down,' I commanded him, 'and tell me how you came to go into the monastery at all. From the few facts you have let slip, you weren't exactly a "holy" young man, were you?'

Sitting down again, he laughed. 'I should hope not. "Holy" people are not usually the right material, they are too busy thinking about themselves instead of God.'

'You mean, I suppose, that they're writing down their good deeds in a heavenly accounts book and working out their balance?'

Lucas nodded. 'I'm afraid no one could have accused me of being holy in any sense of the word.'

'Then why did you do it?'

97

'The primary reason was, I think, that I could no longer endure the emptiness of the life I was living. The second and more important one was that I felt I had a call.'

'Like St Paul?'

'Yes, although it was by no means as dramatic, but it was strong. I'd been pretty well free do to as I liked after I was eighteen when I inherited the money my parents had left. I think I've told you that they died when I was eight. My guardian immediately sent me to Ampleforth where I was reasonably happy. I spent my holidays with him but saw little of him, as he was an elderly bachelor who preferred study to the company of an annoying young boy. I comforted myself with the idea that when I was eighteen I would be free to live my own life without financial worries.'

'And that's what you did?'

'Yes. Instead of going to Oxford, I went to Paris and then to Italy to study art. To my surprise, I discovered that I actually had quite a bit of talent but life was too easy and I didn't apply myself as I should have done.'

'I'm not surprised. Eighteen isn't exactly a mature age.'

'I certainly didn't show much maturity. I learned quite a lot about painting, I even sold a few of my products, but I learned much more about wine, women and the other good things of life. Then the war came. I managed to escape from Paris just before the Germans arrived. At one point, I find myself travelling along a road with crowds of refugees being chased by dive-bombers. I threw myself into a ditch next to a woman with two small children and her husband. The husband had been hit; he was bleeding badly; there was nothing we could do but I stayed with her until he died. Then I travelled with her and the two children until we found some of her relatives. Eventually, after a few more adventures I arrived in London, shocked and exhausted. I still had money but no friends and no family. I intended to volunteer but, before I did this, I felt that I needed a little time to sort myself out.' He stopped and looked at her. 'My whole world had collapsed and I was left realising the total futility of much that I had done.'

'It must have been terrible! What did you do?'

'On an impulse I decided to spend a sort of private retreat at this Trappist monastery. At least, I thought, it will be quiet there and that was what I wanted. For the first three days, I did scarcely anything except sleep. And on the fourth day, I woke up refreshed and ready. But for what? I joined in the prayers of the monastery and I was given a kind of director to talk to.'

'And was it he who persuaded you to enter the monastery?'

'Not at all. He couldn't have done it and he was far too wise to try. I very much enjoyed talking to him and I learned a lot about myself but I was still confused. Until one day just before I was due to leave I found myself remaining in the chapel on my own after Mass. Many things seemed to become clear and I was certain that God was speaking to me and telling me that my proper place was there, in that community. I didn't in the least feel ready or able to do it but the more I resisted, the more insistent the call became. Finally, I submitted and entered on my novitiate. And, as you know, I stayed there for the next twenty years.' He was silent.

'And then you left. Does that mean that you had been mistaken? That God hadn't really called you?'

'I don't think so. I think it simply meant that God now wanted me to move on to something different.' He smiled at me.

I didn't smile back I was far too busy considering what he was saying. 'You mean some people have different vocations at different times? I don't think I've heard any one say that before. People usually say that they must have made a mistake and been deceived by their pride.'

'Perhaps but that isn't necessarily true. I was very happy for many years. As I was studying for the priesthood, I had much to learn and I enjoyed learning. My musical talents were also helpful.'

'Then what changed?'

'I suppose the change really began after my ordination, when the Abbot decided that my artistic talents should be used to help to support the abbey. I was foolish enough to reveal that I had done some work as a potter, so a potter I was destined to be, for the glory of God, of course. I was even sent down to Cornwall to learn the finer points from a famous potter there. Talking with him stimulated my creative ideas and I became pretty good but it all seemed very different when I was working in isolation in the abbey. I suppose if I'd been a good monk, potting and praying would have satisfied me but alas they didn't. Little doubts about my "goodness" began to creep in.'

'By this time weren't you really ready to leave?'

'Yes, but it was very difficult to face the final decision. Fortunately, as you know, I became very ill with cancer. It was neglected and finally I was rushed into hospital for a big operation, two, as it turned out. Then I had to spend some time in convalescence. It was during this time that I had to admit that I couldn't go back. Something vital in me had changed. I now wanted to return to the world on which I had once so readily turned my back.'

'Wasn't this simply a matter of having sinful temptations again?'

'Stop being a devil's advocate, Stella. It doesn't suit you. I just enjoyed being a human being living naturally with others. I enjoyed talking to people, men and women, sharing their joys and sorrows What is so strange about that?'

'Nothing, I suppose, except that it doesn't satisfy me. It's like a religious book written for a child and I can't quite believe it.' I looked at him but he only smiled again. 'What is it that you're not saying?'

'Why should there be anything I'm not saying?'

That convinced me. Suddenly, I was determined to probe. I'd been too long not questioning people. Recently, I had begun once more to realise the importance of truth. 'I don't know but I'm sure there is. A few days ago you said that Eloise recognised a fellow sinner in you. What did you mean?'

He looked at me steadily. 'Are you sure you can take it?'

'Why not? I'm tired of pap.'

'To put it clearly then Eloise, who had a weakness for men, saw that I had a similar weakness for women. We understood each other with few words.'

'I see.' I removed my hand from his. 'You didn't leave the abbey then because you thought it was God's Will?'

'No. Some time after my ordination I began to be tormented by memories of my former life – memories of parties, fine food, good wines and…'

'Seductive women,' I added for him.

'I'm afraid so. It wasn't love. It was lust. I'd never loved anyone.' He stopped obviously waiting for my comment.

I didn't say anything at first. A picture of the past had suddenly come into my mind. It was very clear, although I couldn't remember exactly when it was. I was sitting in Eloise's flat one sunny evening. She had just handed me a gin and tonic and was now mixing herself one. We had been talking about marriage, I think, when she unexpectedly said, 'I'm not like you, Stella. I've never loved any man. I don't think I'm even capable of it but I do enjoy their bodies and the pleasure they can give me. Do I shock you?' Almost without thinking, I had answered, 'No. But I think you're missing the real point of life.' Why had I never remembered this before, I wondered?

'Have I shocked you?' Lucas too wanted an answer.

Once again, I replied, 'No, perhaps because I've just remembered something Eloise once said. You're certainly more alike than I ever realised.' I looked directly at him. 'So why did you really leave the monastery?'

'I did go out because of my illness and the operations that was true but they didn't want me back because of my sinful behaviour.'

'What was that?

'I was sent to a convalescent home for three weeks. In the town I met a married woman and, within days, we were lovers. Naturally neither her husband nor my Abbot approved of this. I didn't want to stay with the woman and I certainly didn't want to return to extra penances, etc.'

'So they chucked you out?'

'To put it crudely, yes.'

'And that's when you came to us?'

'No, that was six humiliating months later. I had struggled to earn my living in a factory. It was a soul-destroying job. I was still ill, terribly alone and a failure who had never learned what was really important. My life seemed totally empty and useless. I felt that God had deserted me. Then I met Patrick and you. In spite of your own problems and difficulties, you welcomed me into your home without any questions. I did nothing to deserve it but you showed me real love, all of you, and suddenly I had friends, home and family. I too began to learn to love. Eloise couldn't understand this but I was changed.'

'And later you were able to help us when everything went so wrong.' Standing up, I began to pile up the lunch dishes when a sudden thought struck me. 'It's funny, isn't? We've been good friends for several years but you've scarcely told me any of this before. Why do you think that is?'

Lucas stood up too, smiling at me. 'You never asked me before, Stella. If you had I would have told you.'

The truth of that remark struck me. 'I don't ask many questions, do I? Not even of myself. Why do you think that is?'

He regarded me steadily. 'At the moment I think it might be as I suggested earlier that you're afraid of the answers you might give yourself. For the same reason you discourage others, even me, from asking questions.'

I felt suddenly challenged. 'What question do you most want me to ask?' I met his steady gaze.

'There are several but I think perhaps the most important is why do you refuse to admit your grief at Eloise's death? You are entitled to grieve at the death of a friend and you are entitled for a time to receive sympathy from those nearest to you. So why don't you expect this? Why do you avoid it?'

'Why are asking me this?' I was puzzled. It wasn't what I had expected.

'Because it seems to me that you've had little understanding or sympathy from Patrick or your children. You have just told me yourself that they resented the time you spent nursing Eloise. They seemed to think that you deprived them of something. And what is more amazing you seem to agree with them. You shouldn't you know. It's nonsense. Most young people are inclined to be selfish but you shouldn't encourage them. And Patrick certainly shouldn't.'

'Patrick has never criticised me. He was very supportive at the funeral. But, of course he has never liked Eloise.'

I could see that Lucas was angry. 'That hardly matters, does it? What really matters is that you are grieving for the terrible and early death of someone dear to you, and you have a right to express that grief and a right to be comforted. That has to be faced before you can solve your other problems. Perhaps, if you can face it, they will go away.'

I tried to answer him but I couldn't. My eyes were suddenly full of tears. In spite of my efforts, they were rolling down my cheeks and I was sobbing. Before I could turn away, Lucas put his arm around me and took me to his couch. Once we were there, he held me close while I cried the tears I had so long repressed. As soon as my sobs had subsided a little, he offered me a box of tissues. 'I'm so sorry,' I sobbed.

'Don't be. You needed to cry. I'm simply glad that you feel that you can trust me. You don't need to talk until you're ready.' After a few minutes asked gently, 'Is there something fresh that has upset you more?

I decided to tell him the whole story. It would such a relief to share it with someone else. 'Eloise herself has made things worse. I know that sounds crazy but it's true.' As quickly as I could I told him about Eloise's unexpected letter and her revelation to Dominic and Patrick of the truth that she was Dominic's mother. 'I know that I was wrong to keep it a secret from Patrick but I had promised her and we had agreed again just before she died that we would keep the secret. When Dominic showed us the letter, I felt utterly betrayed. It reminded me too of my first baby's death. I thought I would lose everything now.'

'But you didn't?'

'No, after the first shock, Patrick was amazingly good about it. Dominic too. Patrick still seemed to be much closer than he had been for a long time. But I still can't think why she did it. We talked a lot when she was ill and I never imagined that she would do something so cruel. It makes me doubt whether she has ever really been my friend at all. Do you understand what I'm saying?'

'I do. But I think you may be wrong. People often see things differently when they're dying. Faced with eternity, it may have seemed to her that it would be better for everyone if certain truths were told, better perhaps most of all for you. Have you thought about that? In any case it didn't do the great damage you expected, did it? Patrick was more resilient than you thought he would be, wasn't he?'

I had to admit that he was right. 'I suppose I always want to protect Patrick too much. Is that what you think?'

'Most certainly. The time has now come, I think, for you to tell him quite firmly that even if he didn't like her, she was your very dear friend, who on more than one occasion gave you help when you most needed it. You shared a lot and you now need time to mourn her. And, if he loves you, he will want to help you.'

'As you have already helped me.'

'Patrick, as your husband, is much more able to help you than I am. Don't you think you should at least give him the chance, Stella?'

'It would help if he asked me as you did.'

'It would, of course. But he obviously finds that almost impossible, so you must help him. He loves you, I'm sure, but he seems at some point to have withdrawn himself so much that he doesn't know how to get back There are reasons for that, as you know but there may be others neither of us knows or can guess.'

'You're very generous to put his point of view so strongly.'

'I'm trying to be because I think that's what you want.'

'You think I should ask him some questions?'

'Why not? It might be better though to try to speak the truth about yourself. Continue what Eloise has started.'

Before answering, I collected up the dishes on to the tray. 'It frightens me,' I said finally.

Taking the tray from me, he answered quickly. 'I know, that's why you have to do it at once.'

'There's Cordelia too.' I turned to look at him as I was about to through the door. 'Do I have to tackle her as well?'

'Of course but I don't think that will be too difficult.' Bending to kiss me on the cheek, he said, 'Be brave, my love. And all things will be well, I'm sure.'

Chapter Ten

Looking at his watch, Patrick realised that it was far too late for him to catch his usual train home. Everyone else had gone; he had spent far longer than was necessary on his last piece of work. It was a long time since he had done this but all day he had been conscious of a growing weariness and an increasingly depressing headache. Although he recognised the symptoms only too well, he could see no reason why they should have come when he and Stella had been so much closer and happier for nearly a week. It was probably, he decided, because he had slept badly the preceding night.

As soon as he had tidied his desk and packed his brief case, he rang home to announce that he would be catching the later train and would arrive an hour after his usual time. Fortunately it was Ben who answered the phone for he did not ask for explanations but cheerfully said he would tell Mum who was busy cooking and then rang off.

Patrick caught the next train easily and was, therefore, able to find a comfortable corner seat. It was his intention during the fifty-minute journey to try to sort out his ideas but, as soon as the familiar scenery began to drift past, the temptation to close his eyes and relax was too great for him. When he opened them again, after what seemed only a few minutes, he realised that the train was in fact just coming into his station. He was the only passenger getting off here; the other regulars had undoubtedly come on the earlier train as they usually did. After showing his season ticket at the barrier, he walked out into the village High street, which ran for about three-quarters of a mile to the other end of the village where his home was situated, the old part of the village as the inhabitants called it.

He walked slowly, for the need to sort out his thoughts had become imperative. There were shops at this end of the street and during the day it was busy with traffic and crowded with shoppers. Now, however, the shops were shut and the street was empty and silent; it was almost possible to believe that the village was deserted. As he looked into the windows of the small department store without noticing any of its offerings, he suddenly found himself admitting what it was that had kept him awake and which had resulted in his daytime headache and weariness. In the middle of the night when Stella lay asleep, his recent feelings of well being and security had been threatened by the thought that there were subjects they had not touched on and many things he ought to tell her. Was this the voice of conscience or simply that of commonsense? Both, he decided, but whatever was the cause it was clear that unless he could speak honestly and persuade her to do the same, their new found happiness would probably not last long.

He strolled on slowly and paused outside the coffee bar, the only place showing lights, the village's one concession to the Sixties. In spite of its brilliant lighting and bright contemporary décor, there were few customers. The youth of the village were apparently reluctant to be converted to these 'new' customs.

He told himself that he had already tried in the past to explain to Stella some of his feelings of guilt and inadequacy and how these feelings had caused him to distance himself from her. She had been wonderfully loving and ready to forgive but she had asked very few questions. It might have made it easier if she had asked more. Perhaps that was how she preferred it and it might be disastrous to force more on her. The whole truth might be too much for her, at present. Yet some of it demanded to be told soon. But not tonight, he told himself as he walked up the path to his front door. Separation from her was the one thing he could never deal with. His years in the Army had made that clear to him. That was why he had accepted the truth about Dominic so calmly. Nevertheless, it had shocked him to know that, in order to please Eloise, Stella had lied to him for years. It strengthened his suspicion that here were other secrets that Stella was keeping from him. Tonight, however, as so often, he needed comfort; he wasn't strong enough to tackle this.

As he shut the front door behind him, he called out to her and she came hurrying into the hall to greet him with a kiss. She did not ask for apologies or explanations, so he returned her kiss and simply told her how glad he was to be home again at last. He joined Stella and his daughters in the breakfast room, where they were still lingering over their coffee. Ben had already gone to the sitting room to watch a favourite television programme and was too absorbed to do more than call out a cheery, 'Hello, Dad!'

'About time,' Julia greeted him cheerfully as he took his place at the table. 'What happened? Did you decide to crawl from the station, Dad? Or did you stop off for a quick one?'

'Neither. The train was a bit late and I must have walked slowly.' No one made any further comment. Cordelia passed his supper to him from the Aga where it had been kept warm and Stella filled his glass with wine. For the moment he felt cheered and relaxed.

'Have you had a difficult day?' Stella asked sympathetically.

Picking up his wine glass, he smiled at her. 'Not really. It was just that I found it difficult to concentrate and became rather slow as a result. I'm sorry because it made me late. It's good to be back.'

'I was fed up this afternoon,' Julia suddenly burst out. 'And praying for the bell to go.'

'That's unusual for you.' Stella looked surprised at her younger daughter.

'I know it's just that I'm sick of Sex before Marriage!'

'I wasn't aware that you'd been experimenting,' Patrick said calmly. 'Have I missed something?'

'She doesn't mean the real thing,' Cordelia explained. 'She just means the obligatory lessons we have in the Fifth Form, don't you?'

'Of course. It's alright for you two to laugh,' she turned to her parents, 'but I don't suppose you ever had to put up with such stuff.'

'No, we were allowed to grow up in blissful ignorance,' Stella said.

'Lucky you. Two days ago two Religious periods were devoted to it and today the same thing happened in our Biology lessons. It was called a discussion but it wasn't. Father John told us it was contrary to God's commandments and therefore a mortal sin, etc., etc. And of course like all sins it seems tempting but we know we must wait until we're married.'

'And did Sister Felicity tell you how wicked it was to abuse your body in this way and how much suffering it could bring you?' Cordelia asked sardonically.

'You've got it. I was so relieved when the bell rang because I was getting more and more tempted to ask her how she knew, since she was supposed to be celibate.'

'It was a good job you didn't,' Patrick remarked, 'that would have been a Mortal Sin.'

'Dad,' Julia protested, 'you not supposed to make flippant remarks like that! Tell him Mum. Or are you secretly a bit of a rebel too?' She paused and looked at her parents. 'I've just remembered you two were only eighteen when you got engaged.'

'Good girls didn't misbehave when we were young.' Stella said virtuously.

'And what about the bad boys?' She turned to Patrick.

'They had to do what the good girls told them.'

'Really?' Cordelia queried him. 'Then boys must have changed.' Detecting a certain bitterness in her tone, Stella looked quickly at her daughter but decided that it might be wiser not to speak.

'OK, then it's a Mortal Sin, so why do we have to waste so much time pretending to discuss it, when we can't do anything about it?' Julia was still defiant.

'Oh, it's just a bit more brain washing,' Cordelia remarked scornfully. 'We should be left to decide these things for ourselves. At least I think so. '

'Don't you have to know the doctrines and the arguments first?' Stella asked.

'You can't decide anything without sufficient data, can you?' Patrick asked mildly.

'It's no use expecting our honourable parents to sympathise with us,' Julia said cheerfully. 'They're bound to toe the Party Line. You can't blame them.' She smiled at everyone. 'Have some pie, Dad,' she suggested obviously deciding it was wiser to end the discussion. 'I can recommend it. It's one of Mum's apple pies.'

'In that case, I certainly will. It's funny to think,' he remarked as Julia handed him a large portion and Cordelia passed him the cream, 'that your Mother could only just about boil an egg when we were first married. Of course it didn't matter much as I was off to Germany a month later. And when I came back she was a brilliant cook.' He began to eat his pie with enjoyment.

'Whatever happened, Mum?' Cordelia asked. 'Did he threaten to beat you if you hadn't improved by the time he got back?'

'I wasn't going to risk that. I simply went to cookery classes in the evening and dressmaking ones too. I thought since I had doomed myself to be a housewife, I'd better be good at it. They gave me something to do as well.'

'And they kept you out of mischief too. I don't suppose there were many men doing cookery and dressmaking,' Julia commented. 'Was that your idea, Dad?'

Suddenly serious, Patrick finished his pie before he answered. Then, as he put down his spoon, he answered her more seriously than she had expected. 'I expect it's difficult for you to understand, Julia, that it was a very hard time for us, especially perhaps for me. If I hadn't known I could trust your mother completely, I don't think I could have survived.'

'I'm sorry, Dad.' Julia was subdued. 'I was just being silly.'

'What's new?' Cordelia asked.

'It's time you went to finish your homework,' Stella suggested swiftly to Julia. Turning to Patrick, she smiled at him. 'Would you like some coffee, darling?'

'I'll get it,' Cordelia stood up and moved towards the kitchen.

'Would you like me to wash up as a penance?' Julia asked.

'Certainly not.' Stella sounded very firm. 'Go and do that homework you've been putting off all evening.'

'Alright, Mum. I'll do it in my room, if that's OK? I'll come and say goodnight later.'

As Julia departed, Cordelia came back with Patrick's coffee. 'Why don't you take it into the sitting room and watch the television with Ben,' Stella suggested. 'You need to relax. I'll do the washing up.'

'I ought to help you, at least,' he protested.

'No need,' Cordelia said. 'I'll help Mum. You can watch Ben's favourite soap. He likes company.'

'God help me,' Patrick groaned.

'Just go,' Stella said, 'You can always go to sleep.'

'I'll go quietly. But don't take too long. I could do with an early night.'

'Alright, I'll promise. But, if you don't go, we can't start.' She gave him a light kiss and a friendly push.'

'I thought he'd never go,' Cordelia began to collect up the dirty dishes. 'Do you think we could have a talk, Mum?' she asked unexpectedly as Stella followed her into the kitchen.

'Of course.' Stella began to sort out the dishes, while Cordelia filled a bowl with hot, soapy water. The kitchen which had been built on to the original house was large with ample space for working and eating. The window over the sink looked out on to a side lawn and a plum tree now heavy with fruit. A glass door led into the large conservatory where she and Lucas had eaten their lunch. It was a comfortable, friendly room where many private family chats had been held, probably because when the door to the breakfast room was shut it seemed remote from the rest of the house. All families, Stella thought, need a place like this.

At first Cordelia was busy with the dishes. Stella waited patiently knowing that this would be the best way with her volatile daughter. As she studied Cordelia's profile, she thought, as she had often done, how very like Patrick she was. Her heavy dark hair sprang back from her forehead, as his did. She had the same broad forehead, the same straight but slightly large nose. Her eyes too were widely spaced and brown like his. Both had unexpectedly sensitively curved mouths. Patrick had always been considered handsome and so was his daughter.

'You've been pretty lucky, haven't you, Mum? Cordelia asked suddenly turning to face Stella.

Stella was surprised. 'Not always. I've had my setbacks and difficulties. But then most people have, I suppose.'

'I didn't mean in general. I meant in particular with Dad.'

This seemed even more surprising in many ways. 'We haven't had an easy life. Surely you know that.'

'Oh, I know you've had some pretty awful times but you've always been sure of one thing.' She paused.

'What is that?'

'You've always known that Dad loves you. You were only a few months older than I am when you got engaged and everyone was pleased.'

'Not everyone, certainly not your paternal grandmother. She wasn't at all pleased.'

'But it didn't matter, did it? Because you knew that Dad would always be there for you, that he would always be faithful. It must have been wonderful to know that.'

There were many difficulties Stella could have pointed out but she refrained, realising that they would not be relevant here. 'What is the matter, Cordelia? You don't really want to talk to me about your dad and me, do you? I'm finding it difficult to understand you.'

For a moment there was silence, then Cordelia walked over to the kitchen table and sat down. She seemed to be fighting back her tears. 'Please sit down, Mum, and talk to me. I'm very miserable.' She began to cry properly as Stella sat down next to her and took her hand. 'I should have told you ages ago, I know, but it was difficult because you were away so often and everyone was unsettled.'

'What should you have told me?' Stella asked gently, putting an arm round her daughter's shoulders.

'About Adrian. We got to know one another well last term. We went out several times and just before the end of term, he told me that he loved me.'

'And do you love him?'

'I said I thought I did but I wasn't sure. Then, we didn't see one another much during the holidays, as he had a job. I thought it might be different when we met again this term.

'And was it? Is that why you're so upset?'

'Oh, no it was just the opposite. He was keener than ever.' She stopped and didn't look at her mother.

'And what about you?'

'I realised that I liked him an awful lot. We've been seeing one another as often as we can. I do love him, Mum but .' She began to cry again. Stella hugged her more tightly but said nothing because she felt afraid. Finally, she asked, 'But what?'

After a few moments Cordelia whispered, 'He wants me to sleep with him. He keeps on asking and he says if I really love him, I will.'

'And what have you said?'

111

'I haven't completely agreed yet but I'm afraid he'll leave me, if I don't. That's what my friend Ann says.'

'Ann can't have a very wide experience, can she? Girls have often thought that and undoubtedly there's a certain amount of truth in it. Other people will tell you the opposite. My mother used to warn me for example that, as soon as a boy's got what he wants, he's off.'

'How horrible! It's not like that with Adrian and me. We love one another. Why shouldn't we be happy together? The trouble is that older people have just forgotten what it feels like, if they ever knew.' She turned passionately on her mother. 'You're just as bad! You don't want to talk about it, do you? You simply want to sit there smugly and tell me it's wrong and therefore I should forget about it. Well, I can't and I don't want to.'

'Cordelia, don't be silly! I'm not suggesting you forget about it. I'm simply suggesting you start to think about it.'

'What do you think I've been doing? Anyway, it's too late. I've mind up my mind. I told him yesterday that I would as soon as we could arrange it. It's time parents stopped thinking they can run their children's lives. Young people believe these days that they have a right to be free. Lots of them are. It's nineteen sixty-nine now and things are different than they were when you were young!'

'I see.' Stella moved apart a little from her daughter. 'Then why are you telling me? And, even more important, why are you so unhappy?'

'I don't know. It seemed marvellous when I agreed and we were so happy. It's silly but I suppose I'm a bit frightened.'

Stella put her arm around her again. 'I'm very glad you are. You'd be foolish, if you weren't? Your head is telling you that you've made a very big decision without any proper thought. Can you trust Adrian?'

'Of course I trust him. We love one another. It's no use, Mum, I intend to do it. I just thought I ought to tell you, because you've always told us to be honest.'

'In that case,' Stella replied calmly. 'You'd better make up your mind to break two rules of the church. That would be less disastrous than only breaking one.'

'Whatever do you mean?'

'It's quite clear surely? If you break the rule against chastity, you'd be wise to break the other one against birth control. You do know that all forms of birth control are prohibited, that the Pope finally ruled against them last year in his encyclical, even the Pill? Of course, you do. We spoke about it at the time.'

'Why are you making everything seem so horrid?' Cordelia asked furiously.

'I'm not intending to do that. I'm simply reminding you of certain facts which you really should consider before you and Adrian decide to take such an important step. Have you talked about them?'

'Not exactly,' Cordelia muttered.

'I suppose that means not at all.'

'He loves me and I trust him and...'

Although Stella knew that Cordelia was extremely angry with her, she was nevertheless determined to force her to face the necessary truths. 'I don't think you're are aware how much you will be trusting him. You can ruin your life, maybe his too. It's so easy in a moment of strong feeling to do something utterly silly and irrevocable. Please, Cordelia, at least listen to me. I do know how you feel but I also know what can happen. I must try to warn you. I love you too much not to do so.' Cordelia was about to stand up but she restrained her gently. 'You may think I'm a stupid interfering mother, that I don't really know what I'm talking about but at least have the courage to listen to me and to think about what I'm saying. If, after that, you want to go ahead, then I can't stop you.'

'Alright, I'll listen but it won't make any difference.'

'I really thought you wanted to have a career,' Stella began.

'What's that got to do with it? You and Dad were in love but it didn't stop you having a career, did it? But I suppose you were always sensible. You never were madly in love.'

'I do know,' Stella replied very firmly, 'that your father never tried to persuade me to do anything that might harm me. He loved me too much. But, if you listen to Adrian, you may lose everything. Suppose you find yourself pregnant? There would be no happy choice for you to make. You might ruin both your chances by getting married or you might be left to face it on your own.'

Cordelia leapt to her feet. 'Stop it, stop it,' she screamed. 'How can you be so horrid you're spoiling everything. I shouldn't have spoken to you. It's not like that nowadays.'

'I'm afraid it still happens,' Stella told her sadly. 'Last term I spoke privately to a girl in my Lower Sixth German group. I was worried because her work had been so disappointing; she didn't seem to be fulfilling her promise. I won't bore you with all the details but finally she told me that she was five months pregnant. She had told no one, not even her parents and she was desperate. The boy had deserted her. He couldn't cope with the situation he'd helped to create. In any case, she realised now that she didn't want to marry him, even if it were possible. So you see, why I'm so worried about you. It's so easy to make a terrible mistake.'

Cordelia didn't move. At last she said in a quiet voice, 'How terrible for her! What did you do?'

'I helped her to tell her parents. They were shocked and heartbroken but they managed to be kind. They removed her from school. I don't know what will happen after the baby is born. So, please Cordelia promise me you'll think a bit more.' She took Cordelia's hand in hers.

Suddenly they heard the door to the breakfast room opening. 'Oh, there you are!' It was Patrick. 'I've been looking for you everywhere. It's half past ten.' Coming into the room, he looked puzzled at them both. 'I couldn't believe you'd still be washing up.'

'We're not,' Stella answered quickly. 'We've been having a chat. I didn't realise we'd been so long. Cordelia's been telling me about her boyfriend, Adrian.'

'Is that the boy I've seen you talking to outside school a couple of times towards the end of last term? Or is this a new one?' Patrick looked interested.

'No, it's the same one,' Cordelia answered reluctantly. 'I didn't know you'd noticed him.'

'I liked the look of him. That's why. If he's still around, why don't you bring him home one day and let us meet him? Is he studying music the same as you?'

'No, he's doing Maths and Physics. He wants to be an engineer. But I'm not sure he wants to meet you all.'

'Probably not.' Patrick smiled. 'That's quite normal. Most boys are scared of that. It seems too much like committing themselves. If you like him, it's your job to insist. He'll know he can't trifle with you then. Why don't you suggest this Saturday?' Without waiting for an answer, he turned to Stella, 'Do you think you could come to bed now? I told you I was tired.'

'You could have gone by yourself,' Stella suggested, smiling at him.

'Don't be silly. You know that bed's not the same without you.' Putting his arm through hers, he moved her towards the door. Then just before they went out, he turned back to Cordelia. 'What do you think of my suggestion?'

Stella waited anxiously. Had Patrick defused the situation enough? To her relief, Cordelia replied normally. 'I think it's a good idea, Dad. That is, if Mum doesn't mind.'

'Of course not,' Stella said quickly. 'This Saturday would be fine or the following one.'

'Well, that's settled.' Patrick sounded pleasantly indifferent. 'You'd better come to bed too, hadn't you?'

'I won't be long,' Cordelia promised as they went out.

When they reached their bedroom, Stella suddenly hugged Patrick. 'I'm so glad you turned up. It was all getting very tense. I'm not sure I was dealing with it properly. Your matter of fact tone was just right.' She hugged him again.

'I'm glad to think I still have my uses, particularly when I get rewarded with one of your best hugs. What was it all about anyway?'

As they undressed, she told him. 'Do you think I said the right things?' she asked him worriedly at the end.

'I couldn't have done it half as well.'

'But you made it all normal again at the end and that was good.'

'Yes, maybe, but you were right to tell her that a relationship must be based on honesty and trust.'

Once they were in bed, he thought over his words, remembering his earlier resolution to be more honest with Stella.

115

It was too late now but at the same time he wondered if it might not have been a mistake. Might it not be better not to risk disturbing the fresh start they had so recently made?

For her part, Stella silently reflected on the irony of her day. The woman who had spent her afternoon discussing her problems with Lucas had, a few hours later, become the adviser of her teenage daughter. Should one not perhaps heal oneself first? Finding herself too drowsy even to consider that, she yielded to sleep.

Chapter Eleven

The next day, however, Eloise interfered in my life again. This had happened so often over the years that I suppose that I should not have been surprised at it happening even now that she was dead. At the moment when her coffin began to disappear I had felt a certain relief mixed with my sadness. I was free now, I had foolishly thought, and could perhaps begin to sort out some of my own problems.

My adoption of Dominic had brought us closer together and had kept us close, even though I might not hear from her for several months. It was especially important as Patrick knew nothing. For many years Eloise and I wanted it to remain that way and she did not fail from time to time to make use of this fact. But she herself had revealed it and I had thought that must be the end. I was, however, living in a fool's paradise.

The bombshell came by post. I was working in the study preparing my lessons for that Friday afternoon when I heard the noise of several letters dropping on the mat. Thinking that none of them could be important, I continued with my work. After that, I gave no further thought to them until I stumbled over them as I was rushing out of the front door, rather later than I had intended to be, on my way to work. Without really looking at them I gathered them up in a pile and put them on the hall table.

I found them waiting for me on my return nearly three hours later. It was fortunate that I was the first person to arrive home. Scooping them up I took them into the kitchen; put them on the table and prepared to make myself a refreshing cup of tea. It was one of those hot, sultry days which sometimes come at the end of September, so I took my tea on to the patio, where it seemed cooler in the shade. The sky was a perfect blue; the sun tinged the heavily laden fruit trees with gold. The hollyhocks and the late roses seemed to droop in the warmth. As I sipped my tea, I leaned back meditating rather than thinking actively. I felt enfolded in peace and joy.

It must have been nearly half an hour later when I returned to the kitchen and noticed the letters still lying on the table. Three of them were advertising circulars which I immediately threw away. The next was a Scientific Journal which came every fortnight for Patrick. Putting this on one side I inspected the last three. They were a bill, a letter from my parents and a large official looking envelope addressed to me. Having an instinctive dislike of the official, I slipped it into my school bag intending to read it later and turned eagerly to the letter from my parents.

I was still reading this rather long letter when Ben returned home, followed soon by Julia and Cordelia. I made coffee and produced some scones for the hungry horde. The next half hour passed swiftly in cheerful family talk. We lingered longer than usual because it was Friday but eventually Julia and Ben slipped away to change out of their school uniform, leaving Cordelia and myself alone.

Obviously she had been waiting for this for, as soon as they had gone, she said a little hesitantly, 'Adrian has agreed to come tomorrow, Mum. He seemed pleased when I asked him.' As soon as I had expressed my pleasure, however, she went on quickly to say, 'He may not be what you expect. His family are quite poor and he has had to work very hard.'

'You surely don't think that will worry me?' I asked. 'After all, as you know, I was in pretty much the same position myself. My parents were definitely what was called working class. I'm sure your Grandad Fitzgerald would be very pleased to meet your Adrian.'

'So am I. But what about Dad?'

'Don't be ridiculous!' I was almost angry with her and with her desire to create dramatic difficulties. 'Your dad married me. Remember? And he wouldn't have done that if he'd been a snob. His mother certainly was but she's dead now and Grandpa Gestenge is too busy enjoying his retirement to bother about your boyfriends. The only thing that matters is whether he's a decent boy or not. You haven't told us much about him. We don't even know his surname.'

'He's eighteen just, a few months older than I am. His name's Adrian Murphy. He lives in Tonbridge. His father works as a garage mechanic and his mother has recently started to work two days a week in the new supermarket. He has two older brothers and an older sister but they've all left home. None of them stayed at school after they were fifteen and so Adrian's very much an exception. They live in a small, terraced house. They don't read books or anything like that. His father often goes to the pub and his mother stays at home watching "rubbish" as Adrian calls it on the television. So, you can see, Mum, that his background is very different from mine.' Looking anxiously at me, she stopped.

I could see now what was worrying her. It was not really what I had expected. 'Does it worry you? Because that's what really matters.'

'Sometimes when I think about it but not when I'm with him. We get on so well.'

It was puzzling to try to decide from her brief description what they could possibly have in common but I guessed there were other things she hadn't mentioned which might become clear when I met him, so I made no comment. 'When is he arriving?'

'I invited him to come in the afternoon. He can meet everyone; stay to tea and then we thought we might go out together in the evening, if that's OK.'

'It sounds fine. I suppose he'll come by the bus. It's more convenient than the train.'

'Actually,' she hesitated, 'he's coming on his motor bike.'

'His motor bike! You didn't tell me about that. How long has he had that?'

'He's had a bike of sorts ever since he was sixteen, when he started with a scooter. He's mad about them. He buys old ones and does them up. He's just finished doing this one up. I haven't seen it yet. It's pretty powerful, I believe.'

I was amazed. Her eyes were shining. I found it difficult to imagine my beautiful, often elegant daughter in this context. Trying to avoid saying anything wounding, I contented myself with asking, 'However does he afford it? It must cost a lot.'

'Well, he does all the work himself and he works in a garage in the holidays. He also sells them and makes quite a profit.'

'He sounds very enterprising.'

'He is, Mum. That's one of the things I like most about him. He's so independent and he's determined not to stay poor and live a dreary life in the back streets of Tonbridge like the rest of his family.'

'And what do they think of him?'

She shrugged her shoulders. 'I don't think that they bother much. He says they think he's a bit mad but as long as they don't interfere, it doesn't worry him.'

'You did say, didn't you that he's hoping to go to University to do Engineering?'

'Yes and he works hard but he might not go if he gets a better idea.'

Before I could ask more Ben came hurtling in, flourishing a beautifully decorated pottery bowl. 'Just look what Lucas has given me! He was firing an order today and he promised he'd make an extra one for me and he did.' He showed it to me. 'It's special, isn't it. It's got my name on it. Look!' Ben had a great admiration for Lucas's talents and his present ambition was to be a potter like him.

While we were admiring it, Lucas himself came in. 'I gather that the firing has been successful?' I asked him.

He smiled at me. 'Very. I'm just planning to deliver them and get my fee. Do you mind if Ben comes with me? I promise to bring him back in time for supper.'

'Fine. Why don't you join us yourself for supper?'

'Thanks I will. And since I expect to be well paid, I'll buy us a special bottle. Come on, Ben.' He turned to go out again. 'You can help me carry the boxes to the car.' They were gone.

Suddenly I noticed that Cordelia was frowning. 'Lucas doesn't have to be around tomorrow, does he?' she asked.

'I expect he'll be busy. But does it matter?'

'Don't you ever think, Mum, how it must look to other people?'

'Whatever do you mean?' I stared at her.

'Having a spare man around, particularly when you spend quite a lot of time alone with him.'

I resisted a temptation to become angry. 'As you well know, Cordelia, he's a family friend and he works with me illustrating my books. If some people want to make something nasty out of it, I can't stop them. If they want to know the truth, they can ask me. But I've no intention of starting to worry about what people may or may not think. I don't think you should either. It's a waste of time.'

'How lucky you are, Mum,' she suddenly burst out. 'You really don't worry about such things, do you? It's not a pose. It's just you.' She gazed seriously at me. 'You actually remind me of Adrian or perhaps I should put it the other way. I don't believe he allows other people to affect him in the least, not if he believes that what he's doing is right.'

'Perhaps we shall like each other then, in spite of all your worries. And if what you say is true, then Lucas won't bother him, will he?'

'Probably not. I suppose I'm the one who worries all the time about silly things and makes ridiculous scenes.'

Smiling at her, I said, 'Don't worry. We all love you very much as you are.' As I spoke the clock in the hall struck. 'Oh, God, I exclaimed, 'it can't be six, surely?'

'I'm afraid it is.' Cordelia looked at her watch. 'Don't worry, Mum, since I've taken up so much of your time, I'll help you get the supper.'

From that time on until bedtime there didn't seem to be a spare moment. Lucas's arrival with a bottle of wine changed the supper into a party. Patrick seemed to be unusually relaxed and he and Lucas vied with one another in telling amusing stories until it was quite late when Lucas left.

Some time afterwards on my way to bed I stopped outside Cordelia's room and tapped on her door. When she called out to me, I went in. She was already in bed. 'Didn't you say something earlier,' I asked her, 'about Adrian taking you out tomorrow evening?'

'Yes, but not till about seven o'clock.'

'Where are you going?'

'Oh, just to a disco.'

I raised my eyebrows. 'I didn't think you liked discos much.'

'I don't but Adrian says this is special.'

'And where is it?'

She hesitated, then answered reluctantly. 'At The Highwayman.' We both knew that this was a large pub in the depths of the country, frequented by bikers and their girl friends. It didn't have a good reputation; in fact it was pretty notorious. 'You're not going to say I can't go, are you? I know how to behave myself and Adrian will look after me.'

'I suppose you're planning to go on the back of his bike? She nodded. I turned towards the door, not quite sure what to say. It was late and I was too tired to want to risk a scene. As I reached the door, I paused. 'I think I'd better see what your dad thinks.'

Patrick was already in bed when I came into our bedroom. I noticed he was reading his magazine and briefly I remembered the letter I had slipped into my school bag but I felt it could wait. As I got into bed next to him, I took away his magazine and told him all I had learned about Adrian. After some discussion we decided to wait until we had met him before we made a decision. 'It should be an interesting encounter at least,' Patrick said as we kissed goodnight.

★

I was standing on the drive talking to Lucas on the Saturday afternoon when Adrian arrived. His motor bike came round the bend with a roar; then slowing down he came quietly to a stop in front of us. My first thought was that this was not the right scenario; Lucas should not have been here.

For a few moments Adrian sat aside his motor bike while he gave a final check to the controls. Since he was wearing a helmet and visor, I couldn't see his face but he looked lean and impressive in his heavy weight jeans, leather jacket and gloves. When he lifted up his visor and removed his helmet, my first thought was how very attractive he was – not simply attractive but handsome. Strangely enough, Cordelia hadn't mentioned this.

His dark hair was cut short but still tried to curl. His features were regular, almost classical and he had unusual dark blue eyes. He smiled a warm, friendly smile as he came up to me and held out his hand. 'I'm sorry, I'm a bit early, I'm afraid. There was less traffic than I expected.' He seemed to be completely at ease with no signs of the nervous inferiority, which Cordelia had led me to expect.

Smiling back I welcomed him warmly, then to my embarrassment, he turned to Lucas, obviously thinking he must be Cordelia's father. He was not, however, in the least put out as I hastily introduced Lucas. 'Cordelia has told me about you,' he remarked, 'you make beautiful pottery and illustrate Mrs Gestenge's books.' Fortunately at that moment Patrick and Cordelia arrived while Lucas disappeared discreetly.

Before following Patrick and Cordelia down the path to the back garden, Adrian stopped for a moment and studied the front of the house. 'I like it,' he said to me, 'it looks real.'

Understanding what he was trying to express, I agreed with him. 'Yes, it's the sort of house children draw all square and solid.'

'And very secure and safe,' he added. As we smiled at each other, I knew I was going to like him, in spite of all my misgivings.

We joined Ben and Julia who were sitting at the table on the patio in front of the study. Cordelia introduced them, rather nervously. She had discarded the short sheath dress she had been wearing earlier and was wearing ordinary jeans but with one of her artistic and unusual tops. She and Adrian made an attractive pair. I looked at Patrick to try to discover his opinion but after a few words, he had already returned to his lounger and his magazine.

After an awkward pause, I suggested drinks might be welcome since it was a sultry afternoon. Since everyone seemed to agree, I took Ben with me to help to carry the glasses. When we returned, we found that Julia with her usual desire for information was asking Adrian about motor bikes. She wanted to know how he acquired them and how he had learned to repair and rebuild them. She was most impressed that he had worked since he was sixteen at the weekends and in the holidays and had not only bought his own bikes but had saved money. Adrian for his part made no attempt to impress, admitting frankly that his family's poverty made it necessary for him to be independent. 'You could do it,' he added, 'but you don't need to so why should you bother?'

'I wouldn't want to,' Cordelia remarked, 'if I'm to be a good musician, I need most of my spare time to practise.'

Adrian turned to her. 'That's what you should do. You're lucky to have a real talent. You'd be wrong not to make the most of it.' Cordelia flushed with pleasure.

Patrick, who had seemed not to be listening, nodded approvingly. 'I'm glad to hear you say that. Cordelia doesn't always realise how lucky she is.'

Soon after this at Ben's suggestion they went to look at Adrian's latest acquisition. 'What do you think of him?' I asked Patrick as soon as we were alone.

'He seems pretty sensible – more than I expected. But not really Cordelia's type – at least I wouldn't think so. What do you think?'

'I think he's honest. I like that.' Then I added, 'Cordelia's very much in love with him.'

Patrick sat up. 'How do you know?'

'She glows with happiness. Her eyes are shining. You must have noticed, surely?'

'I hope you're wrong. She's much too young.'

I laughed. 'I don't know how you of all people dare say that!'

'You and I were different. We'd known one another most of our lives. That makes a difference.'

'I suppose it does.' I was going to say more but Julia came back to say that Cordelia and Adrian were going for a walk and Ben had gone off to see his best friend. They would all be back for tea. She settled down to read under the shade of an apple tree while I leaned back and wondered how and why Cordelia had given me such a wrong impression of Adrian. He was certainly not the awkward working class boy she had described nor did he try to impress. On the contrary he seemed to be surprisingly at ease with everyone. I could tell that he admired Cordelia but I doubted if he was truly in love with her. She would obviously be disappointed if that was so but it might really be the best outcome for her.

Everyone came back punctually for tea. Since the storm which had been hovering around for some time seemed to be about to break we moved into the conservatory. As I sat down to eat after seeing that everyone else was settled, I was surprised to find Adrian taking the seat next to me. It was obviously his intention to get to know me better. Perhaps he thought it would be good policy?

Immersed in my own thoughts, I was surprised when he suddenly asked me, 'Do you really believe in all this God business, Mrs Gestenge?'

Turning to face him, I found his dark blue eyes fixed on me with a challenging look. I couldn't imagine why he wanted to challenge me but I felt certain that I must meet the challenge and answer him honestly. 'Of course I do.'

'Would you mind if I asked you why?' He was sill looking straight into my eyes and I sensed that for some reason this question and my answer were important to him.

'I don't mind. I believe in God because He made himself known to me when I was very young. And something happened then which changed my life. Similar experiences have happened several times since. Does that satisfy you?'

For a moment he was silent then he replied slowly, 'Yes. And thank you for being honest. Not many people are.'

'Perhaps because they're afraid of being laughed at.'

'Maybe but more likely they don't think that someone like me can be serious. That didn't worry you?'

'No. Why should it?'

'Do you mind if I ask you one more question?' Taking my smile for an answer, he continued. Everyone was listening now. 'You believe in God but you don't accept all the stuff the Catholic Church tries to shove down our throats do you?'

'I'm not quite sure I know what you mean?'

'I mean all this stuff about how we should live our lives and how we'll be damned if we don't follow their stupid rules. All this latest rubbish about birth control for example.'

'You're asking the right person!' Julia exclaimed. 'Mum was so angry about it that she wrote to the pope, telling him he didn't have any idea about how ordinary women had to live.'

'Of course it didn't get anywhere,' Cordelia added.

'Except, I imagine, to the waste paper basket,' I said, 'still it did me good to write it.'

'I bet it did,' Adrian said. 'I hope you didn't let it stop there?'

'No and I actually found one Archbishop, retired of course, who encouraged me. But what about your parents, what do they think about these matters? I wouldn't want them to think that I'm leading you astray.'

'They don't think much. But in any case I reckon I'm old enough to make up my own mind, don't you?'

I hesitated. As I did, Cordelia intervened, 'That's a good question for you, Mum. What do you think? When are people old enough to make up their own minds.'

It was Julia with her usual quickness who diverted us, 'It's stopped raining,' she said. 'But it'll be dark soon. 'I think we'd better clear everything into the kitchen.' She began to pile things on to a tray. In a few minutes everything had been transferred and I began to sort out, preparatory to washing up, while the others helped.

Cordelia looked at the kitchen clock, as we finished. 'It's getting late. What time should we leave Adrian?'

'In about half an hour.'

'Will I do as I am? She smiled at him.

'You're just perfect. I've brought the spare helmet as I promised. You'd better find a good padded jacket.'

'You're not going to ride on the back of the bike, are you?' Julia asked. 'I'd be scared, particularly at night. Wouldn't you be, Mum?'

'I don't know,' I replied. 'No one ever asked me when I was young. And I'm a bit too old now…'

'I just don't believe that,' Adrian declared. 'I bet, if I dared you now, you're do it and I'm sure you would have done so, when you were young.'

'Perhaps,' I said.

'I'll remember that, Mum,' Cordelia remarked. 'Now I'd better find a jacket or we'll be late.'

'Late for what?' Patrick asked. He had just come in from the conservatory with Ben where he had been stacking up some of the chairs.

'Late for our trip to the Disco,' Cordelia said.

'What disco?' There was a silence as everyone realised that Patrick didn't seem to know.

'The disco at the Highwayman,' Cordelia replied with a slight touch of defiance. 'Surely you remember, Dad?'

'And how are you going to get there? There are no buses.'

Cordelia looked at Adrian. 'I'm going to take Cordelia on the back of my bike,' he said.

'I don't think so,' Patrick said firmly. 'It's a tricky road at the best of times. And on a dark night with wet surfaces, it's not at all safe.'

'Don't be silly, Dad,' Cordelia begged him. 'Adrian's experienced. He won't take any risks, will you?' She turned to him.

'Of course, I won't,' Adrian replied quickly. 'I promise you, Mr Gestenge. I'll go very carefully. And we won't have a drop of alcohol.'

'I should hope not.' Patrick was becoming angry. I could see that. Ben, accustomed to these storms was already sidling out of the kitchen. 'But, apart from all that,' Patrick continued, 'I don't think the Highwayman is a suitable place for you. The police were called there only last weekend. I don't want you to go there, Cordelia. And, if you must go to a disco, there's one in the village hall tonight.'

Cordelia laughed. 'That's rubbish, Dad. Isn't it Julia?'

Before Julia could answer, Patrick said. 'There's no point in arguing. You're not going, Cordelia and that's that.' He turned to leave the kitchen.

'You can't stop me,' Cordelia shouted with tears in her eyes. 'I'm nearly eighteen. I'm not a baby any more.'

'Then don't act like one,' was Patrick's reply. 'There are plenty of other things you and Adrian can do.'

'Such as? It's no use, Dad, I'm going. You can't stop me. Mum doesn't mind, so why should you?'

That was a mistake but Cordelia, who so resembled Patrick in many ways, often made mistakes like that. Now, Patrick turned furiously to me. 'Is that true, Stella? I don't remember discussing it with you. But, perhaps you don't think that is necessary?'

'I did mention it to you last night and I haven't exactly given my permission,' I tried to keep calm. 'But…'

'Don't let Dad bully you, Mum,' Cordelia interrupted angrily.

'You did say you'd probably have enjoyed it when you were young, didn't you?'

'That has nothing to do with it.' Patrick's anger was growing. 'I don't want you to go on this outing and that's final. It's neither safe nor suitable.' He moved towards the door.

'I'm going anyway,' Cordelia insisted. 'You didn't let your father stop you from doing things you wanted to do when you were my age, so why should I? The trouble is you don't know me or care about me, really. You never have. You just want to stop me being happy. I suppose it's because you're so miserable yourself most of the time.' She moved up to him glaring at him. For one terrible moment, I thought he might hit her, then abruptly all the anger left him. 'You're probably right. I'd better leave you to deal with this Stella.' Without another word, he went.

'Well done, Cordelia,' Julia said, looking coldly at her sister. 'You certainly know how to hurt people.' She too left.

Cordelia was crying now. 'Dad has hurt me. After all, I've always stuck up for him.'

Adrian looked at me. 'We can always take a bus and go into town. I didn't mean to cause a row.'

'You wouldn't have done in any normal family,' Cordelia sobbed, 'but we aren't normal, at least Dad isn't.'

'What do you think, Mrs Gestenge?' Adrian urged me.

'I think Cordelia's father has a perfect right to object to something which he thinks is unwise and perhaps dangerous but in the end I have to say that I believe you are old enough to make your own decisions. But that means you also have to be responsible for what you decide. I've always made that clear to you, Cordelia. Just as my father made it clear to me. So what do you want to do?'

'In plain words,' Adrian explained, 'if you make your own decisions, don't blame your parents then, if things go wrong.

Cordelia didn't stop to think. 'Go, of course! Thanks Mum I knew you'd understand. I'll go and get my jacket. Tell Dad I'm sorry, won't you?' She rushed out of the room.

'I'll give up the idea,' Adrian offered unexpectedly, 'if that'll make things easier. It's no big deal.'

'Thanks. But I doubt if Cordelia will want to give way now.

Just promise me two things: take care and be back before midnight.'

He looked straight at me. 'You can rely on me. I'd better go and get the spare helmet and check the bike.'

Feeling weary and despondent, I sat down. My school bag was lying near by in the corner where I had left it the day before. As I picked it up I noticed the official letter which I had not yet read. It was about time I found out who had sent it. As soon as I opened it I realised that it had come from Eloise's solicitors. Immediately I felt apprehensive, especially when I noticed another envelope addressed to me in Eloise's handwriting.

I read the solicitor's letter through twice before I clearly grasped the astounding fact that in her latest will, just discovered, Eloise had made me her heir. Before I could read the copy of the will they had sent me, Cordelia and Adrian rushed in to say goodbye with firm promises to be back before midnight.

Putting the papers back in the envelope, I decided to go to the study where I might read them in peace but, as I came out of the breakfast room, Julia came up to me. 'Dad's gone up to his bedroom. He's very upset, Mum. Cordelia was a bitch. I think you'd better go to him. He won't want anyone else.' She looked very worried.

When I entered the bedroom, Patrick was lying on his side with his back towards me. 'I have a bad headache,' he said, 'but I don't want anything. Just leave me alone.'

Ignoring that, I walked over to the bed and sat down on the side near him. 'It's me, Patrick.'

He looked at me as if I were a stranger. 'I suppose you gave them your permission and everyone's happy. You made it quite clear that you don't care about my opinion, so why have you come to bother me?'

'You know,' I replied, 'that I didn't say anything I haven't always believed. I've always said that young people have the right to make their own decisions and learn to be independent. Like me, you believed that when you were young. You took your own decisions, so why do you want to deny Cordelia that right?'

'Perhaps,' he said slowly and sadly, 'it's because I don't want her to ruin her life when she's so young.'

'Surely you don't believe that? Has marrying me ruined your life?'

'No. But, if you're honest you must admit that your life would have been much better if you'd listened to your father. I've done you no good at all. In fact I've done you a lot of harm. You can't deny it, Stella.'

'I can and I do,' I said firmly. Knowing how much he suffered, I wanted to try to comfort him. The letter and the will could wait.

Chapter Twelve

It was the following Sunday afternoon before Stella was able to find the time and the privacy to read Eloise's letter. As she fingered the bulky envelope and stared once again at her name inscribed on it in Eloise's familiar flowing script she was tempted to burn it unread. She had a strong premonition that this would be a disturbing letter. Why else would Eloise have bothered to write it? And I don't need any more disturbances, Stella thought, as she sat fingering the letter and recalling her long and turbulent relationship with Eloise.

'She has left me her money but how shall I have to pay for it?' Still she hesitated. She was tired and needed peace and relaxation. This letter she was sure held no promise of either. Could she have destroyed both the letter and the will she would have done so but, if she accepted the will, she knew that she must accept the letter.

She had spent several hours during the evening after Cordelia left trying to resume contact with Patrick who was retreating again into his own dark world. Over and over again his answer had been the same frightening words, 'I know you're too loyal to want to admit it, Stella but you can't deny that I have ruined your life. Every decision I've made has been a disaster. Tonight was just one more example.'

Was it loyalty that made her refuse to consider what he said or was it a primitive fear, which she refused to acknowledge? All she could do was to insist on the love she had for him and the need she had of him. A fortnight earlier it had seemed to bring them together but did not now have the same effect. And this she couldn't understand.

She could not know because Patrick felt unable to tell her how much he wanted her to stop trying to comfort him and instead to look for the truth which she with her clear and rational mind might be able to discover and express, as he could not.

In the end, he yielded to the consolations she offered him as years before she had offered sweets to the children. He dutifully kissed her as she hugged him. She had become the mother he had never really had but what words were there to explain to her that this was not what he truly wanted – now.

The sound of Adrian's bike stopping outside at a quarter to twelve confirmed Patrick's belief that on this occasion Stella had been right. Adrian only stopped for a couple of minutes, after which they were relieved to hear Cordelia coming swiftly up to bed. 'You were right, as I said,' he murmured. Her only reply was to hug him more closely. After kissing her again he submitted, pretending to sleep. It seemed better that way. Now, after Sunday dinner he had retired to his bed, complaining of a headache and wanting only to be left alone.

The family had gone their separate ways and Stella was now sitting in her study, still holding Eloise's unopened letter. Had she really been right about Cordelia, she wondered? Her daughter had not been very happy after her evening out; in fact she had seemed quiet and even depressed. Stella had not tried to question her, as she seemed to be avoiding everyone. Now, she had gone to the Parish church as she often did on a Sunday afternoon to practise on the organ. After which, she was usually invited to tea with the vicar and his wife.

At last, Stella forced herself to open the letter. It was dated August 1969 and seemed therefore to have been written in the last weeks of Eloise's illness. It was longer than she had expected.

Dear Stella,

I think I know you well enough to be sure that you will be completely surprised when you discover that I have left you my not inconsiderable fortune (the size of which is largely due to my ex-husband's generosity). I want you to know that I'm sure that what you did for me in the past when you took my son and more recently since I have been seriously ill has been done out of disinterested love and I am grateful.

It is because I am grateful that I know I must write this letter. At the present moment I can think clearly and I don't know how long this may last, so I want to take this opportunity for doing what I should have done long ago.

Before I say any more, however, I want you to know that my primary reason for leaving you my money is so that you may be free for the first time in your life. It may surprise you when I say this but, if you try to look back honestly, I think you'll admit that your life has always been dominated first by your love for your father and for Patrick and from the time you were eighteen by your love for Patrick alone. I think that it's now time that you had a chance to be yourself and you can't do that, as you're presently situated without money.

I hope it won't shock you when I tell you that you are the only person I have ever loved and that my love for you has been the finest and most important feeling in my life. I have always wanted to advise, help and comfort you whenever I could. But, although you cared for me, you never truly reciprocated my love. Perhaps you were afraid? Whatever the reason, however, you always held back and worried about other people who were incapable of appreciating you and loving you as I did.

When we were at school I struggled to get you to myself and thought I had succeeded until you suddenly produced Patrick at the school dance. I don't suppose you can imagine what a terrible shock it was for me to meet him and to realise that, although you had scarcely spoken of him, he had always been first with you. And he although he was incapable of loving you as I did, or so I thought, was determined that it should remain so.

I hated him and his influence on you and was determined to detach him from you. Many men have found me attractive and I didn't see why he should be any different. Quite soon, I discovered that, although he didn't like me, he was not totally immune to my charms. At about the same time I realised to my amazement that I was not totally immune to his. In fact Patrick was the first man I ever found attractive. I didn't love him. How could I? You were my only love but I wanted him – not the whole of him, just his body.

My first real chance arrived when I came to visit you during your second term at Oxford, when Patrick was also there on the Army course he had so cleverly managed to arrange. Naturally I met him several times with you but one day, when you were busy, I persuaded him to meet me by myself. We spent two hours together in his rooms. And, although nothing much happened, it was quite clear that he was as attracted to me as I was to him. We arranged to meet again but he changed his mind. I didn't see him again until your wedding day.

After that, of course, he was away for over two years in the Army and you and I had a happy time renewing our close friendship. I was not particularly pleased when he came back and was again the centre of your life. I saw little of either of you after that until you so innocently offered me the flat in your house. Even then, I saw little of him until you went away for four days without him to see your mother who was ill. He seemed to resent that and, since we had been left alone together, I tried to console him.

I will be honest and admit that I took the initiative but I wasn't repulsed. Soon after that, you may remember, I left chiefly because I suspected I was pregnant. I'm not saying that Patrick was the father of my baby, for it wasn't possible, since we never became intimate. I liked to think of him, however, as Dominic's father because that strengthened the bond between us. My giving my baby to you and your loving acceptance of him brought us very close, especially when you agreed that Patrick should never know. I felt that Dominic was now our baby.

We were almost totally separated for four years after that. For me there was New York, marriage etc.; more babies and disasters for you. I loved your courage and detested the way Patrick made use of you. That was why I gave you the money to pay off the bank debt Patrick had incurred about the time of the death of your last baby. Again I persuaded you not to tell him, not because I wanted to spare him the humiliation, as you thought, but because I was determined to keep you close to me.

I avoided meeting Patrick again until about five years ago. Soon after he started his job in London, we met accidentally and I invited him to have a drink with me. To my surprise, he accepted. The old attraction still worked it seemed. I soon realised that he was unhappy and that you and he were no longer so close, especially physically. It was very wrong of me but I was lonely too at that time and so I was tempted to offer him consolation and to help him to realise that he was not as completely impotent and unattractive as he apparently thought. I had some success, although not in the normal way. He would have considered that adultery. Less normal relations were more tempting to him. I don't think I need to spell it out crudely. I'm sure you'll understand.

Suddenly I came to my senses and admitted that I couldn't continue in this way because it would cut me off from you and I couldn't bear that. We met again soon after and all was well with us. There seemed to be no point in telling you since I had decided to have nothing more to do with Patrick and I didn't want to make things more difficult for you.

I'm not quite sure why I did all these things. I suppose they gratified my vanity and my jealousy.

They were all pointless, however.

Now I feel that I must tell you the truth and ask your forgiveness before I die, as it seems likely that I shall do soon. I also think that you who are so honest and so loving deserve to know the truth about Patrick. No, not just about Patrick but also about yourself. His turning to me was no more that the desperate action of an isolated and unhappy man. I was pretty sure then and I am now that he loves you deeply but I think he has suspected for some time that you don't love him and perhaps never have loved him, as he wants to be loved.

Do you remember that when you became engaged I told you that you were not in love with him?

You laughed because you thought I had no idea of what I was talking about. You were wrong, however. I did know what I was talking about because I was in love with you, although I daren't tell you that because I knew it would frighten you away. You thought you knew more about loving than I did and in one sense you were right, as I know so well at the moment. Weaker beings, however like Patrick and me can't be satisfied with universal benevolence; we want to be special and we want a dash of Eros too, or passion, if you prefer that word.

Oh, dearest Stella, how I wish you could have been brave enough to come to me! But then I'm not sure that you ever really wanted to, although we often talked about the exciting things we would do after the war.

There's one more thing that, even now, puzzles me. Why did you insist on having so many babies, even at the risk of your life? Was it to prove to Patrick that you loved him? If so, it was a mistake. And if not that, what was the reason? I only know that you terrified me and in the end you overwhelmed Patrick. I suppose I was the only person who understood how he felt. I, however, had the advantage of money and strength and so I could help. He had nothing. Perhaps that is why I felt sorry for him briefly when I met him in London. I'm not sure if that is right. It's perhaps more likely that I followed my wicked desire to come between you two.

My money, I hope, will give you the freedom to face the truth and to sort out your life. If you're sure you don't want to, you need no longer stay with Patrick. But promise me, you'll make a proper decision only after talking honestly with him. When I'm dead, he'll be your only friend left.

My little strength is almost gone, so that I only have time left to tell you how much I value the real love you have shown to me during my illness. It would have been unendurable without you. You gave your love generously and I'm trying now to give back as generously as I can.

Be free and be happy, my dearest,

All my love Eloise.

As soon as she had finished reading the letter, Stella let it fall into her lap. Her first feeling was of utter shock. After a few minutes she re-read it slowly, as if she might have been mistaken in her understanding of what Eloise had written. There had however been no mistake. Carefully refolding it, she put it back in its envelope, and hid it in a drawer together with the copy of the Will. Then walking towards the open patio door she stared down the empty garden. She had a sudden vision of Eloise, her golden hair immaculate as always, the provocative glance of her brilliant blue eyes, her scarlet lips curved into a tantalizing and slightly mocking smile. She had trained her body and face to be the means of her obtaining power. And she had been successful; notably with Conrad Lestrange and with many other men she had used. But she never loved anyone, at least up till now that was what Stella had thought. If she was to believe this letter, however then she had been mistaken. Mistaken in many other matters too, even in her estimate of her own character and motives.

If, in fact, she did believe Eloise's letter then it seemed that there was little she had ever truly understood. As she continued to think over the letter she began to feel like a once blind person seeing herself for the first time in a mirror and finding in her reflection no resemblance to the image she had had of herself. No, perhaps it was more exact to say that she was like someone looking at her portrait painted by a trusted friend which revealed hitherto unsuspected, unflattering facets of her character. Could it possibly be a true picture?

Sitting down on the chair at her desk, she tried to bring her whirling thoughts into some kind of order. How should she begin? Perhaps it would be better to show the letter to Patrick and wait for his reaction. But, might he not be tempted to lie and, if he did, would she know? How could a marriage be real if it wasn't based on mutual honesty and trust? Patrick and she had agreed from their earliest years that they would always try to be completely honest with one another. She had always tried to be so, she told herself, except when Patrick's mental collapse made him unapproachable.

'Doesn't that mean no secrets?' A quiet, little voice seemed to shatter her self-complacency. 'And, if there are to be no secrets, what about Richard Alexander?' 'But that was different,' she said aloud, hoping to drown the little voice. 'That was before we were married and when I thought Patrick had deserted me.' It was no use.

Long suppressed memories suddenly came flooding in, overwhelming her carefully constructed defences. Going to her desk, she unlocked a small drawer, out of which she took an envelope from which she extracted some papers and finally a photograph of a young man in army officer's uniform. After many years she saw again the honest look of his grey eyes, the trusting friendliness of his smile and remembered once again his courage and vulnerability.

It is an evening in mid-March, 1945 and they have just accidentally met. Obviously lost he has asked her the way to the nearest tube station and she has volunteered to lead him to it as it is on her way home. They chat freely and he tells her that he has just arrived in London at the start of a fourteen days' leave from the Army in France. She tells him that she is in her final year as a student, training to be a teacher.

As the subdued lights of the tube station come into view, she turns to go but he stops her with a hesitant request. 'I wonder if you'd be willing to have a meal with me?' Interpreting her hesitation, he adds with a smile, 'I mean a meal and nothing else. I've never been in London before, you see. I know no one here and I haven't a clue where to go. It would be a kind action.'

Looking into his grey eyes she feels that she can trust him. Unusually, she too faces a lonely evening. 'Alright, I'll trust you.' Her smile encourages him.

'I promise you won't regret it. Now where shall we go? You're in charge.' She chooses the Oxford Street Corner House, since it will be cheerful, crowded and fairly inexpensive. It proves to be a good choice and in less than half an hour they are both relaxed and talking as easily as old friends. So much so that at the end of the meal, as it is still quite early, she agrees to go with him to see a new French film at the Academy cinema.

It is just before midnight when he is about to leave her outside the front door of the house where she has a room. To her relief he does not attempt to kiss her but, after thanking her for a pleasant evening, turns to leave. Before she can open her front door, however, he surprises her with an unexpected question. 'Would you meet me for lunch tomorrow? I would like it very much if you could. And, if you have the free time, perhaps we could visit somewhere interesting afterwards?' He is shy but determined. 'What do you think?'

She finds herself unable to resist either his pleading look or his hopeful smile. 'I could be free by lunch time. I don't want to spend all day studying.'

'Good.' He says before she can say any more. 'I'll turn up here at twelve thirty. We can decide where to go over lunch.' With a quick salute he has gone, giving her no chance to change her mind.

The next few days pass like a dream as they explore London together discovering how much they have in common. There seems to be nothing they cannot talk about freely. Every morning she wakes up with the happy thought that she will meet him some time that day. He has apparently forgotten his original intention of spending part of his leave with his elderly aunt who has been for many years his only close living relative. He seems to have mercifully forgotten too the horrors of the battle he has left and to which he must return. Even the missiles still falling on London do not disturb them. They live only for each joyous moment together.

Then, on the seventh day he makes a declaration. After exploring Kew Gardens they are having tea in a quiet corner of the café. She has just picked up the tea pot when he unexpectedly leans forward, fixes his eyes earnestly upon her, saying quietly but with great emphasis, 'I'm seriously in love with you, Stella. If for some reason you don't want us to go any further, say so now and I'll go out of your life. It's your decision.'

She has never doubted his honesty and she does not now. Unnerved by his directness, unsure too of her reply, she continues to fill his cup with tea, unable to look into his eyes. He is still waiting. She must say something. 'Aren't you going to visit your aunt then?'

'That depends on you.' He is unyielding. 'Look at me, please.'

Slowly she raises her eyes to his. 'Won't she be disappointed?'

'Stop being evasive,' he says gently. 'Time is short. I must have an honest reply. You've told me that for many years there was someone important in your life but you had parted and that was over. Perhaps that wasn't really true? Perhaps in spite of all that has happened, you still love him. If that is so, then just tell me. I'll understand and go.'

'You want me to commit myself now? Aren't you asking a lot?'

'No more than I'm prepared to give. I've been close to death in the last few months. My best friend, a tank commander like myself, was blown to pieces a few days before I came on leave. I was lonely and afraid until I met you. Now I don't want to waste any opportunity by running away. I've come to understand that life is so fragile that it needs courage to accept happiness, especially when we realise our vulnerability. Easier not to, really. I'm sorry I'm not sure I'm making myself very clear.'

'You are,' she whispers. 'You want to know if I have that courage. I think I have. I want to be brave like you. Please don't go.' She puts her hand out to him and he takes it in his, almost crushing it as they smile radiantly at each other. Trusting to her honesty he asks no more questions about the past. 'The next seven days are ours then?'

As he releases her hand, she passes the cup of tea to him. 'And after that?

'The rest of our lives, I hope.'

'Hello Mum!' Startled, Stella looked up. Hastily, she thrust the letters and the photograph into the envelope. Cordelia had just come hurrying in through the open door. She was smiling cheerfully and carrying her music case. Too absorbed in her own news she didn't notice her mother's abstracted look. 'I'm back earlier, because I didn't stop for tea as the vicar has a visitor. You'll never guess who it is!' Without waiting for Stella to reply, she announced, 'It's David Hancock!' As Stella still made no obvious reaction, she continued somewhat disappointed, 'You must remember him? He's the cathedral organist.'

With a great effort, Stella brought her mind back through twenty-four years to the present. 'Of course I remember him. Didn't we hear him give a recital last spring?'

'Yes and we thought he was brilliant. Well, he's a friend of the vicar's and the vicar asked him to come and hear me play this afternoon. I didn't know until I got there. I was petrified when he told me but…'

'I gather that all went well,' Stella smiled at her obviously happy daughter.

'Marvellously. He asked me to play three pieces, and then he sat and listened to me without a word. I got more and more nervous. I was sure I must be doing very badly but, when I had finished, he smiled at me and said he thought I had a real talent for music in general and for the organ in particular. I had faults, he said, but they could soon be put right with advanced tuition. Then he asked me what my future plans were. When I told him he said I was not aiming high enough. I would do better to try for an Organ Scholarship at Oxford or Cambridge. He said he would willingly take me on as a pupil and could also arrange for me to have extra tuition in the holidays with a famous organist in Switzerland. I was completely dazed and the vicar suggested that I should discuss it with you and Dad and then we could all have a talk with Mr Hancock. Mr Hancock gave me this note for you and Dad and I came home.' Handing a letter to her mother, she looked anxiously at her.

'Do you really want to do this?' Stella asked.

'I think it would be wonderful!' Cordelia's happiness was obvious. 'But I'm afraid it'll cost too much money. It means staying on at school for an extra year and paying for all these extra lessons. It wouldn't be fair for me to expect it. Things are already too difficult, I know. Still it's nice to know that Mr Hancock thinks I'm good enough, isn't it?'

Stella considered her daughter carefully. 'Leave the money to me. I think that might be arranged. But, first of all, I want to know how much you have thought about this. How sure are you that you really want to do this? Are you ready for the dedication required? It means hours of extra study, not only in term time but also in the holidays. Your friends will be leaving and you will have to stay on at school. Are you prepared for this?'

'Why shouldn't I be?' Cordelia demanded passionately. 'You did something like that. But I suppose you think I'm inferior and Dad is sure to agree with you!'

'Is that your real opinion?' Stella looked unhappily at her daughter. 'I'm sorry if it is but perhaps it's understandable. But at the moment it seems more important to me that you should consider Adrian.'

'Adrian? I don't see what it has to do with him. He's going to be an engineer. I want to be a musician.'

'If you follow this new course, it will probably separate you. I thought that might be important to you since you have been telling me how fond you are of him. Or have you already decided that you're not really suited?'

'Why do you say that?' Cordelia's tone was still hostile.

'Because, although you haven't actually said anything, I don't believe that you enjoyed your outing with him last night. Perhaps you realised then that you had little in common. Or am I mistaken?'

Cordelia hesitated a moment before she answered. 'As a matter of fact I didn't enjoy it much. I thought most of the music was appalling. It was crowded and noisy and a lot of the people were pretty drunk. It definitely wasn't my scene. It was interesting to try it. But I don't want to do it again. Especially now, that I know I've got better use for my time.' She stared at her mother. 'That should please you, surely. I know you made it possible for me to go but you didn't really want me to, did you? You were just subtler than Dad.'

Ignoring her comments, Stella said. 'Did you say any of this to Adrian?'

'Not in so many words but I think he got the idea. I didn't want to upset him.'

'You'll have to tell him about your change of plans for your future, won't you? Don't you think that will upset him?'

'I don't see why we can't still have fun together but, if I have to choose between him and music then I'll certainly choose music. I'm ambitious, you see. I don't understand why you weren't more ambitious, Mum. You were brilliant. You could have done all kinds of things.'

'You mean instead of marrying and having a family. There were reasons. One of them was love.' Stella smiled a little ironically at her daughter.

'That seems to be an awful trap for a girl.' Cordelia said as if she had suddenly become wise. 'I think I'll avoid getting caught too soon. Are you sure, Mum,' she asked suddenly, 'that you can manage the money? It's wonderful of you!'

'Mum!' Julia's voice interrupted them before Stella could reply. 'Mr Regan's at the front door,' she announced as she came into the room. 'He wants to have a word with Dad.'

'What about?'

'I think his wife's been kept in hospital with a suspected miscarriage and he wants to know if Dad will take him to see her.'

'Not again!' Cordelia exclaimed.

Stella ignored her. 'Don't keep him standing in the porch. Take him into the breakfast room and give him a cup of tea and a cake or something. In the meantime, I'd better rouse your father.' She didn't sound very pleased at the idea but she made no further comment.

'What's wrong with Mum?' Julia asked.

Cordelia shrugged. 'Nothing as far as I know. But we've no time to talk about it now. You'd better go to Mr Regan and I'll start the tea.'

Chapter Thirteen

It was obvious that Patrick was in a grim mood when he returned from taking Mike Regan to the hospital. After sitting down, he refused all offers of refreshment from Julia and Cordelia who were already laying the table for supper.

'How was Mrs Regan?' Cordelia asked, hoping to make some contact with him.

'Not very well – pretty weak in fact.'

'I'm sorry,' Julia exclaimed. 'But have they managed to save the baby?'

'They say they have but she'll still have to be careful.'

'That's something at least.' Cordelia sounded relieved 'Then why are you so depressed, Dad?'

'Where's your mother?' Patrick asked without attempting to answer her.

'She's in the kitchen,' Cordelia told him, glad to be able to change the subject. 'She's making a special salad for supper. She found a new recipe in one of her books and thought she'd like to try it.'

'We've been dismissed,' Julia added, 'and given the inferior job of laying the table.'

'Then, why aren't you getting on with it?' Stella's voice startled them as she came in carrying a large bowl, which she placed in the centre of the empty table.

'Sorry, Mum,' Julia explained. 'We were talking to Dad. He's just come back.'

Stella turned apparently seeing Patrick for the first time. 'How was she, then?' she asked him.

'Pretty weak but they've saved the baby. She'll be allowed home in a day or two but they told her she'll have to rest.'

'We can't talk about it now. I must make this special dressing.'

'What's the hurry, Mum?' Cordelia asked. 'It's only Sunday evening supper. A pretty moveable feast I'd have thought.'

'Not this week,' Stella said briskly. 'Ben's bringing his friend and Lucas has invited himself. So you'd better lay the table for seven and be ready in quarter of an hour.' She disappeared again into the kitchen.

'Hard luck,' Julia said sympathetically. 'Mum's has suddenly decided to be the perfect housewife and we've all got to play our parts.'

'I think I'll make myself a cup of coffee, after all.' Standing up, Patrick followed his wife into the kitchen.

'Poor, old Dad,' Cordelia said. 'He's obviously very depressed and needs a bit of Mum's extra comforting.'

'I don't think he'll get it at this moment,' Julia sounded worried. 'Mum seems to be in a strange sort of mood. Or haven't you noticed?'

'I'm not sure,' Cordelia was thoughtful. 'She was a bit odd when I first came in but then she seemed interested in my ideas of a musical career. She even said she thought we'd be able to manage the money, which amazed me. She does seem distant now, though.'

'Perhaps she doesn't like to think about babies being born dead,' Julia suggested. 'Because of her own experience.'

'I expect you're right. I don't imagine a woman ever gets over an experience like that. I read in some book that it was the worst thing that could happen to a woman.' Cordelia turned to her sister. 'In that case we'd better get on with what we're supposed to do.' She began to lay small plates on the table and Julia picked up the cutlery she had earlier taken from the drawer.

Stella busily whisking something in a bowl did not stop when Patrick came into the kitchen. 'Do you want something?'

'I'll make myself a cup of coffee.' After switching on the kettle he took down a mug from the rack and reached for the jar of coffee. As soon as he had made his coffee, he sat down at the table to drink it. At the same time Stella stopped her whisking and sat down opposite him but she still didn't speak.

'It was pretty grim,' he said as he sipped his coffee, 'she looked so ill and vulnerable. I don't think Mike Regan's got a clue about what to do.'

'I should doubt it. He's not the thoughtful type, is he? More the sort who gets drunk every Friday night and comes home to complete his pleasure with his wife, regardless of the consequences.'

'I'm afraid you may be right.' Patrick hesitated to say more, wondering as he often did how much resentment Stella still had because of her own sufferings in the past.

Stella was obviously disinclined to say any more. 'I think I've got this dressing right,' she remarked as if completely dismissing any further discussion of Mary Regan's fate.

'Please Stella,' Patrick put out his hand to her. 'Don't do this to me. I realise you've never really accepted what happened nine years ago…'

'We've sorted that out surely? We're still together – a happy couple,' she interrupted him.

'I'd recently begun to think that we had; that we might again be as we once were but that's just an illusion, isn't it? You weren't being truthful, were you?'

'How truthful have you been?' Before he could answer her, she rushed on, 'But, for God's sake can't you understand that I don't want to talk about it now. I'm sorry for poor Mary Regan. Sorry that you found it so unpleasant but I don't want to talk about it. I don't know if I'll ever want to talk about it.' Picking up her salad dressing and a pile of plates she moved quickly towards the breakfast room, leaving him feeling bewildered and rejected.

Before he could move, however she returned. 'I'm sorry, Patrick,' she said, speaking more calmly. 'I'm upset and confused at present about a lot of things. I know I shouldn't be so irritable but I am. I agree we should try to talk but I can't do it yet. And we certainly can't do it with all the family around.'

'Of course not.' He was glad that she had at least given him some kind of explanation. As he moved towards the breakfast room she stopped him. 'I don't suppose you've had a chance to talk to Cordelia yet? The cathedral organist came to the vicarage to hear her play this afternoon and was apparently very complimentary.' Quickly she told him all that Cordelia had told her and her reply, not wanting him to feel that he had been ignored.

At first he was very pleased. 'I always thought she was very talented and I wouldn't want her to miss her chance. But do you think that you should have said that about the money? It's bound to cost quite a lot and we do have to think about the others. And you know I can't expect to contribute much.'

Seeing his worried look, she was sorry but she was determined not to confide in him yet. 'There may be ways,' she replied evasively. 'In fact, there will be, I'm sure, so let's not worry about it until we have to. I'd like to talk to you about that – later but not just now.'

'Do you think she's sufficiently dedicated? After all, she already has a boy friend.'

'I doubt very much if she'll let Adrian or anyone else deter her from having what she wants. She's made of sterner stuff than some of us.'

'From you, you mean? She won't be led astray like you were?'

'Cordelia and I are different. We have different aims.'

'And Adrian's not like me, fortunately?'

'Probably not.' The noisy arrival of Ben and his best friend followed by Lucas prevented any further intimate conversation between them.

Supper was a noisy and cheerful affair. Ben and his friend gave a riotous account of the village cricket match they been watching. Everyone was interested in Cordelia's new prospects, especially Lucas who had been the first to encourage her to take up playing the organ. The cake baked by Julia with typical, mathematical precision was pronounced a great success and a worthy complement to Stella's delicious salad. No one, except Cordelia, seemed to notice that Patrick contributed little but she was consoled when he smiled and quietly told her how pleased he was. 'Mum was consoling about the money aspect,' she said to him, 'but I'm not sure.' 'There's plenty of time to sort that out,' he replied, marvelling at himself for saying it.

'Anyone looking in would think we are a really happy family,' Stella thought looking round.

It was only when Ben and his friend had gone to watch the television that the subject of the Regans came up again. Patrick had been telling Lucas briefly about it and, as he finished, Julia remarked, 'I don't see how she's going to rest, when she's already got four children under six at home.

'Neither do I,' Cordelia agreed. 'The last baby's only about ten months old isn't it, Mum?'

'I believe so.' Stella's tone was not encouraging.

'Poor woman!' Julia exclaimed.

'But how ridiculous!' Cordelia sounded genuinely shocked. 'Why do people have so many babies when they can't cope with them?' She turned towards her mother, expecting a helpful reply.

To her surprise, however, Stella only gazed back at her seeming to be at a loss for words. To Stella, in fact, it seemed at that moment as if Eloise's questions must be known to everyone, as if they had been branded on her for all to see. 'Why did you have so many babies? Was it because you wanted to persuade Patrick that you loved him? In the end, you know, you only overwhelmed him.' Struggling to free herself, she managed at last to answer her daughter. 'I really don't know. I suppose you might say that about me or anyone who has several children with difficulties.'

Cordelia reacted immediately with obvious distress. 'Don't be silly, Mum. There's no comparison between you and Mrs Regan. You had a choice and you chose to have a family. Besides, you've always coped marvellously. She simply can't cope. Four children are clearly too much for her and now she's having a fifth.'

'I don't see how you're going to stop it,' Julia remarked.

'I'm not sure but perhaps if women were educated more and given more choices they might be happier.'

'And dare I say it, knew more about contraception,' Julia added boldly.

'I think this conversation has gone far enough,' Patrick startled everyone by interrupting suddenly. 'I don't think it's good to speculate about people's private lives, especially when you're speaking from ignorance.'

'I agree,' Lucas stood up. 'We all know that gossip should be avoided. In any case it's time we all helped to clear away the supper. Not you, Stella,' he added, as she stood up. 'You've done enough.'

'Thanks.' Stella smiled at him as she stood up. 'I think I'd better retire to the study to do some marking.' As she passed Patrick, she murmured to him, 'Join me later, when you can. There's something I must tell you, privately.'

'Perhaps it's just this love you're so keen on,' Julia whispered mischievously to Cordelia as they went into the kitchen.

'What is? Oh you mean, Mrs Regan? I doubt it.'

'You'll find out when you marry Adrian, I expect.'

'I intend to have a career.'

'I hope you do but babies seem to have a habit of getting in the way. I don't intend to get married unless I can find a man who agrees with me.'

'So you say now.' Seeing Lucas close behind them, they both became busy sorting out the dishes he and Patrick were bringing into the kitchen.

About forty minutes later, Lucas came into the study bearing a cup of coffee. 'I thought you might be glad of this,' he said as he put it down on the desk.

'Thanks. It's just what I wanted. How about you?'

'Mine's waiting for me in the kitchen. We've just finished sorting out.'

'I feel I ought to be available.'

'There's no need. Ben is on his way to bed. The girls are about to settle down to the Sunday film. And Patrick's just about to give Ben's friend a lift home. Everything's under control.' As he was walking towards the door, he suddenly stopped. 'What's the matter, Stella? Something has upset you hasn't it?'

'Have I made it as obvious as that?'

'No, of course not. It's simply that I care about you and I notice. You know that.'

'Yes, I do and I'm grateful for that.'

Turning back towards her, he replied quickly, 'Why don't you share it with me now. Perhaps I can help.'

She hesitated and then said resolutely, 'I can't. I must speak to Patrick first. Perhaps afterwards.'

'I'm going home now. I have a piece of work to finish. Come round to coffee tomorrow morning as soon as you can.' Without waiting for her reply, he bent and kissed her lightly on the cheek. 'See you tomorrow.' The door closed behind him.

It was some half an hour later when Patrick came in to her. As she looked up he was standing by the door. 'I'm afraid it's a bit late but you did say you wanted to talk to me. We can leave it until tomorrow, if you'd prefer that.'

'No, I'd rather do it now.' She put aside her pile of exercise books and took the letter from her desk. Holding it out to him, she explained, 'I think you ought to read this.' It was simply the solicitor's letter and the copy of the will. She felt it would be better to keep Eloise's letter to herself for the moment. 'It came on Friday but I didn't find time to read until this afternoon and I want you to be the first person to hear about it.'

He moved towards her but made no attempt to take the letter. Puzzled by a certain coolness and even hostility in her tone, he was unsure how to react. 'What is it?'

Irritated, she replied quickly pushing the letter at him. 'It would be better if you sat down and read it. It's from Eloise's solicitors.'

Taking the letter from her, he sat down on the couch and began to read it. When he had finished, he folded it up carefully and put it back in its envelope. 'It seems that she has left her fortune to you. Had you any idea that she would do this?'

'Of course not. We never talked about anything like that. She was too ill, most of the time. You surely don't think I looked after her just to get a reward?'

'I know you too well to think anything like that, Stella. Was there anyone else, however, she might have left her money to?'

'I suppose there isn't really. Her mother died twenty years ago of breast cancer and her father was killed ten years ago in an accident. As you know she had no brothers or sisters, I was her only close friend.' She did not mention the special position of Dominic, which had begun to worry her.

'She always loved you.' Although she waited, he made no further comment. 'I loved her, too.' As he still made no comment, she decided to ask a factual question which had been puzzling her.

Do you understand what they mean when they say that I am her "residuary legatee"?'

'As far as I understand it, it means that when the stated legacies have been paid out, the rest of the estate whatever it is comes to you. I should imagine it will be quite a large sum. I can understand now why you made what I thought was a rather rash promise to Cordelia. If money is all that is needed, then her future career is assured.'

'The others can be helped too when they need it. Don't you see it will solve a lot of problems we've hardly begun to think about?'

'I'm sure it will and I'm sure that Eloise had that in mind. She has always wanted to solve your problems, hasn't she?'

Surprised at the bitterness of his tone, she challenged him. 'You don't sound very pleased?'

'I'm not. I wish it hadn't happened.'

'Whatever makes you say that? Can't you even be pleased at our good fortune?'

'We could have managed without it. I'm not even sure it is good fortune. At least, not as far as our relationship is concerned.'

'I don't understand you. Why don't you say what you really mean for once?'

Suddenly, he stood up. 'Very well, then I will. I'm sorry that Eloise had to die so early and in such a painful way but, at least, I thought we might be free of her, at last. Free to live our own lives and to sort out our own problems. But she obviously decided otherwise. First there was the business of Dominic, now this. Must she always be in the background?'

Leaping to her feet, she faced him angrily. 'Why are you saying these horrid things? This isn't my fault. I didn't know she was going to do this. But I don't see why you shouldn't see it as a useful gift for both of us, instead of sounding almost jealous? You know I love you.' Her eyes were full of tears suddenly.

'I know you love me and I know you loved Eloise too. The trouble is that she can help you more than I can, even now. I can't feel special. I'm sorry if that sounds petty but there it is.'

As she was about to answer him passionately, the memory of Eloise's letter stopped her. What Patrick had just said was so similar to what Eloise had written. Had they both felt the same? Were they right? It seemed impossible for her to think clearly. Forcing back her tears, she tried to speak calmly. 'I think it would be better not to talk about it any more tonight, I'm feeling too upset. Receiving this has brought it all back.'

He agreed quickly. 'I understand. I'm glad you told me. There's not much more to say anyway, is there? Have you decided what you'll do?'

'I think I'd better ring the solicitors tomorrow and make an appointment to see them. What do you think?' She desperately wanted him to say something friendly and perhaps comforting but she didn't know how to reach him.

'I can't think of anything better to do,' was all he said, as he turned to leave the room. At the door, he paused, 'Will you be finished soon?'

'I doubt it. I've got more to do than I realised. What are you going to do?'

'I think I shall go to bed quite soon. My headache hasn't been improved by the events of the day.'

As he seemed to be about to go without another word, she tried to appeal to him. 'Don't go, Patrick. Not like that please.'

'I thought you didn't want to talk any more tonight. Was I wrong?'

'I think I wanted some kindness, perhaps even understanding. But that seems unlikely.'

'I'm sorry.' He sounded weary and depressed. 'I was very affected by Mary Regan's state, I suppose. It seemed so wrong.'

Stella stared at him. 'Damn Mary Regan! I'm sorry for her too but what about me? I don't think that any of you, certainly not you, understood how painful and hard it was looking after Eloise and watching her die in agony. You all thought I could come back and everything could be just the same as it had been before. I thought I had managed until the funeral and now this. But now I realise that I've simply been pretending, not just to you all but to myself. It's a shock when someone you love dies prematurely and painfully. It affects your view of life and of yourself. You can't accept it. You need help.' As he moved a step towards her, she sat down again at her desk. 'Don't try. There's nothing you can say. Just go.'

After hesitating a moment as if intending to protest, he suddenly turned and went.

As the door closed behind him, she allowed the long repressed tears to fall freely.

Chapter Fourteen

'Whatever had I expected?' I asked myself as I walked along the Strand the following Wednesday morning. I had just spent nearly an hour with Eloise's solicitor who had carefully explained all the details to me. I had listened politely until suddenly feeling that I could endure it no longer, that I must get away and think, I had refused coffee on the grounds that I had an appointment to meet my son and had made my escape, clutching several more papers and the key to Eloise's house.

Now, stumbling into the nearest café, I chose the first vacant table and ordered a cup of black coffee, together with a comforting cream cake. I looked at my watch. I had promised to meet Dominic but there was at least an hour before I needed to set off for that and I felt that I needed every minute of that hour. Stirring my coffee, I asked myself again. 'Whatever had I expected? Why was I so shocked?' The first reason was of course that Eloise had left me far more than I had expected, for I had not at any time considered the money she had extracted from Conrad Lestrange. As a result of this Eloise had not been simply comfortably off, she had been rich. My inheritance, therefore, was not just something extra to smooth my way through life; it was a corrupting temptation, or so it seemed to me at that moment.

Since I had spoken to Patrick on the Sunday evening he and I had said no more about this subject, in fact our communications in general had been minimal. I had talked to Lucas on the Monday morning about the will but had avoided any discussion. All I had said to Patrick was that I was taking a day off to go to London to see Eloise's solicitor about some details. To my surprise, he had accepted it without question but unfortunately he had mentioned it to Dominic on the phone and Dominic had immediately insisted on my meeting him for lunch. He urgently wanted to talk to me, it appeared. Patrick had not suggested joining us, neither had I asked him.

The contents of Eloise's letter I had kept to myself. This I needed more time to consider; for it was this, even more than the amount of my inheritance, that had shocked me. Eloise had challenged my view both of myself and of my life. Now, sitting by myself in the café where no one knew me I felt I must begin to meet this challenge. Would she, I asked myself, have written anything untrue at the time when she was dying? That seemed unlikely but at the same time her belief in the truth of what she was saying was no guarantee of its accuracy. I didn't have to accept it.

Nevertheless, it was clear that she had believed what she had written. She had even shown considerable sympathy for Patrick seeing him apparently as a 'fellow victim'. She hadn't actually used that word but I felt was what she had been implying. They were both victims of my 'so-called love' that was what she had been saying. And then I remembered what Patrick had replied to me, 'I can never be special.' Wasn't he, therefore saying something very similar? I had not attempted to answer him but had attacked him instead accusing him of a lack of sympathy and love.

As I finished my cake, I realised that it was about time for me to set out to meet Dominic. We had arranged to meet at a Chinese restaurant just off Shaftesbury Avenue, so I walked there while I tried to rearrange my ideas. The more I tried, the more impossible it seemed. I didn't want to meet Dominic. I was convinced that I wouldn't be able to love him in the same way. I was wrong, of course. As soon as I saw him standing there, tall and fair haired, smiling his usual loving smile and greeting me enthusiastically, I simply loved him as I had always done.

'They do quite a nice cheap lunch,' he said. 'I've been studying the menus.'

'Forget that. We'll have a banquet – a celebration.' For a moment I enjoyed the thought that I need not worry about the expense.'

'Are you sure?' Dominic, considerate as always, looked a little troubled.

'I'm sure. It isn't every day I have the chance to go out to lunch with a handsome young man. Now come on and help me choose.'

It took us some time to choose a meal that was to our mutual satisfaction but, once that was over and the many dishes were in front of us, we were able to settle down. At first Dominic wanted to hear family news and, in particular, to discuss Cordelia's changed prospects. 'Do you think it will really happen? Won't it be very expensive?'

I was cautious. 'I think Cordelia has the ability to make it happen if she really wants to but that has to be left to her. As for the money, we can manage it. I've promised her that.'

Dominic looked at me admiringly. 'You're always so confident, mum. It's amazing! But I suppose that is really why our family has kept afloat. How does Dad feel?'

'He's worried, I think but he's willing to leave it to me. Now let's forget all this for a time and get down to what really matters.' I smiled at him.

'What do you mean?'

'What was the real reason why you so urgently wanted to meet me when Dad told you I was coming to London today?' Seeing him still hesitating, I continued, 'Don't waste your time pretending, please.'

'I won't then. It's impossible anyway with you. It's about my future.'

I frowned a little. 'I thought that was settled, at least until you were within striking distance of your degree? And that's nearly two years away.'

'I'm not sure that I want to continue with my degree,' he replied slowly, obviously worried about my reaction.

Mastering the irritation I felt, I managed to say coolly, 'Why not? You passed your first year exams well. Surely nothing drastic can have happened in the first week of the new year?' Helping myself to some sweet and sour pork, I waited for him to answer.

'No, of course not. It's not that I can't do the work, it's just that I don't see where it's going to get me.'

'I thought we'd been through all this before you finally decided to apply for Law. And you may remember you decided on Law because you thought you'd enjoy the study and even more importantly because you thought it would be a useful opening to several professions. All that's still true, so what's changed?' I returned to my meal.

There was silence for a moment, then Dominic looked at me almost defiantly. 'I've changed. At least, I've learned more about myself and so I now know that what I've always wanted to do, is probably right. You see, I always wanted to be a journalist and then when Eloise told me that she was my mother, it all fell into place. She was a journalist and a pretty successful one I've discovered, so it's clear that I've inherited that talent from her. And now I feel confident enough to say that's what I want to do.'

I cursed Eloise silently. Would she never stop interfering? For the first time I understood Patrick's reaction. Upset though I was, I prayed for guidance and tried to proceed with care and caution.

'Surely, there is no reason why you shouldn't be a journalist when you've taken your degree? I know that there are graduate training courses. Many well known journalists have been to University.'

'Eloise didn't, did she? And I think I'm like her. I'm clever but I'm not really academic. I don't want to waste time, I want to get started.'

'And have you any idea how to do that?'

'I've been looking into it this last week. Many big provincial newspapers have very good training courses and many ambitious people get from there to London. I've got an application form for the Medway newspapers but I wanted to talk to you before I sent it off.' When I didn't immediately answer, he continued, 'I know it's upsetting for you but please don't be cross with me, Mum. Try to think about it as you would with one of your pupils and give me your best advice. I know that will be good.' He smiled hopefully at me.

'Very well, since you've asked me to, I will treat you like one of my pupils and try to be completely objective, so don't waste any more time on flattery.' He was so obviously disconcerted that I had to smile.

He rallied well, however. 'So what do you want your pupil to do?'

'Let me look at the application form, first.' Without a further word he handed it over to me, then watched anxiously while I studied it. Finally, I put it down. 'Well, that seems pretty straightforward, particularly since you had that month's work experience in the Tonbridge newspaper office.'

'You arranged that,' he reminded me.

'Yes, and you weren't very keen when I suggested it.'

'I know but I enjoyed it when I did it and the editor would give me a reference I'm sure. So what do you think, is it alright for me to send the form in?'

'Don't you think that your dad ought to be consulted first?' I really didn't want Patrick to feel ignored again.

'If you think it's the right thing, he won't object. You know that.'

'But is it the right thing? Or have you simply got some romantic notion about Eloise? You seemed to think that she was a pretty selfish person when you last spoke about her.'

He flushed. 'I still do. But knowing that she was a successful journalist convinced me in my idea that journalism was the career for me. She wasn't academic and neither am I. I did well at school because you encouraged me but it was always a slog. And University isn't even a slog, it's just boring a lot of the time. I'll make far better use of my life, if I have to get down to something practical.'

As I listened to him, I had a vivid memory of Eloise saying things like that when I'd tried to persuade her to try for Oxford with me. She'd been right and perhaps Dominic was. For the first time he reminded me of her.

Seeing my hesitation, he pressed on. 'You're an academic and so's Julia. She'll do brilliantly just as you did but I've never enjoyed learning and the search for knowledge and all that. I'll just slack off and waste my time. But give me a practical goal and I'll go for it. You know I'm right, Mum.'

'Perhaps but I still think you should speak to your dad first.'

'There's isn't time. The form has to be in on Friday and there may not be another chance for a year. You don't want me to miss it, do you?'

I smiled recognising familiar pressurising tactics and the need the young always feel to get everything settled at once. 'Why do you need my approval?'

'Because I respect your judgment and I don't want to disappoint you.'

I considered this for a moment, then I smiled at him. 'I see no reason why you shouldn't fill in the form and send it off. If you're successful, then you have my blessing but, if you're not, I think you should wait until you've taken your degree. What do you say?'

'I think you're a wonderful, Mum! I won't ever let you down. Will you tell, Dad?'

I sighed. 'If you insist. Now I suggest we continue with our lunch. This food's too good to waste.'

The rest of our time together passed pleasantly and quickly, then I sent him off to fill in his form. As I walked away from him, returning his cheerful waves, I realised I had only added yet another problem to my list, for Patrick would certainly think I had capitulated too readily.

I should have made my way to Charing Cross and taken the first train home. Instead I found myself wandering along the Embankment. Leaning on the parapet, I watched the boats go by. A light breeze was stirring the water into ripples which glistened in the sun. I had to admit to myself that I didn't want to go home, at least not yet. Deciding, therefore, to miss the first train, I sat down on a nearby bench.

My only companion was an old man sitting huddled in the corner to my right. Since he appeared to be asleep, I studied him idly. His stained and shabby trousers were tucked into worn boots and appeared to be secured round the waist with a piece of cord. Over this he wore what had been an expensive jacket but which was now much battered and which only just fastened round his heavy figure. A bright, many-coloured woollen scarf completed his outfit. His hair was very white and had grown down almost to his collar. Obviously, a vagrant, I decided.

'I imagine, you'll know me next time you meet me.' Startled, I turned completely towards him and found myself being scrutinised by a pair of extraordinarily bright and vivid blue eyes. His voice was rather hoarse but he spoke like an educated man. From the little smile that hovered round his mouth, I realised that he was not offended, so I did not attempt a trite apology. 'Not if you change your clothes,' I answered returning his smile.

Even before I had finished my silly little reply, I realised that I was wrong for his face was not one to be easily forgotten.

Although he was old and weary, I could still see that he had been an independent and intelligent man. His firm mouth and determined chin told me he was still a strong man, while his bright blue eyes flashed with insight and humour. He might have become a vagrant but life had not defeated him. 'I was wrong,' I added suddenly, 'I would recognise you whatever clothes you were wearing.'

He laughed. 'You mean you think I'm not quite what I seemed at first look? You're no longer sure that I'm just an old beggar with a hard luck story?'

'I hadn't quite got round to thinking that but now I think you might be someone worth talking to.'

He laughed again. 'You'll probably be surprised then when I tell you that you're the first person who has bothered to speak to me for months. I was surprised you even sat on the same bench – most people find another one.'

'Which only shows how stupid most people are. They're mostly afraid to meet anyone outside their ordinary rut.'

He smiled. 'But then they haven't your confidence, have they?'

'My confidence?' I frowned. 'Why do you say that? I don't actually feel confident about anything at the moment.'

He was obviously amused. 'Why should a good-looking, intelligent young woman like you expect an ugly, penniless, old tramp like me to believe that?'

'Because it's true and I think you are the sort of person who might believe the truth, however incredible it seems.' I was amazed at myself for speaking to him like this but it was a relief to speak freely.

'Try me.'

Without stopping to think, I did just that. 'First of all, I've been left a fortune but it doesn't make me happy because it's too much and because I mistrust the motives of the person who left it to me.' I stopped waiting for some expression of incredulity but there was none. 'Do you actually believe me?'

'Why not? Why would you bother to tell me a lie? But there must be more. To be given too much money might be annoying to an independent person but why should it destroy your confidence?'

'Because there was a letter with the will which made me feel that I had never properly understood the writer who was a good friend, nor my husband nor, worst of all, myself. I think I may have been deceived or may have been deceiving myself for years. So, no confidence.' When he said nothing, I laughed, mocking myself, 'Such a sad, little story from a poor, little rich girl, isn't it?'

He considered me carefully with those brilliant blue eyes. 'It is a sad, little story but it needn't have a sad ending. It isn't finished yet. Go on fighting the good fight bravely. You must never accept defeat, lass, until the final curtain. I've learned that and I've also learned not to accept other people's opinions, especially not those about yourself.' He smiled encouragingly. 'Go back home and face 'em all straightaway.'

I suddenly knew why I had spoken to him. He looked like my father and he spoke like my father whom I had always trusted and who had never failed me. 'Thanks. You're right. I'd better stop trying to run away.' We smiled at each other. 'But what about you? A man like you shouldn't be sitting on this bench with nothing. Or is that just how it seems.'

'No, it's the truth. I have nothing but these clothes and a few coins for a night's lodging. Don't worry', he added serenely, 'I made the choice and I don't regret it. I was a slave to Mammon once but I decided to be free. The price was high but it was worth it. If we meet again I'll maybe tell you the story but not now. You shouldn't waste any more time.'

'You're right.' I stood up, feeling much stronger suddenly.

'Be true to yourself. That's what really matters.' He sank back into his corner again. Our talk was obviously at an end. Before I turned to go, I took out my purse. 'Don't,' he said firmly. 'I don't need it.'

By hurrying I caught the last train home before the rush hour started. As I settled down in my corner seat while the train flashed by the London slums, I considered the old man's last bit of advice to me. 'Be true to yourself.' My dad had often said that to me and years ago it had seemed easy but now I was puzzled. What was my true self? For years it seemed I had thought of myself as Patrick's wife and our children's mother. Their needs had long been paramount. I had told myself I was happy and fulfilled but now I wondered. 'Where is Stella?' I asked myself. 'Have I been true to her?' Somehow Stella's needs and her personality had slipped out of sight and been forgotten, not only by me but also by everyone.

Soon the children would be gone and need me no more. That left Patrick and now it seemed, if I believed Eloise's letter, that I had not really known Patrick. One thing now seemed clear to me. I did not want to go home either to Patrick or even to the children. I wanted to run away to my childhood home where helped by the love and understanding of my dad I might find myself again. The old man had brought my father back to my mind so vividly that I felt homesick, as I had not done for twenty-five years. 'This is stupid,' I told myself angrily. The old man had told me that I must not give in and I knew my dad would say the same. I must fight to establish the truth and my own position. It would be hard but I must do it.

I remained strong and optimistic until I got off the train and walked into the familiar High Street, when a terrible weariness seemed to overwhelm me. I was tired of struggling. I wanted to rest. Establishing the truth about Patrick and Eloise and my love for them no longer seemed to matter. I wanted to escape from the worry of them. They seemed to have dominated too much of my life. Eloise saying she wanted to set me free seemed merely a mockery.

As I turned into the familiar drive, I didn't go towards the front of the house but turned towards Lucas' studio. I knew suddenly what I wanted. I wanted to love and be loved. It was wrong. It might make more problems than it solved but that was what I wanted and only Lucas could give it to me. As the studio door was slightly open, I was able to walk in softly. Lucas with his back to me was touching up a painting. I said nothing, simply stood there waiting until he became aware of me and turned round.

'Stella!' he exclaimed. Dropping his paintbrush, he moved towards me. 'How was it?'

'It was shattering.' After moving closer to him, I looked up at him, tempting him deliberately and not caring. 'I feel frightened,' I said. 'I need a hug.'

For a moment, he hesitated, then he put his arms round me. 'I can't believe it was so bad,' he tried to tease me. 'Solicitors aren't usually unkind to wealthy clients.'

'It wasn't the solicitor. It was the money. It's far too much. I don't think I want it.'

'You can always give it away – when you have it,' he suggested, smiling at me.

'Perhaps I will. You don't care for money. You must help me.' I lifted up my face and looked imploringly into his eyes. 'Kiss me, Lucas. I need comforting. I need loving. I've been alone too long and so have you.' Feeling, as I knew he did, how could he resist me?

For a few moments we exchanged the passionate kisses we had always avoided before. It would have been so easy to have been swept away, as we both wanted to be. I felt utterly reckless but suddenly I seemed to see Eloise with her familiar ironical smile and hear her say in her light, clear voice, 'Is it Lucas you love now?'

I tore myself from his encircling arms. 'No!' I exclaimed. 'We mustn't. I don't want to destroy you as well. Please, Lucas, don't stop me from going. Just forgive me.' Before he could answer, I had gone.

He caught up with me just as I was opening the front door. Seizing my arm, he exclaimed, 'You can't run away like this! You owe me some kind of explanation, surely?'

'I can't give you one now. Ben will be home soon, anyway.'

'That still sounds like running away to me.' His voice was quiet but I sensed that he was angry.

Pulling my arm away, I faced him. 'I'm sorry, I can't give you any clear explanation – yet. When I feel able to do so, I will. Now, please, let me go.'

'Very well. I'll be there when you want me.' His voice was gentler and he smiled as he turned away. I went in to prepare for the family and for Patrick.

Chapter Fifteen

On his return journey home that same evening Patrick considered the recent worsening of his relationship with Stella. The vehemence of her outburst on the Sunday evening and her almost violent rejection of him had greatly upset him and yet in the intervening three days he had done nothing about it. He had simply retreated once more behind the barriers he himself had erected to lick his wounds and to hide his pain. Stella, for her part, had made no attempt to reach him. When she had come to bed, he had pretended to be asleep and by the next morning she had seemed to be once more her usual calm, loving but remote self.

The disappointment was all the greater because for a brief time before that they had seemed to have come closer after he had defended her against Cordelia's unthinking attack. She had admitted her need for him and he had been able to comfort her. But it had not been enough.

Staring out of the window at the Kentish countryside passing by, he noticed the familiar signs of autumn. The fruit in the orchards had all been picked. The leaves in the woodlands were changing colour and he saw them in a glory of gold and orange as the last rays of the sun lit them up. The day was ending; it would be dark by the time he reached home. Another weary year had almost passed.

For over eight years life had been like this and he had allowed it to continue. It was, he remembered, over ten years since they had moved to this large country house. Ben had only been a baby. They had come with high hopes, or so he thought. This was to be their first settled home. At last, he had a job which had seemed more promising and more permanent than the many unsatisfying jobs he had struggled unsuccessfully to keep during the first years of their married life. With the help of a legacy and relying on his apparently more settled future they had bought this house, big enough and comfortable enough to be a real home.

It had not turned out, however, as he had expected. He had not wanted any more children but Stella, in spite of all her difficulties, had wanted them. He had never been quite sure why but had accepted the fact that, as a devout Catholic, artificial contraception now seemed wrong to her, although she hadn't felt like that when they had first been married. He had tried to accept this but he had been too weak for it. With the result that, after Ben, there had been another miscarriage and then the last baby which should never have been conceived. Even now, he could hardly bear to remember the agony of those days, when her life had hung in the balance. Her womb, weakened by three previous Caesarians, had ruptured at six and a half months. The baby had died and Stella had only been saved by two operations, which had left her sterile.

The feeling of guilt that had attacked him as soon as he had known of her pregnancy had never left. Without Stella's help, which he felt he was no longer entitled to expect, he had struggled in vain against depression and despair. Even now he dared not allow himself to think too long on those dark months of hell. Stella had somehow saved the family and she had never reproached him as he felt he deserved to be reproached. Perhaps it would have been easier, if she had?

Suddenly, he became aware that the train was slowing down. In a few minutes it would reach his station and ten minutes after that he would be home. Once more, he had wasted time in regrets without coming to any positive decision. As he folded up his newspaper and put it in his briefcase, he decided that he would no longer go on like this. Eloise's death was an important moment for him as well as for Stella. He had been unfeeling in not understanding the reality of Stella's pain but he could not deny that for him it was a relief. It seemed to him that if they could only be bold enough and honest enough that there was a chance for them to start again. And that was what he wanted.

By the time he was putting his key in his front door, he had decided with unusual firmness that he would make a start that evening. He would try to break down the barriers which he had erected and which Stella had apparently accepted.

There was no chance until after the evening meal when at last they were left alone to drink their coffee together. To his surprise Stella seemed quite ready to stay and talk. Before she could start, however, he made the apology which he had determined he must make first before anything else was discussed. As he handed her the cup of coffee he had made for her he said firmly, 'Before we talk about anything else, Stella, I want to tell you how very sorry I am for what I said to you on Sunday evening about Eloise. It was cruel and thoughtless of me and showed, I'm afraid, that I have had no real understanding of what you have been feeling. I'm very ashamed of myself for being so self-centred. Can you possibly forgive me?'

'Of course,' she replied quietly after a moment's hesitation. 'I'm sorry too for reacting so violently. It was wrong of me.'

Slowly putting out his hand to took hold of her hand, which was lying near to him on the table. Without resisting him, she allowed her hand to stay in his. He had a longing to put his arms round her, to hold her close and to comfort her but, before he could move, she lifted her head and looked steadily at him as if she wanted to seek out the inmost secrets of his soul, then gently she took her hand away. The moment had passed.

'I must tell you about today.' She sipped her coffee. The words didn't seem to come easily.

'I suppose that you had more information from the solicitor?'

'Yes.' She still seemed to speak reluctantly. 'It was rather overwhelming, in fact. But, before I talk to you about that I'd like to talk to you about Dominic.'

'So there was some reason for his wanting to see you? I thought there might be.'

'Yes.' As quickly as she could, she told him about Dominic's desire to leave University and to start his training as a journalist.

'What, if anything, has he done about it?' Patrick could not hide his disapproval of his son's plans. He felt, as he had sometimes done in the past, that Stella was inclined to indulge Dominic. Before, this had puzzled him but now he wondered if it was because he was Eloise's son.

'He has taken the trouble to obtain an application form and to fill it in but he wanted to discuss it before he sent it off.'

'Not with me, apparently. But, I imagine he thought that you would give him the better advice. I hope you did.'

'Naturally I questioned him and put all the objections, trying to persuade him to wait until he had finished his course at University.'

'Am I to gather from the way you put it that you failed to persuade him?'

'I wouldn't say that I failed. I think it would be better to say that I compromised. I agreed to his sending in the application form, which had to be in by Friday, and he agreed that, if this application were unsuccessful, he wouldn't apply again until after he had taken his degree. Do you object? He very much hopes that you will approve.'

'I don't think that this matters much now, do you?' He was hurt and angry because of the way in which he had been sidelined but determined not to show it too much. 'But I did think that when he talked about it before, we both agreed that he should wait. In fact, I thought he had agreed that he would wait. Why has he suddenly changed his mind?'

She hesitated. 'I think, perhaps it was when he learned that Eloise was his natural mother. I think that made him feel that he had perhaps inherited her talent and, since she had been so successful, he might hope to be. I must admit that he reminded me very much of her when he was talking about himself and his ambitions. I felt because of that that it might be wrong to stop him from trying. Do you understand what I'm trying to say?'

'Only too clearly. Eloise has managed once more to have her way, even after her death. Are we never going to be able to say "no" to her?' He couldn't hide the bitterness that he felt.

'Don't you think you're overreacting? He is her son. He's bound to resemble her. Surely, that is natural? Do you want me to tell Dominic that you object?'

'If I wanted to, I would tell him myself but there is no point now, is there? I yield to your decision. Now perhaps you'd better tell me about the information you had from the solicitor, unless of course, you want to keep it to yourself.'

'Of course not! Why would I want to do that?'

'I can't think of any reason. It's simply that you seemed reluctant to tell me just now.'

'I suppose it's because I found it rather shattering, that's all.'

'Shattering? What do you mean?' He was irritated by her evasion, as it seemed to him.

She was afraid because she desperately wanted his support and understanding, for without it, she knew that she might be tempted to turn to Lucas again. 'I mean that it was far more than I had expected. I hadn't realised, for example, that she owned her house and that it would fetch such a high price if it were sold today. I hadn't known before either just how much she had extracted from her ex-husband.' She stopped looking almost fearfully at him.

'I see. You won't just be a little better off; you'll be quite wealthy. All your troubles are over. Surely, that is cause for you to rejoice. You'll be able to give up your job now, won't you?'

His unfriendly tone wounded her. 'I don't want to give up my job!' she almost shouted. 'I enjoy it. You must know that. I'm looking forward to teaching full-time next term. I don't understand why she has left me so much.'

'But surely you do. It was to show her great love for you and her appreciation of your love for her.'

She stared at him. 'Why are you talking like this Patrick? I did no more for Eloise than I would have done for any old friend who was in her desperate situation. I loved her but not in the way you seem to be suggesting. Surely, you know me well enough to believe me?'

Looking steadily at her as if he were considering the question, he answered slowly. 'I think I do believe you. Your trouble is that Eloise didn't or didn't want to. Now, therefore, she has left you this problem. She still wants to change your life and at last she has found the perfect answer. She still intends to be in control. And it's difficult to see how you can stop her, particularly as that is what you appear to want.'

'Why are you talking like this? I can't bear it! Please Patrick, don't do this!'

'Don't do what? I'm just describing your situation as clearly as I can. I'm sorry but there it is.'

'Why are you separating yourself from me? It's not just my problem. It's yours too. You're my husband. We should share everything as we have always done.' She put out her hand towards him but he didn't take it. Her eyes filled with tears. 'Why are you doing this?'

'I don't want any part of it. Our life has been controlled by Eloise's wishes too often. I want no more of it. I want to free myself. In fact, I must free myself or lose all self-respect.' As he spoke he realised with horror that this was so very different from what he had intended to happen that evening. He could not, however, take back the words, for they were true.

'But that was not what Eloise intended,' she began, then stopped, as the thought struck that it might be just what Eloise had intended. 'Why do you say that our life has been controlled by Eloise's wishes too often. What are you referring to?'

'Surely I don't have to spell it out? As soon as she met me, she wanted me out of your life. She opposed our engagement first, then our marriage. By what right?'

'I suppose she simply thought that it was friendly advice. But it didn't make any difference, did it? I told you about it. We got engaged, we got married. So how can you say that her wishes prevailed? In any case it's a long time ago. Surely you can't still resent something like that after all these years?'

She was no more amazed than Patrick himself that he had said these things. This was not how he had intended to talk to her. As he thought about it, however, it seemed clear to him that he must actually have resented Eloise from that time onwards. 'It's not as simple as that but, when I look back, it seems to me that it was then that I first began to feel that she was always around. You had other friends but they were never as intrusive as she was, nor would you have allowed them to be.'

'So you're blaming me?'

'I suppose I must in part. When we were married, it was not exactly as I hoped and expected.'

'You never said anything.'

'Of course not. We only had a short time together and I didn't want to spoil it. When I came out of the Army two years later, I realised that you had spent a lot of time with her and she was in many ways much closer to you than I was.'

'Surely, you didn't expect me to spend all my time on my own, especially as you scarcely ever wrote to me?'

'No. I suppose I hoped that you would put me first, as you had done once.'

She frowned at him. 'I don't know why you're saying these silly things. Or what it has to do with us now. I want to talk about the future.'

'The past affects the future. I think I'm trying to get you to understand why I said what I did on Sunday night, that I was glad in a way that Eloise was dead. I thought we might have a fresh chance, perhaps.'

'And now you don't?' She was hurt and angry again. 'I never realised that you had always been so stupidly jealous.'

'If I had been jealous, though I'm not at all sure that is the right word, it wouldn't have been surprising, would it? When we moved out of little flat into our first house, she soon became our lodger for several months – not an ideal arrangement. You can't deny that, can you?'

'No, but neither can you deny why we had to have her. It was because we wanted to have a baby and you weren't earning enough so we had to have a lodger.'

'Did it have to be Eloise? Wouldn't a stranger have been better?'

'I don't believe you found Eloise so objectionable at the time.' She remembered Eloise's letter but decided to say no more at the moment.

'Perhaps not but it wasn't an ideal arrangement and it led to one of the worse happenings of all – the fact that she persuaded you to take Dominic without consulting me or even telling me.'

'I thought you had forgiven that.'

'I've forgiven it because I love Dominic and I pitied you but it was still a wrong thing to do. You know that. When I learned that, I think I began to look back and see everything in a different light. I saw that I had never been first with you, as you were with me, poor husband though I know I was. That hurt.'

Stella felt unable to reply to him. 'I admit it was wrong,' she said finally, 'very wrong but I thought that you understood that I wasn't really myself at that terrible time. How could I be?'

'And all the years afterwards?' Was all he said.

What could she answer? 'We were struggling and life was

difficult. I didn't want to upset you. And Eloise wasn't around for years. She was in America. I scarcely thought of her.'

'Perhaps not. But she came back and, when things were really bad, when you weren't very fit and I became ill, it was to her you turned, wasn't it?'

'I desperately needed a friend. Lucas helped too but that doesn't seem to bother you. Why not? You were completely unable to help me. Someone had to help me.'

'You made a secret agreement with her again, didn't you?'

'What do you mean?'

'She gave you the money to cover the debt I had incurred and again you agreed that I was not to be told.'

She stared at him. 'How did you come to know that?' She knew that she had told no one.

Realising that he had said more than he had ever meant to, Patrick tried to avoid a direct answer. 'I think that Lucas may have mentioned it to me.'

'He couldn't have done. He knew nothing about it. I let him assume that my father had given me the money.' For a moment she waited for him to say more but, when he didn't, she continued, 'It was Eloise, wasn't it? It was Eloise herself who told you?' She waited for his answer. When it didn't come, she returned to the attack. 'It was her. It must have been. No one else could have told you. Don't try to lie to me, Patrick. It was her, wasn't it?'

'Yes. It was Eloise.' He wished that he could lie but he knew it was impossible and unhappy words would now have to be spoken. He didn't want to make Stella suffer any more but how could he avoid it?

'When did she tell you?'

'Sometime ago. I can't exactly remember when. Does it matter?' He turned to look at her, praying that she would go no further. 'After all, this isn't exactly what we were talking about, is it?'

Ignoring his last remark, she persisted. 'I think it was about five years ago. Am I right?'

There was to be no escape. 'It might have been.'

'Don't try to be evasive, Patrick. It was five years ago. You met her in London and had a close relationship of some kind for a time.'

'How do you know that?'

She laughed suddenly. 'Eloise herself told me in the letter she sent to me with her will. It's funny, isn't it? She double-crossed us both, as one might say. Only of course, it isn't funny; it's horrible.' The pain she felt was so violent that she could hardly bear to speak but she forced herself to continue. 'You both have always said that you love me but you have both betrayed me. And what is worse you both seem to suggest that it was I who was lacking in love. How can you be so cruel?' She stood up. 'There's not much else for me to say, is there? In that letter, she makes it clear that on several occasion you were apparently attracted to each other but you resisted it until then. It's quite clear why you don't want to have anything to do with her money. It actually makes you feel guilty.'

As she moved towards the door, he too stood up and barred her way. 'It wasn't like that. And you know it, Stella. Eloise occasionally made it clear that she was attracted to me but it wasn't important to her and I was never interested in her. You know that. I've always loved you and I still do love you. You're the only woman I've ever cared about.'

'You expect me to believe that when I now know that you had an intimate relationship with my best friend and discussed me with her? You must think I'm very stupid!'

'I don't know what Eloise has told you but the truth is that we met when we were both lonely and unhappy and we discovered that we had one thing in common.'

'And what was that?'

It was terrible but he had to go on; evasion wasn't an option now. 'We both felt,' he spoke very reluctantly, 'that you had never loved us, as we loved you and as we wanted to be loved in return.' There was a painful silence. He put out his hand to her but she ignored it.

'I see,' she said quietly at last. She brushed him aside as he tried to stop her from leaving. 'Please, don't say any more, Patrick. There is nothing you can say, at the moment. I'm going to the study. Please tell the children that I have a bad headache and don't want to be disturbed.' The door closed behind her and Patrick was left alone to face the destruction he had unintentionally caused.

Chapter Sixteen

After shutting the study door firmly behind her, Stella flung herself down on the sofa, crying bitterly, although she wasn't quite sure of the reason for her tears. Was she weeping because Patrick had so casually admitted to his relationship with Eloise? Surely not? She had, after all, known about that since she had first received Eloise's letter; furthermore it had been brief, and had finished years ago. No, it wasn't simply that.

She sat up trying to discover the source of her anguish. The pain was so poignant that she instinctively put her hand on her heart as if might ease it and so find the ability to think. One word flashed into her brain – betrayal! That was it! She felt betrayed by the two people she had loved and trusted for years. They, who had always sworn that they loved her, had come together secretly only to decide apparently that she did not love them as they wanted to be loved. She who had always loved so faithfully was now decided to be the one at fault. That had been their excuse for comforting one another. And she had been allowed no defence.

It was intolerable. For a time, she raged passionately against them both, reminding herself of the many ways in which she had proved her love for them. After Patrick had not only failed utterly but had also lied to her, she had remained loyal and had scarcely reproached him. For Eloise's sake she had taken her baby, even deceiving Patrick. Her reward had been to have this disastrous secret revealed, even though she had spent many hours comforting and nursing Eloise during her last terrible weeks. Why had they both hidden their true feelings from her? What had she failed to give? What had they wanted? Was it that they had been stupidly jealous of each other? That seemed the only explanation for Patrick's present attitude. And yet it was so unlike him.

Unexpected a scene came vividly into her mind. She had been sitting by Eloise during one of the long, lonely evenings praying as she often did, when Eloise had suddenly asked what she was doing. She had tried to explain simply, although she knew that Eloise did not share her faith. 'I'm praying,' she had said. 'It's God's love that has always sustained me. He would sustain you, if you would let him.'

Before she could explain more, Eloise had interrupted her, 'I suppose He has sent you to give me that love?' As Stella had agreed, she had continued, 'Doesn't it make Patrick angry, perhaps even jealous?'

Shocked, she had replied swiftly, 'Whatever do you mean, Eloise? Do you think that Patrick might be jealous of you, even of God?'

'It might upset him to think that you only love him because God wants you to, don't you think? It might have been anyone you loved, mightn't it?'

She had smiled. 'That's always true, isn't it? We can only choose to love those we come to know.' Wanting only to comfort Eloise and without considering the further implications of her questions, she had continued, 'Since God knows everyone, he loves everyone, especially one who is suffering as you are.' Eloise had seemed to be satisfied but perhaps her thoughts had been quite different.

Could it be possible, Stella wondered that her expression of her belief in the power of God's love, which had guided her since she had been a small child, had aroused some kind of unreasonable jealousy in Eloise? Having no faith herself had she perhaps misunderstand Stella's words thinking of them as an expression of lukewarmness towards herself? Had she perhaps seen Stella as doing what she did only out of a sense of duty and nothing more? If this was so would she have written so warmly in her last letter? Would she, in fact, have left her 'dutiful' friend all her money? It seemed unlikely.

And surely none of this could possibly apply to Patrick, who to some degree shared her faith and who had even greater reason to believe in her love for him. No, she told herself, the answer could not lie here. She had been betrayed by both of them and especially by Patrick, who was obviously trying to blame her, instead of admitting his own guilty feelings.

After wiping her eyes, she stood up and walked across the

room. The curtains had not been drawn across the patio doors. Pausing before she drew them, she stared out into the darkness of the garden but only saw her own face reflected. Her large hazel eyes stared back at her; her short, dark hair framed her face in soft waves. She looked tranquil as always. There was no sign of the inner anguish, which made it impossible for her to sit and think calmly. As she drew the curtains together, there was a knock at the door.

'It's me.' Patrick spoke quietly but urgently. 'I must speak to you, Stella.' Before she could reply, he had opened the door and stepped into the room. 'We can't leave it like this.' He moved towards her. 'I intended us to have quite a different conversation. I wanted us to try to make a fresh start but it all went wrong. Can't we try again?'

'I don't think so, not now, anyway.' She made no move towards him.

'You know I love you. I've always loved you.'

That angered her more but she only said ironically, 'But your love has never been in question, has it? Apparently, it's only my love that is, and always has been.' She moved towards her flat topped walnut desk on which there was a pile of books and papers and switched on her reading lamp. 'Please go away. I can't talk any more tonight and I have some preparation I must do before tomorrow.'

For a moment he stood there, as if hoping to say more but as she opened one of the exercise books, he turned and went away without another word.

She felt a momentary pang of regret but decided it would be better to speak to him later in their bedroom when she might feel calmer. They had always made a practice of resolving their disagreements as far as possible before they went to sleep. This could not be so easily resolved but at least they might restore communication.

She forced herself to do the work she had to do but it took longer than she had expected. The house was very quiet when she had finally finished. Obviously, Patrick had advised the children not to disturb her. As she went quietly up the stairs she was surprised to see that their bedroom door was shut. When she opened the door, it was even more surprising to her to find that the room was in complete darkness. Patrick had evidently gone to sleep without waiting for her.

Annoyed by his apparent indifference, she switched on the main light only to find that he was not in the bed. The room seemed empty and unusually tidy and, as she looked around she realised why. Patrick's dressing gown was no longer hanging behind the door and all his toilet articles including his shaving mirror had been removed from the top of the chest of drawers. Even his little pile of scientific magazines and papers had gone.

It was then that she saw the note propped up on her dressing table. It was short. 'Dear Stella,' he had written, 'I've decided to spend the night in Dominic's room since I think that this is what you would prefer at present. I shall be leaving early in the morning but perhaps you will feel able to talk to me soon. I'm sorry. I never intended our conversation to take the turn it did. Patrick.'

It seemed unbelievable that he should have done this, without attempting to come to some agreement. Only in his darkest moments had he ever before withdrawn so completely. It seemed unbearable – a further pain added. Sitting down on the bed, she tried to think what to do. Always in the past, she would have gone after him and persuaded him, even if it took a long time, to talk to her so that there might not be a complete breach. He knew how much she would hate this. 'Is this then his much vaunted love?' she asked herself.

But then he had apparently persuaded himself that she was the one who was lacking in love. Why should she then trouble to run after him? Why should she care, since it seemingly mattered so little to him. 'I won't go,' she told herself. 'I need to rethink much of my life before I say any more. I'm certainly too tired to make any effort tonight. Let him have it as he wants it.' She began to undress resolutely. The only trouble was that she had no idea how she was going to sort out these problems.

Lying in bed in Dominic's room, pretending to read, Patrick heard Stella come up the stairs and then go into their bedroom. He waited, hoping that she would make some reaction to his note. He hoped to hear her coming along the landing and opening his door but nothing happened. After a few minutes he was forced to admit to himself that nothing was going to happen.

It seemed impossible to imagine how he could have allowed himself to be put in this position. On his return home, he had only wanted to talk to Stella and to try to come closer to her. Instead, he found himself further away than he had ever been and mostly it had been his own fault. Although he had intended to try to understand and sympathise with Stella's grief, he had been unable to contain his longing to be free of Eloise and her interference in their life. The realisation that they might be living on her money had been intolerable to him and still was. But it had been cruel and foolish of him to reveal his knowledge of Eloise's loan, which had made clear his brief intimacy with Eloise.

How could he expect Stella to forgive that when she was already so unhappy? And yet as he tried to recollect their conversation he had a strong feeling that it had not been a total surprise to her. Eloise must have told her in the letter she had sent with her will. Surely that must be the end of all that Eloise could do? But how could it be now that she had left Stella all her money?

He couldn't leave it like this. The thought of life without Stella was intolerable to him, as it always had been. But there seemed to be nothing he could do now. If that were what she now wanted, he would have to accept separation from her. It must be possible, however, to make one more effort. He prayed for a sign from Stella but none came. Finally, in the small hours, he fell asleep.

Patrick had already left when Stella came down to prepare the breakfast after an almost sleepless night. The children accepted his absence without much comment and that was a relief. At six o'clock that evening, however, he telephoned to say that he had an unexpected editorial conference and would not be home before ten. Stella, unsure as to whether this was the truth or simply an excuse to avoid her, made no comment but contented herself with asking him whether she should keep a meal for him. That was unnecessary, he told her, as he and his editor were about to go for a quick meal at a nearby pub.

It was nearly ten thirty when he finally returned home. The

family had already retired to bed but Stella, as she normally did when he was late, was waiting with a pot of coffee and some sandwiches. They sat down at the table in the breakfast room. The dark red curtains were drawn, only two side lights were lit, the kettle was humming on the top of the Aga stove from which a pleasant warmth emanated. It all seemed homely and comforting on this chilly October night, particularly after a slow and draughty journey down from London after a long day.

After handing him his plate of sandwiches, Stella poured out coffee for them both. She was looking very attractive in a long jade green housecoat, which emphasised the green of her eyes and the delicacy of her complexion. She seemed completely relaxed. For a few moments she didn't speak but allowed him to enjoy his coffee and the food. Suddenly she said quietly, 'I've moved your things back from Dominic's room. I hope you don't object.'

Putting down the sandwich he was holding he stared at her, a flicker of hope stirred within him. Perhaps she was beginning to get over her anger and he might be able to talk to her.

Before he could speak, however, she continued. 'It seems ridiculous for us to act so dramatically after being together for so many years. We can surely, in time, arrange matters much better than that?' She took a sip of her coffee.

His disappointment was intense. How could she be so apparently calm? Picking up his sandwich, he tried to speak as calmly. 'You may be right. I'm not sure. I thought you were so angry that you might prefer me to do that. Was I wrong?'

'I'm still angry and deeply hurt by your betrayal and Eloise's betrayal. I don't see how you can expect me to be otherwise. But I don't want the girls and Ben to be unnecessarily upset. We haven't yet decided what we should do, so we should spare them as much as we can. Don't you agree?'

'Of course. I love them, too, but are they likely to be upset by a simple change? Why should they imagine anything threatening?'

'Because divorce is becoming much more common these days and they will think of that as we would never have done. Only last week Julia was telling me how upset one of her friends was because her mother and father were separating. She said they felt that they had no home and no security and that it must in some way be their fault. I want us to avoid putting them in that situation if we can. Don't you agree?'

'Of course. I'm perfectly happy to come back to our room.' He was puzzled by her attitude. 'I only intended to move out temporarily to give you a chance to see things clearly. Surely, now we can discuss our difficulties, as we should have done years ago. That was all I intended to do last night but it all went wrong. I'm very sorry. I hope you can forgive me and we can try again. You know Stella that I love you very much and always have done. Life without you would be intolerable. I need you.'

'But you don't think I have ever loved you as you wanted me to. Perhaps you're right. In which case it might be better for us to separate.'

'For God's sake, don't say things like that. I never meant what you seemed to think I meant. I was upset. Can't you understand?'

She appeared not to have heard what he said as she replied thoughtfully, 'Eloise said something similar in her last letter and suggested that it was that which brought you and her together briefly. Perhaps our relationship isn't, therefore, really a very healthy one.'

'I don't understand you but surely we can discuss it, as we've discussed things in the past.'

'This is different. It's fundamental. I can't talk about it with you, yet. It seems that I may have been deceiving myself for years. I need to discover the truth, somehow. How can I talk to you when I can't understand myself?'

'Can't I help. I want to. Believe me, I know I'm not much use but I do want to help you.'

'But you can't – not now.' Putting down her coffee cup, she stood up. 'I'm going to bed. Come up as soon as you're ready.' She was gone.

On the following day Lucas decided that it was time he sought out Stella and insisted on having an explanation of her upsetting behaviour on the Wednesday afternoon after her return from London. He had expected that she would come to him but when this didn't happen, he decided that he must take the initiative. He prepared his campaign carefully and, as soon as she arrived home after Friday morning school, he knocked on the kitchen door, following up his knock with an immediate entry.

'No need for you to bother with lunch,' he smiled at her as she turned round startled from the kitchen sink where she was just filling the kettle. 'I've made it for us both. It's already set out in my place. You'd better come quickly or the soup will get cold.' Holding the door open, he stood waiting for her. He obviously didn't intend to take 'no' for an answer.

After regarding him steadily for a moment, she suddenly smiled back. 'Since it's clear that I haven't any choice, I'll come quietly.'

Lucas's home in their converted garage was as always very welcoming. The living room took most of the ground floor, except for a small kitchen area at the far end, which was curtained off. It was light and airy but pleasantly warmed by a glowing electric fire. His small table with two chairs was placed near to the fire. A lunch, consisting of homemade soup, fresh rolls, ham and salad was attractively set out on it. There was a pleasant smell of coffee. The rest of the room was taken up with an easel, stacks of canvases, a comfortable but shabby sofa, two similar armchairs and several bookcases overflowing with books. It achieved a surprising order without any clutter. It gave the impression that this was the room of a man who was finally at ease with himself.

Feeling comforted and grateful, Stella took her usual chair and helped herself to a roll. Lucas sat down opposite her. 'This is very welcome,' she said.

'I thought it might be. I suggest we eat first and talk later. For talk we must. You do realise that, don't you?' She nodded but, instead of replying, helped herself to a roll. It was some twenty minutes later, as he was pouring out the coffee, that Lucas came back to the attack. 'Why? Why did you tempt me in that way? Why now? We have known each other for years and I was attracted by you very soon after I first met you and I was often convinced that you felt the same about me. But we never did anything about it, because I realised, and I believe that you did too that an affair between us could only result in much misery for the people we both cared deeply about and finally, therefore, in misery for ourselves. Is that a fair summary?'

'Very fair.' She met the piercing gaze of his dark eyes without flinching. Although his black hair was now considerably flecked with grey and his face more lined he was still the same man who had impressed her with his underlying strength and his capacity to survive. Somehow, he had imparted to her the strength to survive in what had been perhaps her darkest time.

'Then why did you act so differently without warning? You realise that I was too surprised to have any defences?'

'That was wrong of me but I can only say that I desperately needed your strength and the comfort you can give.' Quickly she gave him an outline of the events of her day. 'When I left the old man I felt quite cheerful. He reminded me of my father and he gave the kind of encouraging advice my father would have given me. Then as I walked home from the station it all seemed to evaporate. I felt frightened and lonely and I longed to be loved and comforted, so almost without thinking, I just came to you.'

'Why not Patrick? Was it simply that I was there and he wasn't?'

'Patrick is part of the trouble. There is so much he doesn't understand or refuses to understand. He has betrayed me too.' She stopped suddenly.

Having waited in vain for her to continue, he questioned her again. 'If I'm to understand, don't you think you'll have to explain that last remark. Without explanation I don't see how I can easily believe that of Patrick.'

She shook her head. 'I can't give you an explanation. I shouldn't have said it. It might be truer, perhaps, to say that I've betrayed him.'

'That I do not believe and I can't think why you're saying it to me, of all people.'

'I no longer seem to be sure of anything, least of all myself. Eloise and Patrick have recently destroyed my whole view of myself.'

'What do you mean?'

She wanted to avoid answering him but it was impossible as he took a firm hold of her hands and gazed into her eyes. It had never been easy to evade Lucas. She wished that he would simply comfort her, as she wanted to be comforted. He was aware of what she wanted but he was equally aware that it was not what she needed at that moment. He had tried to comfort her two days before and that had only resulted in her running away. 'You must give me some explanation.' He continued to hold her hands firmly.

Surrendering, she gave the only explanation that she had. 'I thought I might have said that I loved them both, especially Patrick but they apparently didn't seem to think so. They even compared notes apparently.'

Lucas was amazed. 'What utter nonsense! Why are you even considering it? You and I both know it isn't true.' When she didn't reply, he repeated his question. 'You do know it isn't true, don't you?'

'Perhaps in some strange way it is true. Suddenly I don't feel sure about anything, least of all myself. I need time to look over my life. There is something I must face, I think. But what?'

To her surprise Lucas no longer opposed her, in fact he made no answer immediately. Finally, he said slowly. 'You may be right, Stella. I don't know. But I do know that I was not a whole person until I brought out into the open a hidden failing of my own and faced it. Perhaps there is something you have to face and accept. Was that why you ran away from me?'

'Yes. I think I was tempted to use you as an easy way out. To run away from everything with you. But I don't want to do that. You are too valuable to me.'

'You are very dear to me. Remember that I am ready to help you if I can. You may have to face something on your own but I'll be there waiting if you need me. Don't be too hard on Patrick. Try talking to him. Perhaps you've misunderstood him. You know he loves you and he needs you.'

'I'm not ready to talk to Patrick. But, don't worry, I won't desert him.' Releasing her hands from his, she stood up. 'I must go now and prepare for the hungry horde who will soon be returning.'

'I'm afraid I haven't been much use to you.' Standing up he followed her towards the door.

'No one could have done more. You've given me comfort and courage, without asking for anything in return.' As she went through the door, she turned towards him and he bent and kissed her on the lips. 'Remember you always have my friendship,' he said.

With a smile she turned to walk to her own house, only to become aware that Cordelia was coming down the path. As she waited for her daughter she could not help wondering if she had seen that last kiss and, if she had, what might be her thoughts.

Chapter Seventeen

'You're home early, aren't you?' Stella asked, as she opened the kitchen door.

'Yes. I caught the earlier bus and left before the last period.'

Noticing as they walked into the house that Cordelia looked very pale and sounded languid, Stella felt suddenly concerned. For now she forgot her worry that Cordelia might have seen her parting from Lucas. 'Why was that? Are you ill?'

'It's nothing much but I've got a nasty period pain and I feel cold. I just wanted to get home. Since I was free in the last period, I slipped out.'

'You'd better lie down straightaway in the breakfast room where it's nice and warm.' Quickly, she helped Cordelia out of her coat, then settled her on the old settee with a couple of extra cushions and a rug. 'I'll get you some painkillers, then a hot bottle and a warm drink. You'll feel better, in no time.' Without wasting a moment, she hurried away and without delay had everything arranged for Cordelia's comfort.

Lying back, hugging her bottle and sipping tea, Cordelia soon began to feel much better. This was what she had longed for since midday, comfort, warmth and above all loving kindness. 'I'm so glad you are at home, Mum. It makes all the difference. You're very good at tlc.'

'Tlc?' Stella raised her eyebrows.

'Tender, loving care. Surely, you've heard that before?'

'I don't think so but surely anyone would have done the same?'

'Perhaps. But not as well as you. You're particularly good at looking after people when they're ill or feeling down.' She was tempted to add, 'I suppose that was why Eloise wanted to have you with her.' But decided that might be a painful remark for her mother. So she said, instead, 'I know that Dad would agree with me, to say nothing of the rest of the family.' She suddenly felt very ashamed of the jealously she had felt and expressed because of Stella's care for her dying friend. 'We all need you.'

'That's good.' Smiling at her daughter, Stella helped herself to a cup of tea. She felt happy, as she always did, when she was taking care of someone. She drew the curtains, to keep out the growing dark and switched on a light. It was very peaceful, sitting with Cordelia, while they sipped their tea. All worries seemed to have slipped away.

About ten minutes later, noticing that Cordelia's eyes were shut, Stella stood up, preparing to move away quietly into the kitchen where she might start preparing tea for the others who would soon be home. 'Don't go yet, Mum,' Cordelia's voice unexpectedly stopped her.

'I thought you were asleep. How's the pain now?'

'Much better, thanks. Sit down again, Mum. It's so nice just the two of us together. You don't have to do anything yet, do you?'

Stella looked at her watch. 'I was thinking that I ought to start getting tea ready but I think I can leave it for another few minutes.' She sat down. She, too, was enjoying this quiet time alone with her elder daughter.

'Do you mind if I ask you a question, Mum?' Cordelia asked after a moment's pause. 'You don't have to answer it, if you don't want to or, if you think that I have no right to ask it.'

'That sounds a bit intimidating.' Stella tried to smile but she felt suddenly worried, almost afraid.

'It isn't meant to be.' Cordelia hesitated, then asked her question. 'Is Lucas in love with you, Mum?'

Although perhaps she ought not to have been, Stella was unprepared for this and felt unable to give a proper answer. 'What makes you ask that?'

'Well, I have wondered before in the last few months. I suppose I notice things more, since I've fallen in love with Adrian. I've noticed the way he looks at you sometimes and then today I saw him kiss you as you came away. It wasn't his usual, friendly peck, was it?' She was carefully not asking her mother about her feelings.

'Do you really mean to ask whether we are lovers or likely to become so?' Stella's directness silenced Cordelia for a moment but she was still obviously waiting for some kind of answer. 'The simple, honest answer is – we are not. Whatever you may imagine that Lucas feels, I have no such intention.' Her voice was cold.

'You're angry. I'm sorry. I suppose you think I haven't any right to ask?'

'Do you think you have?'

'Well, if you were, it would concern me and all the family, wouldn't it? I'm not trying to blame you or anything like that Mum. Although he's quite old, Lucas is very attractive, I think and you certainly are. I just want you to know, if you ever feel tempted, that we would all hate it. We don't want our family to be split up, as so many seem to be.'

Stella laughed. 'Don't you think that you're letting your imagination run away with you? You know you do sometimes. I went to talk to Lucas this afternoon because I was feeling sad and depressed and I couldn't face an empty house. He was very kind and he was only trying to be a bit extra comforting. He understands how much I've been upset about Eloise.'

'He is always understanding,' Cordelia agreed. 'And we've been pretty selfish, especially me. I'm sorry. I'll try to be better. Can we kiss and make up?' She lifted her face up to Stella.

'Of course,' bending over her, Stella kissed her. 'Now I really must go and get the tea ready. You enjoy your last few minutes of quiet.'

As she went into the kitchen, Stella decided that she hadn't really been dishonest with her daughter. She had merely avoided going into too many details and into discussing matters, which couldn't possibly be discussed first with her daughter.

That evening after managing to get Patrick alone before supper, she suggested that with his agreement, she should tell the family about Eloise's will and their increase of fortune, although she would avoid going into details, saying that she couldn't possibly know yet exactly how much money it would amount to when everything was sorted out. She waited with some trepidation for his reply but, when it was slow in coming, she added, 'I think it's better to tell them the main truth now, especially as I told Dominic when we met. I don't like secrets.

Cordelia too will be relieved that she doesn't have to worry about taking too many of our limited resources for her Oxbridge ambitions. So do you agree?'

Feeling that Stella was manoeuvring him into a false position, Patrick was annoyed without being able to think of any acceptable objection to put forward. 'Obviously, I can't object to your telling the family if that's what you want to do but I had hoped that we might have had a chance to sort things out between ourselves first. Surely, that's not impossible?' Although he didn't want to sound cold and indifferent, he was aware that he did and that he had aroused Stella's hostility.

'I don't think we can wait for that. But I do want to be certain that you won't say how much you hate the idea. I don't want the girls and Ben to be worried by the thought that we are seriously at odds about this, especially as the girls are already worried about their mock exams.'

'You know I wouldn't want to upset them.' He was hurt that she should even suggest that. 'But I don't see how you can expect me to say that I like what has happened. I'll just stay neutral.'

'I suppose I can't expect more.' She turned away, as if there was no need of any more conversation between them.

'Stella, please,' putting out his hand towards her, he tried to stop her. When she seemed to ignore him, he took hold of her arm. 'Please don't turn away from me like this. You must know I love you, as I always have.'

Stopping, she turned to look at him. 'Nothing seems clear to me any more. I don't even understand myself and certainly not you or Eloise. I must have time to think. You'll have to accept that, Patrick.'

She had gone, leaving him without hope. It was a long time since he had felt so close to despair.

As they were finishing supper, she told the family the news about her unexpected legacy, carefully choosing the moment when Patrick had just gone into the kitchen to make coffee. Since she didn't emphasis the amount, her announcement made far less stir than might have been expected. Cordelia was the first to respond, 'That's good! Then it won't bankrupt you if I do choose Oxbridge and music. It was nice of Eloise to leave you something. You certainly deserve it.' She hugged her mother warmly.

'I'll be able to have a new bike for Christmas then, won't I?' Ben asked. Apparently he had no further ambitions.

'What about you, Julia?' Stella asked as Patrick came back into the room. 'I don't want much at the moment – except perhaps a really good microscope of my own. But that would be rather expensive, I'm afraid.'

'I don't think you need worry about that,' Patrick said before Stella could answer her.

'I know what I'd like,' Cordelia suddenly said, 'a really posh celebration for my eighteenth birthday next month. Perhaps we could all go to a theatre and a restaurant in London? What do you say, Mum?'

'I don't think that will be too difficult.' Stella turned towards Patrick, 'But I think your dad's the best person to arrange that, don't you?'

Without waiting for Patrick's reply Cordelia turned eagerly towards him. 'Can I borrow your evening paper? Julia and I can look for the best shows.' Without a comment, he took it out of his briefcase and handed it to her.

When a whole busy weekend had passed without there being time to think, Stella began to feel desperate. How could she ever get time to herself, she wondered? She knew that this was not just a whim but something that she urgently needed, if she was to survive. She tried to tell herself that she was being stupid and melodramatic but it made no difference.

A few days later it was Lucas who suggested to her a possible opportunity, by reminding me that in a few day's time she had her half term holiday which unusually came a week before the children's. 'You should have plenty of time to think, then with everyone out of the way all day. I'll be around but I promise to keep away if you want to be on your own or be available to mop up your tears if that's what you want.'

Although she thanked him, Stella was not convinced that this was enough. She felt that she wanted to get away from everyone even Lucas. But how could she do this without upsetting Patrick and most of all her family?

The solution was offered to her two days later in a letter from her father. They corresponded regularly but this was not one of his usual letters full of news; it was a plea for her to come and visit him and her mother before the onset of winter. He reminded her that, because of the time she had spent caring for Eloise, it was over a year since she had visited them. 'Your mother is far from well,' he wrote. 'She's been ailing for some time, as you know but just recently it's got worse and the doctor has suggested that she should go into the hospital for some tests. This scares her. She asked me not to tell you because she reckons that you have enough problems of your own. But I think that a visit from you would be just the thing to set her up. Do you think you could manage it at half term, if it's only for a couple of days? I'm afraid we can't manage to put the family up any more but I'm sure they'll understand. Let me know as soon as you can and remember that your old dad would be glad to see you too. I'm not getting any younger either.'

She didn't need any excuse to respond to this. She was upset that she had neglected them and was even more concerned at this appeal coming from her usually independent and strong-minded father.

Everyone having agreed that she should go, it was easily arranged by a short telephone call to her father that she should travel on the Monday and return before the following weekend. To Stella's relief, her father sounded as cheerful and as confident as usual, which encouraged her to believe that his letter had been more an attempt to get her to visit them than a serious call for help. Everything would be as it had always been or so she told herself. This visit was what she had wanted since she had met the old man on the Embankment. She hoped it would restore her confidence and help her to find her true self again.

Having been repulsed in all his attempts to come closer to her, Patrick was forced to remain at a distance not only unhappy but also bewildered. Why did she not even want to try to improve their relationship, he asked himself? But then he had to admit to himself that for years it had been he, who had been deeply withdrawn, forcing Stella to find her satisfaction in her work and in the family. He had for many years been content to let things slide while Stella took most of the responsibility. Even then, however there had been a bond between them and there had been times when he had been able to comfort and to help her. Now she seemed to want to deny even the existence of this bond.

On the Sunday evening before she was due to leave on her visit, he was tempted to make one last try. They were in their bedroom and free to speak without fear of interruption. He was already in bed with a scientific paper he had been trying to study while had been waiting for her to join him. She was sitting at the dressing table brushing her hair. 'Have you done all your packing?' he asked her.

'Mostly but I shall have time to check in the morning, as I'm not leaving till half past eleven. I hope to catch the 2 p.m. train from Euston.'

'What are you going to do about lunch? I could meet your train and we could have a quick lunch together. Or have you already arranged to meet Dominic?'

'I've not arranged to meet anyone. I'm not sure how much time I shall have, so I shall go straight to Euston and get a snack there.' Her tone was chillingly neutral.

Patrick, however, was determined to persist. 'Can't we at least come to some little understanding before you go away?'

'I'm not sure that I understand you?' She didn't even turn to look at him.

'Won't you even allow me to say how sorry I am for deceiving you briefly.'

'You have already said that more than once, I think.'

'But you can't forgive me, is that it? It was such a stupid business and it lasted for such a short time. Surely you can't let that wipe out years of faithful love?'

Now, she turned to look at him, putting down her hairbrush first. 'You don't understand, do you? It isn't primarily that. I knew about that episode before you were forced to tell me. Eloise told me in the letter that was enclosed with her will.'

He was shocked. 'Why didn't you say something to me? How long were you intending to keep silent?'

'I don't know. You were already so unsympathetic about my sadness at Eloise's death that I didn't want to speak to you. I felt betrayed by both of you, especially you.'

'So it is what I just said?'

'Not exactly. It wasn't the physical betrayal. It was the fact that the two people I had loved and trusted most secretly got together to discuss me, then decided that in some way I had failed them both. That I had never loved them, as they wanted to be loved. Until you spoke about it, I hadn't realised what had actually happened. That hurt more than I can say. Surely, you can understand that? I don't feel at all sure that Eloise had any right to expect more of me. She was only a friend. You might think that you had but, if you did, shouldn't you have said something to me?'

'I can only ask you once more to forgive me. I was still depressed and lost at that time and Eloise offered me friendly comfort, as I thought.' Seeing her somewhat cynical smile, he added, 'Of course I should have known that Eloise would have a hidden agenda but I didn't think of it, until it was too late and then I despised myself even more than I had before. How could I tell you this when you had already suffered so much because of me? You were always loving and kind. I've never deserved you. Don't reject me now!'

Paying little attention to his last appeal, Stella followed her own thoughts. 'It's not a matter for forgiveness. It's a matter of what is true. This is forcing me to see my whole life differently, to re-examine my view of myself. I must know the truth before I can decide anything.'

Patrick suddenly felt afraid as he met the gaze of her honest hazel eyes. She had never spoken like this before. 'What do you mean?'

'Perhaps you're right. Perhaps I have never loved you, as you wanted to be loved? Perhaps I have never loved anyone properly. It all started I suppose when I prayed for my grandad and believed that I experienced the love of God and that I was chosen to pass this love on to others. Perhaps it was simply a childish delusion, which became spiritual pride?' She paused, waiting for his answer.

'Don't say things like that! They're not true. You know they're not. Your love has always been important to me. Young, though we both were, you were the first person who loved me. I knew nothing about love before then. My life would have been a total failure without your love. You know that.'

'I expect you believe that but it may not be true. Perhaps something else would have suited us both better.' Standing up unexpectedly, she seemed to dismiss the whole discussion, as if it were trivial. 'I can't talk any more now. It's late and I'm tired.' Slipping out of her dressing gown, she stood up. 'I promised Cordelia that I would remind you about her birthday celebration. Have you booked the theatre tickets yet?'

He found it difficult to adjust to her change of tone. 'No, I actually planned to do it tomorrow.'

'That's good because you'd better get an extra one. She would like Adrian to come.'

'Adrian? I'm not sure that's a good idea. Are you?'

'Why not? They're very fond of each other. It's her birthday celebration and she wants him there.'

'But, don't you see that it makes it all seem more serious? It makes him like one of the family. They're so different, I can't see it lasting, can you?'

'Perhaps it won't but we don't know, do we? It's not for us to decide.'

'It's not a very good idea if she really wants to have a serious musical career, is it?' Stella's disinterested attitude irritated him, not for the first time.

'Surely, that's another decision she must make for herself?

'Do I gather that you have agreed?'

'More or less. I didn't think that you would have any serious objections. If you're worried about the family aspect, why don't you invite Lucas as well?' Pulling back the covers, she slipped into the bed beside him but didn't touch him.

'Very well. I surrender. I can see there's no point in trying to argue with you tonight. But, Stella, be careful.'

'What do you mean?'

'Going back to your parents and to your old home might not make you as happy as you seem to think.'

Switching out the light, she replied firmly, 'I'm going home because my mother is ill, as you know.' Turning her back to him she settled down. She did not intend to have any further discussion.

On the Monday morning clouds obscured the blue skies of

the last few days and there was a light, chilly rain. The house was very empty now that everyone had departed for work or school. Stella felt depressed at the thought of the long walk through the village to the station with no one to accompany her and no one to see her off. Her travel bag too seemed heavier that she had thought. As she picked up her warm winter coat which seemed more suitable than the jacket which she had intended to wear, the front door bell rang.

Feeling irritated at the thought of an unwanted caller, she ran down stairs and opened the door to find Lucas in the porch. 'I've come to offer you a lift to the station,' he said cheerfully. 'As it is raining and Patrick has already gone, I thought you might be glad of it.' Before she could answer, he had made his way into the hall.

'I told Patrick I didn't need a lift.' She felt she ought to excuse her husband's apparent indifference.

'But now you do.' Lucas, not to be deterred by her apparent lack of welcome, walked quickly to the breakfast room. 'Since I've come early we have time for a coffee before you go.'

Although she welcomed the coffee and the offer of a lift, she was apprehensive that he too might want to have a talk with her as Patrick had. She decided that she would resist all attempts, only to discover that her fears were unnecessary, for Lucas apparently had no wish except to give her a friendly and comfortable start to her journey. As she done so many times in the past she welcomed his friendship. Since they arrived at the station with time to spare so he bought her a morning paper and when the train came in he lifted her bag on top the luggage rack, gave her a quick, friendly kiss and stood waving until the train had drawn out of the station. It was a more encouraging start than she had anticipated.

Chapter Eighteen

Soon after her arrival at her parents' home, Stella began to feel that she had made a great mistake, not in coming to see them but in imagining that a return to her childhood home could give her some kind of spiritual renewal. During the long journey, she had felt quite optimistic but as soon as she arrived at the grimy station of the northern industrial town where she had been born, an unexpected feeling of melancholy touched her.

Perhaps it was because it was greyer and colder here than in the south; there it was still mellow autumn, but here winter had already begun to advance. She shivered as she stepped into the station forecourt and felt the first blasts of wind from the cold, forbidding moors which surrounded the town. At the same time the thought struck her that it was over twenty years since she had come here by herself. But that had been her choice, she reminded herself, so it was ridiculous to be sentimental about it.

She was lucky there were several taxis waiting outside the station and she tried not to think as she travelled quickly through the ugly, grey streets to the newer suburb where her parents had always lived and where Patrick's father had come to be the doctor. It was strange but never before had she so clearly realised how much Patrick and his mother must have hated the move here from Surrey which his father for financial reasons had forced on them.

There had been no doubt, however, about the warmth of her parents' welcome. As soon as he had heard the taxi arrive her father had come hurrying to the gate to welcome her. He had at first seemed mercifully unchanged. He was the same confident, cheerful man who brought with him a sense of security and permanence, the same feeling that the old man on the Embankment had given her. She relaxed. This was what she had come for.

Her mother had remained in the living room by the brightly

blazing fire. She had turned immediately to welcome her daughter with a loving smile at the same time lifting her face to be kissed. 'Well, here she is Mother, safe and sound,' her father had exclaimed triumphantly. 'I told you she would be. Your mother was worried about you travelling on your own,' he explained to Stella. 'I reminded her you were a big girl now with children of your own but she wasn't happy about it.'

'We mothers always worry, don't we?' Stella's mother said gently. 'Men don't understand. But it's lovely to see you again, Stella dear. Shall we move to the table? The tea's ready and waiting. It's a proper North Country tea. We thought you might be hungry after your journey.' She stood helped by her husband and walked slowly to the table. Stella noticed that it was her father who made the tea and who brought to the table the hot plates of bacon and sausages, which were the main dish. So her father had been speaking the truth when he had written that her mother was growing frailer. She was glad that she had come and by herself too.

They had spent a cosy evening by the fire. John Fitzgerald seemed to be just as involved in politics as he had always been and expressed his views as vigorously as he had always done. He approved of what the local Labour party was doing but was extremely critical of the Labour Government and especially of its Prime Minister, Harold Wilson. He had no idea, he asserted, of how to deal with the trouble which had begun in Northern Ireland the year before and had now escalated. The conditions in the Internment camp of Long Kesh were a disgrace to Britain. He considered that in every department the performance of the government fell far behind its promise.

'And there's not much comfort when you look abroad,' he asserted, 'especially when you consider the way the US troops are behaving in Vietnam. It's no wonder that young people everywhere are protesting and rioting. I don't blame them but it's not good. Has your Dominic been involved in any of these student demonstrations?' he asked Stella.

'He's very much against the war, especially since he's met a couple of American students who have come to England to escape the draft and he has taken part in one or two demonstrations but they seemed to have remained peaceful, fortunately.'

'Well I'm glad the lad has the courage to stick up for his opinions,' John replied, 'but it's a shame if he wastes too much time when he should be studying. But then young people today are very ready to kick over the traces.'

'I sometimes think,' Mary, his wife, ventured to say, 'that young people don't respect anyone or anything today. Don't you agree, Stella?'

Before Stella could reply her father interrupted her. 'If that's true, I for one can understand them. It's a pretty awful world we so-called elders and betters are handing over to them.'

'But there are some marvellous things happening,' his wife protested gently. 'Just think, it's only just over three months since those men were landed on the moon. I thought it was wonderful to look at it and to think there are actually men up there.' Her eyes were shining. 'Didn't you Stella?'

'Well, it is really, isn't it?' Stella agreed. 'Some friends of ours had a candle lit party in the garden so that we could see the moon better. It looked large but still so very far away.'

John Fitzgerald stood up and began to clear the table. 'It was just a show,' he said angrily. 'The Americans only wanted to do something spectacular to cock a snook at the Russians. And it cost millions. If that's the best these scientists can do when there's so much poverty and suffering in the world, they'd better give up now and start digging the roads. They might at least do some good that way.' He went out into the kitchen.

Mary Fitzgerald smiled a little apologetically at her daughter. 'Poor John, he hates it that he can no longer be really active in politics as he always has been.'

'But he's not too old, surely?' Even now Stella could not imagine her father being too old.

'It's not just that. I haven't been so well lately and he feels he must stay at home and look after me. He does all the shopping and a lot of the cooking. He's pretty good at it but it's not a man's job.' Stopping abruptly, she turned to speak to her husband as he came back into the living room. 'Leave the dishes and the politics for a bit, John. Stella's only just arrived. And I want to hear her news and how the family's getting on. Surely, you do, don't you?'

'Ay, of course I do.' John sat down again opposite his

daughter. 'I'm glad to know that Patrick's still settled in that editorial job of his. He seems to have found something that suits him, at last. He must have been at it about six years now. Am I right.' He no longer spoke of it but he could not entirely hide his feeling that his daughter had had a poor deal in her marriage, on the whole. He admired her for making a go of it. It was his tough training of her which had helped her to do that, he thought. But, all the same, he wished things had been easier for her.

Mary, always the peacemaker, intervened quickly. 'I was very pleased to hear how well Cordelia is doing with her music. I always thought she had a special talent even when she was a little girl. Do you remember, John, how well she used to pick up hymns and carols when you taught her? She couldn't have been much more than four when they spent that Christmas with us.'

'She was good, I remember. Young Dominic tried to keep up with us on his recorder but he found it hard. More of a scholar that one.' He turned to Stella. 'Has he any idea yet what he wants to do?'

'He has decided that he wants to be a journalist.'

'Like his dad, I suppose?'

'Not exactly He'd like to become a political journalist, I think. But he'll have to learn the trade first. He aims to get an apprenticeship with a large newspaper group, as soon as he can.'

'He could do well at that,' John said with approval. 'As long as he doesn't rush it. Politics is in the blood, you might say. Though I'd rather he went into Parliament. But, you never know he might do that as well. He'll finish his degree first, I suppose?'

'I'm not sure. It rather depends on whether he gets a good opening with the Medway papers in the next few weeks. He's applied for one. He says he wants to get started.'

'There's something to be said for that, I suppose. It shows his heart's in the right place but education's very important.' He turned to Stella. 'What do you think?'

'I think he should perhaps finish his degree but I don't want to stop him having a go now. Patrick is very much against it, however.' As soon as she had mentioned her slight disagreement with Patrick, she wished she hadn't but for once her father had avoided an opportunity for criticising his son-in-law.'

'It's difficult,' he said. 'You can't stop young people from striking out. They succeed sometimes just because they don't see the difficulties we older people worry so much about.'

And so the conversation had proceeded pleasantly until John had insisted on taking Mary to bed, so that she would not be too tired to enjoy the next day. By the time he came down again, Stella had cleared away and was washing up in the kitchen. Putting on an apron, he joined her and began to wipe up the dishes. This had seemed an appropriate moment, to Stella, for her to begin to confide in him and ask his advice as she had so often done when she was younger.

Before she could speak, however, her father put down his cloth with a sigh. 'I expect you find us a bit changed. Your mother needs a lot of care these days. She's not well. You must have noticed that.'

'She is frailer,' Stella agreed. 'What is wrong?'

'Something to do with her kidneys, they think but they don't seem sure. In fact the doctor has suggested that she go into the hospital for some tests. It should be in a couple of weeks' time.' He looked at his daughter wanting to seek some comfort and even perhaps to ask advice. It was hard for him, however, for never in his life had he been accustomed to doing this. He waited but she was obviously not going to say more unless her asked her. 'What do you think?'

'It seems a good idea. I'm sure they'll be able to find out what is wrong and put it right. I don't really think that Mother looks seriously ill. She's never been robust, has she? But she's always kept going. And with you to look after her, I'm sure she'll soon be alright again.' She had been so confident that he would be ready to give her the reassurance she had been accustomed to have from him that his reply came as a shock.

'I wish I could feel as sure as you seem to do.' He sat down wearily on the kitchen chair. 'I've been trying to do my best for her. I don't mind that. You know what I mean. You've had a bit of that yourself at one time, although I'm glad to know that Patrick's settled down now. When you marry you promise to take the bad as well as the good.' He paused.

'You mean for better for worse, for richer for poorer, in

sickness and in health. I'm not sure I've got it quite right but that's it, isn't it?'

'Until death do us part,' her father ended it for her slowly and sadly. 'And that's the bit we never think about, because it frightens us. And now I have to think about it and I don't know how to face it, Stella.'

It was at that moment that she began to realise how foolish and immature she had been in rushing to get from help from her parents who now had no strength to spare. It was not until the next day, however, when she was able to talk to her mother on her own that she was able to appreciate how much she had been deceived in the past or perhaps, more truthfully, how much she had deceived herself.

It was Wednesday evening and they were sitting comfortably on either side of the fire. John Fitzgerald seizing the opportunity of Stella's visit had gone to a Parish Council meeting in the church hall, leaving his wife in the care of her daughter. Mary, who had been steadily regarding her daughter for some moments, spoke first, 'You have to understand Stella that your father finds it very hard to cope at the moment. He can't get used to our changed circumstances.'

Stella was puzzled. 'I can see that he has more to do but surely it's not so terrible? You're still very much in charge in the home it seems to me. You're frailer but you're not desperately ill, are you?'

Although she smiled, Mary did not answer straightaway. She understood the reasons for her daughter's bewilderment but found it hard to choose the right words in which to convey the truth to her, a truth that up till now had been hidden from her. 'No,' she replied slowly at last. 'I'm not desperately ill, at least not at present but we both know that I'm likely to get worse, although probably quite slowly, very slowly, perhaps.'

'But Dad's afraid you're going to die. He hinted at that last night. But, surely, it's rather silly, isn't it; to anticipate it and be unhappy long before you need to be? Dad's always appeared to be the kind of person who could deal with problems and worries. I've often heard him encourage other people and give them confidence.'

'And that's what you expect from him, isn't it? Perhaps you have come wanting a little reassurance and even advice.'

'That wouldn't be surprising, would it? He's often given both to me.' She felt irritated by her mother.

'Of course, it wouldn't be surprising. I quite understand how you feel but I must tell you that I don't think it will be very likely that you'll get it this time. He is more likely to need your reassurance. He feels rather lost. For years, you see, he has been a public figure, much admired and looked up to. Now, he's suddenly been deprived of all that. He's not only had to retire from all of it but he's had to take up domestic chores to help me.'

'But surely he wants to do that? He loves you.'

'Certainly, he's very good to me but he's lost his public image and become an ordinary man and, as a result he's lost much of his confidence. He doesn't know himself any more. Can you understand?'

'I'm not sure I can.'

'This home with me in it was his base from which he went to conquer the world and he did conquer it, going out with my support and coming back to my admiration and sometimes for my advice.'

Stella was silent for a few minutes while she tried to understand exactly what her mother was saying. 'It seems to me,' she said at last, 'that you're telling me that you're the strong one, not Dad as I always thought. Am I right?'

Her mother smiled at her. 'Even a strong man needs moral support and so in many ways I've been the strong one, just as you have. In fact, you are stronger than I am. You've had to keep your marriage together throughout the most incredible difficulties without anyone near to support you. I admire that. I'm not sure I would have been capable of it. But things have been better for you in recent years, haven't they? I've been very pleased about it. I am right, aren't I?'

As she met her mother's inquiring gaze, it became perfectly clear to Stella what was expected of her. Her mother needed this reassurance to free her from the worry which she was no longer strong enough to face. 'Much better. Patrick likes his job and is happy doing it. I like my teaching and our joint income is now quite good. The children are settled and doing well, although I'm afraid Ben will never be a star.'

'Perhaps not but he's a good boy all the same and I'm sure he'll never let you down.' Stella's mother was relieved but, nevertheless, not quite satisfied. She knew her daughter too well to be entirely deceived. There was, she was convinced, some special reason for Stella making this long visit on her own. She was tempted for a moment to be satisfied with what Stella had told her. She had been satisfactorily answered. There was no reason for her to probe further but her love for her daughter compelled her to. 'But that's not the whole story, is it? Something is worrying you or at least disturbing you? I am right, aren't I?'

Stella hesitated wondering what to say. She knew she could not tell a direct lie successfully but it was possible to prevaricate. 'You know me only too well, Mother and that means that you're right, of course. There is something I'd like to talk over with you but it's not anything you need to worry about. Quite the contrary, I suppose you'd say.'

'I knew I was right.' Her mother was pleased and relieved. 'What is it then?'

'It concerns Eloise. You know I visited her and looked after her before she died? In fact we became quite close again. Then, a few days ago, I discovered that she had left me all her money including her house in Surrey. I don't know if that surprises you but it shocked me.'

'It doesn't entirely surprise me. I always knew she thought a lot of you. She visited me several times when you were in Oxford and she made her feelings quite clear. In any case you were very good to her in her last months. But why haven't you told us about this before?'

'I found it upsetting. I wasn't even sure that I wanted to accept it but the solicitor made it quite clear that there wasn't really any alternative. After all, I could do what I liked with it afterwards. I didn't even tell Patrick for several days.'

Her mother nodded. 'I suppose you thought it might upset the happiness you'd managed to achieve. It's bound to change your way of life. Too much money can sometimes be more trouble than too little, especially when it's the wife who has the money. Men are so proud and I don't suppose that Patrick's any different. Am I right?'

'You're about right.' Stella agreed. 'It hasn't been as difficult in some ways as I expected but we haven't really decided anything. I still feel confused, about what is the right thing to do. I thought visiting you would offer me a good opportunity to get away by myself and to talk it over with someone not involved. I don't want to worry you and Dad, however.'

Her mother smiled. 'I don't see why we should worry about good news but I can see a little advice might help. Your father should certainly have some useful advice in that area. He's always been clever with money. Furthermore it will do him good to have something like that to think about. He'll be back soon. You must put it to him.'

'I will after supper.' She stood up. 'And talking of supper, I think I ought to do something about it. You sit still and tell me what.' She wished she could have said more but since her mother seemed to be satisfied it was better to leave it.

Before she could move, however, her mother spoke again. 'But it's not just the money, is it, Stella? There's something else upsetting you. Is it Eloise?'

Stella stared at her. 'Why do you say that?' It seemed incredible to her.

'Well, it's obvious that her illness and death must have upset you a lot. You behaved very generously towards her and I'm sure that that you felt that it was the only thing you could do in the circumstances but I sometimes wondered if your family, especially Patrick, might not have resented this at times. And if they did, then Patrick, especially, might feel that he doesn't want this money. It might seem to him that Eloise is still able to influence you. He might, in fact, be jealous, in a funny sort of way. It may be that Eloise did have some thought like that. Who knows? She could be quite unpleasant at times. In fact, I don't think I ever really trusted her.'

'If Patrick feels like that he ought to be ashamed of himself.' Stella knew that this was an inadequate answer but she was too upset by her mother's observations to think of anything better to say.

'Perhaps he is,' her mother agreed, 'but then people are not always as perfect as they'd like to be are they?

Before Stella could find an answer, they heard John's key in the front door. 'We'll talk about it tomorrow,' her mother said quickly. 'But do discuss your money arrangements with you father. He'll enjoy it.'

Chapter Nineteen

It was not until the following afternoon that I was able to have some time alone with my mother. After questioning me on the Tuesday evening, my father had spent a happy couple of hours on the Wednesday morning talking about investments and how I might make the best use of the money Eloise had left me. He enjoyed this so much that I began to think I would never have a chance to talk to my mother. At lunchtime, however, she suggested that he should visit an old army friend who was ill. It would be much better for her she told him if he did it while I was there to keep her company. After demurring a little, he accepted the idea and, at last, we were alone for two or three hours.

We did not immediately come to the subject of Eloise, for Mother had several bits of gossip she enjoyed sharing with me. She was not malicious but she liked to know about people and to speculate about the reasons for their somewhat strange actions. After a little while it seemed quite natural for me to ask, 'When did you first feel that you couldn't trust Eloise? And more importantly what made you feel that?' Strangely enough it was that remark which seemed to have disturbed me most.

'I suppose it was quite soon when I first realised how she managed to separate you from your other friends at primary school, even Margery. I didn't say anything because you seemed to be quite happy but I was glad when they left the area.'

'I don't know that I was entirely happy about it but it seemed silly to make a fuss and Eloise was a more interesting companion. And I couldn't see any reason why Margery shouldn't join in with us.'

'I thought that too,' Mother agreed, 'but, nevertheless, I was glad when Eloise left and none too pleased when she came back later and joined you at secondary school. Soon after that, I noticed you stopped being friendly with that very nice girl, Elizabeth, and several other people. It seemed to me that she was a possessive friend who wanted to get you to herself.'

'Patrick said something like that but I didn't take it too seriously.'

'I was afraid that she would come between you and Patrick and spoil the friendship you two had had for so long. But it never happened.'

'Because she didn't know about Patrick until we were sixteen and he came to the school dance. I think I was a bit worried that he might find her more attractive than me.'

Mother laughed. 'Patrick had far too much sense and, in any case he loved you far too much to bother about anyone as shallow as Eloise. I know he has his faults but I'm sure there has never been anyone else for him since he met you when he was only three. You've been very lucky. Not many people are so blessed. It's difficult, I expect, when someone loves you like that but it must be wonderful too.'

Her words pierced my heart like a dagger. Even if I had intended to confess to her my doubts and my own recent feeling, I couldn't have done so now for it was clear that I would never be able to make her understand. Before I could think of an answer, however, Mother continued, obviously following her own line of thought. 'Of course, it isn't really fair to say that it was all Eloise's fault. You encouraged her, just as you did Margery before her.'

'I not sure that I know what you mean?'

Looking seriously at me, Mother seemed to consider this. 'I don't believe you do,' she said finally. 'I think you thought everyone was like yourself, honest and loving but very independent. The trouble was you attracted to yourself lonely, insecure people who needed someone to lean on and you made them feel special.'

'And what was wrong with that?'

'Nothing, except that you never seemed to understand how grateful they were to have your friendship and how much they wanted to keep you to themselves.'

'You mean that they were jealous of my other friends?' I had to admit to myself that I'd never thought about this. It might have been true of Margery but hardly of Eloise. I laughed. 'But that's ridiculous!'

Mother smiled. 'Jealousy certainly isn't ridiculous. I

remember your telling me once about Shakespeare's *Othello* and the terrible things he did because of his jealousy. You didn't think that was ridiculous, did you?'

'No, but that's different. You're talking about ordinary people in ordinary life.'

'Well, they can be jealous too. I know that from my own experience. I was very jealous at one time.'

'You!' Looking at my normally gentle mother I was amazed.

'Yes, I was jealous of Polly.'

'Polly! You don't mean Auntie Polly surely? Why on earth should you be jealous of her?' The idea seemed ludicrous to me.

'I thought that your dad told her things before he told them to me and that he cared more for her advice than he did for mine. It took me quite a time to realise that he loved me more than he did her and that nothing else really mattered. I expect you think it was silly?'

'Well, it was rather but I think I can understand. Polly has a strong personality. And you did get over it, after all.'

'Yes, but even after that I was tempted to believe that you loved your Auntie Polly more than me. She seemed to understand you better than I did.'

'I did love her a lot. She was different from the others and she understood that I felt different too. I suppose that brought us together but you were my mother. No one could take your place.'

'I came to realise that, especially when Polly went away to train as a nurse and you weren't particularly upset. But to come back to what I was saying. People can be jealous, even unlikely people.'

'Are you trying to suggest that Patrick was too?'

'I don't know but he might well have been at one time. I'm only thinking of when you were first engaged. He can't have had any reason to be since you were married. No one could have been a more loyal wife than you. But has it ever occurred to you recently that he might have been a bit upset by your spending so much time with Eloise in her last few months? Of course he would blame himself for feeling that but he might still have felt it, don't you think?'

'Perhaps but I couldn't really avoid it. There was no one else.

In fact, it never seemed that Eloise's family cared much about her after she left school. She made that clear to me years ago. In any case by this time both her parents had been dead for years.'

'Did she never tell you anything? For instance, did she tell you that she never came home, even when her mother was dying?'

I hesitated here for a moment because I knew that her pregnancy was the reason why Eloise had not come home then but I decided not to say anything about this, since it might lead to other questions, the answers to which could only worry my mother. 'No, she never said much and I never really liked to ask. She always put me off. And now it's too late.'

'Well, if you still want to know more about Eloise's family, particularly after you left for Oxford and she began to work as a journalist, and about the time when her mother was ill, you should speak to your Auntie Polly.'

'Auntie Polly?' I was surprised. 'I was hoping I might see her, especially as it's such a long time since I did. But why should I speak to her about Eloise and her mother?'

'She nursed Eloise's mother during her last weeks and I know they talked a lot, although Polly never told me much.'

'But I thought that Eloise's mother died at home? Wasn't Auntie Polly a sister in the hospital?'

'No, don't you remember that she surprised us all again by suddenly giving up her very good job in the hospital and deciding to take it easier for a time by just doing some private nursing when she felt like it? Polly was always one for surprising the family.'

I looked back to my early childhood when Auntie Polly had been the person I loved best after my parents. 'I think she dropped a bombshell when she decided to take up nursing, didn't she? I was rather too young to know exactly what was going on but I felt the family wasn't very pleased. It upset me but only because I realised that she would be going away to train and I wouldn't see her very often. When was it?'

'It was just after your grandad died. You would be about seven, I think. He left her the house and some money and everyone thought she would settle down and look after your Uncle Bill who wasn't married. But not Polly! She'd decided that it was time she lived her own life before it was too late. She told no one except your dad and he encouraged her.'

'He would.' I laughed. 'Even if only to annoy the others.'

'It was partly that, I expect,' Mother agreed, 'but he also thought she had the intelligence and the strength to do it, while the others laughed at the idea. He was right, of course. She not only did it but she did it well. She worked very hard during the war as a sister in our hospital, if you remember. Then a year or two later she gave it up and went into private nursing. That's how she came to know Eloise's mother. I probably told you about it but I expect you've forgotten. You had plenty of your own problems at that time.'

'I'm afraid I lost touch with lots of people after I left home, even Auntie Polly. I was totally amazed when she suddenly married Martin O'Brien. I had no idea she would do anything like that.'

'You weren't the only one. Even your dad was taken by surprise then. We knew that she was friendly with him but we had no idea that after all those years saying she never would get married that she would actually do it so quickly and quietly.'

'I remember that I was not only surprised but disappointed because I couldn't even get to the wedding because it was only about two weeks before Cordelia was due to be born.'

'There were only about half a dozen people there. He was a widower, of course, and I suppose he didn't want any fuss. Soon after they came back from their honeymoon, his job took him to Durham, where he bought a house. None of us saw much of them after that, although when they did come to visit, Polly seemed very happy and your dad and I liked her husband.'

As I listened to my mother I realised very forcibly that the loss of Auntie Polly's loving influence was one of the things I regretted most. 'I did try at first to keep in touch. We even planned a visit but by then I was expecting Julia and I wasn't at all well, so Patrick said we must put it off. After that, of course I had neither the time nor the money. We wrote to each other but it's never the same and we practically lost touch. It must have been about ten years ago that her husband first became ill, wasn't it?'

'It must have been about that. It was his heart, so after that, they didn't travel. Polly stayed with us two or three times but only for two or three days. She didn't want to leave him, you see. It must have been about five years ago that he died.'

'She didn't come straight back here, did she?'

'No, she only came back when your Uncle Bill became ill. She nursed him for a few months and then when he died she inherited your grandad's house. We thought she would sell it and go back to Durham where she had lots of interests but she took us by surprise again by selling the house in Durham and deciding to live in Grandad's house. It seemed strange to me but she asked your dad's advice and he seemed to think that she'd be happier in her old home with her family close by.'

'I meant to see her the last time we visited but there seemed so much to do in a short time that it never happened. I wrote and told her I was very sorry and she wrote and said I must come on my next visit. Does she know I'm here now?'

'Of course, she visited us last week and I told her. She wondered if you could go and see her this Thursday afternoon and stay for tea. I said I would ask you. I meant to mention it before but we've had so much to talk about. Still, it's not too late, is it?'

'Of course not. I'll certainly go tomorrow, if that's alright with you? Or would you and Dad like to come with me?'

'I think she'd rather have you to herself.' Mother sighed. 'In any case, the journey's a bit too much for me these days. You have to change buses in the town centre, you remember? And sometimes you have to wait about. Polly comes here usually or your dad goes to see her by himself. They're both very fit and active.' She smiled at me. 'I envy them sometimes, although I know I shouldn't.'

Not quite knowing how to reply, I gave her a quick hug and a kiss. I was very glad that I'd come but I understood now that they could not help me and neither could I do much to help them. It was sad but inevitable. Noticing that Mother was looking at me curiously, I said quickly and cheerfully. 'I'll go tomorrow afternoon then. It'll be fun to see her again.'

'She's on the phone now, so why don't you give her a call?' On seeing my surprised look, she added, 'Although she's kept the old house, she's spared no money in modernising it. Martin left her well provided for and she's made herself very comfortable. She's more up to date than your dad is. Tell her you'll catch the two thirty bus tomorrow and you'll stay for tea. She'll be very pleased.'

Mother was right. Auntie Polly was delighted at the prospect of seeing me. She sounded as loving as she had always been and just as cheerful and bright. When I came back from the phone, I realised how very pleased I was at the thought of seeing her again. She was the only one of all my aunts and uncles who had always been my friend when I had been a little girl. She had always known when to comfort me with a hug and with sweets conveniently found in her pocket.

As I prepared a cup of tea for myself and my mother, I remembered vividly how she alone had understand my grief and my fear that my grandad might die without knowing that I loved him. She had understood how hard I had prayed in Grandad's garden on that cold, February day. I think she suspected, although I had never told her in words that I had experienced the warmth of Jesus' love on that day. It was certain that she alone had believed with me in the miracle of Grandad's recovery and repentance. That day had changed my life and me and suddenly I understood that it was that to which I needed to return. Perhaps, although I had not realised it, that had been the chief reason for my coming back. Irrationally I began to feel that I might now begin to find the answer to questions I had scarcely formulated.

It was about nine o'clock that I remembered that Patrick had been the only other person to whom I had confided the story of Grandad's miracle. He had believed it but he had been even more impressed by the wonderful thought of being loved, something which he had scarcely experienced in his young life. It was then that I had promised that I would always love him. I had never remembered that promise more clearly than I did at that moment.

Suddenly I decided that I wanted to tell Patrick that I was going to meet Auntie Polly. I was sure he would be interested for, although he had only met her occasionally, he had shared my love for her and she had always seemed to have a special fondness for him. In any case since I had not telephoned home since Monday when I had told them of my safe arrival, it was time that I rang again.

I was disappointed however, for although I let the telephone ring for several minutes, there was no answer. I decided that he had probably taken them all out for a meal and they would not return until quite late. I comforted myself with the thought that I would have more to tell Patrick on the Thursday evening. Nevertheless, I wished I could at least let them know that I had tried to get in touch. I debated whether or not to ring Lucas, finally deciding against this. It might be unwise. As I returned to my parents I felt strangely cut off from all my family.

Chapter Twenty

Eloise dominated my thoughts as I went to bed that night. My mother's remarks troubled me. She had seemed in some way to be blaming me; without knowing it, she had given support to what Eloise had written in her last letter.

Could it possibly be true? Because I had wanted to be kind and understanding had I given Eloise false expectations? It was certainly true that we had been good friends. We had shared many interests, particularly in literature and in the theatre. I recalled many lively discussions over cups of coffee in the Sidona Café; many visits to the library and bookshops. We were both studying English and French in the Sixth Form so that was a bond between us, although our ultimate ambitions were very different.

Eloise prided herself on being unconventional and avant-garde. She read *The New Statesman*, talked light-heartedly and even frivolously about 'free love' and homosexuality. With my strict religious and Labour Party background my outlook was more traditional and serious. Nevertheless, I enjoyed these discussions and was eager to consider new and 'shocking' ideas.

At the same time, however, Patrick had been my real confidant. It was with him that I talked about faith, religion, life and death and how the world must be changed after the war. Eloise was entertaining but she passionately longed for success and money, things I cared little for. She must have had some idea of this surely? If she hadn't, why hadn't she?

As I lay down half-awake, half-dreaming, I slipped back into the past... a beautiful summer morning; Eloise and I are drifting down the River Avon at Stratford. I look up and watch fluffy, cotton wool boats sailing across placid, blue skies. As I dip my fingers into the cool water, I notice two elegant swans drifting indifferently past us. It is hot but there is a slight breeze. The trees on the river bank bend down as if to examine their reflections and offer us a welcome shade.

Eloise is looking as attractive as always, wearing a deep blue cotton dress scattered with a pattern of crisp, white daisies. The blue of the dress emphasises the unusual blue of her eyes. In the sunshine, her golden hair looks more brilliant than ever. Her lips are scarlet.

It is 1942 but war is far from our minds. In the autumn I shall be going to Oxford; Patrick will be going into the Army; Eloise will be starting her first job as a junior reporter on our local paper. Her first step to Fleet Street and fame, she confidently calls it. 'Isn't this brilliant?' She smiles at me. 'It was a marvellous idea of yours that we should have a holiday at Stratford together.'

Smiling back, I agree. I don't mention that my first plan had been to spend this week with Patrick before he went into the Army. Although he was not a Shakespeare devotee like me, he had been very keen. It was only my mother's shock and horror that I should even mention such an idea that had forced us to give up the plan. It had simply never occurred to us what people might think until Mother shattered our or at least my innocence.

I had then turned to Eloise who delighted with the idea helped me to persuade my still reluctant mother. As a result we are now in the middle of a week in a boarding house in Stratford-on-Avon, conveniently near to the theatre which we had already visited five times, enjoying each performance to the full.

The thought crosses my mind, as we discuss our hopes for the performance of *Macbeth* that evening and our admiration for the leading man, that Patrick might not have been so enthusiastic about such a rich diet of Shakespeare. Eloise and I, however, are enjoying it to the full... My thoughts wander.

Suddenly, I was fully awake as I remembered that it was on that holiday that Eloise had talked so much of our sharing a flat in London after the War. She would, of course, have arrived in Fleet Street, and I, she had decided, would have given up teaching to become a successful translator of the newest French literature. The flat was to be in Bloomsbury. Where else could it be? She apparently had our future lives all planned, even the smallest details of the flat which would be within easy reach of the theatres, the bookshops and the British Museum. This place would be our home, a haven of security for both of us.

To me this had all been a delightful daydream – a story we invented to amuse ourselves. It did not, however, have any relation to the future which I hoped would be mine. My future was to be with Patrick. Patrick and I were sure about this but I didn't talk to anyone else about it, not even to Eloise because I was convinced that the idea would arouse ridicule and opposition which would damage us. But I imagined that Eloise really knew this. Now for the first time I understood what a shock it must have been to her when Patrick and I announced our engagement a few weeks later. No wonder she had been angry and opposed it.

I had been hurt by her lack of understanding. She, however, must have felt that I had deceived and rejected her, although until this moment I had never seen it this way. For a time I sat up ashamed of my insensitivity. Without a thought I had destroyed her dreams and had never even acknowledged it.

After a while I lay down and tried once more to sleep. It was stupid, I told myself, to waste time on fruitless regrets so many years later. I could only admit that the misunderstanding had been mostly of my making. I had always found it difficult to share my most intimate thoughts and feeling. I still did, in fact. Without meaning to, therefore, I had misled Eloise. At the same time, I had misunderstood her. I had failed to realise the importance of our relationship to her. Since she had always seemed to express her feelings so easily I had wrongly assumed that they were superficial and had treated them more lightly than I should have done.

Yet she had still hoped and persevered. Why? Again, as I was drifting off to sleep, I found myself back once more in the past. The year is 1947. I have been teaching for two years since my marriage to Patrick. For the first time in my life I have some spare money and I am determined to have an exciting holiday. I want to break free from the constraints of rations and scarcities in the immediate post-war England.

The geography teacher at my school has given me the address of a pension in Switzerland where he had stayed before the war. Immediately I decide I will go to Switzerland. It is difficult all these years later to remember how exciting an adventure that seemed in that time. Unless they have been with the Army, people of my age have never spent a day out of England. Currency is restricted; there are no travel agencies; one has to be bold and self-reliant.

Determined though I am, I realise that I need someone to travel with. This is a problem. Patrick is still overseas with the army and therefore unavailable for two or three months before he is demobbed. The first friend I ask refuses instantly. Then I think of Eloise who has just come out of the ATS and is hoping to resume her journalistic career. She accepts the idea with enthusiasm.

After journeying all night through war-shattered France, we arrive in Switzerland in the early morning, immediately realising that we are entering another world. There is real black coffee with cream accompanied by fresh rolls and croissants with unlimited butter and honey. We seize on these delights, denied to us for seven years. We are smiling, the fatigues of the journey forgotten. The sun is shining. We are sure that this is going to be the best holiday we have ever had. We are right.

We change trains at Berne and take the mountain railway to the village, four thousand feet up in the mountains, where we are staying. The air is fresh and invigorating. Everything is so clean and amazingly undamaged. From the pension window we can see the breathtakingly beautiful Alps; below us we can hear the mountain river hurrying ceaselessly over the rocks. Every day is filled with new joys. We struggle up mountain tracks, stopping on lonely ledges to eat our tasty picnics of dried meat and cheese. We feast on cream cakes in the village restaurant. One day we take a long trip by car over the mountain passes to the Rhone glacier, amazed to find that we can walk in it. Our enjoyment is shared and we have no disagreements. We even manage to share a double bed successfully!

One early morning in the middle of the holiday it occurs to me that Patrick doesn't even know where I am. All I had told him was that I hoped to visit Switzerland early in the holidays before he came home. This though for some reason gives me a strange feeling of freedom. Another day when we are enjoying a rest after our picnic Eloise unexpectedly asks me why I have not waited to go on this wonderful holiday until Patrick can come with me.

'Because I don't know exactly when he will come back for, as you know, he doesn't write very often and I wanted to be sure of it.' I look at her in surprise. 'You're not sorry I asked you, are you?'

'Of course not. I'm loving it. I only wondered whether you might not prefer to have him with you?'

'I never thought about it. It simply didn't seem possible. Besides, I was sure that you would be a good companion and you are. Patrick and I can have another holiday when he comes back.' As I speak I realise that, after two years, I have become accustomed to being without Patrick. I look forward to settling down one day but, for the moment I am enjoying my freedom.'

Eloise looks sharply at me. 'You're very lucky, you know. You have freedom to enjoy yourself but you also have your future settled. Not many people can say that.'

'You wouldn't want that, would you? You're too ambitious.'

'I might, if I could have it with the right person.' For a moment she looks a little thoughtful then suddenly she jumps up. 'If we're going to go as far as we intended, then we'd better not waste any more time. Come on lazy bones.' Setting off without a pause, she beckons me to follow her.

I am jerked awake again. It had indeed been a good holiday. I remembered that clearly, although I had not thought about it for years. I was sure that I had nothing to reproach myself with during that time. If we had disagreed about anything I did not remember it. Then, why did I have this nagging thought that there was something I had always wanted to forget? I told myself I was being ridiculous and that I must try to get some sleep. I was allowing Eloise to obsess me. As I lay down, however, a long and deeply repressed memory flashed into my mind.

It is the last evening. We are both sad to be leaving both the pension where they have made us so welcome and also Switzerland which has enchanted us with its beauty and peace. The proprietor, a cheerful widow, who delights in making people comfortable, has prepared a special meal for us. After the meal, she and her son, Martin, join us for a coffee and a cognac. Two young English women holidaying together, both attractive but both apparently without any romantic ambitions, have intrigued them, I fancy and now they would like to know more. The knowledge that I am married also puzzles them even though I explain that my husband is still in the Army overseas.

We are already friendly with Martin, who has taken us on a couple of car trips over the Alps. His main job is to act as a guide to mountain climbers and this evening he presents us both with a parting gift of edelweiss plucked on the summit that morning. We promise to press it and to keep it. He is a bachelor in his late twenties. Tall but slim he moves with surprising grace but, at the same time he gives an impression of great toughness and strength. He is an attractive man with fair hair and blue eyes that look even more vivid in contrast with his deeply tanned skin. He talks easily, even in English, smiles readily and obviously enjoys female company.

The sort of man, whom Eloise will charm, I think. And she responds to him as she automatically does to all attractive men but, to my surprise, he gives his entire attention to me and Eloise has to make do with Madame, his mother, who also talks easily and wittily.

As we finally retreat to our bedroom, Eloise seems to express a little chagrin. 'It's really not fair! Every desirable male we meet starts by responding to my charms but ends up preferring you! It's especially unfair when one remembers that you already have Patrick firmly tied up!'

'What do you mean?' I'm a little startled. 'I hope you're not suggesting…'

'Of course not. I know that you're completely faithful to Patrick but it is noticeable and seems to give the lie to the old saying that "gentlemen prefer blondes". The truth is they prefer large, soulful dark eyes and a sweet understanding smile.'

'What nonsense!'

'Well, you can't deny that Martin was quite taken by you. In fact, he ignored me practically and flirted outrageously with you.'

'I'm used to that.' I smile at her.

'What do you mean?'

'He's a bachelor. He likes to flirt but he prefers to do it with a married woman. He feels safe. He can enjoy a flirtation with me but still feel safe.'

Eloise laughs. 'I never realised that you were so cynical.'

'I'm not. I'm simply realistic.'

'And it seems to me that my good little friend has just admitted that she does enjoy a little flirting. You can't deny it, can you?'

'I seem to have given myself away, don't I?'

Before we undress we go to stand on our little balcony for a last look at the shadowy mountains surrounding us, the moon highlighting the whiteness of their snowy peaks. The river is still tumbling noisily beneath us. We take deep breaths of clean air, then reluctantly I turn away to undress. 'I hate leaving here,' Eloise says with a sadness that surprises me. 'I feel that nothing will ever be as good again.'

'I hope you're not right, though I know what you mean.' I start to undress but Eloise stays longer on the balcony. I am lying in bed almost asleep when she undresses. She makes some little remark but I don't want to reply. I want to preserve my solitude. She moves very quietly towards the bed obviously convinced that I am asleep. To my surprise she doesn't get into bed but bends over me, lovingly strokes my hair and finally kisses me, 'Good night, my dearest,' she whispers.

I dare not stir, praying that she won't realise that I'm awake. I lie rigid while she gets into the big bed which we share. I'm afraid of what may happen next. To my relief, turning on her side, she keeps well away from me. For a long time I lie awake, dreading that, if I move, she may be encouraged to attempt something more. At last, I fall asleep. The next morning I say nothing and, as Eloise behaves exactly as usual, I almost begin to wonder if I have dreamed it all. I never say anything, however, because I do not want to hurt Eloise. Nor do I want to risk the embarrassment. How many times do we refrain from speaking what perhaps would be better spoken, because we tell ourselves we are too kind-hearted to want to reject the other person? When perhaps what we really mean is that we don't want to risk putting ourselves in an awkward position?

As I remembered this over twenty years later I had to admit that I was no longer sure why I had remained silent. I had always been so convinced that my motives had been as pure as I had always thought them to be. Could the truth actually have been that I had been afraid that Eloise might attract me? Even, if that was not the truth it was obvious that, because I had not clearly rejected her, we had remained close, much closer, I now realised than I had ever admitted. When she had been temporarily without a home in London, I had offered her a flat in our house, in spite of Patrick's protests; I had taken her baby and brought him up as my own, without even telling Patrick. I had accepted her help when I was desperate for money, again agreeing to keep it a secret. And when she was dying, I had rushed to her help and done far more for her than most women in my position would have felt it necessary or even possible to do.

As I considered all these happenings for the first time, together with other less important ones which had proved our intimacy I understood why she had left me her money and how that might be interpreted. I began to view Patrick's anger and his desire to be rid of her much more sympathetically than I had ever done before. It was not because he didn't understand my grief at Eloise's death, but because he understood too well or so he was convinced. His last hope of having me to himself seemed to have been denied him.

As I once more tried to sleep, I admitted to myself that Patrick had been wronged by me in many ways. I had failed to speak the truth to Eloise, and thereby had wrongly encouraged her; therefore, I must no longer fail to speak the truth to Patrick. But, first I must discover what it was.

Chapter Twenty-One

As she stood outside the front door of her grandfather's terrace house, Stella was overwhelmed by the memories of the past, which had been coming back to her on her long bus journey to this northern suburb of the town on the edge of the moors. She and Patrick had so often travelled this way and further to the village in the centre of the moors from where they had started their favourite walks. Patrick was still very much in her thoughts, although she felt no nearer to understanding him or his present behaviour.

When she was only a small child she had come here to visit her grandfather and her aunt and uncle who lived with him. Pausing at the top of the steps which led to the heavy door of the grey stone house with its slate roof she felt that she had slipped back forty years. Looking to right and left along the narrow, windswept steep street, it seemed that nothing had changed. It was frightening.

Hastily, she rapped firmly with the same old knocker. The familiar sound of footsteps coming quickly down the hall. The door opened. Auntie Polly stood before her. The past was swept away, for this was a different Auntie Polly from the one she remembered from her early childhood. At least, she was certainly not living in the past. She was, of course, still small and slight but instead of the nervous, youngest aunt wearing a shabby dress mostly covered with a voluminous overall, a well-dressed, confident woman in her late sixties stood before her. The grey hair fashionably cut and waved framed a face whose sharp contours had rounded to make less obvious the firm mouth and the obstinate line of her chin. The smile, however, was still as friendly and her voice was just as welcoming.

'Come in, Stella! I can't say you haven't changed but you'll always be the same to me.' Opening the door more widely, she stood back so that Stella could enter the hall. Then, after closing the door, she led Stella through to what had been the old kitchen. Stella gasped as she looked around. Her mother had certainly been right when she had said, 'You'll find things much changed, not only Polly but the house also.' What had been the old fashioned kitchen had been transformed into a comfortable, modern living room with an open fireplace in which a bright fire burned. The floor was carpeted; the much-enlarged window was framed with heavy velvet curtains. Instead of the rough kitchen table and heavy horsehair chairs there were several modern armchairs and occasional tables. The whole room was tastefully lit with several well-positioned lights. 'How do you like it?' Auntie Polly asked with obvious pride.

'It's marvellous, rather like the transformation scene in a pantomime!'

'Come and see the kitchen.' Smiling, her aunt led her to what had once been the scullery and wash house. This had been transformed into a shining modern kitchen with every convenience. 'I'll show you the rest of the house later,' her aunt promised, leading her back to the living room, 'but first we'll relax and get to know one another again.'

Stella had hardly sat down before her aunt had begun to ask questions in the quick, lively way she remembered. 'Your mum and dad have always kept me informed of any important happenings but I want you to fill in the details. After all, you were my favourite niece when you were young and we were at one time very close or so I think.'

'We were,' Stella agreed, 'and I've always remembered that.' For the next half-hour she cheerfully answered all her aunt's questions about her present life with Patrick and their family. Feeling that she had put forward a happy story, without touching on any of the darker aspects, she smiled at her aunt who seemed for a moment to have no more questions. 'Now you must tell me about yourself. It's far too long since we last met and you too have changed a lot.'

'There's plenty of time for that,' her aunt replied. As she looked at Stella she was wondering what she should say. Should she accept unquestioningly all that her niece had told her or should she follow her instinct? That instinct which told her that something was very wrong. It was silly she supposed to expect the middle aged Stella to have the same innocence and openness that had been so remarkable about the younger Stella. Thoughtfully, she gazed back at Stella with her keen, grey eyes. No, she decided, I won't accept her story at its face value. I may hurt her but I may help her. I must not let that opportunity pass.

Leaning forward, she looked straight into Stella's eyes. 'It seems that everything is now fine. At last, Patrick seems settled in a job that he enjoys. You have a job, which you will enjoy even more when you take over more responsibility. The older children seem to be doing very well and Ben, although not so gifted, is a dear boy. You have a nice home and at present no great money worries. It's a good picture. Am I right?'

'Yes, things are pretty good now, although, as you know, they haven't always been so good.'

'Then why are you so unhappy?'

Stella felt as if a bomb had exploded in front of her. 'Why do you say that? I haven't said I am unhappy, have I?'

'No, you've been very careful not to but your eyes give you away. They tell me a different story.' She put out her hand and touched Stella gently. 'My instinct tells me that there is another version, an unhappy story. Am I right?'

It was only possible to be honest. 'Yes, you are, Auntie Polly.'

'Do your parents know? '

'No, I had hoped to be able to talk to Dad, as I always used to but I can't because he's changed. I didn't feel that I could burden them with my troubles. What has happened to Dad? He seems so different.'

'Your father has been forced to realise that he is growing old. He has spent most of his life, as you know, trying to improve the education, the working condition and the pay of the workers. It was the great passion of his life and he had considerable success.'

'Then why has he given up so completely? Surely, that wasn't necessary?'

Her Aunt smiled at her. It is always difficult she thought to make the young understand how difficult it can be to grow old but she must try since she wanted Stella to admire her father still and to appreciate his love. 'There are two chief reasons, I believe.

The first is something, which he rarely speaks of but which is nevertheless very important to him. I mean, of course, his great love for your mother, which you may have underestimated. Love, as I'm sure you know, sometimes demands that we make sacrifices and he cheerfully made his for her, giving up many of his activities.'

'I appreciate that,' Stella interrupted, 'but why all of them? That's what puzzles me.'

'That brings me to his second reason. Having given up many of his activities, he discovered, as we all do at some time, how quickly his place was filled. Other people had quickly stepped in – some he had considered his friends. There was no going back; he was no longer needed. He gave up the rest with some bitterness, I imagine, although he has never said so.'

'And now he dreads that Mother will die and he'll be left with nothing. How terrible! How can I help?'

'You can't except by showing your love for him. He is sensible and wise enough to accept, in time, what we all have to accept. At least he has understood that love is the most important thing in anyone's life. No one, I'm sure, comforts himself on his deathbed by thinking of the money he has accumulated or the votes he has gained. It is the love we have given and received that matters then.'

'I'm sure you're right,' Stella agreed.

Her aunt had more to say, however. 'I'm sure that you, Stella, have always understood the importance of love from your earliest years. Your marriage to Patrick proves that. But now you obviously have some difficulties and have come home, or so it seems to me to get a little advice. Well your parents may be preoccupied but I'm not. Why don't you try telling me? It might help, don't you think?'

'I'm sure it would. You always used to understand me. The trouble is the more I think about it, the harder it is to tell. I don't even know where to begin.'

Moving back a little, her aunt answered in a matter of fact tone, 'Why don't you start at the beginning?'

'I'm not exactly sure where that is.' Suddenly standing up Stella walked across the room to the window. Although it was a grey day it was not dark yet and she could see the little patch of garden. She was sure she could see the patch where she had knelt on the stones praying for her grandfather. She wished she could feel again the warmth of love she had felt then and the conviction she had had that miracles could happen. In fact, a miracle had happened and only Auntie Polly had ever known anything about it – Auntie Polly and Patrick.

Turning round she spoke to her aunt. 'Do you remember finding me praying that day when Grandad was supposed to be dying and I refused to kiss him?'

'Of course, I do! A miracle happened that day. Father was converted. I never told anyone because I didn't think you wanted me to.'

'I didn't want you to. I only told Patrick. It affected him a lot because he didn't know much about love. It was then I promised to love him.'

'It was a promise made in faith and you've kept that promise, although it must have been very difficult at times.'

'I'm not sure I have. But I don't want to talk about that for the moment. I want to talk about my friend, Eloise. Do you remember her?'

'I never met her very often but I've heard quite a lot about her. Why are you asking me?'

'I thought you might know things I don't know. Mother told me yesterday that you nursed her mother when she was dying of cancer. Is that right?'

Auntie Polly leaned back in her chair and closed her eyes as if trying to recall something more clearly. Sitting up she replied firmly, 'Yes, that's right. I remember Celia Marshall very clearly, not because of her suffering, nor because she resented dying so young but because she was so unhappy. She was angry and full of guilt about the way she had treated her daughter. Before she died she wanted to make her peace with Eloise but she couldn't get in touch with her.'

'Oh, no! How terrible! Why should she feel like that?'

Auntie Polly fixed her penetrating gaze once more on Stella. Could Stella really be as shocked as she sounded? 'But surely you know that she never came to see her mother during those last terrible months, so there was no chance for Celia to ask her daughter's forgiveness. Of course I know that Celia Marshall was a pretty selfish, vain woman, not much of a mother but I don't think anyone deserves that, do you?'

'No, of course not.' She paused to think, then she asked, 'That would be just over twenty years ago, wouldn't it?' Her aunt nodded. 'Then Eloise couldn't have come to see her; and she might not have been particularly welcome if she had.'

'What possible excuse could there be? You surprise me, Stella. I know she was your friend but…'

'She was pregnant and I imagine that she was just over giving birth at the time of the funeral. Even I didn't know until after the baby was born and she didn't tell me then about her mother's illness and death. Her own problems were rather overwhelming, I think. And I don't think that she thought her mother would have time for her. At least that's what she told me eventually.'

'So Celia's repentance came too late, it seems?'

'Why was she repenting? What had she done wrong?'

'Chiefly her lack of love for her daughter.'

'I don't understand that. I always thought that Eloise was very much petted and spoilt. Sometimes, I almost envied her.'

'You had no need to do that. She was spoilt when she was young, because she was like a pretty doll but as she grew older, her mother began to resent it more and more that her daughter was better looking, younger and therefore more attractive than she was and she made her resentment clear. When she was dying she was very lonely. She was forced to realise that her husband's love was superficial and she had driven her daughter away and now she longed to talk to her. But she couldn't get in touch with her.'

'Eloise cut herself off from everyone – even from me for a time. Then, after the birth, she asked me to take the baby, because she wanted to be sure that he would have a good home.'

'And what did you say?'

'I agreed, of course. My first baby had just been stillborn. She had a baby needing a home and I had a home needing a baby. It seemed the right thing to do.'

'Are you telling me that Dominic is actually Eloise's son?'

Polly was amazed at what Stella had so long concealed and now so calmly revealed.

'Yes.'

'That was unusually generous of you and Patrick!'

'Patrick had nothing to do with it. He knew nothing about it. As far as he was concerned Dominic came from the adoption society.'

Polly stared at her niece whom she had always thought she had known so well. 'I can hardly believe you! Why ever did you do something like that?'

'I did it because Eloise begged me to do it. She thought that Patrick might refuse to take her baby and I was afraid that she might be right.'

'You must have loved her a lot. Her mother always insisted that her daughter loved you but I never imagined that you had similar feelings for her.'

'I don't know that I did.' Stella felt unable to explain her feelings at the time. 'It simply seemed the best thing to do for both of us and for the baby.'

'Perhaps it did but it wasn't very fair to Patrick, was it?'

'I don't know that it was. But I'm not sure that I've ever been fair to Patrick But I don't want to talk about Patrick at the moment. Later, perhaps but not now.'

'Then what do you want to talk about?' Polly felt herself to be baffled by her niece.

'I need to talk about Eloise for the moment. I feel that I've often misunderstood her and been unkind to her, although I don't think I ever really meant to be.'

'Don't get the wrong idea,' Polly protested, 'although her mother was sorry for her lack of love and wanted to tell her so, she made it quite clear that Eloise was no saint.'

'How do you mean?'

'She said that from her earliest years Eloise was very ready to snatch anything she wanted and to keep a firm grip on it when she had acquired it.'

'I find that quite easy to believe. I suppose, in a sense, that was what she did to me.'

'Then why are you so worried? What has brought all this back to your mind? I suppose that you are still upset by her premature death. That is always a shock, although it must be nearly three months since she died.'

'It was very upsetting, the more so because I spent so much time with her. I was, however, getting over her death or so I thought until she approached me from beyond the grave. I haven't told you about that, have I?'

'No. Whatever do you mean?' It seemed to her aunt that Stella was getting a little morbid about her friend's death, which it must have affected her more than she was prepared to admit.

'First of all, she wrote to Dominic telling him that she was his natural mother, although just before she died she had said that she would not do this. The letter was sent to him not long after her funeral. Dominic was upset but Patrick was even more so, as he had never been told.'

'That was a dreadful thing to do! Why did she do it?'

'In another letter, which came later to me, she explained that she thought that it was time for various truths to be told. She also told me that I had never understood how much she had loved me. In fact; I had never loved Patrick or her, as they deserved to be loved. The proof of her love for me came in her will, in which she left me her house and all her money.' Stella tried to speak calmly but it was obvious that she was making a big effort to control her emotions. Her eyes filled with tears but she blinked them back. 'I didn't read the letter to Patrick but I had to tell him about the will. He was very angry, much more upset than I had expected. He was tired, he said, of having his life dominated by Eloise. He had hoped that we would make a fresh start now that she was dead but obviously her money would make this impossible. He seemed to be saying that I had to choose between him and Eloise's money. I refused to make a decision and came here.'

'You poor child!' Standing up her aunt walked over to her and put her arm round Stella's shoulders. 'You really do need some one to help you.' For a moment, Stella's tears ran freely, as she accepted her aunt's comfort. Although, it was true, that Lucas had tried to comfort her, she realised now that she desperately needed a comfort that was friendly and unbiased.

Sitting down next to her on the settee, her aunt kissed her and then passed her some tissues from a nearby little table. When Stella seemed calm again, she began to speak, 'I suppose it is possible to understand Patrick's attitude but, since you have been a loving friend and wife to him for most of your lives, I find it difficult to forgive him for being so jealous. The strange thing is that Eloise to whom you had always been such a good friend seemed to have had rather similar feelings. You must find this hard to understand.' It was becoming clear to her even as she spoke that there must be much more that Stella hadn't told her. She was sure, also, that it would be good for Stella to tell the rest of the story if she could be persuaded. When Stella didn't comment, she asked a further question, 'Why did you say that you weren't sure that you had ever been fair to Patrick? I can't see how that can possibly be right?'

Moving away a little from her aunt, Stella sat up. 'It has taken me some time to understand. I'm not sure I do, even now. But, as I look back, as I have been, I'm not sure that I was ever fair to Eloise or Patrick, especially not to Patrick. It's quite a long story. I'm not sure I should burden you with it.'

'What nonsense! How can it be a burden to me, especially if it will help you? What can I possibly have to do which is more important?' She stood up suddenly. 'I think we should have a little break and have tea first. It's all ready in the dining room. I only need a few minutes to boil the kettle, etc. Why don't you have a look at the County magazine while you're waiting?'

Stella stood up too. 'I think I'd rather walk down the garden. Moving over to the window, she looked out. 'The sun's still setting. It looks quite beautiful. Have you still kept the little Lourdes grotto that used to be there? You remember the place where I prayed when I was so afraid that Grandad was going to die without knowing that I loved him?'

'Of course I remember. That was a wonderful experience for you, wasn't it? I've altered lots of things but not that. That is special. I believe that you met Jesus there, didn't you?'

'Yes, I believe I did and I think it might help me to go back. Perhaps I shall be helped to understand everything better, including myself. What do you think, Auntie Polly?'

As her aunt took her in her arms and kissed her, it seemed as if the years had rolled back and she was that little girl again. She had been unhappy and confused then and she had been helped. Perhaps she would be again. 'You don't think I'm being stupid, do you?'

'Of course not! Go now before the sun sets. It's always seemed a peaceful spot to me. Stay as long as you need to.'

'Thank you.' After kissing her aunt again, Stella went quickly.

'God bless you,' Auntie Polly whispered as she watched her go.

Chapter Twenty-Two

As a child she had never appreciated the view since she had scarcely been able to look over the top of the dry stone wall at the end of the garden. Now, she was entranced by it.

Her grandfather's house was on high ground at the end of the town, so that over the wall she could see a few more scattered houses lower down, one or two farms and then on the horizon the outcrops of black rocks on the moors. The same dark, mysterious moors which had always fascinated her with their promise of freedom and of danger.

Overall was a wide stretch of sky, at this sunset hour incredibly beautiful. The Master Painter had swept his brush across the pale azure background with broad strokes of orange, indigo and gold. Seen in silhouette against this, the distant black rocks looked more menacing than ever.

She scarcely glanced at the little shrine at which she had prayed as a child. She simply stood, absorbed into eternity. All was quiet, cold and clear. She was not conscious of words or thoughts. She simply reached out and was swept away.

Years ago, the six-year-old Stella had felt herself enveloped in warmth and love. Now, it was completely different. There were no words to describe her feelings. She wasn't aware of how long she had stood there when she noticed that the colours were changing and fading. Night was almost upon her. Reluctantly, she turned and walked slowly back towards the house. As she walked back she had the feeling that much had been made clear to her. It seemed as if her tormented soul had been washed clean. Without speaking of it, even to herself, she had come looking for the truth. Including the truth about herself. And now miraculously it seemed that she might have found it, although she had yet to put it into words. All her worries and guilt seemed to have vanished before the clear light of infinity.

'Are you alright?' her aunt asked her as she came in. 'You look pale. You must be cold. You should have put your coat on.'

'I'm fine, though it did grow chilly as the sun disappeared. But it did me good. I hadn't realised before what an amazing view you have. The sky too was indescribably lovely.'

'Good.' Her aunt smiled at her. 'I'm sure a hot cup of tea will soon warm you up. It's all ready.' She led the way to the one time parlour which had been transformed into a comfortable dining room with thick carpet and highly polished oak furniture, in place of the cold lino and hard, shiny horsehair sofa and chairs.

Auntie Polly had prepared a real North Country High tea with home cooked ham and hard-boiled eggs, fresh bread rolls, home made scones and a temptingly rich fruitcake. As she poured out the tea, she was relieved to see Stella relax and her colour return.

'This looks delicious!' Stella exclaimed, helping herself to some ham and eggs. 'It reminds me of many meals I had with you when I was younger.'

'This is better cooked, I hope! Martin enjoyed good food so I learned to cook well before we were married. I'd never bothered before. There'd always been someone else to do it. But then it seemed worth while to make the effort for him.'

'I hope he appreciated it.'

'He certainly did. He was always an appreciative husband.' The firm, almost hard lines of Polly's face softened as smiled at the thought of her dead husband.

'You must miss him.'

'Very much. But we had sixteen happy years together. I consider that I was lucky to get the chance at forty-eight. It is a great blessing to have a close companion who loves you as you love him. Other successes seem unimportant, as you grow older. Love alone gives real meaning to life. But you don't need me to tell you that.'

She didn't look at Stella or wait for an answer but poured herself a cup of tea. She had decided that it would be intrusive to ask any more questions. It was now better to wait patiently until she was ready to make further confidences, if in fact she did. Stella, she thought, must be free to decide.

After a few moments Stella broke the silence. 'I'd really forgotten how impressive the view was from the end of the garden, if in fact I ever saw it properly before. Tonight the sunset was so beautiful that I just stood and stared and forgot my worries. I didn't pray or even think in words but I had an amazing sense of peace and clarity. As I came down the garden, I think I understand Eloise and our relations with each other for the first time. It seemed that we could now both be at peace. I'd been so angry with her, you see, for betraying me and then for reproaching me by saying that I had never loved her as she wanted to be loved.'

Her aunt nodded but said nothing, although she was surprised that Stella's main preoccupation was still with Eloise and not with Patrick. It seemed to her, however, that it would be wiser not to make any comment at this point.

'Her mother was right,' Stella continued. 'Eloise did snatch at things she wanted and she did cling on to them pretty selfishly. She tried to do that with me, of course. The trouble was that I didn't understand or perhaps I didn't want to understand. It's difficult to explain but I realise now that Eloise didn't just love me as a friend. She was "in love" with me. I can't think of any other way to express it.' She stopped, wondering how her aunt would receive this.

'You mean that she wanted a Lesbian relationship with you?' To Stella's relief her aunt seemed to accept this idea calmly.

'I think so.'

'That wasn't your fault.'

'Perhaps not but I think that in my innocence I encouraged her. When we were eighteen she often talked of our living together in London. In my heart I knew that this would never happen because of Patrick but I never said so. In fact, I pretended to go along with the idea. And, on another occasion when I should definitely have spoken out, I didn't. I'm afraid that, in a way, I enjoyed her love and didn't want to lose her. As a result she kept trying to bring us together and to separate me from Patrick.' She stopped suddenly. It was difficult to continue.

'Even Dominic was part of this, I suppose?'

'Yes, she sometimes called him "our baby" and I didn't object. How could I?'

'Your relationship must have been very tormented.'

'It was. Sometimes I thought she was very selfish, almost evil, but most of the time I loved her as a friend. Before she died, I think she came to understand. It was about this time, I imagine, that she wrote me her last letter. She appreciated my love, she said, but she regretted that she had never been as special with me as she had wanted to be. Then she warned me that she thought that Patrick felt the same and was unhappy, so unhappy that she had tried to console him. I was very angry and very hurt but now I understand, I think, and am at peace with her.'

'Is that why you said earlier that you always had failed Patrick?'

'Yes, and that is worse.'

'Don't you think that you're blaming yourself too much? After all, you were happy for years and I'm sure that you love him.'

'I was never "in love" with him, even when I married him. When I first became engaged to him, I didn't realise it. Eloise tried to warn me but I ignored her.'

'I imagine many young girls were like that in those days. You knew so little, after all.'

'That was true when we first became engaged but it wasn't true when I married him.'

'How could that be? What do you mean?'

'During the time Patrick was in France and our engagement was at an end, I met someone else and we fell passionately in love.'

'But you didn't marry him.'

'No, not because I fell out of love but because he was killed a few days after he went back to France.'

'You poor child! I never heard anything about that before.'

'No one did. He died before I had time to tell anyone about him, so I decided it would be easier to keep it all to myself. And so when Patrick came back and asked my forgiveness I agreed to marry him. It seemed the only chance of happiness still left to me.'

'Patrick must have been very upset when you told him about the other man.'

'I never told him. I didn't see what good it would do. He still doesn't know.'

'Aren't you ever going to tell him? Don't you think it might make things easier if you did?'

'Perhaps. As she was dying, Eloise decided that there had been too many secrets for too long and so she revealed some but even she didn't know about Richard. Do you think it is now time for me to do as she suggested?' She looked directly at her aunt and waited for her reply.

'I need time to consider that.' Her aunt thoughtfully buttered a roll and avoided looking at her niece.

Stella was surprised. 'I though you would be in favour of telling the truth.'

'Mostly yes but not invariably.' She didn't seem prepared to say any more so for a time they ate in silence. 'The question is,' her aunt said at last. 'Do you think that Patrick is strong enough to bear such a truth now after such a long silence?'

'Why shouldn't he be? I'm not sure that I know what you mean.'

Her aunt was irritated. It seemed to her that Stella was deliberately pretending not to understand. 'Of course you know what I mean. You know that Patrick has felt able to rely on your loyalty and love ever since he was a boy. And, before you protest about that being unfair, I think I should remind you that you have always had the support of his love too and that your life would have been the poorer without it.'

'Perhaps I should remind you that he had a brief relationship with Eloise about six years ago. He's not perhaps as perfect as you seem to think.' Her voice expressed the anger, which she felt.

Her aunt, however, did not react as she might have expected. 'And why was that, do you think? Was it perhaps that he badly needed comfort and that Eloise, unpredictable as always, offered it to him? I don't suppose it satisfied either of them, since as you have been telling me, they both wanted you. Am I right?'

After a brief pause Stella answered reluctantly, 'That's pretty much what Eloise wrote to me. She was still in favour, however of speaking the truth.'

'But she didn't know about your earlier lover, did she? So she couldn't know how devastating the truth might be to Patrick.'

'I suppose you're right.'

'That's why I'm concerned that the truth might be destructive. Don't you think that you might be risking plunging him back into that hell of suicidal depression, which might be fatal?'

'Are you telling me that I must resign myself to spending the rest of my life as a prop to Patrick?'

For the first time her aunt was really shocked. She had never expected to hear Stella speak so callously as this seemed to her. 'How can you talk like that! I thought you loved him, that he was your friend. He's also the father of your children. Surely all that matters? The young man you've been talking about died nearly twenty-five years ago. What is the point of resurrecting his memory now and wrecking your marriage?'

'Our marriage hasn't really been much of a success since our last baby died. For several reasons Patrick and I have not been close since then. He retreated into his own world and I became immersed in earning our living and running the family. We were in the same house but not together. Now, Eloise although she is dead, seems to have become a big problem. Patrick, it appears, has always resented my friendship with her. He wants at last to be free of her and is furious that she has left me all her money. I'm not sure what he wants me to do about it and I don't much care. There was a great gulf between us and, although Patrick wanted to try and bridge it, I found that I was quite unwilling.'

'So you came away with nothing resolved? Wasn't that rather unkind?'

'Perhaps it was. But I desperately wanted to try to understand myself and my relations with Patrick and Eloise.'

'And have you got anywhere with that?'

'I think so. At least, I no longer feel guilty about Eloise but I also feel, more strongly than ever, that I should never have married Patrick.'

'Don't you think it's a bit late to be thinking that now that you have been married for so many years and have a family?' Her aunt was finding it difficult to be sympathetic.

'I can understand your saying that but the truth is that I desperately long to be free to live my own life. I seem to have been in a kind of prison for years.'

'I don't see how you can expect to do that now. Aren't you being a little immature?'

'There's one thing I haven't told you.'

'I thought there might be,' her aunt said dryly.

'You see I think I've fallen seriously in love with someone else and I don't see why I should be expected to give up this second chance of happiness.'

'Are you willing to tell me about this?'

For a moment Stella hesitated, then as quickly and as briefly as she could she told her aunt about Lucas and the recent change in their relationship which she herself had precipitated.

'Why ever did you do that after eight years?' Her aunt was puzzled. Such behaviour seemed quite alien to her.

'I suppose I suddenly felt terribly vulnerable and unloved. I think it was Eloise's death which made me think differently about the future. It made me realise how brief and fragile life is and how important it is, therefore, to seize any happiness which is offered.'

'Surely you're not telling me, Stella, that Patrick's love and your children's love doesn't matter to you? Don't you think that they need you?'

'Of course, I won't desert the children but in any case they're growing up and won't need me soon. As for Patrick. I not sure that he really does love me, any more. I think that he simply depends on me as he has done for years. He even told Eloise that he never felt specially loved by me, although he wanted to be.'

'Perhaps he's not so wrong in what he thinks.'

'It may be that he isn't. That's why I said to you that I'm not sure that I've ever been fair to him. What other truth is there for me to tell him?'

'Only you can know that.'

'I believe that with Lucas I have the chance to achieve again the happiness I so briefly had with Richard. I lost that through no fault of my own. I don't want to lose this because I'm too cowardly to take it. Eloise's money offers us the chance to live separately. I shall need no financial help from Patrick and he can live comfortably on what he earns and be independent. He can see the children whenever he wants.'

'It sounds as if you've already decided.' Her aunt suddenly felt unable to argue against Stella's new view of life which seemed to her completely unrealistic.

'I think I have. Now, that I've been away from Lucas for several days, I realise more than ever how much he means to me.

I'm sorry because I know you don't approve but that seems to be the truth.'

Sitting up very straight her aunt suddenly put down her cup firmly. She could no longer restrain herself. 'I'm shocked! I never imagined that you of all people would talk like this! You seem to have forgotten utterly that you, as a Christian, made solemn vows before God. "Till death do us part" that was the agreement, wasn't it? How can you talk so calmly of breaking that vow? Do you think you will ever forgive yourself if you do?'

'I think it might be more honest than perpetuating our marriage. People can make mistakes. Surely you know that?'

'What about your children? Are they supposed to pay for your mistakes too? Or don't you love them either?'

'You know I do. I've worked hard to give them some security. They won't be separated from Patrick. Fortunately they know Lucas well and they are very fond of him as he is of them.'

'You seem to be quite sure about all that. But doesn't it worry you that the Church will disapprove and your union will be unblessed? I've always thought of you as a good Catholic.'

'I prefer to think of myself as a Christian. I think the time has come for the Church to stop trying to run people's lives and instead to leave them free to make personal decisions as God does. I rather thought you might agree with that.'

'To a certain extent, I do but perhaps I should remind you that it's God's rules you're breaking, not just the Church's. "Thou shalt not commit adultery", is a commandment of God's, I believe.' Before Stella could begin to argue, Polly went on quickly. 'But that apart, I think you're making a big mistake. You're allowing the past to dominate your life.'

'What do you mean?'

'It seems to me that you have never come to terms with the sad death of that young man, Richard. You told no one. You simply shut it away, which is a dangerous thing to do. Now you seem to think that you can make everything right by substituting Lucas for Richard and ignoring all that has happened in between. It won't work. We can't let ourselves be dominated by our past. We must live in the present as perfectly as we can, for the past has gone and the future is unknown. Surely you understand what I'm trying to say?'

After staring at her aunt for several moments, Stella replied wearily, 'I suppose I do. The truth is that, although I felt tonight that I understood some things for the first time, I'm still very confused.'

'Then must you make a decision yet?' Polly felt a return of love and sympathy for her niece, as she remembered the loving and confident little child she had known so well. 'You've had a difficult life but you've done bravely so far. Don't ruin it all now by running away. You must understand that you don't even know that you would have been so happy with Richard or even if you would have married him when Patrick returned. Thoughts of what might have been can be so deceiving. Your marriage with Patrick is a reality. You can't compare the two. Illusions are always very tempting.'

'And you think that I'm transferring my dream to Lucas?'

'It may be. That is what you must try to discover. What is most important to you?'

'I've always thought that love was most important since I was a child. You know that.'

'Yes, I know but what does that mean now? What is this love? There are many kinds of love. That is what you must ask yourself. I can't solve that problem. I can only suggest caution.' For a moment they were both silent, knowing that there could be no immediate answer, then Polly continued in her usual brisk manner. 'It's getting late, I'm afraid. We must hurry to finish our meal, if you're to catch your bus. You must have a piece of cake before you go. I made it specially for you.' She smiled encouragingly.

As she took the cake, Stella smiled back. 'I'm sorry I've done my best to spoil your lovely meal but it's been a great help talking freely to you. You've reminded me of truths I wanted to forget and you've helped to make things clearer. I don't know yet what I shall do but I promise you it won't be anything rash.'

'That's all I want to know for the moment,' her aunt replied. 'I trust you to try to do what is right.'

Chapter Twenty-Three

Sitting in the express train moving swiftly towards Euston, I reflected that everything was proceeding as it was supposed to do with one important exception. I was travelling on the nine o'clock train instead of the eleven thirty, as originally planned. Why? It was simple really. In the evening after my return from my aunt's there had been two phone calls for me.

The first, from Julia, had been to make sure, ostensibly at least, that I was coming home on the Friday as I had originally promised. 'Of course,' I told her cheerfully, trying to hide the fact that I felt a little guilty because I had not spoken to anyone at home since Monday: 'I would have let you know if there had been any reason to change it. Surely you know that?'

'I see.' Julia obviously didn't but she wasn't going to argue. 'It's just that we were disappointed that you didn't ring again. We've missed you a lot.'

'But I did.' I was defensive. 'I tried twice on Wednesday but no one was in.'

'That was because Dad was very kind and took us all out for a meal. We'd run through the food you'd left prepared and Cordelia and I had a lot of homework and hadn't really got time to cook a meal.'

'That was very understanding of Dad,' I said quickly to hide my feeling of discomfort. 'What are you doing tonight?'

'Dad's going to be a bit late but he's promised to pick up some fish and chips in the village, so that will be easy.'

'That seems a good idea. And I promise you that I'll be home when you get back from school tomorrow with tea waiting and a meal on the way. Does that reassure you?'

'Marvellous! I'll tell the others. They all send their love. We've missed you a lot, especially Dad, I think. We don't want you going away any more. You've had to be away too much in the last few months.'

'I'm sorry,' I replied quickly. 'But no need to worry, I'll be there tomorrow.'

'I'm glad, but Mum,' Julia hesitated.

'But what?' Why did I dread what she might say?

Perhaps my tone was forbidding but, whatever the cause, she retreated. 'Nothing. I'll see you tomorrow. Give our love to Grannie and Grandad. Lots of love to you.' She rang off. This odd, incomplete call left me somewhat disturbed but there seemed to be nothing I could do.

To my surprise there was another call to me about an hour later. An even bigger surprise – it came from Lucas. He too wanted to know when I was returning. As soon as I told him the time, he asked me if I could possibly come on an earlier train, so that we might have time to talk. When I hesitated, he added, 'I've missed you a lot, Stella. Surely, you feel the same, don't you?'

I knew what he meant. Hadn't I told Auntie Polly how much I had missed him? Briefly I thought of Patrick but he, apparently, didn't care enough to ring me. Quite quickly I told Lucas that I would catch the nine o'clock train which would give us an extra couple of hours. He was pleased.

So, here I was travelling on the nine o'clock train to Euston. It would be hard to say whether or not I was surprised when I saw Lucas waiting for me at the barrier, but I was definitely pleased. As soon as I had given in my ticket, he took control. After kissing me with startling warmth, he took my case, slipped his hand through my arm and began to carve a way for us through the crowds to where his car was parked.

'This isn't part of the plan,' I say to myself. 'What plan?' I then ask myself. Suddenly, I have to admit that, although I haven't really any plan, Lucas most certainly has. Weakly but happily I submit. It is delightful to be looked after.

So, just after two hours later, here we are arriving in Lucas's studio, having stopped for a brief lunch on the way. He hasn't said much on the journey but he has obviously been very happy and so have I.

As soon as he has shut the door, he takes me in his arms and kisses me as passionately as he had that afternoon when I tempted him and then ran away. This time I don't run away. 'Why should I?' I ask myself.

'Darling Stella, you have made me so happy. I can dream again. I thought I'd given that up years ago.' And so we dream. Dreams are so seductive. I forget Auntie Polly's warning as Lucas settles me comfortably next to him on the couch with his arms around me. 'When we've sorted everything out.' He kisses me so that I can't protest. 'I know it'll take some time but we will do it and you and I can be together. We'll go abroad for a time.'

I don't ask, 'how?' as I should have done but simply, 'where?' Lucas has obviously been thinking a lot about this, since I've been away. I realise that he has been lonely and, for some reason, remote from the family but I don't ask why. I simply listen. He wants to take me to the places where he studied before the war. Paris, Rome Florence, Assisi – so many magical names. These are places I've never had a chance to visit, scarcely thought about. He wants to share the beauty and the glory with me.

'We'll visit the Louvre, Versailles, St Peter's, the Sistine chapel. There's so much to see. You'll love it, Stella,' he promises. The sky will be blue, the sun will be shining and best of all, we'll be in love. We'll start life again. We both need to, don't you think?'

Part of me is saying, this is crazy but I ignore it. I don't even ask about money. I have plenty now anyway. I suppose I assume the children will be with us. I don't bother to consider this but snuggle closer to him as he kisses me. I'm the girl I was once before with Richard. But this time it can last. There is no war now.

I'm not quite sure what breaks the spell but it is broken. I looked at my watch. 'I must go, Lucas.' I began to detach myself from him. 'Why now? It's only three o'clock.'

'I promised Julia I'd be waiting for them with a meal in the oven. She sounded unhappy. Are they? Do you know?' As I freed myself, I didn't quite look at him but I was aware of his penetrating gaze. He was searching for the truth. What would he find, I wondered? I would like to know.

'I don't know,' he spoke slowly. 'I've hardly seen any of them, except for Ben. I feel they've closed ranks against me. Do you know why?'

'No,' I answered shortly. Was I lying? I wasn't sure. 'Perhaps it was because my relations with Patrick were pretty bad when I left.'

'Surely, they don't blame me?'

'I don't see why they should.' As I stood up I remembered Cordelia's suspicions but it didn't seem worth mentioning them. 'The meat's still in the freezer compartment,' I explained as I moved towards the door.

He caught up with me just as I was opening the door. 'You can't go like this, Stella. When will I see you again?'

'Why don't you come round for coffee after supper as you often do?'

'I might. But you know I didn't mean that.' He was hurt and angry. I was sorry but suddenly afraid. He took hold of my shoulders. 'You must be honest with Patrick. You know that. We can't go on pretending.'

I knew that but I refused to think about it. 'I will, but I can't say anything tonight. It would be too cruel. Surely, you understand that?'

'Of course but it must be soon.' As we kissed passionately, it was as if the sunshine was shining again. Wanting to reassure him, I hugged him before I left with a whispered promise, 'It won't be long.'

Reality took over completely as I entered the house. There was a lot to be done in a short time and, like the competent housewife I'd been for so long, I did it. An hour later the casserole was in the oven. It would be ready in time for the evening meal and its pleasing aroma would greet them as they came in off the school bus. The final duty was to lay a little welcoming tea in the breakfast room. Luckily there was the remains of the delicious fruitcake which Auntie Polly had insisted on my taking away. Ben would like that.

I had over half an hour to wait so I sat down in the armchair near the Aga. I intended to think, knowing that I really needed to but my mind seemed strangely unwilling, so I closed my eyes and tried to relax. I had just done this when the back door bell rang. Annoyed at being disturbed, I opened the back door somewhat violently to find myself looking down on the Regan's eldest child Johnny, aged seven and three-quarters or thereabouts.

As always he was grubby, his hair was unkempt and he was wearing a shabby jersey about two sizes too big for him and a pair of short trousers much too small. My first feeling was one of irritation. I wondered why he was here and why his mother couldn't at least have washed his face first. The next moment I looked into the worried blue eyes staring up at me and realised from his expression that the child was upset and that my look had done nothing to reassure him. Repentant, I smiled at him. 'What is it, Johnny? Do you want something?'

'Mum asked me to give you this.' He held out an envelope, which he was clasping in his hand. 'Come into the kitchen while I read it.' As I opened the door more widely, he ventured in, actually wiping his muddy shoes on the mat. 'Mum says will you please send an answer back when you've read it.'

'In that case you'd better have a glass of milk and a biscuit while I read it.' While I poured out the milk, he chose the richest chocolate biscuit on the plate. I had obviously pleased him. Sitting down at the kitchen table I opened the envelope with some curiosity. The note inside was written in pencil on cheap lined paper in the round unformed hand of the barely literate. Surprisingly, however, it was correctly spelt and well expressed.

Dear Mrs Gestenge

I'm sorry to bother you but I don't know where to turn. You and your husband have always been kind to me and Mike. And I hope you might be able to give me some advice now. I've not been well since I came home from the hospital and yesterday I started to bleed and today it's got much worse. I don't know what to do. Would you be able to come and see what you think? If you can't do that, please tell me what you think I should do. I'm very sorry to bother you but I don't know who else to turn to.

Yours sincerely, Mary Regan.

Obviously there was only one thing to do. I must take Johnny back and see what the situation was for myself. While he was finishing his milk I wrote a hasty note to the family and left it on the breakfast room table. 'Sorry I'm not here as I promised but I've gone to see Mrs Regan who is ill and worried. Help yourselves to tea. If I am delayed, there's a casserole in the oven, ready about 5.30. See you soon. Lots of love, Mum.'

As the sun was fading the air was becoming quite chilly so,

after putting on a warm jacket, I took Johnny's hand and we set out to walk the length of the village street. The Regans lived in one of the railway cottages near the station, just past all the shops. They were entitled to one of these as Mike Regan worked on the railway. On the way there Rosemary Taylor, one of the leaders of our little Catholic congregation, stopped me. She was noted for being very devout and also our organiser of fundraising activities. She was warmly and smartly dressed in a fur-trimmed coat and hat as she came out of our only department store. As soon as she had greeted me, she looked astonished at Johnny. 'Where are you taking Johnny?' Then in a lower tone to me, 'I do think his mother might wash his hands and face, at least, before she lets him out, don't you?'

'I don't think she thought about it. Johnny came to tell me that she's not very well, so I'm taking him home to find out what's wrong.'

'How very charitable of you! I hope you won't be too shocked when you get there!'

'I don't expect I shall. I've been before. I must hurry now before she gets worried.'

'Of course. Well let me know if there's anything I can do, won't you?'

Thanking her, I moved on with Johnny as quickly as I could. At last we reached the row of small, shabby cottages. No 5 where the Regans lived was the most dilapidated. The paint was coming off the door and the net curtains were grey instead of white. Before I could knock on the door, Johnny had opened it and called out, 'Mrs Gestenge has come back with me, Mum!'

I followed him through the front door straight into the living room, which was usually untidy but today was chaotic. Broken toys, tattered books and children's clothes were scattered all over every available surface, so that I had to tread with great care. The table in the centre of the room was covered with a much stained cloth and on it were laid several plates, knives, an open wrapped, sliced loaf, a jar of jam and a dish of margarine. One child about four years old was seated at the table spreading jam thickly on himself as well as on a slice of bread.

Suddenly as I stumbled over a battered, naked doll, I heard

Mrs Regan say, 'It's very kind of you to come, Mrs Gestenge, especially when you've got so much to do yourself.' Turning quickly I saw Mary Regan lying on a couch near the open fire, covered with a shabby eiderdown. Johnny was now standing near to her.

Carefully, I made my way towards her. She was very pale except for a brilliant red patch on either cheek. Bending over her, I stroked her forehead. I thought she might have a temperature but it was difficult to be sure. After moving some clothes off a chair, I sat down next to her. 'Can you give me some idea of what's wrong?'

Before she answered me, she turned to Johnny, telling him to go into the kitchen to help his Grannie. 'I don't want him to know,' she whispered.

'I didn't know your mother was here,' I replied, wondering why she had sent for me.

'She only came a few minutes ago on the bus. She's been working all day but she says she can stay until Mike comes home about eight. She'll give the kids a meal and do her best.' She looked at me pleadingly. 'But she doesn't know what to do. I don't want to make a fuss but I think it's getting worse. Will you help me, please.'

'Of course. That's why I came. How much bleeding is there?' As she drew back the eiderdown and lifted up her nightdress, I looked reluctantly. I shrank from this. 'I put two towels underneath me,' she explained, 'because the pads get soaked so quickly. I don't think I should leave it any longer, do you?' As I looked, I saw that the pads were soaked and the blood was already oozing on to the towels.

Covering her up again hastily, I realised that I had to make a quick decision. 'I must get you straight to hospital. I don't think you should wait for an ambulance, so I'll go and get the car. I'll be as quick as possible.' Without waiting to hear her thanks I hurried into the street.

There were very few people in the streets but, as I came up to the station I suddenly recognised the familiar figure of Patrick coming down the steps towards the street. I had not expected him to be home so early but there he was. Never had I been more pleased to see him. He wasn't looking in my direction, so I ran towards him calling his name. Surprised, he came quickly to meet me.

Before he could ask me any questions, I explained the situation to him as clearly as I could. As I expected, he responded without hesitation to an emergency. 'I'll go home and get the car,' he decided, 'I'll be much faster than you. You go back and get her ready. They'll never manage without you.'

In a moment he had disappeared round the bend as I turned to run back to the Regan's house. He was quite right; they would never have managed without me. It was Johnny who showed the most sense, while Grannie simply held the baby and panicked. Mary was just about ready when Patrick knocked on the door. Johnny held the door open while Patrick, without hesitating picked Mary up in his arms and carried her out to the car.

Johnny, bright boy, went ahead to open the car door, while I followed with her few necessities in a shopping bag. The children, clustered around their Grannie in the doorway, waved goodbye. As soon as we were sure that Mary was as comfortable as possible, Patrick drove off. It was about nine miles to the hospital and he didn't intend to waste any time. I leaned back confident that I could leave this tricky journey to him while I held Mary's hand and tried to comfort her.

As soon as he had parked the car outside the hospital, Patrick leapt out and disappeared through the front door. In a surprisingly short time he returned not only with a wheel chair but also with someone to push it who knew exactly where to go. In a very short time we reached the Emergency Department, which was practically empty. Almost at once, a nurse came to push her to a cubicle. Since Mary insisted on holding my hand I went with her. After making a quick examination, the nurse hurried off to find a doctor, leaving us alone.

Clutching my hand even more firmly, Mary whispered to me, 'I don't know how to thank you both. She hesitated for a moment, then continued, 'Do you think you can give me some advice when I'm better? I don't want to go through this any more. Mike and I love each other but he doesn't know what to do either. That's why he gets drunk sometimes. I want to make a good home but I don't have the time or the strength as things are. Please can you help?

Ashamed of ever having criticised Mike or her, I hastily promised to do the best I could. How rash we often are in judging others, I thought. It was impossible to say more as the nurse returned followed by the doctor. 'We'll wait until we know what's happening,' I added, as I left the cubicle. I joined Patrick who was already sitting in the waiting area. Immediately he dashed off to get coffee and sandwiches before the refreshment counter closed. While I was waiting, I tried to think what I could to help Mary Regan but I still found coherent thought difficult.

After a few minutes I was pleased to see Patrick returned carrying two coffees and two buns. 'The sandwiches looked very tired,' he explained as I looked with some distaste at the very solid bun. 'I didn't expect to see you,' I remarked valiantly biting my bun.

'I took an earlier train because I wanted to welcome you. I was so sorry about the way we parted.'

'It wasn't your fault.' There was so much to say but even now I wasn't sure exactly what it should be. 'This is reality', I'm telling myself but I still don't seem to know exactly what that means. This is, however, neither the right time nor the right place in which to discuss it, so I tell him about Mary's desperate appeal. 'Poor woman! Do you think you can help her?' 'I hope so.' It is difficult to know what to say next, so we sit in silence.

Golden sun, blue skies, Rome, Paris, all those dreams I have so recently shared with Lucas just fade away. 'So is this reality, then?' I ask myself. Blood, pain and loss. Sadness almost overwhelms me. I don't know how to bear it. Suddenly, without a word Patrick takes my hand firmly and comfortingly in his. I know that he is willing his strength and love into me. I also know that he is remembering me as I was. I am not alone. 'What nonsense,' I tell myself angrily the next moment. 'What's the matter with you, woman, going on in this sentimental way?' But my hand still remains in Patrick's. I am back eight years in a bed in this same hospital. I have just been brought back from the operating theatre and have been told as gently as possible that my baby is dead and that my womb has had to be removed. I hardly seem to care I feel so weak and so tired. I simply want to drift away.

Then the curtain round the cubicle is drawn back a little and I'm aware that Patrick has come in. I want to say something but I can't. 'Don't try to speak, Stella darling,' he says quietly as he sits on the chair by my bed and takes my hand firmly in his.

As he holds my hand so firmly I suddenly feel warmth and love flooding into me. His strength enters into me. 'You saved my life that day,' I tell him.

'I tried to. After waiting for hours thinking that you were going to die and making a poor attempt at praying, at last there was something I could do. I could give you my strength and my love or so I thought.'

'You could and you did and it worked. It was a miracle.'

'We've never spoken of it but I've always hoped that it did work.'

'I've tried not to remember it again all these years. But Mary's pain and the blood and the rush to the hospital brought it all back I couldn't escape it. It has seemed to bring you back too. Oh why, have I been so stupid all these years?'

'Don't say that!' He tightens his hold on my hand. 'I'm the one who was completely stupid.'

'But why were we? We stare at one another, finding no easy answer. 'I suppose,' I suggest finally. 'that we both ran away from the pain and in different directions too.'

'Not you,' he protests. 'I was the one who took refuge in despair and left you unprotected.'

'And I forgot I was a wife as well as a mother. That was my refuge. It's not the first time I ran away from a loss but now miraculously we've come together again, and we mustn't let go.' As he grasps my hand even more firmly, Patrick agrees.

'Oh God,' I think to myself. 'Why have I made things so much worse, only today. Why was I so mad?' But I'm determined to hold on to Patrick.

Chapter Twenty-Four

They were still sitting silently together holding hands when the nurse came to ask them if they would like to speak to Mary before she was taken to the ward. 'How is she now?' Patrick asked as they followed her.

'Much more comfortable. The doctor has set up a drip and a blood transfusion. But it was lucky you brought her in when you did. She might have died if you hadn't.'

'Do you know when she'll be ready to come home?' Stella asked.

The nurse, a kindly middle-aged woman, shook her head. 'The gynaecologist will see her tomorrow as she may need a small operation to remove the rest of the foetus. But I would say that she desperately needs a few days' rest, more than anything else.' Agreeing wholeheartedly with that, they followed her through the curtain.

Mary certainly looked better. Her hair had been brushed and she had some colour in her cheeks. Her eyes filled with tears as she thanked them both again. Stella told her that she must try to have a good night's sleep and Patrick told her that he would make sure that her husband, Mike, had all the news. 'Would you like me to bring him in to see you tomorrow?' he asked.

'Thank you very much but there's no need for you to do that,' she said with more firmness than they expected. 'If he wants to see me, he can come by bus while my Mum looks after the children. Just ask him to ring up, please.' As they were about to leave she caught hold of Stella's hand with an appealing look. It was clear what she meant. 'I won't forget what we talked about,' Stella reassured her. 'When you're a bit better, I'll try to help you to sort things out. In the meantime, do your best to get well.'

'I'll do my best,' she promised. 'And would you mind making sure, Mr Gestenge, that Mike knows that I don't want any fuss, I just need a bit of peace and quiet.'

'Certainly, I will,' Patrick promised. 'It seems as if Mary Regan has decided to become more assertive,' he remarked as they left the ward. 'Is that your influence?'

Although his tone was neutral, she looked suspiciously at him but he only smiled at her. 'Surely, you not going to deny that you are somewhat inclined to be rebellious?'

'I suppose I can't, at least not to you but in Mary Regan's case I don't think that it has anything to do with me. I think she feels very strongly that she can't endure her life any longer. She wants to make a change. Does that surprise you?'

'Certainly not. Furthermore, I'm pleased that you're prepared to help her, if you can. But, please Stella, don't commit yourself too much. Your family does feel that they have a right to see more of you. You've been away rather a lot in the last few months.'

'Is that what they've been saying?'

Noticing the sudden sharpness of her tone, Patrick thought it wiser to avoid any direct answer here. 'They missed you a lot last week. As you must know I'm not an entirely successful substitute.'

'On the contrary Julia told me how good you'd been taking them out for a meal and buying fish and chips.'

He smiled. 'At least I wasn't a total failure then.' Although he wanted to say more, he hesitated.

'Were there difficulties then?' She sensed that there was something he had not said.

To her annoyance, he avoided answering her by stopping at the telephone box in the hospital foyer. 'I think it would be a good idea to telephone the family. We should be home soon after six, so they might as well wait for us before eating.'

'Won't we be back before then?'

'I'm allowing time for seeing the Regans first.' Before she could comment, he had removed himself from her by shutting the door of the box and putting in his money. After a short conversation, he rejoined her. 'Cordelia was delighted to hear the news,' he told her as they set off for the car park.

Determined not to be sidetracked, she returned to her earlier question. 'What difficulties did you have then?'

She wondered at first if he was going to answer her but, after a pause, he said slowly, 'It was more an irritation. I found it increasingly difficult to be patient with Cordelia's growing infatuation with Adrian.'

She frowned disliking his use of the word 'infatuation' but decided that it would be wiser to ignore it. She felt very sad that the intimacy and understanding that they had experienced in the hospital waiting room seemed to have vanished completely.

She couldn't know how much he longed to take her hand and to be able to talk freely with her, feeling sure of her sympathy. 'She spent far more time,' he continued, 'thinking about Adrian than about her work. I don't see how she can possibly hope to achieve her ambition without more commitment. I hope you'll be able to talk to her.'

Suddenly, she felt very weary. This was not what she wanted. She remembered the earlier hours of the day spent with Lucas. She had told herself sternly that this happiness was an illusion and life must be lived in reality but now she found herself wondering if that decision had been the wrong one. What was reality? Whatever the truth was she could not believe in any way that she had the right to destroy Cordelia's dreams. 'I will try to talk to her but she has to be allowed to make her own choices. You know that is what I believe.'

'I accept that but surely some good advice wouldn't do any harm?' Without waiting for her answer he started the car. The subject was closed, it seemed, for during their journey he only talked about her visit to her parents. Anxious to avoid a disagreement, she made no objections.

They arrived home soon after 6 p.m. to an enthusiastic welcome and were soon sitting down to a cheerful, family meal. 'This is delicious, Mum,' Julia exclaimed, 'we've really missed your cooking.'

'Dad did his best,' Cordelia added quickly, 'but—'

'I'm not a cook,' Patrick swiftly intervened.

'Boys don't have to cook. That's a girl's job,' Ben announced amidst general laughter.

'You've got a lot to learn,' Cordelia told him. 'The world's changed. Women aren't so ready to be household slaves any more.'

'I think we should leave him in blissful ignorance a little

longer,' Julia suggested. She turned towards Stella. 'How is Mrs Regan, Mum? What was the matter?'

Quickly Stella told her, simplifying the story as much as possible because of Ben.

'What a good thing you went to see her! The poor woman might have died!'

'It was very lucky I saw your dad coming out of the station. It would have been much slower if I had had to do it by myself.'

'You make a good team,' Cordelia commented. 'Not many people would have realised so quickly what had to be done and then done it without wasting any time. I would always be glad to have you two around in an emergency. But, it's going to be terrible for her when she comes home isn't it? How will she possibly cope when she's so weak?'

'I suppose her mother will try to help her,' Stella said, 'but the trouble is she isn't very competent either. I think…'

'You're not to think of it, Mum,' Cordelia interrupted quickly. 'You've done enough. Don't you agree with me, Dad?'

'I'm afraid I do,' Patrick replied reluctantly, knowing how much this might annoy Stella.

'What about Mr Regan?' Julia asked.

'Can you imagine him looking after his sick wife, four children and the house?' Cordelia asked scornfully.

'He has to earn their living,' Patrick reminded her, 'Money is scarce enough as it is.'

'It seems to me', Julia said, 'that it's obviously the duty of all us so-called Christians to do our bit. And I don't mean just you Mum.'

'Who are you suggesting?' Cordelia asked. 'Mrs Taylor perhaps? I can't quite see her scrubbing a floor in the Regan's cottage, can you?'

'Probably not,' Stella answered quickly before Julia could respond. 'But I'm sure she'd be pleased to find some people who might help.'

'Right,' Julia responded. 'We'll leave that to you, Mum. I'm sure you'll be very tactful.

But in the meantime I don't see why Cordelia and I shouldn't do something tomorrow morning.'

'Hold on,' Cordelia said swiftly, 'you may wish to polish your halo but I have no inclination for scrubbing floors and washing nappies. Count me out.'

'I'm afraid that you wouldn't be much good at either of those jobs,' Stella commented.

'But there must be something we can do,' Julia was disappointed.

'I'm sure there is.' Stella thought for a moment. 'I know, if there's no objection you could gather together all the dirty washing and take it to the launderette. Your dad or I could drive you there. You just sort it out and keep your eye on it till it's ready. You've done that before. It wouldn't take much more than an hour.'

'OK, that doesn't sound too bad. What do you say, Cordelia?'

'I'll agree if Dad thinks I can spare the time from my work. What do you say, Dad?' She was being deliberately provocative.

Before Patrick could respond, Stella intervened. 'I hardly think that an hour of good works would spoil your future prospects. Do you?'

'Perhaps you should ask, Dad. He seems to think I've been wasting too much time recently.'

'And have you?' Stella looked squarely at her daughter. 'And if so, in what way?'

'I'm happy to answer for myself.' Patrick spoke quietly. He was deeply hurt by Cordelia's attitude but he was determined to show neither his hurt nor his anger. 'Cordelia knows that I think that she has spent far too much time with Adrian or thinking about Adrian and far too little time on the necessary preparation for her exams. But I hardly think that this is the time to discuss it.'

Julia and Ben both looked relieved but to their surprise Stella said, 'I don't see why we shouldn't discuss it amicably and learn something. Are you saying that your dad is completely wrong, Cordelia?' She waited as Cordelia hesitated. Both Julia and Ben looked meaningfully at her.'

'Perhaps not,' she replied at last. 'But it's very hard to decide.'

'If you want to be a successful musician,' Patrick said, 'You'll have to give a lot of time to it. There's no easy way.'

'You're right, I expect,' Cordelia answered her father passionately, 'but you don't seem to realise how difficult it is. I love music but I also love Adrian. You seem to have forgotten what it's like.'

'It's always difficult,' Stella answered her, 'but growing up means making choices. There's no way round it. You can't do everything or have everything. And what is worse, you can't spend years making your choices or you may find you haven't got any left.'

'It's rather horrible though,' Julia said, as Cordelia remained rebelliously silent, 'to have to make some of the most important decisions of your life when you're far too young to know enough.'

'However old we are we never know enough. We're always making decisions in the dark. That's one of the conditions of our lives.' What would they say, she wondered, if they knew that she was in exactly that position at the moment? But surely I should have more certainty that they do at their age? And, if I don't seem to have does that mean that I really do know the answer but I don't want to admit it?

'You're not going to tell me then that I must give up Adrian,' Cordelia demanded aggressively, 'because I can't.'

'No, I'm telling you that you must make your own choice but that you must think carefully before you make it. But do remember that, if you don't make it fairly soon, you may have lost your musical chances.'

'What does Adrian think?' Patrick asked unexpectedly. 'Perhaps he thinks you are talented and really wants you to work hard at your music. That's how I felt about your mother. We managed, although not without difficulties at times. I'm right, aren't I?' He turned towards Stella.

'Yes,' she agreed, suddenly remembering vividly that time in their lives. 'You were pretty understanding. I was grateful.'

'There you are then,' Julia said, 'that's the first thing you have to do. Discuss it with Adrian.'

Before Cordelia could reply, they were interrupted by a knock at the back door. 'Whoever can that be? she asked, instead of answering Julia.

Guiltily, Stella remembered her invitation to Lucas. 'It must be Lucas. I saw him earlier and suggested that he might join us for coffee.'

'Oh, no,' Cordelia exclaimed, 'we wanted this to be a family evening.'

'But Uncle Lucas is family,' Ben said as he hurried to the back door.

'You may think so but I don't,' Cordelia retorted. Ben, however, was already at the back door and didn't hear her. Stella waited for someone to contradict Cordelia but Julia avoided her gaze and Patrick seemed unaware of the sudden change in the atmosphere. He did, however greet Lucas warmly as Ben brought him in and suggested that Ben bring another chair up to the table.

'I hope I haven't come too soon,' Lucas said. He didn't seem his usual relaxed self.

'It's just the right time,' Ben replied enthusiastically while looking round cheerfully.

'Mum didn't have time to make a pudding as she's only just come back from the hospital, so we're going to have coffee and Auntie Polly's cake. It's very good.'

'The hospital?' Startled Lucas turned towards Stella. 'There's nothing wrong with you is there?' His concern was very obvious.

'No, it was Mrs Regan. Patrick will tell you about it, while I make the coffee.' She hurried into the kitchen only to find that Cordelia and Julia soon followed her, carrying piles of plates.

'We'll help you, Mum,' Cordelia said.

'Don't be ridiculous. I can manage. You should help to entertain our visitor.'

'We'd rather help you,' Julia said firmly. 'Besides Dad can tell him all about Mrs Regan far better than we can. In any case, we've missed you.' Suddenly she came up to Stella and gave her a quick hug. To Stella's amazement Cordelia followed suit. 'I feel calmer about things already, Mum,' she said unexpectedly. 'Anyway, you must be tired. You've had a hectic day.'

'I surrender. I am rather tired.' Stella realised as she said the words, that they were undeniably true. 'It's nice to have some help.' She made no further reference to Lucas and their obvious unwillingness to have him as a guest. Apparently he had been right when he had said that they had recently made him feel like an outsider. The situation was clear but not the reason and she didn't intend to probe into that at the moment.

'I see you've found another lame duck,' Lucas remarked as she came into the breakfast room with the coffee, followed closely by Cordelia and Julia carrying plates and the cake. 'I'd hoped that you were going to have a quiet life for a time.'

'So did we all', Patrick said, smiling at Stella as he took a cup of coffee from her.

'Do you think people said that to the Good Samaritan?' Julia asked somewhat sharply.

'I just happened to be there,' Stella protested. 'I don't think that anyone with any proper feeling could have refused to help that poor woman. In any case I couldn't have been half as effective without your help, Patrick,' she turned towards her husband. 'So I don't want any criticism from you. You're just as bad as I am.'

'I wasn't criticising,' Lucas protested. 'I'm only hoping, as I'm sure everyone else is that you won't get yourself too involved.'

'No need to worry,' Cordelia said quickly. 'Mum's already passed on the flag to Julia and me. We're to do our bit tomorrow morning. This is a family affair.' And you're not included. Those words weren't spoken but they seemed to hover in the air.

Fortunately the uncomfortable silence was broken by Ben asking Lucas if he could come round to the studio in the morning. 'You can help me stack the latest batch of mugs into the kiln,' Lucas told him. 'If that's not too boring.'

'I love doing that. I'm going to be a potter one day.'

'Perhaps you'd better make sure you do your homework first,' Cordelia warned him. 'You know you leave it to the last minute.'

'So do you,' Ben retorted with unusual boldness. 'Anyway, it is half term.'

Sensing that it might be a good time to intervene, Stella quickly asked if anyone would like more coffee and then offered the last piece of cake to Lucas. 'I think it should be yours. Everyone else has already had a piece.'

'What about Dad?' Julia asked quickly. 'He hasn't had any before. We're always fair in this family, aren't we?'

Patrick laughed, 'In that case may I be allowed to withdraw my claim. I really can't eat any more.' He handed the plate to Lucas. 'It's all yours. But', he added turning to Stella, 'I would like another cup of coffee.'

It was soon after this that Cordelia and Julia announced that they would like to watch television since this was the beginning of the half term holidays. Ben followed them, after making sure that he could help Lucas on the Saturday morning. Left alone with Patrick and Lucas, Stella felt unhappy. She had promised Lucas to speak to Patrick but, after the last few friendly hours she had spent with Patrick, she found herself unwilling even to think of doing so. It would be cruel, she told herself. Surely Lucas would be prepared to wait a little while? Taking a surreptitious look at him, she found his dark eyes fixed on her. There was an obvious question in that look. Afraid that he might even now say something, she turned to Patrick who had retreated from the table to an armchair with his second cup of coffee.

'If you've finished?' she asked him, 'I'd like to finish clearing up.' Without a word, he handed her his cup, then leaned back even more comfortably and closed his eyes. For the first time she noticed how pale and tired he looked. Suddenly she was determined that Lucas should not try to force any issue now. Standing up she began to collect the cups and plates on a tray which she handed to Lucas. 'Would you mind carrying this into the kitchen for me?'

Obviously pleased at the opportunity, he followed her quickly into the kitchen, closing the door behind him. Before she could object to this, he had put down the tray and taken her into his arms. She tried to avoid his passionate kisses but it was impossible, impossible also, it seemed, to control her own response. 'When are you going to tell him?' he demanded. With a great effort, she managed to release herself. 'Not now, please,' she begged him. 'You can see that Patrick is very tired; it would be too unkind. Surely, you can understand that?'

'Very well but I don't intend to be kept waiting too long. We've waited long enough. I don't want to see you always working to help others; I want to make you happy. I want to give you the kind of life you deserve. Surely, that isn't wrong?'

She was too weary to argue. 'I want to be happy, of course but just at the moment I want even more to clear up this mess and have a rest. Surely, you can understand that?' She smiled at him, longing for his agreement.'

'Very well,' he said somewhat reluctantly. 'I'll do that and then I'll go. But I must talk to you tomorrow.' She could only agree.

It was about a quarter of an hour later that they came back to the breakfast room where an apologetic Patrick seemed to be dozing. 'Don't worry,' Lucas reassured him, 'I was intending to go any way. I've several jobs waiting to be done.'

He was gone and they were alone. 'Do you want to go to bed?' she asked Patrick. 'You look very tired.'

'I am. I haven't slept much while you've been away. I've had a lot to think about, especially after the way we parted.'

'That was wrong of me. I'm truly sorry.'

'That doesn't matter now. In fact, I suppose it helped me to come to a decision.'

She was suddenly afraid. He sounded so calm and decided. 'Do we have to talk about it now? We're both tired.'

'No. I think it would be better to leave it. I have certain reservations now, I think.'

'Reservations about what?'

'Well, I was going to say that I'd decided that I should now leave you.'

She stared at him, astounded. Of course in the past he had said things like this but they had always been said in an outburst of rage and despair and she had known that he would never do it. But this was different.

Knowing her so well, as he did, he could guess her thoughts, so he added quickly, 'I'm serious, Stella. I've been thinking about it a lot while you've been away.'

'Is this what you really want? Do you mean that you don't love me any more?'

'No, it's not that. I've come to believe that if you truly love someone, you want their happiness, even more than your own. Perhaps I've just begun to grow up.'

'Don't you think that you should consult me after all our years together?' Her voice was quiet but the anguish she felt showed in her eyes. After a moment's thought she added, 'But you said also that you now have reservations. Have you?'

'Yes. That's another reason for not discussing it any more tonight. Will you agree to that? Can we have a truce like we used to when we were kids. Do you remember? When we'd go involved in some impossible disagreement we'd decide to have a truce and leave it.'

'Of course I remember but a truce always involved a friendly hug. What about that?

'It seems a good idea to me.'

'Good. You look very tired, so you go to bed and when, I've sent Ben to bed, I'll bring up some hot milky drinks and we'll have a soothing chat about nothing in particular.'

'Why not. It sounds comfortable.' As she moved towards the door, he noticed that she was smiling. 'Why the smile?'

'I was thinking how strange life is.'

'What does that mean?'

'I too now have reservations now about something I was going to say to you.' Before he could form his question, she added. 'Don't ask me, I've no intention of saying any more tonight. Agreed?'

'I'll accept that as one of the terms of the truce. Is that what you want?'

'It's not open to discussion. Now go. I must deal with Ben.' As he went through the door, she was amazed at what she had said. 'How have I come to this point,' she wondered. What about Lucas? There's plenty of time to sort things out, she told herself as she went to deal firmly with her son. I'm too tired tonight.

Chapter Twenty-Five

'Patrick! Patrick! Where are you?' The frantic voice awoke Patrick from his deep, dreamless sleep. For a moment as he lay in the darkness trying to think where he was he thought it was a dream. Then it came again, 'Patrick, where are you?' He struggled to come awake. It was Stella's voice. She had come back, he remembered. Where was she? What was wrong? As he turned he felt her body close to his. Of course they had come to bed together. As he touched her, he realised she must be asleep and dreaming. 'Patrick!' She called again, even more frantically.

'I'm here! Stella, it's alright!' He took her hand and held it firmly in his. 'Wake up! I'm here, next to you.' Suddenly she moved. As his eyes became accustomed to the darkness, he could see the outlines of her pale, frightened face. He would have liked to have taken her in his arms to comfort her but shrinking from that he simply held her hand more firmly. 'You don't need to be frightened. It's only a dream.'

Slowly her head sank back on to the pillow. 'It was horrible, but I don't know why.' As he moved a little, she cried out, 'Don't let go of me.' 'I won't,' he promised. Comforted, she moved a little and put her head on his shoulder. For a few moments they remained silent, then he asked gently, 'Would you like to tell me about it? It might help.'

'I don't think I can remember all of it. It's rather trivial, I suppose, but I was terrified.'

'Dreams are sometimes like that. It's your feeling that matters.'

'I was walking in a strange city with Lucas. It was a beautiful place and I was happy until I realised that we were lost. Lucas pretended he wasn't and we walked on until Lucas suddenly decided to turn off to the left. I was sure that was wrong and I tried to stop him but he wouldn't take any notice. Then I saw you coming towards me. I called you and you came to me. I was so pleased to see you. Lucas seemed to have vanished but I didn't seem to notice. When I told you I was lost, you said you knew the way and I must follow you, so we set off on a different road from the one Lucas had taken. I was following you, when some people got in the way and, when they had gone past, I couldn't see you any more. I hurried down the street but there were two turnings and I didn't know which one to take. I couldn't see any sign of you. I was terribly frightened. I felt I was lost for ever. There were people around but they took no notice. It was growing dark. It always is in my bad dreams. I began to call you, then you must have woken me up. I'm so glad you did! That was all it was. It was a bit silly, wasn't it? I'm sorry I woke you, especially when you were so tired.'

'I'm glad I was here.'

'So am I.' They continued to lie quietly together still holding hands.

He wondered if she realised how much she had given away but decided that she had no idea. 'So it is Lucas?' he asked her at last.

'I'm not sure that I know what you mean.' Although she sounded a little annoyed, she made not attempt to remove her hand from his, which encouraged him.

'I'm suggesting that Lucas is in love with you.'

'Whatever made you think that? I didn't say anything about that, except that I was with Lucas at first.'

'I suppose that's what brought it to my mind and caused me to remember what Cordelia and Julia said to me when you were away.'

She could have pretended a little more and kept away from the truth but with Patrick comforting her and holding her hand so firmly, it seemed wrong. 'I think I can guess what they said. They said that Lucas was in love with me, is that right?'

'It was Cordelia first, I believe. She discussed it with Julia and apparently convinced her and they both warned me.'

'And that's why they were so unfriendly to him tonight – almost rude, in fact. Is that right?'

'I'm afraid so. Cordelia has decided that he's too disloyal to be considered any more as a member of the family. And Julia doesn't disagree.'

'But you weren't unpleasant to him. Didn't you believe them?'

'It was all pretty wild, I thought. One of Cordelia's fancies. But tonight I had a glimpse of what she meant when I caught him looking at you a couple of times. But that didn't mean that I wanted to be unkind to him. Why should it? You're an attractive woman. I suppose I should be surprised that it hadn't happened before.'

It was perhaps because he didn't ask for any confessions that she told him. 'It wouldn't have happened now, at least I don't think so if I hadn't tempted him. I did it because I felt lonely and unhappy, deserted and betrayed by you and Eloise. She had made me feel that I had never properly loved you or her. I suppose I felt bereft.'

'I know how you felt, I can understand.'

'How can you?'

'Because I've felt like that.' Suddenly lying close to her, holding her hand in the darkness and the silence with no likelihood of interruption, it seemed possible at last for them to talk honestly as they should have done many times before. He paused for a moment, hoping that she would encourage him.

She did. 'Tell me,' she said gently, moving a little closer to him.

'It was when I realised without any doubt that you were not in love with me when you married me. There had been times when I'd wondered, convinced that things were not quite as they should be but one day I discovered the truth you'd always kept from me.'

'What do you mean?' She was afraid. 'If you're thinking about Eloise, you're wrong. I've understood a lot about my relationship with her during the last few days. I know now that she was in love with me and that it took her quite a long time to realise that I was not in love with her and never could be. I was partly to blame, I should have been more open with her but I was never sure what she really felt. I never meant to hurt either her or you. You must believe me.'

'I do.' He lifted her hand to his lips and kissed it. 'It isn't Eloise. It's Richard Alexander.' He felt the shock run through her body.

'How do you know about him? I never told anyone – not even Eloise.'

'And you certainly didn't tell me.' His quiet unemotional tone made her feel guiltier.

'I should have done, I admit. But how did you find out about him?'

'It was quite accidentally about six years ago. I urgently needed a stamp. You weren't about, so I went to look in your desk, as I know you often keep stamps there. I found the envelope in your drawer.'

'I keep it locked, so how could you?'

'I don't know why but it wasn't locked that day, so I searched through it. I didn't find any stamps but I found this big buff envelope and on it you had written, "Richard Alexander. Born: January 1922; Died: March 31st, 1945." I was very curious and in the end I gave in to my curiosity. I opened it and read the contents. For the first time I learned about your tragic romance which apparently ended in his death just about five months before we were married. It was a great shock but at the same time it made clear to me several things which had been puzzling me for years. I knew now that what I had sometimes suspected was right. You were not in love with me when you married me and you had never been in love with me since. Richard Alexander's ghost had always been between us. I'd never been special.'

'That's what Eloise said in her letter with her will. That was one of her statements, which upset me most. She also said that you felt the same.' A sudden thought struck. 'You said it was about six years ago, didn't you? Then that was when you and Eloise…'

'Had our stupid, little affair. Yes. We tried to console each other but it didn't work. She didn't care for me and I didn't care for her. The end result was I think that we both felt lonelier than ever. I certainly did.' He seemed to be about to release her hand but she held on to him tightly.

'Don't go away now,' she begged him. 'We shall lose all we have gained if you do.' She was quite sure that the new closeness, which had begun in the hospital, must not be allowed to fade away.

'I won't.' He understood what she meant. He too was convinced that they might never have another chance if they threw this one away.

'But why didn't you tell me? Why didn't you ask me about it?'

'I think that the more important question is why didn't you tell me after I returned and asked you to marry me?'

'I was afraid.'

'Surely you didn't think that after all we had shared that I would be unforgiving and reject you?'

'I suppose that came into it but I didn't put it to myself like that. I was so empty and lonely. I was terribly afraid of the future. It was wonderful that you had come back and I simply wanted us to stay together. I didn't think there would ever be anyone else with whom I could be as happy as I would be with you. I didn't realise how it might be for you. I'm sorry, Patrick.'

'I was the one who went wrong first. I should never have deserted you all those months.'

'But don't you think it would have better if you'd told me what you'd discovered when you discovered it?'

'I couldn't. I didn't have the confidence. I had only just begun to get well. I had let you down so badly and caused you so much unnecessary suffering that I couldn't believe that you could possibly want me now. It seemed to me that I was lucky that you allowed me to stay with you. The best thing I could do was to respect your memories and keep my distance.'

'And that is why you rarely came at all close to me? Never tried to make love to me?'

'Yes. Sometimes I wanted to try but I didn't think that I had the right any more.'

'And I just thought that you had lost interest in me. And neither of us said anything. How foolish we were!' They continued to hold hands but they didn't speak for a time.

'I suppose there seemed to be so much to say and it was too difficult to know where to begin.' Patrick said at last. 'Then there was always Eloise. I felt by this time that I was no more important to you than she was. Perhaps even less.'

'I should have realised.' She lifted her head a little so that she could move a little closer. 'Auntie Polly was right!'

'What do you mean?'

'She made me tell her everything. I don't know how she did, but she did.' She wondered if he would be angry to hear that she had told her aunt before him.

'She was always good at getting at the truth.' That was all he said.

Relieved, she continued: 'She said I was very wrong to have allowed the past to dominate my life. And I had helped this to happen by not telling any one, particularly you. She said that we couldn't cling to the dead. We had to allow them to die.'

'Because they don't change in our eyes and everyone else does. Is that what she meant?'

'I think so. She said it had become a dream. She pointed out that I might not have wanted to marry Richard, even if he had come back, that, however important my feeling seemed to be, it might not have lasted, I began to see that she was right and that dreams, illusions I prefer to say, are very powerful but can be very dangerous. She told me that I'd never been afraid to be honest in the past and that I should be brave enough to be that now.'

'And what did you think?'

'I thought I had agreed with her and came home determined to sort things out.'

'Which seems to bring us back to Lucas, where we started. Or am I wrong? We've agreed, I think, that he's in love with you but you have carefully said nothing about your feelings. Isn't it perhaps time that you did?' This seemed to him to be the crisis. Stella had at last spoken fully and truthfully about the past. But what of the present? He waited.

When she didn't speak, he asked a little impatiently, 'Don't you know what to say? Or is there something you still don't want to say? If so, why not? We've had a time of truth. We've told each other many things, which should have been said a long time ago. So, why hesitate now? This may be our last chance! Surely you understand that? Without a proper understanding, I see no point in my staying. Now, you have Eloise's money, you don't need any financial support from me and I can live in London on what I earn.' It was obviously necessary to remind her, he thought, of the decisions he had reached in her absence.

She was startled. For the first time she remembered what he had said before they went to bed. She obviously had not taken it seriously enough. 'You've never said anything like that before. Surely, you can't possibly mean it, just like that? You've always said that you couldn't bear us to be separated.'

'I told you before we came to bed that I'd grown up recently and begun to understand that if you truly love someone, you want their happiness even more than you want your own. I meant that, Stella. If you will be happier without me, then I'm prepared to go, not without regrets, of course. Now, it's for you to say whether you would prefer me to go.'

'Of course I don't.' The thought of a future without Patrick terrified her. Why had she ever thought that it might not, she asked herself? She remembered her frightening dream. It was Patrick she had cried out for, not Lucas. Had Patrick understood that? She turned towards Patrick. 'I'll try to tell you the last bit, as truthfully as I can.' Suddenly the complete revelation of the foolish things she had done and said hit her. 'How could I have been so stupid again. I think I've treated Lucas just as I treated Eloise. But with her I had an excuse. I didn't really understand what I was doing. How can I say that about Lucas? What a despicable person I am! I don't deserve your love!'

She tried to pull her hand away from his but he held her more firmly. 'What do you mean? What are you trying to say? Don't waste any more time, my love. Simply tell me the whole story.'

'You might want to leave me then!'

Putting his other arm around her he asked her gently, 'Do you really think so?'

'I'll have to risk it, won't I?' Burying her face in his shoulder she began to speak very quietly. 'I thought I was really beginning to get things sorted out when I left Auntie Polly. I had told her about Lucas, you see, and she was shocked, utterly shocked that I should think of behaving in such a way. It was quite clear to her that I was just trying to run away from reality again. I decided that I would discuss everything with you first, then that evening Lucas rang me up. I hadn't quite understand before then how seriously he had taken the situation until he told how much he had been thinking about me, about us. He begged me to come home on an earlier train, so that we might have time to talk before I met the children and you.'

'And what did you say?'

'I agreed. I see now that it was very wrong of me but it all seemed very attractive. To my surprise, he met me at Euston and greeted me like a lover. We had lunch on the way down and then I went to his flat.' She paused. It seemed disloyal to Lucas to be telling these matters to Patrick but, if she didn't, she would be even more disloyal to Patrick, her husband and her friend.

'And did you talk?' It was difficult to tell from Patrick's voice what he felt, for he was determined not to influence her by showing too much emotion at this point. He was afraid, however, of what she might say.

'Yes. We didn't make love. We hugged and kissed and talked of the wonderful times we might have together. Lucas wanted to take me to Paris, Rome and all the beautiful cities he knew before the War. It was like being enchanted. I wanted something beautiful to happen to me, I suppose, after all the horror of Eloise's death and feeling so isolated from you and everyone for so long. I'm so sorry.'

'I should have realised.' Patrick lifted her hand and kissed it gently. 'I have been so self-centred for years. I'm sorry too.'

'I see now that it was only dreaming. In spite of all I had understood about my relationship with Eloise, I was now treating Lucas in the same way. When she talked about us having a flat in London, I went along with it, although I knew it wouldn't happen. Now, I was doing the same thing with Lucas, playing a cruel game and not even realising it. Oh, Patrick, how could I do it?'

He held her closer. 'You desperately needed love, which I had selfishly withheld from you, pretending to myself that it was what you wanted.'

'As soon as I came back into our home, it all vanished. Reality took over again. I prepared the meal very quickly, I had just sat down when Johnny came to the door and after that there was no time to think. Suddenly, you and I were together again. You shared my feelings and my sadness. I didn't have to tell you. It was right as it always used to be. You felt the same, didn't you?'

'Of course and now at last we've been able to speak the truth. I don't think we've ever been so close for years. In the darkness and the quiet, the truth had to be spoken. We love each other, as we always have and we have to stay together because we would be incomplete apart. You know that, don't you?'

'Yes, I do now. But Patrick what shall I do?'

'You have to speak the truth to Lucas now. Be brave. It will hurt him less than pretending. You know that.'

'I'll do it somehow.'

'You talked to Cordelia about having to make choices. What you said was very wise, I thought. You have had to make a choice tonight. You must give Lucas the chance to make his.'

'What do you mean?'

'He must decide whether to stay or go away.'

'It's a terrible thing I've done to him.'

'He's wise enough to understand. He knew he was taking a risk. It was his decision as much as yours. There is nothing more to think about now. Everything is and must remain clear.'

'You're right, I suppose.' She didn't think that she could possibly sleep but still holding Patrick's hand, tiredness overcame her. She yielded tomorrow's worries to tomorrow.

Chapter Twenty-Six

Tomorrow is now today. Stella has no excuse not to talk to Lucas. It is nine thirty on the Saturday morning and she is eating a solitary breakfast of toast and coffee. Patrick who is still in bed has given her a kiss and his good wishes. When she asked him for support, he had merely said, 'This has to be done by you, darling. Only you can confess your sins. As for me, I find it quite morale boosting to know that even you have sins to confess.' To take away any sting from his words, he kissed her again. Acknowledging the justice of his words, she makes no protest. Nevertheless it doesn't make it easier.

Suddenly, the peace is shattered as the back door is pushed open violently, followed quickly by someone fiercely shoving open the breakfast room door. Ben hurtles into the room, ignoring her, even though she calls to him and without pausing disappears through the door into the hall. At the bottom of the stairs his progress is stopped as he apparently runs into Cordelia who quickly expresses her outrage. Obviously Ben is in one of his 'moods'.

After a brief but heated altercation, Stella hears them going upstairs. Good; for the present, Cordelia is dealing with him but, as his mother knows only too well, this can only be a brief respite. For a few blessed moments there is silence but from past experience, Stella knows that another problem is threatening, so she hastily finishes her toast and coffee. She has barely finished when the door from the hall opens again and Cordelia bursts in. There are obvious signs that Ben has communicated his 'mood' to her. 'What is wrong?' Stella asks mildly.

'Mum! You'll have to deal with Ben. I can't do anything with him. He's in quite a state. You know what he's like.'

'What's the reason? Did you get any idea?' Stella stands up as she prepares to go.

'Not much, except that it's something to do with Lucas.'

'Has he been with Lucas then?'

'Yes, surely you remember that Lucas said he could help him this morning, so Ben, after an early breakfast went round to the Studio.'

'I don't see why that should have upset him. He's done that many times.' Stella admits to herself that she has considerable reluctance to being drawn into this, although she knows that it is unavoidable.

'I don't know what's gone wrong either.' Cordelia sounds angry. 'But it's obvious that Lucas has said something which has upset Ben a lot. I think that he has too much influence on Ben. You'll have to deal with it, Mum.'

'I'll do my best. In the meantime, you'd better have your breakfast and get Julia to have hers. I shall want to take you to the Regans soon.'

As soon as she opens Ben's bedroom door, she sees him lying face downwards on his bed. Hurrying across the room, she sits down on the bed and speaks gently to him. 'Whatever has upset you Ben? Surely you can tell me. Cordelia says it's something to do with Lucas. Is that right?'

Between sobs Ben manages to say, 'Lucas told me that he is going away soon.'

'Going away! What do you mean? Did he say where?'

'Yes. He says he wants to go back to Europe and travel around like he used to do before the war. He wants to go to Paris and Rome and places like that. And, I think, he's got a friend to go with.'

Stella feels very angry. How dare Lucas talk like this to Ben? Almost immediately she has to remind herself that she is also to blame. 'Perhaps, Lucas only meant,' she suggests, 'that he is thinking of having a holiday. After all he hasn't had one for a long time, has he?'

Ben doesn't answer at once but his sobs become fewer and slowly he lifts his head to look at her. His face is still tear stained but he looks more hopeful. 'Do you really think I've got the wrong idea? I often do, I know.'

'Perhaps you have.' She strokes his unruly hair. 'But I think you'd better tell me how you came to be talking about this. What did you say?'

'He seemed so pleased with what I was doing this morning, so I asked him if he thought I could become a potter, if I worked very hard. I'm not much good at most things, not clever like the others but I think I would like to be a potter like Lucas.' His eyes filled with tears again.

'What did Lucas say?'

'He said he thought I could. He said I had a real gift for things like that. Then I asked him, since I couldn't learn at school, if he would give me regular lessons so that I could be his assistant when I left school. I thought he'd be pleased. I really did, Mum.' He sobbed again, although he tried to stop it. 'You see he's always been so good to me and I like him an awful lot. Not as much as you and Dad but almost as much and I thought he liked me a lot.'

'I'm sure he does.' Stella strokes his hair again.

'Then why did he say he didn't think it would be a good idea? He said it wouldn't be possible and when I asked why, he said this about going away. He said I shouldn't be upset, because there were other things I could do. Then I told him he was horrid, that he didn't understand and then I ran away.'

'Perhaps he was thinking that you ought to speak to your Dad first or to me or that you shouldn't decide too soon what you wanted to do.'

'Perhaps.' Ben is not really convinced but is trying to be hopeful for he knows that he sometimes misunderstands other people. 'Do you think you could speak to him, Mum, and find out? Will you please, please, Mum.'

After kissing him, Stella stands up. 'Of course I will. I must speak to your Dad first and then I'll go and see Lucas. Stay here until I come back.'

'I will, Mum. Thanks.'

Patrick has already been awakened by the noise. After telling him briefly what has happened, she announces that she is going to see Lucas to try to sort things out. 'Do you think you can?' Patrick doesn't look very convinced.

'I've no alternative have I? I'm the fool who's helped to cause all this.'

'Don't be too hard on yourself. Remember that Lucas has to make his choices just like everyone else. He may not have realised before this, just what that means. I think you can help him.'

'I'll try. But will you please get up and take the girls to the Regans and to the launderette?'

'It's difficult being your husband. One gets such strange duties but I'll do it for you. But I want payment – a kiss before you go.' After kissing him, Stella hurries away, only stopping to tell Cordelia and Julia that their Dad will be helping them.

Just as she is leaving, Cordelia stops her with a question, 'Was I right about Ben? Were you able to talk to him?'

'I was able to talk to him and you were right in thinking that it's Lucas who has upset him and I'm going to talk to Lucas now; that's why Dad is taking you.'

'Damn Lucas!' Cordelia's anger surprises both Stella and Julia. 'It's about time he stopped interfering in our family.'

'I don't think you're being fair,' Julia protests. 'We've often been glad of his help.'

'Well, we aren't now! And you know why.'

Stella decides that the time has come for her to be more honest. 'Dad has told me what you said to him about Lucas being in love with me because I wanted to know why you were both unfriendly towards him last night. Whatever your so-called reasons, you were rude to my guest.'

Cordelia shrugs her shoulders but Julia apologises. Ignoring Cordelia's resentment, Stella continues, 'You should know from experience, Cordelia, even if Julia doesn't, that people don't plan to fall in love. And, once it has happened, it's difficult to stop the feeling.'

'Well, I think you should be able to, if you know it's wrong.' Cordelia glares at her mother.

'Do you? Well, then I think you should stop being in love with Adrian, because, if you don't your career plans are going to be ruined and all our efforts and money wasted. Your being in love with Adrian seems wrong to your Dad, so why don't you stop it?'

'That's different.'

'Not really,' Julia objects.

Cordelia rounds on Stella. 'That isn't what you said last night. You were much more reasonable then. You said I should learn to make mature choices. Now, you seem to be saying that you think

I should have a choice forced on me. You can't do that. It isn't right. I can't just stop loving him because you say it's wrong!'

'Mum's just trying to prove to you,' Julia intervenes quickly, 'that you can't blame Lucas. It's just as hard for him. Am I right, Mum?'

'That's about it,' Stella agrees. 'Can you feel a bit more sympathetic now?' she asks her elder daughter.

'I suppose so.' As Stella begins to turn away, she adds unexpectedly: 'I've been thinking a lot about what you said, you know. It's alright to talk about choices but the trouble is that I want both.'

'Then, you'll have to talk honestly to Adrian about it all and see if he's willing to share you with your music. It's no use pretending.'

'Why ever shouldn't he be?' Julia asks unexpectedly. 'Why shouldn't a woman have a career, which really matters to her? I wouldn't marry anyone who didn't agree to that.'

'You might not,' Cordelia retorts. 'But I know I don't want to lose Adrian. I'm sure I'll never be as happy with anyone else. '

'Don't say that,' Stella says sharply.

'Why ever not?'

'Because nothing and no one is ever perfect and you can ruin your life by clinging to an illusion. Try to be realistic.' Mindful, as she now is, of the unhappiness she has created by her treasured dream of Richard Alexander, she feels she must give her daughter a warning, inadequate though it is. She turns to go, anxious to avoid further questioning. 'I must go. Ben is waiting to hear from me.'

She hurries out of the house, then hesitates and walks very slowly towards the studio. What can she possibly say to Lucas, she wonders? Pushing open the door, she enters and sees him sitting on his couch almost immediately opposite to her. He is unaware of her entrance for she has come in very silently. For a moment she studies him. He is sitting in the middle of the couch with his hands clasped loosely between his knees and his head bent forward. Never before has she seen him look so depressed. She wants to comfort him but knows that she must not. Instead she calls his name, 'Lucas!'

Slowly, he raises his head and stares at her, almost as if he doesn't recognise her. His face is set in unhappy lines. He looks so much older and wearier than the lover who embraced her so happily the day before that she is filled with guilt. 'Stella! I didn't expect to see you now.'

'It's very hard, isn't it to make choices and to admit the consequences of one's actions?'

'Have you spoken to Ben?'

'Yes, that's partly why I'm here now. He's very upset and wants me to talk to you. I've persuaded him to believe that he might have misunderstood you.'

'Why ever did you do that? You know it isn't true!'

She moved a step towards him. 'Are you sure of that, Lucas? Have you really considered everything? If you're so sure, why do you look so unhappy?'

It is only after a few moments consideration that he answers her and then only indirectly. 'I should never have said what I did to him. Certainly not in that way.'

'If it's true there's no reason why you shouldn't have said it to him, is there? He will have to know. Although I suppose you could have said it more tactfully.'

He is shocked not only by her words but by the cold way in which she speaks. 'I never imagined that you would say that! You have always been so loving.'

'It's not exactly loving to desert one's husband and family, is it? At least, I don't imagine they will think of it as a loving action whatever words I use.'

'I don't think I understand you, Stella. Why are you talking like this?'

'Shall we concentrate on Ben first. I came to speak for him. He is deeply hurt.'

'He was talking about the future as my pupil and then as my apprentice. I couldn't let him go on but I didn't realise he would be so upset.'

'Why not? He loves you and he thinks you have betrayed his trust in you. He has always felt that you appreciated the little talent he had and wanted to help him to develop it. Now you have taken that away from him and he has lost the small amount of self-esteem he had. He will get over it, I suppose. He's only a child. Is that what you think?'

Standing up abruptly Lucas moves towards her. 'Why are saying these things? You know I don't think like that. I thought you loved me.'

'I do love you. That's why I'm saying these things. I'm trying to put you in touch with reality.'

'But only yesterday, I thought you were agreeing with me. Was I completely mistaken? Why did you pretend?' Moving closer to her, he seizes hold of her by her shoulders.

'I wasn't pretending. It was a beautiful dream and I loved it but then I had to leave you and return to reality. Ben is part of that reality. Surely you can understand what I mean? It has become clear to me that if you and I persist in following our romantic dream, others will suffer as Ben has suffered and we shall be destroyed. Surely that is clear to you?'

Slowly he releases her and moves back to the couch. As he sits down, he replies sadly, 'Many things are becoming clearer. Ben had no part in my dreams of a happy life with you. I don't think he played any part in yours either.'

'No. Nor did Patrick, Dominic, Cordelia and Julia. We were dreaming dreams, Lucas. They were wonderful but they were only dreams. We were enchanted by the idea of the ecstatic life we might have together. People are often led astray by illusions, particularly today when the media often seems intent on persuading us that it is possible to have heaven on earth by changing one's partner or even by spending vast sums on the perfect holiday. The more people cease believing in God the readier they are to believe in dreams. But we know better, don't we?'

'You are suddenly very wise, Stella.' His voice has a slightly mocking tone. 'Perhaps you can explain your conversion. Why weren't you so wise yesterday or in the time just before you went on holiday? Have you been playing a game – a somewhat cruel one?'

'Of course not!'

'They why are we in this position now? I've known you for several years and have loved you for most of that time but I never made a move until, I think it's true to say, you initiated this one. Do you deny that?'

'No, although I wish I could. I was very vulnerable at that time. Eloise had just died and I felt that I had been deserted and betrayed not only by her but also by Patrick. In my weakness I turned to you for comfort. But it was selfish and wrong of me. I hope you can forgive me?'

'I'm afraid I was pretty selfish too. I took advantage of you. I refused to think of the consequences. I didn't care whether it was right or wrong. I just wanted to be happy as I thought we could be. Now, it all seems rather ridiculous.'

'That's because Ben has shown you the consequences. Since, as I believe, all love comes from God, it should be good. If it isn't then we know we've got it wrong. Ben showed you that you had got it wrong because he told you that you were destroying all his hopes and his belief in you. And you found that mattered, after all, to you. I'm right, aren't I?'

He isn't ready to agree. 'That's your analysis. A bit simplistic, don't you think?'

'Perhaps but that doesn't mean it isn't true. We all have to make choices. I've made my choice. I don't want to leave Patrick or our children. I would destroy their lives and my own if I did. I can't deny the love that Patrick and I have had for so many years and I don't want to destroy the trust my children should rightly be able to have in me. It is simple in fact.'

As he considers it, he realises that her calm, unemotional manner doesn't actually surprise him. This is the Stella he has known for years. 'You have a choice. You are fortunate.' There is bitterness in his voice.

'So do you.'

'I don't see it.'

'You can go away and start your life afresh if you want to or you can stay here and become once more a part of our family.' When he does not answer her, she moves across the room and sits down next to him on the couch. 'I know it's hard Lucas – harder for you than for me – or so it must seem.' She puts her hand gently on his.

Furiously he moves his hand away. 'Of course it's easier for you. You can remain with Patrick and your family after conveniently filing away this entertaining little incident with me. I am the fool who thought you loved me and my reward is to lose everything, although it could be said that I deserve it.'

'You're very wrong. First of all, it was no pretence, I was deeply attracted to you but I've come to realise that I must stamp out that feeling, as you must. It's too dangerously destructive. That can be done. I know.' She pauses for a moment but when he makes no response, she continues. 'Furthermore, you do have a choice, if you'll only think about it.'

'I don't want a hypocritical sermon, Stella, especially from you of all people.' He is very angry with her. 'Be honest, if you can. What can there possibly be for me if I stay here as your rejected lover? I've betrayed Patrick's friendship, Ben hates me and it was only too clear last night that your daughters wanted to be rid of me. No, I've no alternative. I must go and start afresh.'

'None of that need be true, if you'll only stop feeling sorry for yourself. Patrick is still your friend. The girls will soon come round, once they know you're not going to take me away and Ben is only too ready to believe that you only meant that you want to go away on a holiday. You're like a second father to him, since you spent so much time with him when Patrick was ill. You can't desert him. You know you can't, Lucas. Please don't think of it.' She takes his hand again and this time he doesn't pull it away.

'I don't think I understood till now how much Ben matters to me. You're right. Some loves are more important. But I think it would be better for everyone, especially me, if I did go away for a few weeks.'

'Where can you go?'

'I could go to Cornwall and stay with my old teacher. I have an open invitation. He's a brilliant artist and there's still a lot I can learn from him. I think it might help me in several ways not only as a teacher. What do you think?'

'I think it's a very good idea. It will give us a chance, especially to get back to normal.' She turns to look at him. Their eyes meet and he realises that, in spite of her outward calm, she too is finding this very difficult.

'Thank you for being braver and wiser than I am.' He kisses her quickly, then moves away.

She stands up, ready to go. 'If you can face it, I would like us to have a special family meal tonight to show that we're still all united. Can you do it?'

'If you can, I can, as long as you can guarantee that I won't be ostracised.'

'I can promise you that. In the meantime, I'll send Ben round and you can tell him your plans. He's probably getting desperate. And you will come to us at seven?'

'I promise.' Before he can say more, she has gone.

★

It was nearly midnight when I finally retired to my bedroom. It had been a successful evening, I thought. The day too had been more successful than I had ever imagined it could be. Cordelia and Julia, helped by Patrick, had done their 'good deed' without complaint. I had managed to send a message to Mary Regan, promising to visit her on Sunday. Lucas had made his peace with Ben.

The evening meal, however, had undoubtedly been the climax of the day. After a brief explanation Cordelia and Julia had cooperated splendidly. Ben had been happily convinced about all the wonderful new things Lucas was going to teach him when he returned from Cornwall. Patrick, in his most relaxed and friendly mood, had cheerfully welcomed Adrian and had even been unruffled by Dominic's phoned announcement that he had been given an interview by the newspaper. At whatever cost to himself (perhaps only I could guess how great) Lucas had returned to his role as honorary uncle.

It seemed that, after a long and difficult climb, we had reached a safe plateau where we might rest for a time, before tackling whatever struggles might lie ahead.

Walking across to the window I looked out before drawing the curtain. The bare trees in the garden and in the orchard behind were touched with magic by the moonlight. It was strangely quiet. The sky was very dark and the stars seemed to be unusually bright. As I looked at them, I felt swept into the immensity of the universe. Suddenly I was vividly conscious of Eloise. I felt that she was close to me begging me for an answer. I knew what she wanted. 'You were special,' I whispered, 'not perhaps in the way you wanted to be but always special.' I knew now that she was at peace.

Suddenly, I felt Patrick close to me. Putting an arm round me he said softly, 'You did well. But now it's time to come to bed. I was filled with a feeling of love for him, a love I had not always recognised but which I now understood had always been the centre of my life. Turning quickly I put my arms round his neck as he drew me close to him. 'You're very special,' I told him, 'you always have been and you always will be.'

'I know that now.' Very deliberately he bent his head and kissed me on my lips. It was a true lover's kiss and I was able to respond fully, perhaps for the first time.

Lightning Source UK Ltd.
Milton Keynes UK
21 January 2010
148894UK00001B/4/A